CLOUDBREAKERS
VALLEN

Kenton J Moore

SoulForge Media

Cover Art by Marco González and J. Paz Díaz

Cover Layout and Design by Kenton J Moore

Map Illustration by Kenton J Moore

First edition 2025

Interior Design by: Kenton J Moore

Edited by: Victoria Helmink and Loretta Cameron

Story Editing by: Lynaya Moore

ISBN (Paperback): 978-1-7770866-8-8

ISBN (Hardcover): 978-1-7770866-9-5

ISBN (eBook): 978-1-7382956-0-9

For all my service brethren in the Canadian Forces, the adventures I shared with you shaped who I am.

For my best friend, Loretta Cameron, who helped me create this wonderful world. I will never forget our world-building sessions.

For my Mother, who has always been my number one fan. Your tenacious and relentless support is unmatched.

And for my children, forever the reason I write.

KINGDOM OF VERDOS
SHADESTEP VILLAGE
HILLMAGE CITY
SAND'S EDGE VILLAGE
EASTBANK VILLAGE
ARBANESS THE FLOATING ESTATE
SOUTHILL CITY
HARROW'S TOWN
ESCORE VILLAGE
HAVELOCK CITY
STONESVALE VILLAGE
THE ERRBRYTE ESTATE
DAVITCH BASIN
THE DRAGON LAKES
VANDRAD CITY
FIRE ISLAND
THE GRINDLEMOOR
RAIDER'S BAY
THE FURIOUS SEA

Prologue

The waitress huffed and took a moment to tuck a few loose strands of her bangs behind her ear once the wooden serving tray she carried was rested on the polished bar. A well-groomed bartender rushed over and tossed his bar towel over his shoulder, nodding to a patron calling for his attention as he did.

"Light, what a night..." the waitress said, leaning against the bar for a moment. She shared an awkward smile with some raucous men sitting at the bar beside her before chiming off the list of orders to be delivered to tables. The bartender nodded and set to work filling ceramic ale mugs and placing them one at a time on the tray. In the span of a moment, he had six mugs filled along with a flagon of mead and two empty glasses on the tray.

"Sun, give me strength!" she said to the bartender as she hefted the tray, balancing it perfectly on her forearm and open palm. He smiled at her and returned to wiping the bar.

The public house was full near to bursting, and it was the fourth bustling night in a row. Stinking of body odour, wood polish, and spilled alcohol, it was a wonder anyone managed to keep their sanity working in such a place. As the woman made her way through the throng, weaving around tables and exuberant patrons like a ballet dancer, many called to her or outright tried to grab her. The crowd was thick and mostly men, steel or coal workers by their clothing and hygiene. She was deft at avoiding them, and her disarming smile and piercing eyes that radiated threat were enough to keep all but the most lecherous of them at bay. Waiting was not a new profession to her.

Twice she stopped as she was flagged down by polite patrons requesting refills at their tables. She kept a mental record of all of them. As she reached the back of the open hall where a line of six tables sat in carved-out booths, her demeanour shifted. Her steps became lighter, her smile became permanent, and her voice raised a pitch or so. Those in the profession called it a service persona, and hers was as finely crafted as they came. As she approached the first table, her persona was in full swing.

The table seated three men and two women, all in crisp military uniforms. Their dark blue coats were cut close to their figure, double-breasted with bright brass fittings and a single lapel on the right side. Underneath they wore white shirts with a high-neck collar. Insignias of rank on the single lapel indicated they were all officers, and their countenance supported this assumption.

"Thank you," said one of the men, seated toward the back of the booth. He bore a short well-trimmed beard specked with streaks of white, and his blue eyes shone like the sky she knew he made his home in. Two brass shoulder epaulets sat atop his jacket, streaming tassels of a stainless white. He leaned toward the end of the table and set down a pouch of coins. "Open a tab, lass. If you could."

The waitress began placing four of the six ales on her tray down on the table, along with the bottle of mead and two glasses. "Not often we see cloudbreakers in here. Let alone officers. Is the Crystal Sky tavern full today?"

The man with the beard smiled as he took one of the glasses and began pouring the mead into it. "Closed actually, for a time. Renovations we're told."

The waitress picked up the coin pouch and dropped it into a pocket on the front of the apron she wore around her waist. "A shame. I imagine the patronage here is a tad rowdier than you're used to."

One of the female officers scoffed and mistakenly made eye contact with a man standing at one of the tables on the general floor of the hall. He smiled a toothless grin back at her, and she shook her head in revulsion. Watching all of this, the bearded officer smiled and sat back in his chair. "Quite."

"Well," the waitress began as she turned to walk away from the table. "Suspect you lot could handle it even better than I can."

With that she was off, heading for a standing table on the far side of the room from the bar. Two men stood at the table as she approached, leaning close and talking in hushed tones. Her service persona faltered for the briefest of moments. These men shook her confidence. Nothing about them was outwardly threatening in appearance. They both wore relatively well-kept clothing. One of them had hung an older-style pea coat of wool dyed a dark brown over the back of his chair. He wore slacks and tall leather boots, with a newsboy cap. His shirt was simple cotton. The other was dressed similarly but carried a leather messenger bag and wore no hat. The hatless man flashed a toothless grin as the waitress approached, an empty eye socket on his left side still somehow seeming to sparkle with questionable intent.

"Heyyyy," the one-eyed man lisped. "There comes our lady!"

The waitress smiled as best she could and went to work setting the mugs on the table. She wordlessly took the coin offered by the man in the hat and vanished into the crowd back toward the bar.

"Y'know... I think she's sweet on you," Ketrick Whitehall said, nodding toward the waitress as she departed into the crowd. He smiled and took off his newsboy hat, leaning back into the chair to take a long drink from his ale. His silvery blonde hair almost shimmered in the dim light of the pub.

"Shite. You think?" said the one-eyed man.

"By the light, no." Ketrick laughed. "Swear on the sun, Eiffert, you're as thick as anything I've ever known."

Eiffert grumbled something that was lost to the din of the crowd and drowned his disappointment with a long drink from his ale. He set the cup down on the table and wiped a bit that ran from the corner of his near-toothless mouth with his sleeve. Ketrick was watching the crowd and sipping from his ale. It was clear he knew the waitress would not be rushing back to top them up, so he had decided to savour his beverage.

"My contact is comin', Ketrick. Swear on the light, she'll be here. She's a good one. You have my word."

Ketrick nodded and leaned back across the table to speak candidly with his one-eyed counterpart. The muscle in his cheek tensed and his jaw set, almost spitting out the words.

"I don't trust her one bit with this, Eiffert. Cousin or not... I'll gut her where she stands if she does not bring the money."

Eiffert swallowed. "She'll pay. I know it."

"She better," Ketrick sat back in his chair. "And she better be discreet. If he finds out what we're doing he'll set the storm on us. You know he will."

Eiffert drank from his mug and watched the crowd, but it was not the patrons he was seeing with his one good eye. His gaze was fixed somewhere far beyond the room.

"Scares me, he does" Eiffert breathed, barely audible over the laughter from a table nearby.

"What are you mumbling?" Ketrick said, leaning forward to hear.

"I said..." Eiffert was cut off as a middle-aged woman approached their table. Her auburn hair was in shambles, pock-marked throughout with dirt and detritus. She looked homeless, and her fidgeting hands betrayed desperation. There was an odd, burned look to the skin around her eyes, like a terrible sunburn coming from within. Her pupils darted around like a spooked cat.

"Eff..." she said through gritted teeth, nodding at her kin. She tried to make eye contact with Ketrick, but her eyes immediately fell to the floor.

"Geneve, you look terrible. You brought our stuff, right?" Eiffert pleaded with her, holding out what remained of his ale in the mug to her. She shook her head vigorously, refusing the offered drink.

"Shite..." Ketrick breathed, watching the woman's every move. "I knew it. You took it, didn't you?"

Immediately Geneve froze, almost as though she had been struck. For a moment, her rapid eye movement stopped.

"Light be damned, you did!" Ketrick laughed out loud. Eiffert looked mortified, his singular gaze bouncing between his dishevelled contact and his cousin. Geneve's head-shaking increased, and her fidgeting returned double what it had been.

"I need more!" She almost screamed before catching herself and toning down her volume. "Please... I need it. I'll pay. I brought extra coin."

Digging inside the loose clothing she wore, Geneve produced a satchel fat with coins that made an audible clink as it hit the table. Eiffert frowned at her, then picked up the satchel and looked inside. He thumbed through the contents quickly before looking at Ketrick.

"Three hundred at least. Maybe more."

Ketrick whistled silently and took the satchel from Eiffert as his cousin addressed Geneve.

"Where'd you come by this much?"

She shrugged. "Places..."

"Places." Eiffert nodded, sensing her shame as he repeated her answer.

"You have some, or don't you?" she pleaded.

Ketrick stood and lifted his coat off the chair behind him. He threw it around himself as he pushed his arms through it, a purposeful motion to show off the quality of the coat fabric. A disarming smile crossed his sharp features. He snatched up the satchel and nodded to Eiffert.

"We do. But not here. Come on."

As Ketrick moved to lead his cohorts out of the public house, he made quick eye contact with one of the cloudbreakers across the bar. He flashed a coy smile from the corner of his mouth as he placed his newsboy cap on his head. Then he tipped it at the cloudbreakers and led the others across the pub and outside.

Not far from the public house, down a cobblestone street, Ketrick ducked into an alleyway between the stone foundations of two tenant buildings. The municipality of King's Ridge had many of these dark alleys, being an older part of town and the slums of Gallenfort. Vagrants littered the alley, but Ketrick led them past, down the sloping alley to where a drainage grate let the foul liquid of the streets flow into the city sewers. He stopped there, shooting a glance back the way they came to be sure they were not followed. Convinced they were in a private place, Ketrick motioned for Eiffert to hand him the leather bag he was carrying.

"That it?" Their ragged contact asked meekly.

"Yeah..." Ketrick said, opening the flap and reaching inside. "This is it."

Ketrick produced a small glass vial from within the bag, stoppered with a metal screw cap. The liquid inside was a dark purple-red ooze that seemed to move on its own as if it were alive. It was like a macabre experiment stuck inside a tube. Every once in a while, a subtle spark flared inside the substance. The remaining space in the vial was filled with a light blue vapour.

Geneve gasped audibly, almost a sigh of relief and reached for the vial instinctively. Ketrick drew it away, a sadistic smile spreading across his face. He looked at Eiffert, and then back at Geneve. He began to twirl the vial in his fingers, taunting Geneve with it as he spoke.

"You were only supposed to sell it."

The woman drew her hand back, her eyes wide and her lips tight. She trembled.

"I'm sorry, I..."

Ketrick danced the vial before her face and moved around the woman like a cat circling a mouse. He held the vial out, waiting for her to reach for it and immediately drawing it back.

"What was it like?"

She said nothing. Another failed attempt at grabbing for the vial.

"Ketrick..." Eiffert pleaded.

"How did it *feel*? Did you see something amazing? What was it?" Ketrick continued.

The woman sobbed. She tried once more when Ketrick offered the vial, and once again failed to secure her prize.

"Please... I paid you double."

Ketrick stopped his circling and stood before Geneve. He drew himself up to his full height, shoulders back, like a proper gentleman. He regarded the vial in his hand.

"Yes. I suppose you did."

The alley fell to silence, save the woman's sobbing and the trickling sound of filth dripping into the drain.

"But," Ketrick drew out his word in the silence. "I can no longer trust you, Geneve. Not that I ever did, mind you. But look at you. Look how *desperate* you are."

The woman flinched like she had been slapped. Ketrick continued.

"I need associates who can *sell* the product, not *use* it. I require discretion. You are most definitely not discreet, and you've clearly used this more than once. You are a *liability* now."

The silence in the alley seemed to stretch on forever before Ketrick spoke again.

"But," he sighed. "I am a compassionate man. I understand. Here."

Ketrick held the vial out in offer, directly before Geneve's face. Her eyes were wide and fixated on the substance within the tube. Just as she reached out for it, Ketrick dropped the vial. Geneve's eyes went wide with horror. She dove for the glass tube as Ketrick stepped out of the way. Too late, she crumpled to the stone as the vial shattered at her fingertips. The ooze, now free of its glass prison, blended with the filth flowing in between the cobblestone towards the drain. Sparks of white light and ethereal flames of blue and yellow danced above the widening puddle, undulating in intensity as it spread. The blue vapour remained visible even in the dimness of the alley, drifting above the firelight from the ooze as it continued to dilute among the sludge.

As Ketrick walked away, dragging a solemn Eiffert with him, the woman began lapping what little remained of the substance off the ground. She sobbed and licked at the stone as though her life itself depended on it. Urine, oils, rainwater, and all other manner of city fluids slurped up with the ooze, yet she was inexorable, unbothered even by the vapour, sparks, or flame. As Ketrick and Eiffert faded into the background of the city, the woman slumped over onto her side. Bathed in sewage and dirt, she drew in a long deep breath. Her limbs ceased their fidgeting. In the darkness of the alley, her eyes began to radiate an eerie blue-purple colour as thin trails of blue vapour drifted up from her open mouth.

Chapter 1

Head in the clouds

Cole

Cole Vallen brushed dirt from the potato he had just pulled from the ground, before tossing it into a nearly filled basket beside him. He stretched his arms and shoulders out, pressed his circular tinted glasses up his nose, and then plunged his potato fork back into the soil. After a quick stomp to drive the forks deeper into the ground, he levered the handle down, causing the metal tines to upend a new pile of dirt filled with more buried potatoes. He repeated this motion; bending down, brushing the potatoes, and placing them in the basket. Twice he wiped sweat from his brow using the sleeve of his cotton shirt, and once more pushed his glasses up his face. The late afternoon sun was high in the air, and the sound of someone approaching caught his attention. He turned to see his father, basket up on his shoulder, approaching across the rows.

"Almost quitting time, Cole?"

Cole looked at his basket, nearly overflowing with potatoes, and realized his mind had been elsewhere again. Working in the fields had that effect on him. Menial labour tended to make his mind drift, and he often lost track of time when it happened. Cole wiped his hands on his pants to clean some of the dirt off and then brushed them through his curly, dark brown hair. He could feel the dirt still on his hands becoming mud in the sweat of his hair. He smiled at his father.

"So it seems. My head was in the clouds again."

Jasper Vallen laughed aloud and walked past his son, heading for their wagon perched on the edge of the field a hundred meters away. Cole took a moment to breathe in the smell of the earth and the plants. He tried to avoid it, but his face turned to the sky anyway. It always did. He watched a handful of crows circling, no doubt waiting for them to clear the field so they could search for worms upended by the digging. It amazed Cole to watch the birds in flight. How their black wings banked so effortlessly, gliding through the air, changing direction on a whim. Behind the crows, and far above in the blue sky, puffy white clouds lazed about like lords above their kingdom.

Cole had always dreamed of the sky; ever since the posters and the radios first spoke about the cloudbreakers and their airships when they entered service during the last few years of the war. Unfortunately for Cole, airships were a rare sight this far north in the kingdom. His community was far removed from the fighting, which took place predominantly in the south. The sky armadas of the allied kingdoms had no business here. That did not temper Cole's obsession, and he spent all the free time he could learning about the machines. Every book the library and the school had, every poster put up around town, and every radio broadcast he could listen to had made Cole a veritable encyclopedia on all things airship. He imagined them a lot like the clouds above; massive metal objects lording over the land below. The cloudbreakers were the crows, waiting to come down and perform their duties on the surface below.

"Cole!" his father called, pulling him from his daydreaming. "Come on. Let's get this load home."

"Coming!" Cole called back.

Despite his skinny frame, Cole was surprisingly strong. He easily hoisted the potato basket to rest on his right shoulder and drew the potato fork from the ground with his other hand. He flicked it higher into the air so he could grab the shaft closer to the tines in a smooth motion, and smiled to himself. The act reminded him of a sword, and he fought the urge to spin the tool in his hands like one.

Dirt fell from Cole's boots as he trudged across the field toward the wagon. Upturning the potato hills made for a bit of mud, and after a day standing in it, one's boots tended to bear a coating of soil. However, moving across dry ground was enough to knock it off, so Cole left a trail behind him. Their land was a meagre plot on the northwest outskirts of Harrow's Town, one of the many settlements making up the north of the Kingdom of Verdos. Harrow's Town was mostly known for farming and every year they held a fall harvest festival. Tomorrow was the beginning of it, and it would last a full week, bringing visitors from all the neighbouring towns. It was an exciting time for locals. Except for Cole.

To Cole, the festival had always meant tedious and hard work. Before, during, *and* after. As one of the smaller farms in the area, the Vallen family depended on trade and commerce from the festival to break even and make it through another year. The war effort had nearly bled them dry. Labourers, in particular, were in the shortest supply as most had been recruited and sent off to fight. Cole had only been eight months away from the mandatory service age of eighteen when news that the war had ended reached Harrow's Town. Cole's father believed the festival this year would put their family back on track. Peace was a foreign concept, but the last year had shown them that almost anything was possible now.

This year was the first year in almost three generations that the farms of Harrow's Town were not required to send tithe shipments to the war effort. No trains would head south with free goods surrendered by farmers this year. The festival was going to be special, or at least that was the rumour. Abundance would bring income, and income would provide for expansion. Better tools. More land cleared. Innovations, improvements, profit. These were the topics discussed at the Vallen dinner table in the last few months, though it was only ever Cole and his father, and his father led the discussions. Cole shared none of the excitement. He knew that the one thing sure to increase this year was people, and people did not rate high among Cole Vallen's interests.

Cole had been born with an exceptionally rare condition that caused a third of his right eye to be a different colour. The condition, which a doctor in his youth had called sectoral heterochromia, did not affect Cole's vision in the slightest, but it did affect his life. Verdosi people were superstitious, and Cole had been marked. He had suffered torment and ridicule almost all of his life. At least until a new friend gave him rare sunshades to help hide his eyes from the world. Some people forgot as time went on, but there were a few who did not, like the town bullies who never missed a chance to weaponize Cole's defect. His mother had the same eye condition, and when she died inexplicably in childbirth, the word cursed was used to label the Vallen family. Cole had grown up wanting to be anywhere else, and the war offered that.

Cole had grown fond of the tantalizing promise of escape that adventure offered, and the news of the war ending shattered him. It was as if his chance to escape the tumultuous world he knew was taken from him. He had become accustomed to the rhetoric sold by the radio and the posters. He wanted to become a cloudbreaker more than anything. See the world outside his small town. Lord over the land below that he had grown up toiling on. Perhaps find a place where his eyes did not solicit hostility and mistrust. Peace had shattered his dreams, but at the same time, it had brought hope to his father.

"Keep walking and you'll make it to town without the wagon, Cole!"

For the second time today his father's words woke him from a daydream. Cole realized he had walked right past the wagon. Feeling foolish, he spun around and strode back to join his father at the back of the open cart. His father took the basket of potatoes from Cole's shoulder while Cole slid the fork into the back alongside all the other baskets of vegetables. There were cabbages, carrots, onion, garlic, and of course, the potatoes, all piled in the back of the wagon. Enough to feed a handful of houses for a full winter. Cole stretched out his shoulders again and leaned against the back of the wagon.

"I'm not working you too hard, am I Cole?"

Cole shook his head and stood up. He removed his glasses to wipe sweat from his face, looked at the sky, and then at his father. He watched to see if his father would react to seeing his eyes. His father simply held out a water canteen. Cole took it gratefully and popped the cap. He paused to reply before taking a drink.

"No, Dad. It's not that."

Jasper waited for Cole to finish his drink and replace the cap before he took it back and pressed the issue.

"So," he began, tossing the canteen into the back of the wagon. "What is it, son?"

"Nothing."

"Come on, Cole. I know you better than that. You're usually excited about the festival."

Cole smiled at that.

"No, I'm not, Dad."

Jasper walked around the side of the wagon and Cole followed. They walked the length of the wagon and as they passed the ladder to the driver's seat, Cole climbed up. Jasper kept walking, heading for the edge of the road where the two workhorses that pulled the wagon were hitched. He untied their leads from the post they were hitched to, led them to the front of the wagon, backed them into their breeching and connected the breeching straps one at a time. He pulled on the backband, girth, and bellyband to ensure they were secure. Once the horses were connected, he tossed the reins up to Cole who caught them and waited.

"Next season will be different, Cole."

"You keep saying that," Cole said as his father climbed into the seat. "Maybe it won't be. Maybe it will just be more of the same."

Jasper settled into the seat beside him and took the reins when Cole offered them, giving them a snap. The horses lurched ahead, and the wagon creaked, rolling forward down the road that led to town.

"Maybe you could buy a power wagon."

Jasper laughed and Cole could not help but look over at him. The wrinkles on his face had deepened this last year, and there was more white in his beard and his curly hair than Cole remembered. He was aging, and a life living off the land as they did was taxing. It showed in his father's gnarled and calloused hands, his fingers with knuckles swollen, cracked and dry skin, looking like misshapen pink carrots. His neck leaned forward, giving him an almost hunched-back posture, and his forehead and cheeks were sun-bleached and blotchy. The dirt on him did not help his appearance either. Cole felt a wave of sadness for the age his father showed. Maybe not for his father, but for the future Cole felt was waiting for him.

"It's not as bad as it looks, son."

Cole blinked in surprise.

"What?"

"Me. My life. Our life. It's not as bad as it looks."

Somehow sensing Cole's hesitation, he continued.

"It's a good life, Cole. Living off the land and feeding people. There's honour in it. Sure, there's little to no adventure... but it's honest work. Good, important work."

"It's not about the work Dad," Cole tapped his glasses in his lap. "It's never been about the work."

"Your eyes..." Jasper sighed.

"Yeah."

"Just don't feel like I belong here anymore, Dad," Cole said after a moment of silent bouncing as the wagon rolled down the road. "Not sure I belong anywhere."

His father let the rein go with his left hand and held it up in front of his face, almost as though he was reading the lines on his skin like a book.

"Vallens have been farming this plot of land for three generations, Cole. Someday, light-willing, you'll be the fourth. I'm sorry about the way folk 'round here treat you. I am. I'm sorry we ain't city folk or high-born lords, so you could do anything your heart desires, but you'll have land. Our land. You'll find a wife and have children of your own, and someday you'll sit beside them, and know you did well. And you'll know it was where you belonged all along."

Cole smiled. His father did this often when Cole was solemn about the future or his condition. Jasper Vallen loved what he did. He loved his place in the world, as his father and his grandfather had as well. They saw the land and the food they grew in a way Cole never could. He wished he did. As he opened his mouth to reply, there was a cracking sound and the wagon lurched. The horses spooked, but Cole's father managed to rein them in without incident. The wagon was stopped.

Cole leaned off the seat on the passenger side and looked backward. The wheel on the back of the wagon had jumped the axle and fallen off. The axle nut sat in the mud a meter or so away on the edge of the road. Cole stood and began to climb off the wagon, setting his glasses down on the bench.

"Lost a wheel?" Jasper asked as he secured the reins and began to climb down as well.

"Looks like the nut spun off again," Cole said. "I thought Shepherd fixed it for you?"

"So did I," his father said as he rounded the back of the wagon. He reached inside the back of the wagon and took out tools to fix the wheel. "But this old girl has seen much better days."

"Maybe next season you can..."

"Buy a power wagon" Jasper interrupted. "Yes, someone told me that a few times before."

Cole caught a thick wooden post that his father tossed to him. He smiled to himself and stuck the post into the dirt under the back of the wagon. He waited for his father to recover the axle nut from the ditch and come back to the side of the wagon. He rolled the wheel out of the way and inspected the connection to the axle that the nut spun onto. The threading was worn.

"Not much thread left on this axle."

Cole waited while his father dug into his toolbox. He produced a can filled with resin and beeswax. Cupping his hand into the can, he scooped out a handful of the goo and smeared it onto the threads of the axel, coating it all around.

"Should hold at least until we get to town. Ready?"

Cole nodded.

"Lift."

Cole put his back under the post and levered the wagon upwards enough that his father could slide the wheel back onto the axle. His legs shook with the effort. When the wheel was in place, Cole slowly let the weight of the wagon rest down on the wheel. Sure that it was aligned and not broken, Cole's father spun the nut onto the axle threads. He connected a tightening rod, and Cole and his father together spun it as tight as they dared. Then Cole picked up the post and returned it to the back of the wagon as his father did the same with the tools. They stood for a moment together at the back of the wagon while Cole's father cleaned the goo off his hand with a rag.

"Yeah, if the festival is what I think it will be this year, I'll look at getting a power wagon next season."

"Rikket's family got one. He won't stop talking about it."

"I'm sure he doesn't. Bet he'll have fun words for you about this too."

"What, losing the wheel again?"

Cole's father nodded, tossing the rag into the back of the wagon on top of the tool bag.

"I won't tell him. Rikket has enough to make fun of me for."

Cole's father sighed, and put his hand on Cole's shoulder, shaking him lightly.

"I'm sorry, Cole. I'm trying."

Cole smiled at his father, as best he could.

"I know Dad. I'm okay."

They made their way back to the driver's seat. Once in, Cole's father gave the snap and the horses started away, but he reined them in a tad slower.

"As for your eyes," Jasper picked up Cole's glasses and handed them to him. "Keep wearing these. Be yourself. Folk will forget about it. Even Rikket."

"Rikket is an ass," Cole said after a time of riding in silence. His father laughed out loud, a hearty laugh that seemed to come from his belly.

"That he can be, Cole. That he can be."

Chapter 2

Destined for better

Cole

The first day of the Harvest Festival was a raucous affair, just as Cole's father had predicted it would be. Endless lines of people, some from as far away as Havelock - the capital city of Verdos and a three-day journey to the south by horse - packed the small town square and beyond. Tents had been set up in some of the empty fields outside the town proper, no doubt because the inn had been full almost immediately.

Harrow's Town was essentially a clustered mass of buildings that expanded outwards like the rings of a spider web. The center of town was an open square, boasting a fountain with a statue of the town's founder: Emijen Harrow. The huge brass statue depicted Emijen leaning against a pitchfork stuck into the ground, his hat removed and his eyes fixed on the far-off horizon. Cole always found it funny that he shared kinship with the town's founder through that glance. He felt the statue was also lamenting about a world far away. Regardless, Harrow's town had rallied around him. At the border of the square was the postal office, town hall, marshall's building, a bank of Verdos, a library, and Harrow's Town's only public house: The Swine and Ale.

Beyond the central square was a crisscross of roads and alleyways designed for horses and foot traffic. Directly to the south of the square was the Ashwind District, home to a few nobles who called the area home, as well as tailor shops and tool makers. Further still to the south was the aptly named Southside District, home to the feed stores and other commercial operations catering to local farmers. North of the square was Butcher's Row. The area was almost exactly as the name implied, filled with meat cutter shops, sausage makers, and delis.

Past the row was the final district in town, which had recently seen its name changed to Sable Hill on account of Rikket's family. Homes and various shops populated this area. It was in this district that Cole and his father found a hastily constructed table with their name on a tag. The rickety table did not look capable of supporting even a single basket of potatoes. Cole and his father spent their first evening at the fair reinforcing the table. Sadly, the post for lifting the wagon had to make the ultimate sacrifice, and Jasper had cut it in two to become extra table legs.

In the morning on the following day, Cole was surprised to see crowds of people already shoulder to shoulder sauntering through the streets and browsing wares. When he and his father arrived and pulled the blankets off their wares, it did not take long to begin making sales. A lot of the first people to visit were travelling merchants. Re-sellers who bought from farmers and sold at higher prices to taverns and estates in Havelock and the other big cities beyond. Noble kitchens, his father had called them. They were the pickiest customers Cole had ever seen, often rejecting potatoes based on too many ears, or carrots because of the slightest malformations. Cole's father always shrugged as though their opinion was worth less than the dirt that dusted their vegetables.

"They'll come back," he said to Cole after one merchant had scoffed and walked off. "All potatoes look the same after a while."

Sure enough, later in the day, the same merchants would come by dragging servants along to carry the crate upon crate they would purchase. Cole did not necessarily hate the work. He loved speaking to so many foreign people. So few of them mentioned his glasses. Often, they sensed the energy of his youthful curiosity and were more than willing to spin yarns of their travels while Cole's father pretended not to listen. A few times, wealthier-looking merchants even tossed Cole an extra coin or two as an investment in his future. This shocked him and silently enraged his father. They called it a 'financial promise' for a better life. Jasper Vallen called it unwanted pity. Enjoying himself or not, Cole was nonetheless enthused to see his best friend Rikket emerge from the crowd with a mischievous grin on his face.

"Cole!" Rikket exclaimed as he burst from the crowd and hugged his friend like they had not seen each other in weeks. "Look at *you,* you dirt worm. How's the festival back here?"

Rikket was a tad taller than Cole but almost twice his size in girth. He was a big lad, stocky in frame. His red hair was straight and parted in the center, hanging down almost to his sharp jawline. His chin sported the early beginnings of a beard, or perhaps a goatee. Either way, it was like the fuzz on a peach but red. He was quite proud of it, his hazel eyes sparkling every time it was mentioned.

"Rikket!" Immediately after stepping back from the hug, Cole reached up and tickled the fuzz on his friend's chin. "Beard is coming in nice. You best start putting the oil to it!"

Rikket punched Cole on the shoulder and ducked a couple of playful jabs sent back in return. Then he stood and reached a hand out to Jasper.

"Mr. Vallen, sir. How are you keepin'?"

Jasper Vallen shot a sideways glance at his son, before taking Rikket's hand and shaking it hard. He gripped so hard he heard the boy's knuckles pop and relished a bit in the wince he saw on his face.

"Rikket. How's your family? Booth seeing many sales?"

Rikket rubbed his hand while trying to hide the obvious pain he felt. He smiled despite the veiled insult and pointed with his thumb over his shoulder toward the town square.

"Mom and Da have it under control, sir. Township gave us a double booth in the square, out front of the marshall's. Mom has her quilts and pillows on the one side, Da the produce on the other. Sales are good I reckon, last I saw. Not much left of the potatoes, just corn and radish to go now."

Rikket caught sight of the pile of potato baskets behind Cole's father and his face went almost as red as his hair. He stuttered a bit and then tried to change the subject as quickly as possible. Rikket's family, the Sables, had moved to Harrow's Town almost ten years ago and had bought a whole series of farms in the area. A lot of rumours accused the Sables of bullying the previous owners into selling, but Cole knew it was simply an issue of money. Rikket's family had made their fortune working for the Gisborne textiles industry out of Havelock. It had always been Lady Sable's dream to live on an estate, and Rikket's father had made that dream happen for his wife. They started with corn when they arrived, quickly dominating and edging out as much competition as possible. Two years ago, they had seeded their first potato crops. It was a product that the Vallen farm had provided. Not long after, there was a sudden vote to name the upper district Sable Hill in their honour. Cole remembered that vote well. He had never seen so many fistfights.

"Cole," Rikket motioned towards the town square. "I heard an airship is coming up from down south. Patron talking to Da mentioned it. Want to come with me and see it?"

Cole's eyes went wide. He immediately looked to his father, who sighed and slapped the tabletop with a handkerchief he had picked up.

"Suppose you won't forgive me if I say no," his father sighed. "Go on. Just be here before dark. I'll need the help to strike down for the night. Stay out of trouble."

Cole barely got the words thank you out before he was off, charging through the crowds following Rikket's red hair like a flag. An airship in Harrow's Town. It was like a dream come true after years of reading about them or hearing stories from travelling merchants. His mind was like a storm, thoughts striking and fading like lightning. *What was it doing here? How long is it staying for? Which one is it?*

Cole ran through a mental checklist of the types of airships he knew about. There were celestial-class warships, storm-glass gunships, and cloud-class cruiser vessels mostly known for being the oldest and least armed of the fleets. Verdos had invented airships about twenty-seven years ago, and the alliance between Verdos and Akoy meant that they could be built quickly. Hundreds had been constructed. The technology had almost single-handedly won the war with the Ciar K'Hen empire to the south. Despite the significant numbers advantage of Ciar K'Hen, the airships proved too powerful.

Cole saw Rikket ahead, almost disappearing through the mass of people. His daydreaming had got the better of him again and he realized his running had slowed. He picked up the pace, trying to close the gap with his friend. The crowd of people was getting thicker as they approached the square, not surprising being that town square was the concentration of most of the booths. A man on high stilts appeared above the crowd and it gave Cole pause for a moment. Especially when the man drew a deep breath and then, holding a torch near his face, blew out a spray of liquid from his mouth that immediately burst into a huge ball of flame to the cheers of the crowd below him.

"Cole!" Rikket called from ahead. "Come on!"

Cole turned his attention away from the performer and saw Rikket standing amid the crowd. People walked across between them, momentarily blocking their sight of one another, but it was enough for Cole to see Rikket pointing enthusiastically down one of the roads that led out of town.

"Simpren's field!" Rikket called out.

"Lookout rock! Got it!" Cole called back.

Once more he plunged into the crowd, this time not paying as much attention to keeping sight of Rikket. He knew where they were headed. It took a little less than an hour to clear the crowds and by this time, Cole had caught up and was walking at a brisk pace, shoulder to shoulder with Rikket. They made small talk about the festival, Jasper's disdain for the Sables, and what peace might mean for either family. When at last they reached the field, they crossed a shallow stream and climbed up a bank to Lookout Rock. It was a place so named for the clear view of all southern approaches to Harrow's Town it provided. As soon as their eye level crested the horizon of the rock they saw the airship.

Barely a mile off, trailing steam and smoke and floating like a steel cloud in the sky just as Cole imagined they would, was an airship of the Verdos fleet. Signature markings of gold and green adorned its hull, with a flag flying high from its mast showing the Verdosi coat of arms - a winged knight clutching a tome in one hand and a sword in the other surrounded by fruitful trees and the sun rising high above. The hull was rounded on the ends and oval in overall shape, with barrels of cannons protruding like the quills of a porcupine along its length. Vapour sails for gathering cloud water to feed the steam engines were closed along the hull. Cole remembered reading that closing sails was a procedure for docking. He surmised that it was likely the ship was going to come to rest in Simpren's field. It made sense, given the available space and their crops already up for the season. Even from this far away, they could hear the ship humming. Sunlight reflected off the vertical glass of its bridge windows at the lower forward end, and they could make out tiny figures of people scurrying atop the flat deck at the top of the ship.

Cole drew a deep breath. He was captivated by the way the great steel machine seemed to hover effortlessly. Again he likened it to the clouds he watched whenever he gazed at the sky. He felt butterflies in his stomach as he took in every detail of the machine that he could see, from the stacks ejecting steam and smoke atop its back to the chopping of the ducted propellers at its rear. He even noted the three distinct circular openings on the side of the hull facing them, deciding they had to be peregrine tubes; deployment shoots for the winged combat specialists the cloudbreakers employed.

"Do you know which one it is?" Rikket asked after whistling softly to express how impressed he was.

Cole squinted, trying to find identifying details at this distance. Faintly, he could make out a hull number painted on the side of the ship just behind the bridge windows and forward of the vapour sails. He removed his glasses to be sure.

"C26..." Cole whispered. "Is that C26? That number there, just behind the bridge windows. See it?"

Rikket squinted too. Cole knew his friend's eyesight was better and waited patiently for confirmation. He racked his brain of all the airship information he could recall from reading and listening to radio broadcasts. C designation usually meant first-era Verdosi; a cloud class. The ship's armament supported that. Cruisers were built for speed and tactical operations, not bombardment or battle command.

"C26" Rikket confirmed.

Cole thought for a moment and then it hit him.

"It's the Cirrus. Second-generation cloud class, I think. A crew of forty-seven. Six peregrines."

Rikket laughed and sank to a squat, picking up a rock and tossing it down the grade of the hill in front of them. Cole sat on the ground beside him, watching the Cirrus approach Harrow's Town.

"I don't know how you know so much, Cole. Sure is somethin' though. A gift. Wish I had half the mind you do for it. Wouldn't be shuckin' corn as much as I do, that's for sure."

Cole looked at Rikket and then at the ground near his feet. He thought of his father and the words he spoke in the wagon yesterday.

"It's a good life, Rikket. Better than we could ask for, I reckon."

"Bullshit, Cole."

"What? What does that even mean, 'bullshit'?"

"You know what it means, Cole. Useless. Good for nothing. Can't even fertilize with it."

Cole laughed.

"I'm serious! It's bullshit."

"What is bullshit?"

"You are! That bullshit you just said is."

The pair laughed and watched the sun beginning to set off in the distance. The pinkish-yellow light made the Cirrus appear even more surreal than it already did. The whole scene before them was like a painting.

"Seriously though, Cole." Rikket said into the silence. "You don't belong here, digging in the dirt. You're meant for better than this."

Cole scoffed. He rolled his glasses in his hands.

"You know that's not true, Rikket."

"Why? Because you have some green in your otherwise brown eyes? Come on, Cole. You're not cursed and you know it."

"How can you know it?"

"I mean it, my friend. I know."

"Right," Cole slipped his glasses on and pressed them up with his finger. "Big ole city lad, you are? Noble Rikket Sable. Knows all there is about curses and such. And shuckin' corn."

"You jest! Go on then. But I know. C26. Verdosi Airship Cirrus. Crew of forty-seven. Six peregrines."

There was a long silence before Rikket finally stood and stretched his back.

"You show me a potato farmer who knows that much... one *half* as smart as you are, and I'll show you another person meant for bigger things. Cursed eyeballs or not."

Cole did not say another word for the remainder of the time they watched the Cirrus approach. Even when the pair of them walked back to town, it was in silence until their farewells when they reached the square. Rikket knew what he was saying. He may be a smug ass sometimes, but he knew Cole. The real Cole. The Cole that hid behind dark glasses and pretended he loved farming. He knew what Cole truly wanted deep down inside, even if Cole could not admit it himself.

Chapter 3

Talking to the dream

Cole

On the second day of the festival, people talked about the Cirrus' arrival more than anything else. There were occasional conversations about weather, peacetime, and discussions amongst locals about the profits already being seen. Mostly though, the conversation was about the Cirrus. Speculation ran rampant about why it was in Harrow's Town for the festival. What was the purpose of the cloudbreakers now that the war was over? Would airships become a common sight among the towns this far north? How much would it cost to buy one if they were to be decommissioned from active service, and how many baskets of produce could one ship carry?

Cole smiled politely at all the conversations as they occurred, mostly as the people passed by their booth. He wished they would stop and talk to him the way they were to one another, but when they did it was about business and prices, and most of them simply passed by without a purchase. Cole was happy to let his father do most of the talking when customers did stop by. That way Cole could listen to all the questions in the crowd and answer them in his mind as though he was a part of the conversation himself. He tried his best to busy himself by sorting potatoes into different baskets based on size. He was doing his best to entice potential buyers by creating the illusion of uniformity in the product as it was offered. Ultimately, it was a vain attempt at distracting himself.

"Yes, sir. I am indeed. Arrived on the Cirrus yesterday."

The words broke Cole's concentration on his task like a thunderclap. He looked up to see a woman turning over a head of cabbage in her hand, inspecting it as she made idle conversation with Cole's father. She was older than Cole for sure, but younger than his father, with short-cropped light brown hair, almost blonde if the sunlight hit her right. There was not a single hint of gray. Her sharp features, easy smile, and hazel eyes marked her as Verdosi, most likely from Havelock or perhaps further south. She wore a dark blue dyed wool coat, double-breasted with brass buttons, and a single lapel. A brass pin depicting a winged man holding a sword straight aloft was on prominent display on her lapel.

"You're a peregrine," Cole said, interrupting his father who was just beginning to ask what he could get the woman. A surprised look came Cole's way, as the woman regarded him briefly before following Cole's gaze to the pin on her lapel.

"Absolutely correct, young sir," the woman began, setting the cabbage back down in the basket in front of Jasper. A look of disappointment flashed on Jasper's face for a moment. Sales had been slow. The woman turned to face Cole, her right hand hooking a thumb through her belt where an empty weapon holster hung, tied at the bottom to her thigh with a leather strap.

"Impressive to tell from just a pin. I am a peregrine. Rather, I was. During the war."

"You stop being a peregrine without war?" Cole asked.

"Cole, watch the tone!" Jasper hissed.

The woman lifted her left hand in a reassuring gesture. Her smile was charismatic and disarming, but warm.

"No offence occurred. It's quite alright as questions go. Yes, and no. That is your answer, young sir. Yes, we no longer have the use of a peregrine in peacetime. But no, I cannot stop being a peregrine."

The woman's smile was intoxicating, and Cole found himself smiling to match.

"My name is Cole Vallen, this is my father."

Cole's father held out his hand to the stranger.

"Jasper Vallen."

The woman took Jasper's hand eagerly and shook it.

"Aislinn Elissan, at your service!"

Aislinn bowed graciously as she released Jasper's hand and reached for Cole's. Her grip was surprisingly firm.

"Tell me, young Cole. How did you recognize the peregrine pin? Have you travelled much to the south?"

"Never," Cole replied, lowering his gaze almost in shame. "I studied the war posters and read any books the library had. Listen to the radio in town square too, when my duties allow."

"Study?" Aislinn leaned against the table, her eyebrows raised. "Impressive. Can you write also?"

"I can."

"Exemplary! It's a wonderful skill to have, Cole Vallen. The literate arts can quite quickly unlock the world, as it stands. Have you thought of enlisting?"

The question immediately sent Cole's gaze to his father. The look on Jasper Vallen's face told Cole everything he already knew.

"For a time, yes. I was close to enlistment age. Eight months to my birthday, when peace was declared."

Aislinn's face fell sombre and she nodded.

"Nasty business, the war was. Be glad for the gift the light has given you, young Cole. There is more in this world for a mind like yours than ever there was in a world at war."

Cole opened his mouth to protest but quickly shut it when he locked eyes with his father. It was a pleading look. *Don't open that box, Cole. You won't like what you find.* Instead, Cole changed the subject.

"Have you always served on the Cirrus? Second generation cloud-class, right?"

Aislinn was even more impressed this time, and she nodded at the correct identification of the vessel.

"I served on two others during the war, and yes you are quite right! Cirrus is a second-generation hull commissioned to the Verdosi fleet before the unveiling of the storm class."

"Radio said the hulls were close to becoming obsolete when the celestial class entered service."

"Did they?" Aislinn laughed. Her laugh was infectious. Even Jasper Vallen smiled. "I doubt they could mothball the old hulls. Tons of uses, you see. But the celestials... the Starfall is indeed a marvel... oh you should see her, Cole. A diamond in the sky, that one."

"Will there only ever be the one constellation class?"

"No chance. Starfall is just the first in the future of airships. More capable than any other hull in the sky. Starfall was the first ship to include a citadel. Do you know what that is?"

Cole shook his head. Aislinn's excitement was palpable.

"Wonder of engineering. See the problem with airships, Cole, is the air! Imagine that. Up among the clouds, it's very hard to breathe. People of great strength gasp for air and fall weak. Temperature so cold, it feels like winter without snow. Airships can't go too high, or they could kill everyone on board without a single shot fired or sword swung. But the Starfall..."

Aislinn paused for dramatic effect, looking into the sky and sweeping her hand like a tavern bard performing a great ballad.

"The Starfall has the citadel. A whole internal structure meant to contain the environment from the surface. Two doors into and out of the hull - we call them airlocks - allow passage in and out, and inside the citadel? Spaces sealed entirely from the world beyond. Special pumps warm the air and send it inside. Never are the two airlock doors open at the same time while the Starfall sails. Inside the citadel, you have air the same as you would on the surface. Warm, breathable air, no matter how high you climb."

Cole's eyes were wide as Aislinn's hand came down, her grand performance complete.

"Folk were never meant to claim the sky," Jasper Vallen said, derisive and jealous of the effect this woman was having on his son. "By the light, if we were, we would have grown wings."

Aislinn winked at Cole, before turning to Jasper Vallen.

"I do have wings, Jasper Vallen. I just left them on my ship."

There was an awkward moment of silence where Aislinn waited for a laugh or anything from the old farmer. Nothing came.

"Well, I believe I have worn out my welcome at your fine locale."

Aislinn produced a coin pouch from her pant pocket and tossed it to Cole's father.

"I'll take two baskets of cabbage, one each of celery and tomato, and four of the potatoes. I'll have our victualler come by with men to collect them."

Aislinn turned to Cole and gave another small bow.

"Farewell, young Cole. Good fortune in your studies."

With that, Aislinn turned and disappeared into the crowd of people heading in the direction of the square. Cole watched her for as long as he could keep eyes on her, taking a measure of the way she walked and how she made idle conversation with anyone who met her gaze. When at last he could no longer see her, he turned back to his task of sorting potatoes. Jasper Vallen opened the pouch of coins and looked inside. After a moment, he threw it down on the table and slammed his fist down beside it.

"Why are you angry?" Cole asked with a touch of resentment in his voice.

"Cocksure snob paid enough for almost twice what she ordered."

Cole could barely contain his disappointment.

"And *that* angers you?"

"You don't understand, Cole."

"*Make* me understand! How can you be upset to be paid *more* for our goods?"

"Because she's insulting us. They all are. This whole *festival* is. Can't you see that? Probably a noble born. Thinks she's being charitable."

"You make no sense."

"Don't I?" Jasper Vallen whirled on his son. "Don't you see, for all your smarts boy, how the world here works? She's a cloudbreaker. Most of these other people are nobles. We're farmers. You and all your studies, your fawning over her, her airships, and her world amid the clouds! She pities you, Cole. Stuck with a failing old farm. Thinks we need charity, and so pays extra."

"So what if she does pity us?" Cole snapped back. It had been a very long time since Cole raised his voice to his father. People walking by stopped for a moment to gawk. Cole did not care and vented his frustration regardless.

"So *what* if she pities *me*? She should!! We have nothing, Father. We *are nothing* here! Broken wagons and horses when the world has power wagons. Set away in tiny stalls way off the ring road where we're out of sight. The whole town laughs at us! They laugh at *me* and call me *cursed* because of some green in my eyes! I'm smarter than all of them. Half of them can't even read, and you're too proud of your hands in the dirt and your *good life* to care!"

"How *dare* you, boy."

"How dare I? *How dare you!*"

Cole stormed out of the booth but stopped in the crowd, onlookers watching the exchange between the two. He whirled and pointed his hand right at his father's face.

"I wish peace never came. Eight more months and I would have had a chance to get away from here. I could have been a cloudbreaker. Could have found a place in the world where people didn't care about *this*!"

Cole ripped the glasses off his face and threw them down onto the table, then turned and stomped off into the crowd toward the square. He heard his father yelling back at him. He ignored it, but the gist of the message was clear. *Go then. Go find your future on your own and don't come back.* Cole wished he could. He wished Aislinn would appear out of the crowd and offer him a job on the Cirrus. He wished he could fly away on that ship and never look back. A crew of forty-eight. But he knew that was not his destiny. This fight had been building inside Cole for a while, and his father had been the unfortunate target. What Cole needed now was a stiff drink and time to cool off. He made a beeline straight through the crowds to the Sable booth.

Rikket was flirting with a young woman and her friends that were shopping at the textiles side of the Sable booth when Cole appeared. The moment Rikket saw Cole's face, he knew. Immediately, he excused himself from the women and draped his arm around Cole's shoulder.

"If ever I saw a man needing a drink, it was you. Come, my friend. To the tavern with you."

Chapter 4

A bit too much

Cole

The Swine and Ale public house, Harrow's Town's only public drinking establishment, was neither built nor staffed for the volume of people it was catering to during the festival. Hastily constructed picnic tables and chairs had been erected in the street and the yard in front of the tavern to accommodate some of the overflow, but still, there was mostly standing room only. Cole was still steaming as Rikket led him through the crowd, pushing and edging past people as they made their way up the three steps leading to the double doors propped permanently open. The main hall inside, which usually felt like adequate space, was a sardine-can of bodies bumping and jostling each other as they tried to make way for servers carrying trays of drinks above their heads.

"Maybe we should grab a bottle and head for Lookout R ock..." Cole grumbled as he was jostled for the fifth time since crossing the threshold of the doors. He was also feeling painfully exposed. "I lost my glasses."

"Nonsense. This will do *just* fine my friend! There's too many people in here for anyone to notice your eyes."

Rikket made a beeline for the bar, where surprisingly enough, a handful of stools stood like security guards standing silent vigil over the barkeep, protecting him from the raving fans that cheered just beyond the live-edge wooden slab that served as the bar. Two bartenders were working feverishly behind the counter, pouring ales like water to travellers in the desert, opening whiskey and rum bottles, and doling out twice as many meads. Cole did not recognize either of the bartenders. Must have been a relative or a volunteer here to help. It was clear the standard staff was overwhelmed.

Rikket leapt up onto one of the barstools and motioned for Cole to join him, slapping the bar with a flat palm and shouting at the barkeep like he owned the place. At the same time, he pulled his coin pouch from his hip pocket and sat it on the bar.

"Two single whiskey, and two ale, if you can be so kind! My friend here is thirsty, and I have half a mind to sate my own thirst with him!"

The barkeep nodded, not quite managing to hide the glance he shot at Rikket's coin pouch. The signal was familiar among locals. It meant the equivalent of *start a tab, sir. We're in for the long haul.*

"What are you getting for yourself?" Cole joked, trying to force a smile, despite his mood. He was still sour over his fight with his father. He imagined it was going to take more than a whiskey and an ale to calm him down.

Rikket raised his eyebrows a few times in quick succession, and making sure neither of the barkeepers were watching, he reached over the counter and snatched up a clean glass. From inside the black vest he wore over his usual gray cotton shirt, he produced a small flat glass mickey of innocuous design.

"Sable reserve," he said as he popped the cork that stoppered the mickey and poured some of the lightly golden liquid into the cup he'd stolen. "Only for special occasions. Da calls it *The Prince's Light*. Ha! Poetic bastard he is."

Rikket slid the glass in front of Cole and then raised the mickey.

"To fathers!" Rikket cheered and slammed a drink straight from the small bottle.

"Shade curse them sometimes..." Cole whispered and tipped the glass into his mouth. Prince's Light indeed. The solution burned like liquid sunshine, all the way across Cole's palette, down his throat and deep into his chest. He felt like he had fire itself inside of him, expressed in earnest by the gasp and cough that followed the drink.

"*Whoa!*" was all Cole could manage to say as Rikket stoppered the mickey and slipped it back into his jacket in time for the barkeep to come by with their ale and whiskey.

"Accurate reaction. They call it honey jack. Dad bought a cask of mead from them Reppareons out west just before Havelock. Ran it through a still he made with old man Turb's help.

He named the batch Prince's Light because light be praised, it sure puts the sun itself in your belly!"

Cole shot the whiskey down his throat to help dull the honey jack's burn. It worked to a fashion, but it was a long drink of ale that finally quelled the fire.

"So," Rikket began, himself also finishing his whiskey and settling into the glass of ale. "Not that I'm complaining in the slightest, but to what do we owe the honour for this impromptu celebration?"

Cole shook his head. "Light, you're dumb when you try to sound smart."

"Ha!" Rikket slapped Cole on the back. "And to think I wasted good honey jack on insults. Speak, friend... or forever pay your own bills."

Cole sat silent for a moment or two, or perhaps a mouthful or two of ale, while he tried to find words to explain himself.

"Cloudbreaker came by the booth. A peregrine who came in on the Cirrus. She paid double for the produce she ordered... and I fought with Dad after she left."

Rikket was nodding as he listened to Cole.

"I said some things..." Cole paused to drink deep from his mug. It was already almost empty, so Rikket motioned to the barkeep for another round and got a nod in return. "Some things I regret already. I could see the pain in Dad's eyes."

"Don't do that Cole."

"Do what?"

"Take his anger on yourself."

"I don't think I am, Rikket. I'm just so frustrated... like the war ended and life is suddenly better for everyone but me."

"That's bullshit and you know it, Cole."

"You keep saying that word like it makes sense, but it doesn't."

"Shut up. Listen, Cole, you have got to be one of the stupidest smart people I've ever met. With that mind you carry on top of your neck, you could do anything in this world. So the war ended and the world has peace. You didn't get to ship off and be a cloudbreaker. How is that the end of your story?"

"I'm not talking about peace, Rikket."

"Light, you're confusing. What are we talking about then?"

Cole opened his eyes wide and stared at Rikket. Without his glasses, the third of bright green shone in his otherwise brown eyes. It was a stark green, like a loose emerald that slipped its mount on someone's broach. Rikket shook his head.

"You and those damn eyes, Cole... you were picked on as a kid. So what? You think that for the rest of your life, you have to wear tinted glasses and farm potatoes because you got a little green stuffed in your shit-brown eyeball?"

Cole turned back to his empty beer.

"I can't explain it, Rikket... you don't understand."

"Yeah Cole," Rikket put his hand on his friend's shoulder. "I do understand. I've known since I met you. You think you're cursed. Light be damned this whole *town* thinks so too. You've suffered because of it. And your ma before you. But Cole... man... just because the war ended and you might not escape as a cloudbreaker does *not mean* you're trapped here! Trust me.

That brain on your shoulders is your gift. Not the marked eyes you see the world through. War isn't your only way out. Stop thinking it was. You probably would have been stabbed in the face by some Ciar K'Hen javelin rifle anyway."

Cole scoffed and Rikket took his hand back.

"I'm serious! It's *war*, Cole. More than half the people who went off to fight in it never came back. Use that damn gift of yours, Cole. *Do* something with your mind. The world is at peace... the options are limitless."

"Not for me, Rikket. Not with this *mark*."

"Now you're being obstinate."

"You don't even know what that means."

"Do so! It means Cole Vallen is an obstinate, pig-headed bastard. Why are your options not limitless, Cole? Give me one good reason that doesn't involve your eyes."

Cole swallowed.

"My father is a farmer. His father was a farmer. I will only ever be a farmer."

"Bullshit."

"Again..."

"*Bullshit, Cole Vallen!*" he hollered, startling the barkeep who was setting the new round of whiskeys and ale in front of the boys. Cole didn't know whether to strike his friend or laugh.

"Look, Cole. Someday, you are going to have to get it through that thick smarter-than-your-own-good skull that your life is *yours* and no one else's. No one outside this town is going to care about your damn eyes. They'll care about your mind. Just leave, Cole. Light... let's go right now. Me and you."

Cole's frustration peaked. He was losing control of what he was truly angry about, and annoyance that Rikket was making actual sense was only adding to the building frustration within him. How could he explain that loyalty and love for his family had built the chains that he knew bound him to his fate? How could anyone other than Cole and his mother understand what it was like to exist marked by superstition? Who would understand that even if he *could* explain it? Maybe Aislinn Elissan could.

"Sorry, Rikket," Cole finally relented, after shooting his second whiskey and taking another sip of the new ale to wash it down. The effects of the alcohol were starting to wear on him, his vision was blurring at the edges, and he felt the numb emotion of inebriation tempering the fire within him. "I hate to admit it, but you're right. Wagon's wheel broke on the way into festival the other night, and Dad had some grand speech about how farming is a good life. Then the Cirrus arriving, meeting that peregrine, this festival being such an affair. I guess I'm just overwhelmed."

Rikket responded by producing the honey jack again from inside his vest. This time, he splashed a shot of it directly into each of their ale mugs.

"Cole Vallen accepts intellectual defeat by the *vastly* superior Rikket Sable! The crowd goes wild."

Cole could not help but smile, and the pair lifted their mugs and clinked them together before downing a long drink in tandem. The honey jack boosted the alcohol level in the ale, but the ale also tempered the heat of it. The result was a pleasing warm glow, like a painted sunset versus the afternoon summer sun. As they nodded in agreement to the addition within their drinks, Rikket nodded toward the far end of the bar.

"One thing to praise the light for..." he began, motioning in the direction of his nod by pointing with the ale in his hand. "Is that you weren't born into that damned Pyrell family."

Cole followed Rikket's indications and saw two of the Pyrell youth at the far end of the bar. A server was caught between them and the pressing crowd of people in the pub. Edam Pyrell was the oldest of the two, roughly two years or so older than Cole and Rikket. The younger was his brother Peter. If the adults of Harrow's Town considered the Sable family as bullies, all the youth knew to fear the Pyrell brothers. They had gained their size and strength faster than most of the other kids in the area and used that physical power to establish themselves as alphas within the community. Edam Pyrell especially. He had bullied Cole for most of his life as he recalled it. Until Rikket moved to town and Cole started wearing glasses to hide his eyes. The Pyrells worked for Rikket's father, so once Cole and Rikket became friends, Edam and his brother left Cole alone. Bullies always remained bullies, however. Edam and Peter were harassing the young server, clear as day. Cole recognized her.

Ellie Rispen. Her father owned the public house they sat in. They had been friends when they were younger.

"Edam!" Cole shouted, the sound of his voice surprising even him.

Edam and Peter looked around, unsure where the shout had come from, and then they saw Cole and Rikket at the end of the bar, both looking straight at them. Edam was holding Ellie by the upper arm while Peter made a disgusting display of looking her up and down like a beef cow he was considering at the slaughter yard. It was clear Ellie was in pain, as she tried to pull herself away without causing a scene.

"Let her go," Cole commanded, loud enough that there was no mistaking his words. The shout caught the attention of the barkeep and a whole handful of the people standing near the bar. Edam looked at the barkeep, who was now staring directly at the brothers. He looked around at the people near him who had stopped to gawk. Then he pushed Ellie away, causing her to bump into people and spill her tray.

Edam and Peter made their way around the bar, shoving past people directly toward Cole and Rikket. They stopped at the empty stool directly to the right of Cole. The barkeep started making his way over as Edam grabbed Cole's mug and tore it away from him.

"Mind your own business, you cursed failure," Edam hissed, titling the mug upright over Cole's head. Not a drop of liquid fell from the empty cup. Cole had already finished it.

"Smooth, Edam," Rikket said as he burst out in laughter.

"Take it outside, boys... last thing we need is a scene," the barkeep ordered, reaching across the bar and yanking the mug out of Edam's hands.

Before Edam could react, Cole had stood from his stool and threw a left cross that staggered Edam back into his brother. The right hay-maker punch that followed toppled Edam to the side so that his head bounced off the bar table and his entire body fell to the ground in an unconscious heap. Peter lunged forward and it was then that Cole realized he was far drunker than he thought when he started the fight. Peter's fist connected with Cole's jaw just to the left of his chin and he stumbled backward into Rikket, who was now standing from his stool and managed to catch Cole under the armpits.

"Cole! You okay?" Rikket said. Cole was laughing.

"He hits like one of your Ma's pillows..." Cole giggled.

Peter kicked at Cole, but his foot caught in the stool Rikket had been sitting on and his dancing to free it caused him to fall into the crowd. The people he bumped into crashed into other people, spilling drinks and breaking mugs. Immediately it was as though a candle had been lit in a hayloft. The whole bar erupted into a cheering, laughing, shoving, and brawling mass of bodies. The sounds of shattering glass, ceramic mugs, and breaking furniture were the percussion to the symphony of utter chaos.

"Time to go..." Rikket whispered in Cole's ears, as he started dragging his laughing best friend through the crowd toward the door.

All around them bottles and mugs flew. Ale, mead, wine, and all other manner of libations sprayed through the air with more than likely a bit of blood and saliva included. People tussled and fell everywhere, and yet to Cole, it was all a blur. At one point two fighting patrons knocked Rikket away and Cole was left leaning against a table. He noticed a mug of ale sitting unattended and added it to the witches' brew already in his stomach. A piece of bread loaf on the same table became a quick snack as well just as Rikket found him and resumed their path to escape.

Cole had lost all sensation of time. The storm of emotions, added to the adrenaline of the fight and all the drink had sent him spiralling into a world of inebriation where all he saw was flashing lights in a dim world and a sound that made no sense. Just as they reached the door and the fresh air of the outside hit them, Cole thought he saw dark blue dyed-wool jackets with single lapels rushing into the crowd, breaking up fights and trying to keep the peace. Then Rikket had them out of the public house and was darting down a small alley leading away from the square.

Chapter 5

What we do for friends

Rikket

Rikket Sable ducked into the narrow alley between Swine and Ale and a lengthy building that contained a pharmacy, a doctor's office, and a general store. They were heading straight north. Rikket wanted to get Cole back to his house, but in his condition, he wasn't sure they could make it that far. With one of Cole's arms draped over his shoulders, his best friend stumbled along beside him. The raucous shouting and sounds of the bar fight seemed distant as they echoed into the alley. The crowd must have been spilling out into the square, with some patrons running to escape the brawl, because now and then the shouts became louder as people ran past the entrance to the alley.

Cole was struggling to stay on his feet. Rikket was working hard to keep him upright, but he knew the Pyrell brothers might find them if they stopped. Rikket figured they would not be able to put up much of a fight in their current state. The magic of

Cole's sucker punch, even with him being as strong as he was, would not catch Edam off guard a second time. Edam was too good a fighter. Years of being the town bully had made sure of that.

Cole stumbled on uneven ground in the alley, and Rikket barely managed to keep him standing. A weak apology and drunken laughter came from his friend. Rikket wondered how it was that Cole had become so drunk off the same amount of liquor that Rikket himself had. He must not have eaten anything today, or very little. And there was the speed at which he was knocking them back. His fight with his father affected him more than Cole would admit. Or something else had. He regretted giving Cole so much of the honey jack he had stolen from home. He should have known better.

Rikket reached the end of the alley and looked both ways. The alley emptied into one of the spider-web roads behind the ring road. A big open yard across from them had a pair of trees and a rudimentary bench. It was still too close to the tavern to stop. Mostly, this road was homes and apartment complexes. The street was sparsely populated by people walking and talking to one another. For the most part, they ignored Rikket and Cole, though a few poked their noses into the air down the length of the alley, trying to ascertain the nature of the far-off commotion. Realizing the narrow alley continued into deeper darkness on the other side of the road, Rikket heaved Cole up and secured himself better under Cole's armpit. Cole smiled, despite his head lolling from side to side.

"Yer a gud freend, 'Ket..." Cole slurred, trying to kiss his friend on the cheek.

"By the light. Okay, Cole... let's go."

Rikket led Cole across the street past the park on their left and into the alley on the other side. This one was narrower and darker than before because it threaded a small space between two tall apartment complexes. They must have been about three stories or so. Trash bags and the occasional stray dog or cat provided ample obstacles to the pair as they made their way deeper and deeper into the alley. Further and further from the chaos they trudged, and at last, the world became quiet.

Two more road crossings and Rikket finally felt safe enough to venture walking down the road itself. He hooked to his left after exiting the alley and started walking amid the houses that lined the street here. Cole was becoming worse for wear. His ambling had become almost a shuffle, and now was more of a drag than a shuffle at all. Rikket was essentially carrying Cole at this point, propping up his weight with one of Cole's arms over his shoulder and his neck directly under Cole's armpit. Cole's feet barely moved anymore, every once in a while stirring to kick at the ground once or twice, but then going limp and dragging in the street. The strain on Rikket was enormous, and more than once, people had looked their way with concern. To Rikket's anger though, none of them had asked to help.

"Light, Cole... for a farmer you clearly don't eat enough. Obviously can't handle your liquor."

Rikket's mission swayed from escaping the Pyrells to finding a safe place to rest. They were not far from where the Vallen table had been set up if they doubled back across Butcher's Row to Sable Hill. Rikket decided against that, as he didn't think Jasper Vallen would still be there given what Cole told him about their fight. He couldn't go to his own family. They would find the stolen Honey Jack and Rikket would have his own health to worry about. He knew he would catch the belt for that. The Sable's were called many things, but to Rikket, 'thief' cut the deepest. Just then, Rikket caught sight of what could be their salvation. Up ahead about a hundred meters on the right-hand side of the street, stood the Harrow's Town Temple of the Light, and beside it, the cemetery.

Verdosi people were a superstitious culture, Cole had been right about that much. They worshipped the sun and light but cursed shade and the darkness. There was no safer place to find amnesty in the waning light of day than a cemetery. Rikket shared none of the religious superstition. He had spent most of his youth in the neighbouring kingdom of Akoy before his parents came to Verdos and eventually Harrow's Town. The cemetery was perfect, and he needed to find a place to catch his own breath while he let Cole rest. The Temple may still have the priests inside too. If Rikket could set Cole to rest in a safe place in the cemetery, maybe he could get into the Temple and fetch Cole some water and food. Something to help sober him up. It may not have been the best plan, but at least Rikket finally had one. He could not run all night, especially carrying Cole. His legs were already burning from the effort of the distance they had travelled.

The cemetery had a tall iron and wood fence surrounding it, lavishly decorated with motifs depicting the eternal dance of sun and moon, light and dark, and good and evil. Written off as an ancient fairy tale, most of Verdos still believed in the Sunlight Prince and his battle with his evil brother, the Shade Wizard. Rikket knew the tale well. It was his father's favourite story to tell. Levi Sable had told him as a child that Akoy had their version of the story and Verdos another. It was the book the Verdosi scholar Aldous Corcoran had written that was Rikket's favourite. The peasant girl whose brother was abducted by monsters strikes off into a world of endless darkness to save her kin and in doing so, save the kingdom. Rikket's father said it was a metaphor for winning. That those who think themselves the weakest yet still press on often endure, and the ripples they leave in their wake changes the world. Rikket thought there was much more to the story.

Rikket found the gate in the cemetery fence and silently slid it open. To his surprise, the iron ushered not a squeak as it swung inward. The priests took great care of the building and the fences. Following the cobblestone pathway inward for a little bit where it passed underneath a large oak tree, Rikket found a great place to rest Cole; a gazebo in the center of the cemetery with a handful of concrete benches. As Rikket entered, and to the great relief of his muscles laid Cole down on a bench, he found that he was not alone in the gazebo. Slowly he stood from laying Cole down, flashing his best innocent smile. Across from him, a priest of the Temple stood over a young man also lying on one of the concrete benches.

"Evening, sir..." Rikket began, holding his hands up to show he was not a threat. "Not what it looks like, I assure you. My friend had a bit too much to drink is all. There was a tavern brawl... and we're just looking for somewhere safe to rest. That's all."

The man on the bench moaned, and the priest turned his hooded face away from Rikket a moment. The priest wore long dark purple robes that almost looked like a midnight sky under a full moon. Two long red thick ribbons were strung over his shoulders around his neck so that they fell down the front of his robes like tassels. The tassels were covered in strange symbols Rikket had never seen before. His hood was drawn up completely, and in the dark, Rikket could only see his chin. Realizing the man on the bench was not moving, the priest turned his attention back to Rikket.

"This is no place for you, boy. Begone from here."

Rikket was confused. Firstly, the priest's accent was Akoyan. Secondly, in his years in Verdos he had never heard of a priest of the Temple of the Light rejecting the needy. In Cole's condition, they were definitely needy. Rikket took a couple of steps toward the priest, closing the gap across the gazebo, and passing by a large fountain taking up the center of the space.

"My friend just needs water. Please, and maybe some food. He's quite sick."

The priest waved his hand at Rikket, as though he were banishing a demon away. In his other hand, Rikket noticed he held something tight in his fist. A stoppered vial perhaps. It was hard to tell in the dark. This priest was like none Rikket had ever seen. He began to suspect this man was not a priest at all.

"You know not what you do, boy. Begone!" The man said again, more forceful this time. Rikket stepped closer still. *Who talks like that?* He thought to himself.

"My friend is sick. We come begging the sanctuary of the Temple..."

"I said *begone!*" The priest roared, lunging at Rikket.

Rikket flinched expecting to be hit, but instead, he found the priest stopped dead in mid-lunge. His shouting must have roused the man on the bench, and he had grabbed the priest by the arm holding the vial, stopping him in his tracks. Growling, the priest spun and slapped the man straight across the face. That was all Rikket needed to see, and he threw himself on the false priest, knocking him back into the wall of the gazebo beside the bench the man was on. As the pair of them wrestled, Rikket noticed the man was grasping desperately for something on the ground. Amid his tackle, he must have knocked the vial free of the false priest's hands. The man's grasping fingers reached it and lifted it from the ground.

"No! Don't let him..." screamed the priest as he fought against Rikket's weight on top of him. The priest's hood was thrown back and Rikket got a bit of a look at the haggard toothless face hiding underneath. Rikket held the priest against the wall as best he could, his attention split between the tussle and the man, as he ripped off the cork of the vial like a starving orphan and downed the entire contents in one quick motion. Rikket froze in shock at the sight, and the false priest used the opportunity to wiggle free and bolt off into the darkness. Rikket's attention was wholly on the man now, whose eyes began to radiate a blinding bluish-purple light. Ethereal fog surrounded him, and the light continued to build inside his eyes until it was coming from his mouth, ears, and nose as well. The entire centre of the man's chest was burning as though it had an otherworldly lantern lit inside him. His face contorted as though he was screaming, but no sound came forth.

Rikket had only a flash of a moment to shoot a glance toward Cole, seeing his best friend's eyes flicker in his drunken stupor, blinded by the light building within the man. Then the entire gazebo exploded with brightness and fire. For a moment, night became day within the cemetery. The dust and sundered stone from the benches and gazebo settled and rained down from the sky which had once more succumbed to night.

A pair of temple priests entered the cemetery from the temple with their lanterns held high. Nothing remained of the gazebo save broken stone and shattered benches. A black scar along the ground radiated outwards like a star pattern burned in the stone where the man had been. There was no sign of Rikket or the glowing man at all. As the priests searched the area for any sign of survivors, a moan from the shadows caught one of their attention.

"Over here!" The taller of the Temple priests yelled. His colleague rushed over.

There, in a crumpled heap at the base of a gravestone, was a barely conscious Cole Vallen. Blood trickled from a gash on his forehead, and his clothing was scorched and still smoldering in places. Pieces of stone from the gazebo lay all around him. As the priest who discovered him bent to check his vital signs, the other rushed off toward the Temple to call for the marshall and find help. Cole's eyes fluttered open for a second and then closed. His breath came in shallow gasps, and with barely a whisper, he uttered the name:

"Rikket."

Chapter 6

Initial investigation

Aislinn

Aislinn Elissan stepped across a large piece of stone rubble and surveyed the scene of the explosion in the cemetery. The gazebo location was mostly isolated from the public by hastily erected barriers of whatever the local marshall could gather in the two days since the incident. Rope and twine, mostly, made a makeshift fence around the scene. In the light of day, the devastation from the explosion was more evident, with parts of the gazebo and nearby headstones completely torn from their locations and scattered about. Two priests stood far off to the left toward the church, speaking with the marshall who promptly left the conversation when he noticed Aislinn moving among the rubble.

The marshall was a pudgy man, well-fed and even more well-rested. He bore a groomed beard below a shining bald head, as though his hair had lost the war with gravity and simply slid down his face. As he came to a stop beside Aislinn, he drew a deep breath to mask how out of breath he was from his short trot. Aislinn smiled, noting the bead of sweat already rolling from his temple down his cheek. The marshall reached out with his mitt-like hand in introduction.

"You must be Aislinn Elissan. Heard you were offering help. Marshall Heff Jemmo. Pleasure to meet you, ma'am."

Aislinn nodded and reached out her hand to clasp Jemmo's paw. His palms were sweaty, and his grip was soft. Aislinn added a surge of grip to her handshake, noting the faint wince on Jemmo's face. She took special note of the way Jemmo rotated his right shoulder as he took his hand back.

"Pleasure is mine, marshall Jemmo. Something wrong with your shoulder?"

The marshall paused a moment, his eyes widening, before rolling his shoulder a second time and reaching across to rub it with his left hand.

"What? Oh. Yes, sir. Old injury. Grew up working the mills here long before I was elected marshall. Gets to me now and then. Impressive you noticed."

Aislinn smiled and nodded.

"Indeed," she replied before motioning to the scene before them. "I suspect the captain briefed you why I would like to offer my services?"

"She did," Jemmo coughed. "Must admit I'm not quite sure what about this case needs the attention of a special investigator though."

Aislinn took a couple of steps closer to the star-pattern scorch marks where the gazebo had been. She stooped down and looked first to her left, where the two priests remained speaking to one other in hushed tones. She looked ahead, seeing the cracked headstone the surviving boy had crashed into when thrown by the explosion. She noted the now-dried blood stains from the survivor's injury. Finally, Aislinn turned her attention to the remains of the fountain in the center of the gazebo ruins. She stood and approached the fountain. Reaching out, she ran her fingertips over the stone for a moment. Lifting her fingers to appraise the film on them, she rubbed them together and sniffed lightly, before turning back to the marshall.

"After the war, the North Alliance decreed that to keep certain talented members of the Airship Service gainfully employed, they would create new functions for us. New roles in which to serve. In testing, I showed exceptional aptitude for investigation and research, and so I was offered assignment to a new unit, the Special Investigative Service."

The marshall's confusion emboldened Aislinn, and she bowed ever so slightly before continuing.

"Cloudbreaker marshalls. So to speak. Fear not, I have no intention of overriding your authority over this matter. Not unless I have to. I'm just offering my assistance while we are here."

Jemmo nodded and swallowed audibly, his gullet jiggling below his thick beard.

"Fair as it stands," Jemmo answered.

"What have you uncovered so far, Marshall Jemmo?"

Jemmo cleared his throat, attempting to insert a dash of charismatic authority like Aislinn was demonstrating. He was unsettled. Aislinn turned up a faint smile in the corner of her lip as Jemmo turned away to begin his debrief. She so enjoyed being the smartest person in the room.

"Witnesses say they heard a commotion in the cemetery on the evening of the incident. They were in the temple preparing for prayers the following morning. There was a blinding flash and an explosion that rattled the windows of the temple. When they arrived outside, they found a local boy injured against that headstone over there, mumbling the name Rikket over and over. Rikket's another local boy. Only son of Leviticus Sable and his wife Seran Se'Baht Sable. No one else was here, and by the *light* you could smell the hooch coming off the Vallen boy. Could smell it from the gate over there."

Aislinn's eyebrow furled. "Cole Vallen?" he asked.

Jemmo nodded.

"The survivor. He's in rough shape. Prime suspect right now. I think he did this or is responsible anyhow. Folk say he started an altercation at the Swine and Ale earlier in the evening. He was dragged out by Rikket Sable."

"And what of Rikket Sable? Was he found? Or have you not identified the remains yet?"

Jemmo coughed and spun to face Aislinn.

"Light no! What remains? I don't see a body here. Rikket's missing. That's all. The Sables are prominent members of the township here. Only Akoyan Nobles I know of that live in these parts. Moved here a few years back. If he was dead..."

"I suspect he is."

Jemmo stared at Aislinn with a stunned expression on his face. Aislinn responded by holding up the two fingers she brushed against the fountain. The ash was red, but the stone was dark gray. She also pointed to the ground at the base of the fountain, and along the edges of the rubble that made up the gazebo walls. Singed gore was evident in abundance. Jemmo's face went white, and he swayed as though he was about to pass out. Aislinn sighed and turned around to walk into the center of the start pattern. She looked around low and high, before speaking slowly.

"Whatever exploded was right here in this very spot judging by the scorch marks and the dispersal of the debris from the gazebo. Everything closest to this spot faced heat high enough to melt the stone on the fountain, and the bench that was on this side."

Aislinn pointed to a slab of stone that looked little more than melted candle wax.

"The explosion would have evaporated anyone who was lying on this bench, but Cole Vallen was on that side, shielded from the blast by the fountain. That's why he survived. He took impact, but not the heat."

Aislinn pointed to the ground a few steps away from where she was, near the fountain but closer to where the wall of the gazebo would have been. There was a break in the charred ground where the stone was clean. The spot looked like foot-prints.

"Someone was standing there when the explosion happened. What vexes me though, is there is no material in the stone. No metal. No wood. No parts of a bomb or explosive in sight. It should have been embedded in the stone. There should have been something..."

As Aislinn bent to continue looking closer at the ground and the surroundings, Jemmo took an opportunity to breathe deep and wipe the sweat pooling on his forehead. He frowned, taking it all in, and then addressed Aislinn hastily.

"Wait... how do you know red ash and scattered gore means Rikket Sable may be dead?"

"For one, you said Cole was repeating the name Rikket. That means he was here with him, and likely the last thing he saw before the explosion. For two..."

Aislinn lowered her head and pointed off at an upward angle across the cemetery. The line she drew was directly from her spot in the center of the star burn, across the clean footprints just to the right of the fountain, above and to the right of where Cole Vallen had been lying on the bench when the explosion occurred. In a tree across the cemetery yard directly where Aislinn was pointing, hidden among the foliage and tangled up amid the branches, was a mutilated and burnt human carcass.

"We have to identify the remains to be sure, but I am reasonably certain that is him. From what you have added, I would infer that Rikket carried Cole here to hide from someone they crossed at the tavern."

Jemmo fought back a gag as Aislinn stood and started walking toward the priests by the temple.

"I have some questions for the witnesses," she said as she passed Jemmo. The marshall seemed pleased with the distraction from the gore in the far-off tree and turned hastily to follow Aislinn. As they approached the pair, Jemmo took the lead and introduced Aislinn.

"Father Impress, Father Ratly, this is... uh... Investigator Aislinn Elissan. She would like to ask you both some questions."

Aislinn bowed courteously.

"Aislinn is fine. I understand you were in the temple when you heard the explosion. How would you describe the sound? Was it a whoosh like a bonfire starting up, or a boom like dynamite would sound?"

The priests looked at one another, confused and shrugging as they tried to recall the details of the night. Impress spoke first, a tall thin man with graying hair and a clean-shaven face. His trailing stole scarf bore the markings of the Order of the Light, and the golden-white tassels at its ends indicated he was one of the ranking priests at the temple. He had striking features, and ice-blue eyes that reflected the sadness inherent in the event he was recounting.

"I was in the grand hall when it happened," he began, making direct eye contact with Aislinn as he recounted his experiences of the event. "The glass in the temple shook, and there was a rumbling that followed, like thunder but inside the walls."

Ratly nodded his bald head, the light mustache that graced his face twitching as he prepared to speak. His hazel-brown deep-set eyes shared the same grief that Impress had shown. He wore the same standard Order of the Light robes as Impress, but no stole scarf to indicate his ranking.

"I was in the foyer, sweeping before mass the following day. What Father Impress says best describes it. It was like thunder indoors, shaking everything. The light was so bright, coming from outside. It was shocking to see such brightness in the dark of night. Dare I say it... it was almost holy."

Aislinn nodded and frowned.

"Did either of you get a good look at the light? Through a clear window? Could you recall a colour to it?"

Both priests paused a moment before Impress spoke first again.

"I apologize, Aislinn Elissan. The glass in the main hall is stained... though I did experience the brightness, I cannot recall a colour."

There was a moment of silence while Ratly pondered the question. Finally, he spoke.

"I never thought to recall, but now that you ask it, I do remember the front doors to the temple were open to let the evening air inside. I do recall a purple-blue flash before white and finally red."

Aislinn nodded.

"And when you rushed outside, what did you see?"

"Horror," Father Impress stated as Ratly nodded beside him. "We saw horror. Flame all around and stone torn asunder. Our cemetery had become the wasteland you see before you, and our gazebo and fountain were gone. And then..."

"That was when you found Cole Vallen?" Aislinn asked.

"Yes," Father Impress spoke first again. "I heard him, moaning in the dark, and I went to him. Found him at the base of Chebbit Astor's tombstone. He was burned pretty badly, and his forehead cut deep. He could not answer questions and was barely conscious. He kept repeating the name Rikket, over and over. The Sables have a son named Rikket... do you suppose that is who he was referring to?"

"It seems quite likely. Was anyone else here? Did you see any other people in the cemetery that night?" Aislinn said almost under her breath.

"No. Not a soul beyond us and young Cole Vallen after the explosion," said Father Impress. Jemmo was white as a cloud.

"Thank you, Fathers. That is all my questions. If I think of anything else, I will call on you."

The priests nodded and blessed Aislinn with customary hand gestures meant to depict a rising sun.

"May the Light forever shine for you, Aislinn Elissan."

Aislinn nodded and started to walk back toward the gazebo. Something was not adding up for her. Her jaw was set, and she was searching the scene with eyes like an eagle scouting for fish in a river far below. She barely took notice when Jemmo slipped away to speak to a deputy at the edge of the cemetery. Based on the hunched and defeated posture of the marshall, and his vague gestures toward the oak tree, Aislinn surmised he was likely instructing his deputy to send for the coroner.

Suddenly Aislinn froze in mid-step. Her gaze fixed on the ground beneath him. There was no path in this section of the cemetery, just dirt and grass that was not burnt from the explosion. Aislinn knelt, reaching out with a finger and lightly brushing a disturbed piece of grass. The sod had been torn up here, revealing a bit of the dirt below, like a small divot. Aislinn turned her head toward the temple and saw more of the same. The marks seemed to form a trail, first to the left, then to the right, separated by an unmistakably human gait. Someone had run past here in a hurry, and not only that, but they had also suddenly veered away from the temple toward the street. Aislinn followed the tracks to the edge of the cemetery where they disappeared. On the iron fence above, Aislinn spotted a small piece of torn cloth hanging from the top. It was dark purple.

Jemmo approached and looked up at the fence.

"I still think the Vallen kid did this. Open and shut. Does seem suspicious though. Why bomb your friend? Jealous of the Sable money, perhaps? Or maybe just drunk farm kids making homemade explosives that got out of hand?"

Aislinn turned to Jemmo, concentrating on keeping emotion off her face so the marshall would not suspect her surprise. Given the state of the investigation before Aislinn's arrival, however, she did not believe hiding *anything* from this man was a difficult task. Except perhaps food.

"I found footprints in the grass there, leading to this fence. Someone else could have been here. Ran away in a hurry and left that clothing up top when they climbed over."

Jemmo bent down and rubbed his finger in the dirt of one of the divots.

"Been a hunter most my life. This looks old... lot of local kids always playing pranks in this place."

Aislinn pressed her teeth together to stem her retort.

"So Cole Vallen is still your suspect?"

"Yes ma'am. You aren't certain? Shade be damned I can *not* see another scenario here. Sables have had to deal with hate since the day they arrived here. The whole town is jealous of them. There is a motive, and the Vallens are cursed. But this..."

Aislinn followed Jemmo's meaty paw as it gestured to the scene before them.

"Just cannot see who else could have done this."

Aislinn's curiosity was suddenly piqued. "What do you mean the Vallens are cursed?"

"Goes a long way back, that story. All folk around here know it. The boy and his mother are marked. You can see it in their eyes. Both are the same or were the same. She died in childbirth. Jasper Vallen has never had a good go of it. Now there's this..."

"Have you spoken with Cole Vallen yet?"

Jemmo shook his head.

"No. The boy is still in the treatment center. Has not woken up just yet."

"Well... let us hope he wakes soon and recalls the evening."

As Jemmo turned to walk away, Aislinn took another look up at the cloth on the fence. The investigation left a sour taste in her mouth. Not only because of the marshall's ineptitude but also because the evidence she was seeing was far beyond what this sleepy town was equipped to handle. Thunder like it was inside. Blueish purple light. Explosions without explosive materials. It was becoming all too familiar. She sighed and followed Jemmo, even though she had had more than his fill of the man. She needed to speak to Cole Vallen and she needed to know if the remains in the tree were Rikket Sable. More than anything, she needed to convince herself she was wrong about what she believed had happened.

Chapter 7

The waking nightmare

Jasper/Cole

Jasper Vallen's gnarled hands hung limp from his knees as he leaned forward in the chair given to him by the treatment center staff. His hunched back looked as though he carried the weight of a full field of potatoes on his shoulders. He emitted a deep sigh and lifted his head to watch his son through tired and bloodshot eyes as the boy fought to breathe each ragged breath. Over the last day or so, Cole's condition had begun to improve, but the danger still felt palpable. Jasper's sun-bleached cheeks were now stained with tears that could no longer fall, and so his eyes puffed and turned red as another wave of emotion battered him.

The treatment center room was a small wooden-walled square with a concrete floor and a single window. When it was dark, a pair of shielded gas lanterns cast a warm glow over everything, seeming to eliminate all shadow. They were off now though, as the mid-day sun provided ample light through the glass. Below the window sat the steel-framed bed that Cole was on. He was covered to his chest in a few thin blankets. A thick bandage covered the wound on his forehead as well as his left eye, which had swollen shut the morning after the explosion. Beside the bed, a table held a chamber pot, some medicine flasks, and other rudimentary medical tools such as scissors and bandages. A nurse strolled into the room just as Cole drew another ragged breath. Jasper nodded at her without a word.

"Good day, Mr. Vallen," the nurse cooed in a sympathetic voice.

"Good day."

The nurse approached Cole's bedside and set down a tray she had brought in with her. There was a bowl on the tray, and Jasper saw a wisp of steam come off it. There was also a flask and some cloth napkins. She was a warm woman, curvaceous and mature, with curly black hair, pulled back into a tight bun. She wore the white robes of her profession and carried herself like a commanding mother-hen. After setting the tray down on the small table and moving other implements around to organize, she leaned forward, listening to Cole breathe for a moment. Her head turned toward Jasper and she gave a smile that lifted his spirits ever so slightly.

"He's sounding better this morning."

Jasper nodded.

"Been like that most of the night and mornin'," Jasper replied as he sat back in the chair and rubbed his left shoulder with his right hand. The nurse nodded and stood, turning away to busy herself with the bowl.

"Have you slept, Mr. Vallen?"

"Not as much as I should, but more than I wanted to…"

"You need your strength to be there for your son, Mr. Vallen. We can bring a cot in for you if you want?"

Jasper continued to rub his shoulder as he thought about her words. He watched her stir the contents of the bowl with a spoon, before placing a napkin under Cole's chin.

"Don't fuss over me, ma'am. I'll be alright."

The nurse nodded. Jasper suspected he was going to see a cot by the end of the day regardless. He had never crossed paths with this woman before, but he knew of her. The town was too small for a person like her not to spread a reputation. She was a true saint.

"That more medicine?" Jasper asked as the nurse began spooning what looked like pudding from the bowl into Cole's mouth.

"Just some porridge. Food to give him strength."

She was gentle with Cole like she was feeding a sick infant. She waited patiently after the spoon was away for Cole's instinct to kick in and swallow. Jasper braced himself for the coughing and choking that had followed each time a nurse had fed Cole to date, but nothing came. Just a silent swallow, over and over, until Cole had nearly finished the whole bowl. The nurse set the bowl down and picked up the flask. She removed the cap and swung it aside, tilting it slowly to Cole's mouth. This time there was a sputter of a cough.

"Dear me," she soothed. "Sorry about that."

She exchanged the flask for a napkin and dabbed away the spilled water from the corner of Cole's mouth. A weak reply seemed to stop time in the room.

"Thank you."

Jasper was frozen a moment, but when the surprised nurse turned to him, he shot to his feet. In a moment, he was at the bedside opposite the nurse.

"Cole?" he whimpered, fresh tears running down his cheeks.

"Dad..." Cole replied, his right eye fluttering open slightly before squinting against the light. "Hurts..."

The nurse immediately understood and moved to draw the curtains across the windows. Shade coated the room as she began to turn the lantern knobs to shed a gentler light than the strong sun. Cole's eye opened and found his father's face in the gloom. Jasper sobbed and took up his son's hand, consciously aware to hold it lightly.

"Cole," the words came rough, strained through intense emotions. "You came back to me, son. You came back."

Cole swallowed and did his best to smile. He opened his mouth to speak but then slipped back into unconsciousness. The nurse leaned forward over him and put an ear close to his mouth. Jasper stroked his hand and sobbed, waiting for the news he hoped she would share.

"He's sleeping," she said as a relieved smile spread across her face. "That was a great sign. I'll fetch the doctor right away, but I think he's going to be just fine."

Over the next two days, Cole's condition steadily improved to the point where he could sit up in bed and feed himself the porridge the treatment center provided. One night, when he moaned about the same food being served again, Jasper was allowed to bring him a soft potato stew. Cole ate two bowls. The doctor visited late in the afternoon on the second day, telling Cole that he had suffered a traumatic head injury and burns to nine percent of his body, mostly his right leg and abdomen. He was told little about what happened, just that there had been an accident and when he was ready, the marshall wanted to speak to him. This made Cole flush with worry. He had been wondering why there was an ankle chain on him.

Cole had noticed the chain on the morning after he first woke up. He had felt an itch and reached down to scratch it, only to find a leather cuff around his right ankle. A thick chain was attached to the cuff, and following it off the edge of the bed, Cole saw that it was anchored to a steel plate bolted into the concrete. The only answer he had been given by the nurses, doctor, and his father was that it was for his protection. The doctor had explained a little further than the others, saying that head injury patients can sometimes wake up not themselves, and often run or injure themselves further. It made sense, but Cole suspected there was more to the story. His suspicions were increased every time his father and caretakers avoided questions about how he ended up in the treatment center.

On the morning of his third day awake, shortly after the nurse had left with his breakfast porridge, the door to his room opened and in walked Marshall Jemmo followed closely by Aislinn Elissan. Jasper Vallen stood and brushed his hands on his thighs. Cole was elated to see Aislinn again, but his excitement collapsed when he saw how nervous his father was as he shook their hands. Marshall Jemmo was the first to approach the foot of Cole's bed. Cole was sitting upright, his back propped by comfortable pillows set against the headboard. The morning sun was shining through the open windows, sparkling off the sweat beading on the top of Jemmo's scalp. Aislinn took up position to Jemmo's left, as Jasper came around past all of them and sat on the edge of Cole's bed. He grasped Cole's hand, and Cole squeezed back, swallowing hard.

"Good morning, Cole," Jemmo began. His gaze darted from Cole's to Jaspers, a brief moment making eye contact with Aislinn, and then back to Cole. He lingered a moment on Cole's bandage still covering his left eye. Cole didn't miss the sigh of relief Jemmo ushered. The marshall cleared his throat. "If you don't mind, Inspector Elissan and I have some questions about the incident that occurred during the festival."

Cole shared a look with his father, Aislinn, and finally made eye contact with Jemmo. There was a slight twitch to the man's beard and a subtle shift in the shape of the man's eyes. His ears bounced upward ever so slightly. He was clenching his jaw.

"Tell me, Cole," the marshall began, taking on an authoritative and almost menacing tone. "What happened? What do you remember?"

Cole swallowed hard, searching his mind. He found only pain, flashes of it. There was light. Anger. He searched further and finally found memories that coalesced. He held onto those and started, which was as clear to him as the room was now.

"I fought with my father," Cole swallowed as his father's grip on his hand tightened. He continued. "At our booth during the festival. It was about my future and how I was feeling trapped. I left and went to the square... I was looking for... for..."

Cole trailed off as realization dawned on him. His father had been here the whole time since he woke up. Doctors and nurses had come to see him. Even Father Impress from the Temple had been by, but Cole had pretended to be asleep for that visit. So many had come, but not his best friend. The name spoken aloud was like a hammer to his chest.

"Rikket."

Aislinn watched Cole intently. The way her eyes burned into him made Cole uneasy. He blinked a tear from his right eye.

"Where is Rikket?" Cole suddenly pleaded. He looked at his father. "Why hasn't Rikket come to see me? Is he okay?"

Jasper Vallen's face scrunched up like he had just been hit with a foul odour, but in his eyes, Cole read pain. His eyebrows crushed in toward one another, bunching up the skin of his forehead into waves like a crackled ocean. Fluid shone at the outer corners of his eyelids where the crow's feet of a hard life became more pronounced in his grimace. His nostrils flared. Cole could tell he wanted to speak, but couldn't. It was Aislinn Elissan who did.

"Cole, please focus. We need to know what happened after you found Rikket."

Cole lingered on his father's face a moment longer. Then he turned to look directly at Aislinn. The sharp bird-like features of the Cloudbreaker were almost emotionless. Everything about her posture was exuding measured professionalism. But there was something in her eyes. Something she wasn't able to hide. A subtle shift to their shape. A glistening of their surface. The woman was excellent at hiding her emotions. *How am I seeing this?* Cole thought to himself. He cleared his throat and continued his story, keeping eye contact with Aislinn.

"Rikket said I was a man who needed a drink, so we headed to the Swine and Ale together. It was packed with people, but we made our way to the bar anyway. There were stools, so we sat at them..."

As Cole recounted the story of what happened, he was also re-living it all in his mind. He could see the greased hairs of the barkeep's mustache. The scratched lines of the bar top. The knots and burs of the live-edge counter. He recalled exactly how the hardwood of the stool felt, polished almost to a glass finish by all the rumps that had perched atop it in its years. He recalled the sound Edam Pyrell's head made as it thudded against the bar. The sting he felt in his knuckles after the punch. The iron taste of the little bit of blood Peter drew when he hit Cole. But the further he made it into the evening, the blurrier everything became. Was he truly that drunk? As Cole's story reached the point of being dragged through the alleys by Rikket during their escape, he faltered.

"I... I can't remember what happened next..."

Cole squinted, losing his eye contact with Aislinn. He focused on the bedsheets covering his legs. His breath quickened. There was a twitch in his right hand. He was panicking.

"What am I forgetting?" he breathed as a touch of anger welled up inside, adding to the anxiety. "Why can I remember everything else in perfect detail... but... then it's just... it's just..."

The twitching in his fingers stopped. His breath caught.

"Light."

Aislinn couldn't contain her surprise. Cole saw it. A spastic jerk in the woman's muscles. She was stepping forward.

"Light," Cole continued. "Light and fire. Fragments. Then nothing... just darkness."

Marshall Jemmo scoffed and turned to Aislinn.

"Cursed," he breathed through gritted teeth. His intent was for Aislinn alone to hear it, but he missed the intended volume. When he turned back to make eye contact with Cole, he found

Jasper's gaze instead. It burned through him. Cole could see the marshall swallow.

"How much had you drank, Cole? Did you and Rikket bring a homemade explosive to the cemetery?"

Cole coughed in surprise.

"A bomb? Do you think I set off a bomb?

The marshall squirmed.

"Did you?" he pressed.

"Of course not!"

"You're a smart lad, Cole Vallen. Boredom and smarts are a dangerous mix. Maybe you were too drunk to remember. Did you bring anything with you?"

"I didn't make a bomb..."

"Was there someone else with you and Rikket? Did anyone else see you in the cemetery that night?"

"I don't remember..."

"Can you prove you didn't make a bomb?"

"I didn't have a bomb!" Cole finally shouted. He had enough of the accusations. He couldn't remember anything. The further he and Rikket made it through the alleys, the more shattered the memories became. By the time he recalled the cold stone of a bench, that was all there was. Cold stone. Followed by light and fire. And pain.

"Ask Rikket. He'll tell you. He was helping me... he..."

Cole sobbed and Aislinn stepped forward. Cole didn't miss the withering glare the cloudbreaker fired at marshall Jemmo. When she made eye contact with Cole it was as though they were the only two in the room. The feeling made Cole swallow involuntarily.

"Cole," Aislinn began in a tone both soothing and firm. "Rikket Sable was killed in an explosion. The same explosion that you were injured in."

The edges of Cole's vision turned gray, and eventually black. The narrowing of his vision continued until the only thing left was Aislinn's face. Cole blinked a few times, and then mercifully fell into that quiet darkness as Aislinn repeated his name.

"Cole. Cole!"

The next time Cole's eyes opened it was to the same frame. The exact place where he had lost consciousness, only this time without Aislinn Elissan's concerned visage. Just the empty upper-right corner of the room from Cole's perspective. It was night. The faint light in the room came from the turned-down lanterns. Jasper Vallen was slumped in the chair on the opposite side of the room. His face was in his hands. There was a subtle tremor in his shoulders.

"Dad," Cole whispered. "Is it true? Is Rikket..."

Jasper Vallen sat up and wiped at his face. He sighed and then stood, crossing the room to sit on the left end of Cole's bed. He took a deep breath and Cole waited for the answer he could already see written all over his father's face.

"Yeah, son. It's true. Funeral for him was yesterday."

Cole swallowed his emotions.

"They think I did it?"

Silence flooded the room as Jasper Vallen fought with his inner turmoil. Cole read every detail of it on his skin.

"Dad," Cole pleaded. "Please."

Jasper Vallen nodded finally.

"Yeah, Cole. Marshall Jemmo thinks you made a bomb and just don't remember. There's going to be a trial, as soon as the doctor clears you."

A tear ran down Cole's face.

"Dad, you know that's not true. I would never..."

Jasper squeezed his son's hand hard.

"I know, Cole. I know."

For what seemed like forever, Jasper and Cole sat in silence with one another, just feeling each other's presence. Occasionally, Jasper would squeeze Cole's hand and receive a light squeeze in turn. It felt like all that was needed for the moment between them, but it was only Cole trying to find the right words for what he needed to say.

"Dad, about our fight," he began. "I said some things I regret. I don't want to be pitied for being a farmer. I insulted you... and our heritage. I'm sorry."

Jasper Vallen did something that surprised Cole at that moment. He laughed.

"Cole. Son. That fight is spilled milk. I said things I regret too. It's behind us. You have nothing to apologize for."

There was another long silence before Cole spoke again.

"We really are cursed, aren't we?"

Jasper shook his head, made eye contact with his son, and then shrugged his weathered shoulders. Somehow, it almost seemed like a weight had been lifted from him.

"Perhaps we are."

Chapter 8

Praying to be wrong

Aislinn

Masons and the temple priests had quickly begun repairing the damage to the cemetery in the days after the marshall cleared the site. Much of the damage had already been repaired, especially the headstones. The gazebo was mostly demolished, but it was going to take a long time to complete its reconstruction. It was a Sunday, so none of the usual workers were in the cemetery when Aislinn Elissan arrived. That suited her fine. She wanted privacy to address some of her burning concerns without the presence of Jemmo.

After their short talk with Cole Vallen, Marshall Jemmo had doubled down on his accusations that implicated Cole in the bombing. He was leaning heavily into the story that Cole had been playing with explosives while drunk. They were calling the charges 'involuntary murder.' It may have sounded as though it carried an air of mistake, but the word murder illustrated what it really was. The town was scared. The only son of the most prominent noble was killed in a bizarre explosion, and they wanted a scapegoat. Cole Vallen was that scapegoat. The mob was ready to lynch him, regardless of the truth of the matter. They whispered of the Vallen curse, in hushed tones while standing in shady corners. Cole set the bomb. He must have.

Aislinn had little success in unearthing the nature of this rumoured curse at first. Eventually, she learned that Cole and his mother both shared unusual eyes. Devil eyes, some had called them. Marked eyes, were the words of others. Aislinn had not yet been able to see this for herself though because the bandages had been covering Cole's left eye when they spoke in the treatment center, and he was wearing those tinted glasses when they first met. The thought had occurred to her that perhaps Cole knew exactly what he was doing by hiding his eyes. This town had shown him its true colours, and it made sense why Cole would hide. She imagined that his mother experienced much of the same. She had died in childbirth. The Vallens had suffered ever since. Now Cole was the sole survivor of the most shocking event to befall this town in living memory. Suspicious indeed.

Aislinn had grown up an orphan, abandoned on the steps of the Imperial Archives as a child along with her twin brother Bayne. Their entire childhood and adolescence had been spent among books, scholars, and wise old men and women. She considered herself an intelligent woman, possessed of a rare set of gifts. Insight and intuition. She could take in the most minute details, and read people and the world around her like words on a page. The talent got her in trouble more often than not in her youth, but it made her excel as a cloudbreaker, and then again later when she took her peregrine training. The same went for her brother. After the war, it was that very same skill set that earned her top marks in the role reassignment tests. The day they gave Aislinn the new rank as the first special investigator in the service of the Kingdom of Verdos was a proud day for her. But insight and intuition were not Aislinn Elissan's only gifts. She was also blessed with a fantastic memory, and it was that memory that nagged her now.

"Thunder inside..." Aislinn whispered as she bent once more in the center of the star-shaped burn on the stone. "An explosion without a bomb..."

"Suppose I shouldn't be surprised to find ya talkin' to yerself," came a grizzly bear of a voice behind her. Aislinn smiled. She didn't need to turn around. She knew exactly who it was. "What are ya doin' here, ya nutter?"

"Lucius," Aislinn said as she kept her gaze on the ground, scanning for any clue she might have missed. Any piece or part of a bomb. "What brings you away from the tavern, Chief? Wrestled everyone out of their coin already?"

"Nah," Lucius grunted. "Not one soul in this town can afford to pay me anyhow. I didn't bother. Came to find you."

Aislinn turned her head to look up at her friend. The huge barrel-chested engineer cut an imposing figure standing over Aislinn; over almost anyone, for that matter. He wore baggy cargo slacks made from leather and canvas, with pockets on his hips and thighs to hold the numerous tools of his trade. A dark reddish cotton shirt covered his massive torso, high-necked and crisscrossed with leather straps and an old pair of suspenders. Over top all of it was his thick dark-brown leather engineer's coat. He was never seen without it. Folk closest to him swore he slept in the thing. Aislinn knew it to be true. He sported graying black hair combed back smooth to his scalp, and a beard that came to a point below his chin groomed straight to match his hair. Aislinn thought of him as a handsome man, but the more you complimented him, the more he would cover himself in grease and oil. Aislinn smiled up at him.

"Find me? What for?"

Lucius shrugged and looked around for a place to sit. He whistled softly at the scene.

"Heard a few whispers 'bout what happened here. Don't do it justice though, ta see it wit' my own eyes."

Aislinn nodded and followed his gaze around the area.

"Yeah. It's quite the mess."

"Hear tell a local boy made himself a bomb?"

Aislinn shook her head and sighed. She stood up, brushed her hands together, and faced her friend.

"I don't think so."

Lucius grunted and then made eye contact with Aislinn. The look on the small woman's face illustrated concern. In all the years Lucius had known Aislinn, he had rarely seen her looking this serious.

"Thunder inside," Aislinn began, almost in a whisper. "Blueish-purple light. A bomb that wasn't a bomb. I've been over this area five times, Lucius. Not a shred of metal in the stone. Not a spec of chemical residue. Just ash. And blood."

If there was colour to his skin below the soils of the airship engineering spaces, it drained from Lucius' skin.

"Can't be..."

Aislinn paced back and forth. She waved her hand in the air making gestures as she spoke.

"Could be some of the weapons made it out of Matan Ba'al after the war, but it's unlikely. And why this far north? There are *much* bigger targets in the south. Gallenfort for sure. Vandrad even. Why an Akoyan noble's son? Why *here*?"

Aislinn stopped and she looked her friend in the eye. Something had occurred to her.

"Neither of the boys were the intended target. Had to be someone else."

Aislinn grabbed Lucius by the shoulders and tried to guide the huge tank of a man into the center of the star pattern. Lucius didn't budge.

"Aislinn," Lucius rolled his eyes.

"Humor me."

Grudgingly, Lucius allowed himself to be piloted by the woman until he was standing perfectly in the center of the star pattern. Once she was satisfied with Lucius' position, she ran around to the other side of the melted fountain and laid down roughly where Cole would have been if his story had been true.

"Aislinn, what are you doing?"

Aislinn looked around and shifted her position a bit. Not yet satisfied, she spun around to put her head on the opposite end of the bench and her feet where her head had been. She could see the unimpressed face of Lucius staring at her across the top of the wrecked fountain.

"Bend down," Aislinn commanded.

"What?"

"Bend down Lucius!"

Lucius grunted and lowered himself. Aislinn could still see the top of his head just peeking over the fountain.

"Bit further."

Lucius obeyed and the last of his hair vanished below the rubble.

"Good! How tall are you, Lucius?"

"Six foot two, give or take. Where ya goin' with this?"

Aislinn was running mental calculations as she looked around for confirmation that she was right.

"And how far have you squatted down do you think?"

There was a moment while Lucius considered the request before his reply.

"Maybe a foot? Just under?"

"Five and a half..." Aislinn whispered. She looked down at his feet.

"Lucius, can you see my feet? Without standing up."

"Yeah," he replied. "From the thigh down, and part of your side. The other leg is hidden."

Aislinn grinned. She had figured out exactly where Cole was lying. What Lucius could see were the exact parts of Cole that had suffered burns.

"Light and fire," Aislinn whispered and then sat up. A pleading glance from Lucius was met by a nod from Aislinn and relieved, the old engineer straightened to full height and stretched his back.

"The boys were not the target. They were just in the wrong place at the wrong time. They must have seen something. I think Rikket set Cole down here to rest and then tried to intervene. He was too close to the blast. He was dead before he hit the tree, and Cole was mostly protected by the fountain here. Cole Vallen is innocent."

A gloomy Lucius walked around and leaned on the fountain, looking down at Aislinn who still sat on the ruined bench.

"Way I hear it, none of that is goin' ta matter."

Aislinn nodded in agreement.

"The whole town thinks the Vallens are cursed. Something to do with their eyes, but I haven't seen them yet so I can't be sure. Cole was wearing glasses when I first met him. Bandages later in the treatment center."

"Strange eyes mean a man's cursed? Lord you Verdosi are a wild lot."

"Just this town, actually," Aislinn began. "I remember an old tome I read mentioning people with strange eyes being lordly. Almost worshipped."

Aislinn suddenly paused and looked up at Lucius thoughtfully.

"Why were you looking for me?"

Lucius grunted.

"Cirrus is leavin'. Cap'n sent me ta fetch ya."

"Leaving?" Aislinn asked more than a little surprised and maybe even a bit disappointed.

"Yeah. Hiram Errbryte's having a birthday party or somethin' at his estate. Cap'ns been ordered ta make an appearance. Means all of us too."

Aislinn whistled.

"The elusive alchemist *and* a visit to the famed Errbryte estate. Now *that* is something."

Lucius held a hand out. He could already tell what his old friend was thinking.

"Yer not thinkin' of staying, Aislinn?"

"I am."

"Aislinn..."

Aislinn Elissan stood and looked her friend straight in the eye. Or rather as close as she could, being significantly shorter.

"I have to, Lucius. Request a leave of absence on my behalf. Ask the Captain to give me three days to stay for the trial and then I will head east to rendezvous with the Cirrus at the estate. I need to find answers here, Lucius. I need to know I'm wrong."

Lucius shook his head and took in all the facts as Aislinn had pointed them out to him. Deep inside, he wanted Aislinn to be wrong also, but the evidence was beginning to stack up and indicate otherwise.

"A'ight," Lucius said. "I'll request the leave for ya. But Aislinn..."

Lucius pointed his finger into the center of Aislinn's chest and leaned in close.

"If ya find out this *was* a flash dart, ya damn well better get word to us! No bein' a hero."

"After the trial," Aislinn answered slowly. "After I help Cole Vallen prove his innocence, I'll meet the ship and tell you everything I know."

Lucius nodded his agreement and turned to walk away. At the edge of the ruined gazebo, he stopped.

"Prove the boy is innocent," he repeated back. "Why do you care? What ya see in him?"

Aislinn shrugged her shoulders and weighed her response. Lucius was one of her oldest friends. He would know if Aislinn was lying.

"Me."

Lucius emitted a solemn laugh as he returned to walking away. His left arm came up in a two-fingered wave. His way of saying see you later. Before he was out of earshot though, he turned back, shouting as he walked backwards.

"Why I feel like we 'bout ta pick up a new stray?"

Aislinn waved back with the two-finger salute just as Lucius turned around. Aislinn watched him as he walked across the cemetery until he stepped through the open gate and vanished into the street past the front of the temple. Once more Aislinn brushed her fingers against the stone fountain, this time on the clean side opposite where the explosion had happened.

"Light and fire," she whispered.

Chapter 9

An unforgettable trial

Cole/Aislinn

The trial of Cole Vallen had quickly escalated into nothing short of a circus. Almost every single person who called Harrow's Town home had shown up. They packed the courthouse and the grounds outside hours before the trial was to start. Speculation and rumour had lit the town on fire. Marshalls had been called in from Havelock and Escore as well as Stonesvale Village to assist Jemmo with keeping the peace. Much of the population was on the side of the Sables, but a lot of the farm folk who had reason to dislike the nobles showed their support for Jasper Vallen. Already, three fights in the streets had resulted in men and women in the treatment center.

As the time of the trial neared, Jasper and Cole waited patiently in a back room at the courthouse. They had been moved there in the early hours of the morning to avoid most of the crowds. It proved not early enough, as the wagon that carried them had come under attack from rotten produce, thrown stones, and hurled insults alike. Onlookers who sided with Cole thought he was taking the whole thing in stride, but Jasper knew better. He knew the look in Cole's eyes. Even with his glasses on, Jasper could see that Cole was defeated. The news of Rikket's death had crushed Cole's spirit. Innocent or not, his son was never going to be the same again.

The marshall who came from Escore stepped into the room with Cole and Jasper. He looked young for a marshall. Maybe mid-thirties. He was muscular and fit, but thin. His hair was a curly mess of bright red that almost looked like fire if the wind caught it right. He had fine features, not the kind that had seen time in fields, and white skin interspersed with freckles. Jasper nodded to the man as he closed the door behind him. The din of human voices drowned out as the wooden slab latched into its frame. Cole pretended he didn't hear any of what the shouting had said.

"Marshall Birsk," Jasper said in greeting. The man reached out and shook Jasper's hand.

"Mr. Vallen," he reached for Cole's hand, momentarily embarrassed when he realized Cole's were shackled together. He withdrew his hand. "Cole. How are you holding up?"

Cole shrugged and raised the shackled hands to the point the chain, which was attached to the floor, would allow. A padlock connected the floor chain to the manacles that held Cole's hands together. He didn't say a word.

"Ah," Birsk began as he stepped forward. "Fair enough."

Birsk produced a key from his belt loop and unlocked the padlock, dropping the tethering chain to the floor. Cole's wrists were still bound by the manacles, but he was now free to stand and move around. Birsk put a hand under Cole's left armpit and helped him stand.

"Is it time?" Jasper asked.

"Yes sir," Birsk replied evenly. "It's time. Are you ready, Cole?"

Behind his glasses, Cole's eyes were wide. He wanted to speak. He could tell Marshall Birsk was empathetic. He had seen it in the way he walked through the door. He heard a tone inflection in his voice when he asked how Cole was holding up. He felt it in the comforting grip the marshall had under his arm. Birsk felt remorse for Cole, and they had never even met until now. Cole wondered why. Still not able to speak, Cole could only nod. Then the marshall led him to the door which opened again to shouts, cheers, and insults. Jasper followed them out and closed the door behind him.

Aislinn sat patiently in the first row of benches behind the stand of the accused in the courtroom. It was not the first time Aislinn had been in court, but never had she attended such a small court packed with so many people. She was squished onto the bench between a farmer who reeked of pig manure and a chubby fellow with soft hands. A merchant, Aislinn thought. Behind them, six more rows of benches were just as tightly packed with a body jammed into every available standing space. To her front was the wooden fence that served to separate the courtroom proper from the observation seating. A tall podium stand sat in the middle of the room with a tether chain for the accused. To its left sat the elevated rows of benches for a jury, to the right a bank of windows letting in the light of the morning, with two rows of stools below. Directly to the front of the podium, about three or four paces was an elevated desk with the Verdosi coat of arms. The judge's seat.

Just as Aislinn began to speculate on what kind of judge would hold Cole Vallen's fate in his hands, silence fell over the room. The doors at the back had opened, and in walked a richly decorated couple. He was a bulky man, not overweight but fit. His white hair was cleanly parted to his right and he bore an expertly trimmed beard with a greased handlebar mustache. Thin wire-frame spectacles sat high on his nose giving him a scholarly appearance. His clothes were fine cotton over a silk shirt, adorned with intricate stitching and brass buttons. A chain ran from his belt to his watch pocket. His appearance screamed noble, and Aislinn instantly knew this had to be Leviticus Sable. Aislinn had asked Jemmo twice to be introduced to the man, but he was being protected. Now, looking at the pair of them walking into the courtroom, Aislinn knew exactly why.

The woman who walked with her arm wound through her husband's arm, moved more like a jungle cat than a human. Even with the click of her heels against the hardwood floor in the courtroom, there was no bob in her shoulders. She was grace incarnate. Floating like a swan across a still pond. Her hair was as white as a cloud, though she looked far too young for it. It sat atop her head in voluminous ringlets. Like her shoulders, it did not move as she walked. She was hauntingly beautiful with flawless skin of a rich darkness that sent shivers down Aislinn's spine. Aislinn searched the woman's face, from the sharp chin to the thin nose, her set and powerful jawline to her thin almost invisible eyebrows. Aislinn was shocked to discover emerald green eyes instead of the metallic silver she expected. Under the woman's tight black corset, the dress she wore was fit for royalty. The silk embroidered gloves that rose above her elbows covered hands that, coiled as they were, made Aislinn think she could strike with the speed of a viper. This woman had Ciar K'hen blood.

The couple strode up the aisle to the very front of the room. On the bench opposite the aisle from Aislinn, three people wordlessly stood to give them space to sit down. Not a word was spoken, and the Sables took their seats. Aislinn took in every detail as though she were the court-appointed artist. Leviticus Sable looked relaxed. Comfortable. Sure. Once seated he smiled intimately at his wife and then folded his hands calmly in his lap. Even nodding and thanking the few people that reached out to offer condolences from the crowd. His wife though, Seran Se'Baht Sable, was a stone statue. She never smiled. Never acknowledged anyone. She just sat there beside her husband, staring intensely straight ahead, like a cat about to pounce on a mouse.

A moment or two after the Sables had seated themselves, the room erupted in noise. Booing and hissing issued from the hall outside the courtroom, cascading closer and closer until the same shouting and hollering had reached the room. Aislinn knew before she visually confirmed it. Cole Vallen was being walked in at the side of one of the loaned marshalls. He shuffled more than he walked, doing his best to move within the constraints of the manacles binding his ankles and his wrists. Jasper Vallen was close behind, his head held low, occasionally returning an offered handshake from the few people in the crowd showing sympathy. Aislinn sighed when she saw the pale skin on Cole's face as he was led past them and up onto the stand. Even with his tinted lenses on, Aislinn could imagine the story those eyes must be telling.

Jasper Vallen took a seat somewhere to the rear of the room when it was offered to him. The way he nodded to the man and shook his hand told Aislinn he must not have recognized the man who sacrificed his place for him. Aislinn could see in the lines on his face, even through the crowd, that his heart was breaking for the way the community was treating his son. He looked lost inside his mind. The words of the people stung him. Aislinn could almost see him flinch as they assaulted his ears. It was like a hive of wasps upended in a field attacking him from every angle. He began to look numb to it. There were simply too many. Aislinn watched in solemn silence as Jasper Vallen dropped his wet face into his hands.

"All rise!" shouted Marshall Birsk, his flame-red hair bouncing. "Judge Sandevall of Havelock will preside."

The judge seemed to appear out of thin air behind his desk, but the way his shoulders elevated, slowed, and then elevated again told Aislinn that there must be a special staircase for the judge behind the raised desk. It had seemed closer to the wall, but now Aislinn realized the desk was hiding a back entrance to the courtroom. She wondered if perhaps it was also meant as an escape if proceedings became unruly. Aislinn's suspicion was confirmed when the jury filed in from behind the desk also and climbed into their seats on the raised benches. Jemmo walked in also, standing beside the judge's desk opposite Birsk. As the judge and the jury seated themselves, Jemmo waddled out into the center of the room in front of Cole.

"Marshall, please read the charges against the accused," the judge mumbled. He looked sleepy and very old. Gnarled fingers gripped a gavel and set it on the edge of his desk within his reach.

"Cole Vallen, you are accused of public mischief, disorderly conduct, and the involuntary murder of Rikket Sable. How do you plead?"

Deafening silence blanketed the courtroom as everyone waited with bated breath to hear the words of the accused. Aislinn leaned forward on the bench and whispered under her breath. *"Come on, Cole..."*

"Innocent," Cole said, his words echoing across the chamber and seemingly igniting a cacophonous explosion of shouts and insults.

Aislinn dared to turn up the corner of her mouth in a wry smile as the shouting continued. As the judge desperately bashed his gavel and called for order, Aislinn shot a glance across at the Sables. Lady Sable was as stone-still as she always was, but Leviticus was smiling. Aislinn turned her attention back to Cole, and for a moment thought she saw his shoulders raise ever so slightly.

"Good lad," Aislinn whispered. "Let's go then."

"Prosecution, call your first witness," bellowed the judge when there was finally enough silence for his voice to carry. "And I will have order, or so help me, this trial will continue behind locked doors!"

"Prosecution calls Edam and Peter Pyrell," Jemmo barked.

Birsk stepped around behind the judge's desk and reappeared a moment later with two lads about Cole's age. They both wore the best clothes Aislinn imagined they could find in their wardrobe. Both of them appeared to have grown out of the finery years ago. A chuckle rumbled through the room, especially regarding the biggest of the two. He looked a lot like a market pig stuffed into a sack half his size.

Aislinn sat back and listened as the two boys shared their version of events during the tavern brawl at the Swine and Ale with the court. They painted a picture of an out-of-control Cole Vallen, who came into the bar with Rikket, spouting all sorts of profanity and threats which made Edam and Peter fear for their lives. Gasps and laughs from the crowd accentuated their wild tale, and Aislinn couldn't help but think of it more like a stage play than an attestation of events. When they finished, the boys were marched to the side of the room where stools had been set up under the windows. Once seated, Aislinn noticed the boys bump fists with each other, no doubt congratulating one another on a job well done.

"Next witness," the judge sighed.

"Prosecution calls Edward Rispen."

The man that walked out to take center stage this time was a barkeep if ever Aislinn had seen one. He had a thickly greased handlebar mustache and wore a striped shirt tucked into cotton pants held up by suspenders. His hair also looked to have enough grease in it to fuel a lantern for a fortnight.

"Name and profession," Jemmo asked, even though not a person in the room didn't know.

"Edward Rispen. I own the Swine and Ale."

"Mr. Rispen. Were you present at the tavern the night in question?"

"Yes sir, I was."

"And can you share with the court your version of events?"

"I don't recall it all in fine detail, sir. The night was so busy what with the festival and all. But I do recall Cole Vallen and Rikket Sable arriving. They sat at the bar. My tender served their drinks. Rikket paid ahead with his coin purse."

"And was Cole Vallen acting strange?"

"He seemed upset, sir. Angry about something. Rikket was trying to cheer him up or maybe calm him down. I was too busy to hear their conversation."

"And did you see the altercation between the Pyrell brothers and the accused?"

"I did."

The crowd was deathly silent.

"Can you tell us, Mr. Rispen?"

Edward Rispen wrung his hands together. Aislinn noticed a gesture of movement; a slight turning of his head as though he were about to look over his shoulder but did not. His head lowered. He was about to do something that seemed to scare him. He was about to tell the truth.

"Cole shouted at Edam and Peter. It caught our attention. I noticed Edam was harassing my daughter Ellie. He had her by the arm. Cole instructed him to let go. Edam stormed over and tried to dump an empty cup on Cole's head, but Cole knocked him out with two punches. That was when Peter joined in and soon the whole tavern."

"That's a damned lie!" shouted Edam as he leapt to his feet. "You're a liar!"

"Order!" The judge yelled to quiet the room as it erupted again. "Marshall, remove that young man from my courtroom!"

Aislinn couldn't help but smile as she watched Birsk drag a screaming Edam Pyrell out of the room. *Two punches to take that boy down?* Aislinn thought to herself. *Impressive.*

The court heard from two other witnesses after Edward Rispen. One was another patron in the tavern who corroborated the barkeep's story which only made Aislinn like Cole more. The second witness was an old lady who saw Rikket dragging a near-unconscious Cole past her park just south of the cemetery. She provided nothing of value to the case, other than setting the stage for the boy's arrival in the cemetery. After her testimony, the court was allowed a short recess. Most of the people in attendance flooded out into the street to gossip about what comes next, as they smoked tobacco and milled about. Aislinn made a beeline directly for Jemmo.

"Inspector Elissan!" Jemmo breathed when he saw her standing at the edge of the room. Birsk was leading Cole out through the hidden back door. Good. The boy needed to rest.

"Marshall Jemmo," Aislinn began as she accepted the man's paw and shook it. "Quite the show so far."

Jemmo huffed.

"No doubt. Wish he would declare guilty and end this farce."

"Yes. About that," Aislinn began. "I want you to call me as a witness."

Jemmo coughed.

"What? Why on earth would I do that."

"I have information I believe the court should hear, and I would like to enter my testimony."

Jemmo's eyes burned with a seething anger. Aislinn knew the man was unable to refuse. If she had to, Aislinn could simply declare herself and enter a statement under her authority as an investigator, but Aislinn wanted to see the man squirm. She knew the marshall was not impartial. He had indicated as much when he mentioned the Vallen curse. With a silent nod, Jemmo turned and walked away toward the back room.

"Thank you, marshall!" Aislinn called as the man never broke stride.

After the recess, the next witnesses called were Fathers Impress and Ratly. Aislinn wasn't surprised. She would have done the same. They were holy men, and so they recounted events exactly as they knew them to be. It was almost word for word to what they had told Aislinn when she first met them. Right down to those same words that sent chills down Aislinn's spine. *Thunder like it was indoors. Blue-purple light, then fire.* Despite the hole in her stomach, she was certain now.

"Prosecution call your next witness," came the judge's words as the Fathers moved to take their place on stools beneath the windows. Aislinn was about to stand up when Jemmo spoke.

"Prosecution calls Leviticus Sable."

A murmur surged through the room as Levi Sable stood from his bench and made his way through the gate into the center of the room. Aislinn could see Cole's shoulders slump at the name, but the most shocking thing of all occurred as Levi passed the podium Cole stood upon. Right there, in the center of the room for all to see, Leviticus Sable climbed the podium and hugged Cole Vallen tight. Aislinn watched as he whispered in the boy's ear, and immediately Cole's shoulders started quaking. No one said a word. Mrs. Sable was still as always.

"Mr. Sable, please approach the court," Jemmo coughed. He looked more shocked than anyone. He continued once Levi stepped down from the accused podium and took his place out front. "State your name and profession."

"Leviticus Sable, industrialist. Owner of the Sable Estate."

"Mr. Sable," Jemmo began. He was thrown, and acting strange. Aislinn watched as he cleared his throat and adjusted his collar. He couldn't make eye contact with Levi Sable. Strange.

"Your son is Rikket Sable, is he not?"

"He was."

The crowd gasped and Jemmo squirmed even more.

"Uh. Yes. And you... uh... have something you wish the court to know?"

Levi drew a deep breath, almost as though he was about to deliver a prepared public speech. Perhaps he was.

"Cole Vallen was my son Rikket's best friend. They grew up together. Worked together. Defended one another. I can never convey the depth of the loss my wife and I feel having to now face this world without our son. But..."

Levi turned away from the judge and faced the crowd.

"I know I have lost my son. I know what happened is a tragic and mysterious event that will live on in the memory of this town for a very *very* long time. But I also know this..." the courtroom hung on his every word as he paused. "Cole Vallen is not guilty of murdering my son."

In the stunned silence, Levi turned back to the judge.

"Should this court find him innocent, I swear this to you all. I will welcome him in my home, just as I would my own son."

Cheers erupted from everyone in the room, and the gavel bash and cries of order added to the cacophony. As Levi walked out of the room without waiting to be dismissed, he paused at Cole's side and laid a hand on his wrist. He nodded to Cole and continued back to his seat. Aislinn's attention was fixed on Mrs. Sable. Finally, she showed movement. A tightening of her jaw muscle. A slight balling of her fingers as she gripped the fabric of her dress. She did not approve. Levi was acting on his own. Aislinn wasn't sure if she understood the theatrics, but she knew that nothing good would come of Cole finding himself alone with the Sables. She had to make sure that never happened, and there was only one thing she could do. She couldn't wait for Jemmo. She had to make her move now.

"Your honour!" Aislinn barked as she rose to her feet. Jemmo froze and the din of the room quieted in surprise at this new turn of events. Aislinn edged herself past Levi Sable as the man was just coming through the gate. She nodded ever so slightly to a surprised Cole Vallen as she passed the dais.

"Special Investigator Aislinn Elissan," she introduced himself to the court, accompanied by her trademark shallow bow. "I invoke my authority under the crown of Verdos as a duly appointed officer and demand to speak in this trial."

"I was just about to call you," hissed Jemmo under his breath. "What are you doing, Elissan?"

Aislinn shrugged as the judge suddenly seemed interested in the case.

"Most unusual Inspector Elissan," the judge mused. "An interesting turn of events indeed. Speak. The court will hear your testimony."

"Your honour," Aislinn used a bit of a flourish to buy herself a moment. Her quick reaction to intervene had not provided the time she needed to flesh out her response. She had to improvise. "People of the jury, and citizens of Harrow's Town, I arrived here a little more than a fortnight ago on the Verdosi Airship Cirrus. I first met Cole and his father Jasper at their booth during the festival. I was hoping to secure fresh lettuce, but alas, I could only find cabbage. Eesh."

Aislinn feigned a motion of disgust, to a few giggles from the room and the jury.

"I was immediately impressed upon meeting Cole Vallen. Here was a youth with a sharp mind, and an eye for the scholarly arts, much like myself."

Aislinn saw Cole fidget a bit at the compliments.

"When next I saw this young man, he was lying in a treatment bed, fighting for his life. He was not yet aware that the incident that harmed him..." Aislinn paused for dramatic effect and watched the crowd. They were shifting in their seats. Nervous. "Also took the life of his best friend."

"I offered my services to the investigation, with the blessing of my captain, because something was amiss with the details as I heard them. Your marshall," Aislinn made a point of thrusting her finger directly at Jemmo. "The wise man that he is, seemed to have a foolproof case on his hands. A drunk boy plays with explosives and kills his best friend. A *cursed* boy."

Jemmo shifted uneasily at the scornful way Aislinn expressed the word cursed. Aislinn paced around the room, specifically holding the gaze of every member of the jury for a moment. Then she approached the dais and whispered to Cole.

"Take off your glasses, Cole."

Cole hesitated a moment, so Aislinn whispered the words *trust me*. Cole relented and removed the glasses. It was the first time Aislinn had a good look at the boy's eyes, and she lightly rapped her fist against the podium railings. She had suspected it all along, but now she had confirmation. Cole's eyes were a shining brown colour, except for a third of his left eye. That one spectacular piece shone a bright emerald green. As Cole looked up at the judge and then the jury, a collective gasp came from all of them. Jemmo looked as though he was about to erupt. Aislinn walked right up to Jemmo and spoke as though directly to him.

"Sectoral heterochromia. Part of Cole Vallen's eyes are a different colour. Your honour, I was raised in the Imperial Archives of Verdos. Abandoned on the steps as a child. I've spent my life among scholars and so I ask you this. Are you aware," Aislinn spun and swept her arm across the whole room. "Are *any of you* aware, that heterochromia was once a mark of royalty in Verdos?"

Silence. Aislinn continued.

"You all judged this young man. You judged his mother before him as I have learned in my time among you. Based on your reaction to this mark, it is clear you were ignorant of the holy nature of it. Father Impress!"

Aislinn's shout startled many in the room. Impress stood.

"Do you recall the Old Testament of the Light?"

Impress shifted his weight from one leg to the other.

"Of course."

"And do you recall Lord Callum, first King of Verdos as written of in the testament?"

"I do."

Aislinn strode toward the priest.

"Would you please recite to the court, sir, verse five, line thirteen of the Old Testament?"

Just as Aislinn knew he would, the priest drew a breath and recited the passage from the Testament.

"And in his eyes, he bore the great green of the wild *and* the deep brown of the land."

Aislinn smiled and nodded to the priest, who returned to his seat.

"Thank you, Father Impress."

Aislinn turned to the audience, now rapt in attention to her words. Mrs. Sable was gone, but Levi remained.

"And in his eyes, he bore," Aislinn repeated dramatically. She motioned for Cole to turn around by spinning her finger in the air, which he did as best the shackles would allow. *"The great green of the wild, and the deep brown of the land."*

Aislinn waited for the hushed tones and whispers of the crowd to subside before moving on.

"Your honour, members of the jury, people of Harrow's Town. Cole Vallen and as I understand it, his mother as well, bear the marking of a long-forgotten lineage. Am I saying that Cole Vallen is descended from our first King? No. It's highly unlikely. He's the son of a potato farmer after all. He is not nobility. He is not royalty. But considering all he has endured in your treatment of him? He *is* kingly. But what does any of this have to do with the incident? How do the boy's eyes affect the outcome of this trial? They shouldn't. But Cole Vallen was pronounced guilty the moment you marched him in here. All of you shouted it as they did. Your own *marshall...*" again Aislinn thrust a finger at Jemmo. "Condemned him. Long before the trial even began. How foolish of all of you."

"Inspector Elissan," Jemmo barked. He was losing control, barely able to contain his anger any longer. "Make your point!"

Aislinn whirled on the marshall. Her voice oozed venom. She had summoned an authority that made even the judge cower.

"When I inspected the site, all three times, I saw no trace whatsoever of material that would indicate a bomb of any kind. For Cole Vallen to be guilty he would have to set off an explosive device, run around a fountain, and pass out on a stone bench in a *very* specific position to survive the ensuing blast. If you were any *remote kind* of *capable* inspector you would have known that, but you were willing to *condemn* a boy because of some green in his otherwise brown eyes!"

Jemmo had lost all the colour in his skin. His eyes darted over Aislinn's left shoulder before coming back. He must have been hoping Aislinn wouldn't notice, but she did. He was looking for approval from someone in the audience. The judge broke the tension.

"Inspector Elissan," the judge leaned forward, his gnarled fingers rolling over the edge of the desk like the talons of a vulture. "Please finish your testimony. What were your findings of the scene?"

Aislinn took a breath and collected herself, pulling back all of the angry authority she had mustered. Something else washed over her now. Fear.

"In the final days of the war your honour, I was a peregrine serving aboard the Akoyan Airship, Windshear. We were pressing a final assault on Matan Ba'al, the capital city of Ciar K'hen. The Windshear was ordered to attack from the north-east. The peregrines, myself included, had orders to attack a sentinel fortress in the desert so the main force could slip through undetected. We attacked shortly after dark... but we were not prepared for what we faced. In their desperation, the Ciar K'hen had developed a terrible weapon. An alchemical substance that turned flesh into fire, delivered to its target by a dart rifle. I saw most of my team... my twin brother..." Aislinn shivered as she relived the memory, and her voice trailed off before she continued. "When our men were hit by these darts, they started to glow... and then they exploded. Violently. The terror we felt when we faced them still haunts my dreams. Those of us who survived that attack describe its effect the same..."

Aislinn turned to face the priests who sat on the edge of their stools.

"... a sound like thunder indoors. Bluish purple flash. And then..."

"Light and fire."

It was Cole Vallen who finished the sentence for Aislinn, speaking aloud to a room stunned into silence. The implications were immense. Even the judge swallowed hard.

"This is deeply disturbing. Do you believe, Inspector Elissan, that such a weapon could be here in Harrow's Town?"

Aislinn could only shrug. Recalling that night had stripped her of her emotional strength.

"I am not yet positive, your honour. My investigation into this matter is only just beginning. But Cole Vallen is innocent. That much I know. With your leave, I would ask that all charges be dropped, and he be remanded into my custody. I believe he has much to offer my investigation, should his memory return."

The judge nodded slowly.

"What will become of him in your charge, Inspector?"

Aislinn turned to face Cole. She took note of the moisture that rimmed the boy's eyes.

"I will take him on as an initiate, your honour. He will train with me. Cole Vallen will become a cloudbreaker to serve his community and kingdom."

The collective boom of voices that went up in the room as the judge's gavel came down was deafening. Aislinn Elissan had achieved her gambit. In a short time, she had turned the Vallen curse into a boon and gave Cole Vallen everything he had been dreaming of. Yet in that moment, in all that emotion, it was the word issued *after* the gavel strike that made Cole's knees buckle.

"Innocent."

Chapter 10

The venom of loss

Jasper/Cole

The moments after the judge's proclamation were a blur for Cole Vallen. All the adrenaline and stress of the trial had erupted from him and taken his strength along with it. When Marshall Birsk approached the podium with a key and began releasing Cole's manacles, his words of congratulation barely registered. Even Aislinn Elissan, who had single-handedly saved Cole's future and delivered his dreams in tandem was a ghost amid the shock Cole was enduring. But then a face appeared that brought reality rushing back in like a broken dam.

"Cole, son, are you okay?"

Jasper Vallen was standing before Cole, leaning down to him in the heap he was at the base of the podium. His arms reached out and scooped Cole into a hug that only a relieved father could give. Cole shuddered and began to sob, the only word he could utter was a weak *"Dad."*

Jasper helped Cole to his feet and stepped down from the podium. Marshall Birsk braced him from the other side. The judge and Jemmo had already vanished through the back door, as had the jury. Father Impress and Father Ratly crossed the room to stand near the podium. They stopped behind Aislinn.

"Inspector Elissan," Impress said as he reached out his hand to shake Aislinn's. "Well done."

"Thank you, Father. And thank you also for your assistance."

Impress gave a sly grin. "You know, Inspector Elissan... that passage had nothing to do with the colour of Lord Callum's eyes. Verse five, Line twelve: And lo, Lord Callum stood upon the peak, and beheld his new Kingdom through grateful eyes."

Aislinn chuckled but said nothing. She simply shook the father's hand a little harder and smiled.

"Impressive," Father Impress said as he released Aislinn's hand. "Very impressive, Inspector. No person deserves condemnation for something they cannot control. You have done the Light's work here."

"You helped, Father."

Fathers Impress and Ratly bowed slightly to Aislinn and then approached Cole and his father.

"May the Light shine upon you, Cole Vallen, and illuminate your path to come."

Cole reached out and shook both of the priest's hands in turn. He swallowed hard.

"I never had the chance to thank you for saving me."

Father Impress smiled and placed his hand on Cole's shoulder.

"And you never have to. Farewell, Cole Vallen. I hope to see you again someday."

"Farewell, Cole," Father Ratly said as Impress turned away. "Walk with the light, young man."

The priests stepped through the gates and made their way into the crowd that was filing out of the courtroom observation benches. Cole watched them go and then turned to Aislinn.

"What was all that about Lord Callum and my eyes? Is that what Father Impress was talking to you about just now?"

Aislinn waved off the question as she came around the podium closer to Cole and the others. Birsk bent down and started removing the manacles from Cole's ankles. His wrists were already free, with one arm draped over Jasper's shoulders and his other bracing himself against the podium. His legs still felt weak.

"My aren't we a curious one," Aislinn chided. "That was just a discussion between fellow scholars. Nothing more."

Cole noted the mischievous grin on Aislinn's face. "Thank you, Aislinn. For everything. You had no reason..."

Aislinn's face fell sullen as she interrupted Cole. "Oh, young Vallen, I most definitely had a reason."

Birsk stood up, holding the manacles. "Well Cole Vallen, you are free to go."

Cole nodded, and Aislinn patted him on the back. Jasper turned to Marshall Birsk as Cole and Aislinn made their way through the gate. He reached out to shake the marshall's hand.

"Thank you Marshall Birsk."

"My pleasure," the marshall returned. "Not the first time I've watched an innocent on trial for crimes they didn't commit."

"I suspected. A family member?"

The marshall nodded. "My daughter. Mimi."

Jasper recoiled. "You look so young to have a daughter!"

"So I am often told."

Jasper shifted, looking over his shoulder a moment as Cole and the others were waiting in the line of the crowd to leave. Spectators were shaking Cole's hand and patting his shoulders. It lifted Jasper's heart to see him accepted for once, especially without his glasses.

"Take care of him," Birsk said as he started to walk away toward the back door.

"Marshall Birsk," Jasper called, turning the man around just before he passed the judge's desk. "What happened to your daughter?"

"Sent to the Forgotten Plains Penitentiary in Akoy," Birsk shrugged, making his best attempt at hiding his pain. "I receive a letter now and then. So that's something."

With that, he left and Jasper, wordless, made his way through the gate to catch up to his son.

Outside the courthouse, the reality of being free was beginning to seep into Cole. His strength was returning, so he drew in a deep breath of the fresh afternoon air. His right hand hurt from all the hands he had shaken in his attempt to leave the courtroom, and his shoulders were raw from all the pats. As was so often the case, he turned his face skyward and watched a few puffy white clouds hovering in the sky. There were no crows today. Aislinn had left a few moments ago to retrieve a power wagon she had rented for her use during her stay. Cole and Jasper now stood alone in the street, with only a handful of people still exiting the courthouse.

Jasper looked more tired now than Cole had ever seen him. He tried to imagine everything his father must have been through. From their fight at the festival to the news of Rikket's death and Cole's injury, and then the trial. Cole wondered what strength his father possessed to shoulder all that happened, and despite looking so haggard and worn out, he still carried it all with such stoicism. Suddenly, a thought occurred to Cole.

"Dad, what happened with the booth?"

Jasper Vallen turned his face to his son. His eyes were wide, and then he laughed his deep guttural laugh that Cole loved to hear. "All this, and you worry *now* about farming?"

Cole was sheepish. "I never thought to ask until now."

Still laughing, Jasper did his best to reply. "No one would blame you for that, Cole. We're fine. After I heard you had been hurt, I liquidated the yield at a discount so I could close the booth. The festival was at its end soon after the explosion anyway. Fear drove the foreign merchants away, and the locals cared more about speculation than cabbage and potatoes."

"Liquidated at a discount? But Dad, you needed that money."

Jasper shrugged, his laughter melting away into a coy grin. "Aislinn paid double, remember? Even practically *giving* the yield away..." he paused and drew a deep breath. There was a sparkle in his eyes. "We earned almost three times our profit from last year."

Cole's breath caught in his throat and his reply came as a whisper. "Three times..."

Jasper nodded, but the rumbling of an engine caught his attention. Aislinn and her power wagon rolled up and stopped just short of them. Instead of a flat cargo back on the truck, this one had been fitted with extra bench seats. Aislinn leaned forward in the driver's seat, her foot depressing the brake as her arms folded over the steering wheel.

"Your chariot has arrived, gentlemen," Aislinn said to them.

Just as Jasper and Cole were about to climb aboard the wagon, a voice called out. "Cole Vallen!"

Cole stopped, one foot up into the chassis of the truck and another still on the ground. He stepped back down and turned to see the Sables approaching him. Behind him, he heard Aislinn whisper something under her breath. Cole had not caught the words, but it was clear she was cursing. Lady Sable sped toward Cole, with Levi desperately trying to stop her. Before Cole or anyone could react, her open palm slashed across Cole's face. The slap nearly took him to the ground. Levi grabbed his wife and pulled her back as Jasper jumped from the truck to tend Cole, and Aislinn slipped the truck gear into park and leapt out.

"Seran! Stop!" Levi was shouting. Lady Sable was coiled fury, pulling against her husband's arms desperate to attack Cole again. Aislinn stepped between her and Cole, menacingly staring down the Sables. In the sunlight, the blue of her uniform coat almost matched the sky.

"You struck my son!" Jasper was yelling.

"I'll do *much* more than that!" Lady Sable yelled back. Levi grunted, trying to hold her place. Tears flowed from both their faces.

"Calm yourselves! Everyone!" Aislinn commanded. Reluctantly, everyone obeyed.

Lady Sable broke free of Levi's grasp and straightened herself. She smoothed her dress and reset her corset where it had been twisted.

"Innocent or not," she seethed as she went about fixing herself. Her eyes were fixed on Cole, and Cole couldn't help but see her as a puma preening before consuming its prey. "Rikket would still *be here* if not for this one. I hold you *accountable*, Cole Vallen, for the death of my *only son!*"

Her words stung Cole far more than the slap, and tears ran freely down his cheeks. He opened his mouth, trying with all his might to usher the words in his heart: *I'm sorry...* but all that came forth was a squeak.

Sure that his son was okay, Jasper stood and whirled on the Sables. Aislinn's arm holding him back was all that stopped him from escalating the violence. Instead, he shot an accusatory finger at the nobles.

"My son had *nothing to do* with Rikket's death! You *heard* what the Inspector said! Not everything is about you, Seran Se'Baht!"

Seran's menace burned a hole through Jasper, but she maintained her composure. "Nothing to do with his death?" She growled. "If not for *your* son, Jasper Vallen, mine would not have been there to be utterly destroyed in that explosion!" A single tear rolled down her otherwise perfect cheeks. "If not for *your* son, mine would not have stolen alcohol from us and been in a tavern brawl! It was *your son's influence* that stole Rikket from this world, and I want him to *know it.* I want it to *haunt him* for the *rest* of his days as it will haunt mine to live without *my* son!"

Jasper's jaw tightened, but there was a slight tremor to it as well. Behind him on the ground, Cole collapsed into a sobbing heap.

"Yes," Seran continued. "Cry, Cole Vallen. *Cry* like I have, every night since my boy was taken. Suffer. As I have."

Levi Sable stepped in front of his wife and tried to lead her away by her shoulders. "Okay, Seran. Let's go. That's enough."

Seran's fists clenched, and she released a banshee wail that shook Cole to his core. "It will *never be enough*!" With that, she allowed Levi to turn her and escort her away toward a power wagon that was waiting for them just down the street.

Jasper bent and tried to lift Cole to his feet. He was shaking and sobbing uncontrollably. All the strength he had gained since breathing the free air outside the courtroom was gone. Part of him wished he was never pronounced innocent. Part of him wanted to be thrown into a deep pit and left to rot. That was how his insides felt at that moment. Rotten. Lost. The community may have been swayed by Aislinn's testimony, but Seran Se'Baht Sable would never forgive him. And in the dark recesses of his thoughts, Cole Vallen wondered if he would ever be able to forgive himself.

Chapter 11

Last night at home

Jasper/Cole

The powered wagon ride out of Harrow's Town to the Vallen farm was more like an evacuation than a leisurely drive. The speed with which Aislinn was able to navigate the streets and reach the main eastern road had scared Jasper more than once. This was the first time Jasper had ever ridden in a truck, which only made matters worse. Aislinn had ripped around the ring road at a breakneck pace before shooting out onto the east road. A few times Aislinn had slapped a raised button in the center of the wheel, blasting a steam whistle that issued a deeper register, more like a horn. The sound always called attention to the truck, and people dove out of the way seeing the vehicle careening toward them.

Clinging to his seat during one of the issuances of the horn, Jasper had asked Aislinn "Do you think this is good for our image after what just happened in court?" In truth, at that moment, Jasper cared very little for public opinion. He just wanted Aislinn to slow down. The cloudbreaker had given no reply to the question, but as soon as the roadside emptied of the buildings and opened into the farmland of the outskirts, Aislinn did indeed slow down. As she backed off pressure on a peddle in the floor, she also depressed a lever on a rod beside her, guiding the rod into a new position before releasing the lever. Very little detail ever seemed to escape the inspector's attention, and so she replied to the question Jasper was holding before it was even asked.

"Gearing," Aislinn began as she motioned to the lever she had just released. "The engine only moves at a single speed, so to create more speed from the same engine, this gearing uses different-sized wheels with teeth on them to transfer the energy."

Jasper grinned at Aislinn. "I have a steam tractor. I know what a transmission is. Just never seen one so small."

Cole sat between Aislinn and his father on the bench seat. He had finally stopped crying, but now silently stared through hollow eyes at the road before them. Jasper had his left arm around Cole and lightly squeezed the boy's shoulder in reassurance. Aislinn sighed.

"If your question was not about the gearing, what was it?"

Jasper turned his head to look past his son at Aislinn. His brown hair was dancing in the wind from the truck. "I was wondering why the hurry? The Sables left, yet you raced out of town like a wolf was on your heels."

Aislinn turned up the corner of her mouth in a thin smile. "I see where Cole gets his smarts."

"From his mother," Jasper corrected, turning his head to the right to watch the fields of wheat they passed. "I see things, sure. But his mother was the one with the smarts. Read all the time, she did." Jasper chuckled at some distant memory. "Even when she should have been farming."

"A good woman, then. Turn here?"

"A great woman, and yes," Jasper corrected her for the second time, just as Aislinn steered the truck off the main road onto a fork. "Ours is the last on the left. Near the foothills."

The rolling landscape before them was truly a sight to behold. Fields of wheat and corn and other crops divided by thin strips of alpine forest stretched out over flat land pockmarked by the occasional hill. Far off in the distance, that flat land gave way to thicker woods and taller hills before it finally rose into sharp peaks and mountains, the northernmost tip of the Rinda mountain range that divided Verdos and Akoy. Harrow's Town sat in a green belt between the mountains in the north and the Grindlemoor rainforest to the south. Fertile erosion soil from the mountains was fed by rains both from Davith Basin in the east, and the Grindlemoor to the south. It was prime agricultural land. The Vallen farm was one of the most northern farms in the region, nestled against the foothills of the mountains and fed by natural springs.

Jasper always loved the approach to home, and as he looked over at Cole, he could see his son was enjoying it too. There was life returning to him as his eyes darted around taking in the sight of the mountains. Then his gaze flicked upwards. Jasper smiled.

Cole never missed an opportunity to stare at the sky. Jasper drew a deep breath and then asked the question that truly bothered him. The one burning in his mind since Aislinn's testimony.

"What happens to Cole now?"

"Cole will become a cloudbreaker," Aislinn began to reply. She was parroting his words from the testimony, and Jasper knew it.

"Yes, but why? The world is at peace, what purpose will he serve?" Jasper interrupted Aislinn. This was his son they were talking about. His only son. If there was one thing Jasper could empathize with from the events of the last few days, it was Seran Se'Baht Sable's loss.

Cole looked from his father to Aislinn, waiting for the cloudbreaker's reply. He was also curious. Aislinn's jaw tightened. "Everything about the explosion raises the hair on my neck. Cole was there. He survived it. Drunk or not, I'm gambling on him remembering something that night that will help me..." Aislinn turned her face to her passengers as she finished her sentence. "Before more people die."

"So," Cole finally spoke as Aislinn turned her head back to the road. "You need me for your investigation."

Aislinn was silent for a moment as the truck rolled down the road. She had broken a bit of her concentration and hit a puddle in the road. The truck bounced, causing them all to grunt. Cole wondered for a moment if the same puddle had been what caused their wagon wheel to fall off before the festival.

"Cole," Aislinn began. "You have a gift. You're smart and very perceptive. You'll make a good investigator with training," she paused to weigh her words. "But I am not offering you this opportunity purely out of charity. If Ciar K'Hen weapons are here in Verdos, it could reignite the war. Hundreds would die... *thousands* potentially. I've seen what those weapons do, and now I believe you have too. I need you to remember that night, so to protect you I had to employ you. It was the best path I could see to keep you away from dangerous people."

"The Sables?" Cole speculated. Aislinn's silent nod confirmed Cole's speculation to whom she was referring.

"I don't think Mr. Sable would hurt me," Cole began before Aislinn interrupted him. "He told me he forgave me in the courtroom, that it wasn't my fault."

"Not him."

There was a malice in Aislinn's eyes that Cole couldn't help but notice. A hatred, not unlike the way Jemmo looked at Cole.

"You hate her," Cole said out loud. "Why?"

"Because I think she's Ciar K'Hen."

"Half," Jasper corrected. "She's only half Ciar K'hen. Seran's family came from a small village in the southeast of Akoy, at least as the story goes. A place called Blightwood."

"I've spent time there," Aislinn added. She stroked the wheel thoughtfully. "It's close to the blood meridian."

"The blood meridian?" Cole asked.

"It's a narrow gap of land between the North Worldspine and the Furious Sea. In the early days of the war, it was no-man's-land. It was the one land passage between Ciar K'hen and Akoy. Eventually, both sides called a stalemate in the area. It's littered with bodies now, and the broken machines of war. A place of ghosts."

"We've never been friends exactly," Jasper continued once Aislinn was finished. "But folk say she was born to a teen mother in Blightwood. After Ciar K'Hen raiders paid a visit."

"It makes sense actually," Aislinn continued to stroke the wheel, deep in thought. "It's not unheard of. Lewd acts on either side to be honest. Explains her green eyes."

"Ciar K'Hen don't have green eyes?" Cole asked.

"Not usually. One of their cultural signatures is steel gray eyes. They almost shine in the darkness, like a cat. Some of our scholars think they evolved that way to help see in the dark of the desert."

The wagon finally arrived at the Vallen farm, and Aislinn rolled the machine to a stop in front of their barn. She stepped down from the driver's seat as Cole and Jasper also climbed out. Jasper went around to the back of the wagon and pulled out a canvas kit bag with Cole's belongings. Cole followed Aislinn to the front of the machine and watched her as she opened a valve to bleed steam from the engine. She flipped a lever inside also and closed a different valve.

"How do they work?" Cole asked, leaning into the space as his curiosity overcame him. Cole had only been this close to a power wagon once before when Levi had picked Rikket up for a trip to Havelock. He knew they operated on steam from books he had read, but he knew little else about their true engineering. "How does the engine generate heat? There's no boiler."

Aislinn smiled and stood back, propping open the engine compartment to help vent the steam. "They use alchemy now. Akoyan engineering built upon the foundations of Verdosi science. I'm not a hundred percent sure how it works, but there is a fuel that reacts when exposed to water, instantly heating it to steam. That's this valve here," Aislinn pointed to the second valve that she had closed and the lever she had flipped. "And this lever. They control the flow of the fuel into the water tanks. This valve here lets me open and close the steam supply from the water tank to the engine."

"Why bleed it off?" Cole asked. He was sure of the answer almost the moment he asked it. "Is that to prevent damage to the piping? Like in our tractor?"

Aislinn nodded as she walked around to the driver's seat. She pulled a rag out from under the seat and wiped off her hands. Jasper had joined them with Cole's bag slung over his shoulder.

"That's correct. The alchemy involved in these engines is powerful. Expose enough fuel, and the entire tank instantly becomes steam, and without somewhere for that steam to go, it's putting constant pressure on the piping. Since we'll be here overnight, it's best to bleed the tank and let the engine cool until tomorrow."

Aislinn's final word hit Cole like another slap. His shoulders slumped.

"Tomorrow?"

Aislinn stopped wiping her hands and tossed the rag back under the seat. Both Jasper and Cole were staring at her. She had kept the sad news from them as long as she could.

"Look," she began as she searched her mind for ways to say it best. "I thought you two had been through enough so I wanted to wait for the right time. Tomorrow morning, I leave for Stonesvale, and beyond that the Errbryte estate. The Cirrus will be waiting for me there and I have to report all of this information to my command chain," she paused for the part she knew would hurt them. "And Cole has to come with me."

Aislinn noticed Jasper Vallen swallow hard as his eyes began to glisten. Ever the father, he simply said "Then we had best get some rest. Tomorrow will be a long day for you both."

Cole had bathed before supper while Aislinn finished her maintenance on the truck. Jasper made a hearty stew of celery, potatoes, corn, and beef chunks and they all sat down to dinner together in the dining room. Aislinn had been offered the guest room, which she graciously accepted and in short order, had fallen asleep. Barely a word further had been spoken between any of them. Jasper had gone off to do some chores, and Cole had cleared the table and washed the dishes. When he was done, he thought about going upstairs to sleep, but instead, he found his legs had carried him on autopilot to a swing hanging from an old oak tree in their front yard.

The swing was a battered old piece of pine fencing board showing its age and years of abuse by weather and the rumps of youth. The board was fastened to a thick tree branch by a pair of rusty metal chains. Cole sank into the swing, uncertain if it would hold when it groaned in protest, but it did. He looked out across the fields in the waning light. Watched as the tops of their corn waved in a gentle breeze, and sighed when that same breeze brought him a slight chill.

"Surprised that thing still holds you up," came his father's voice from behind him. "Old as it is."

"Yeah," Cole replied. He let out a short chuckle. "It almost didn't."

"I have a lot of memories of you on that swing."

Cole rocked the swing a little, not quite daring enough to test its capacity with a full swing. He smiled to himself as he relived a few of those memories himself.

"I kissed Ellie Rispen on this swing," Cole said. Stepping up beside him, he heard his father chuckle as he continued the story. "Was back when her Dad was helping with harvest before they bought the Swine and Ale. I think we were ten? Eleven maybe?"

"About that," Jasper said, himself looking out across the field as he stood with his son.

"I think that's what started Edam Pyrell hating on me so much. He was sweet on her. Word got out at school that we'd kissed... and then kids started saying Ellie had my curse. Like it was a sickness she could get by touching me."

Jasper placed a hand on Cole's shoulder and listened to his son recount the memory. He knew it all by heart already. It was hard to forget.

"But then," Cole continued. "That was when the Sables moved to town. I met Rikket, and he gave me those glasses, and..."

Cole cried, trying to speak through sobs as his father silently squeezed his shoulder like a sentinel guardian.

"Now I'm about to go off on adventures I've always dreamed of but Rikket had to die..."

No longer able to stand, Jasper dropped to his knees and took his son in his arms. Cole cried into his father's shoulder.

"Rikket had to die... and it's all my fault."

"It is *not* your fault, Cole. You forget what that woman said. She's a hurting parent. You can't blame her, and you can't take that guilt on, do you hear me?"

Jasper held Cole at arm's length and wiped the tears from beneath his multi-coloured eye.

"Tomorrow you're going to go with that woman in there. You're going to become a cloudbreaker, just like you always wanted, and you're going to help her find those weapons. And when you do *that* son, you will find who was responsible for Rikket's death."

Cole took in all the pain in his father's eyes. Took in the quiver of his suntanned cheeks. The wrinkled skin of his set jawline hidden under his white unkempt beard. The haunted expression on his face showed a man who had seen his fair share of heartache in his years of life. He loved a woman who was shunned. He lost that same woman when he gained a son bearing the same mark, and now he was about to lose that son too. Yet here he was, his knees in the soil where three generations of his family had worked, telling that son why he should go. Jasper Vallen at last reached an understanding with his son in that moment. Cole finally saw the self-sacrificing man his father was.

"Dad," he croaked. "You'll be alone."

Jasper barked his deep laugh. The laugh Cole loved to hear.

"Cole," he said as he stood to his feet. "You are definitely my son."

"I don't understand, Dad. You laugh at the weirdest things."

Jasper helped Cole stand up from the swing and together they walked toward the house.

"You'll understand one day, Cole. Maybe when you have a son of your own."

Chapter 12

To the Rise

Cole

The two-day journey from Harrow's Town to Stonesvale flew by in a blur for Cole. To get to the road south, they had to travel back through town which was hard on Cole. He found himself sinking into the seat as Aislinn steered around the ring road in the square, somehow feeling like the courthouse building itself was judging him. Yet in what felt like a blink in the journey overall, they had left the farms of his hometown behind and soldiered forward into lands unknown.

To make time, Aislinn had taught Cole to drive the truck so that they could take turns at the wheel while the other slept. The shared duty let them cover incredible distances in short order with only a few breaks at streams to replace water in the tank. To pass the time, Cole asked all sorts of questions about the world, the war, Aislinn's past, and the life of a cloudbreaker. A lot of it he knew from study and conversation with merchants, but it was interesting to hear it all from Aislinn's perspective. Cole learned that Aislinn had a fascination with deep history, and the puzzles of life beyond what was written.

Cole was most surprised to learn that Akoy and Verdos had not always been allies. There was a time long ago when both nations warred with one another, without even knowing what a Ciar K'Hen was. When the hundred-year war with Ciar K'Hen ignited, it was a war over resources. The lands on the north side of the Furious Sea were fertile, abundant, and brimming with assets from wood to farmland to steel. Almost the entirety of the Ciar K'Hen empire was a vast desert, beyond imagination. Their empire vastly outnumbered the population of the entirety of the north, however, and so they went to war with the northern kingdoms for control over this abundance.

When Akoy and Verdos fought their war, resources were not a part of it. Their conflict was solely over culture. The Verdosi people believed in knowledge and the conservation of records and history. To the Verdosi, the world was called Sebria, which in their old tongue meant 'the great cradle.' It was widely believed that life was born from the wild magic of the world, and nature was to be protected as the cradle that provided life. They were stewards of their land, but also fervently explored and searched for knowledge and higher learning. They invented writing and books, and produced scholars who built a massive stone castle in Hilmage City. It would become a vault, dedicated to protecting their gathered knowledge, holding the tomes of collected information their monk scholars brought back from every corner of their land. It was a time of progress and peace;

until they found their way across the Rinda Mountains and discovered Akoy.

Akoyans were a barbaric culture in those days. Nomadic and aggressive. Their name for the world was Thone. There was never a definition discovered for the word specifically. Some scholars in Verdos believed it to be the name of a deity. The Akoyans believed life began as the result of war between their pantheon of Gods during a time they aptly referred to as 'the Godwar.' During this era, Hexen Faris, their greedy God of shadow and death, tricked the others into a war with one another. It was widely held that he did this so he could absorb the essence of Kalissa, Goddess of light and life, and wife of Panas, King of the Gods and lord of justice and battle. During their war, all the Gods were killed or imprisoned, sending the world into chaos. Panas and Hexen Faris were said to have fought as the last survivors, sundering the land of Thone and creating the Furious Sea and the Maelstrom Sands, where storms from their fight still rage to this day.

Of course, Aislinn continued, scholars now knew that the storms in the Furious Sea and the Maelstrom Sands were because of their proximity to the equator of the globe. Regardless, when Akoy and Verdos first discovered one another, they were far more primitive people, and conflict occurred instantly over their differently held beliefs. Eventually, they settled their differences and instead allied to share their collective resources and forge a stronger society together. Akoy with its strength, numbers, and tenacity for construction and building, and Verdos with its science, natural resources, and advanced societal doctrines. In the modern world, it became almost impossible to tell the two cultures apart, aside from minor differences such as their clothing and architecture.

Cole liked that Aislinn shared a similar interest with him in solving mysteries and puzzles. Aislinn felt like the time before written history was the most fascinating puzzle of all, and she loved to talk about her theories that everything was connected. She believed there was truth in tales and stories because, before written history, that was the only way to share lessons across time. The Old Testament of the Light, Tome of the Godwar, and even fairy tales like Legend of the Sunlight Prince and Legend of the Fire Dragons were puzzle pieces that painted the true history of the world in Aislinn's eyes. The implications of her theories captured Cole's imagination. In every moment they spent awake, Cole pressed Aislinn for more knowledge. More learning. When at last the truck rolled up and over a ridge, showing the village of Stonesvale before them, Cole felt a small rush of disappointment.

Stonesvale was nestled into an arm of the Rinda range just like Harrow's Town was, but where Harrow's Town was fertile farming land amid the rolling foothills of the north, Stonesvale was more central and the peaks surrounded it rose in jagged cliffs and steep hills to dizzying heights above them. Right at the edge of the Grindlemoor rainforest, the small village had quickly become a bit of a transportation hub for travel between the three main cities of Verdos. A network of roads all culminated in the village, and as the truck rolled to a stop in front of the huge local inn, Cole immediately understood why.

"It's a port village," Aislinn said as they stepped out of the truck and stretched. She pointed to the south where the land sloped downward and met a few hundred meters of wooden docks. Steamboats, paddle wheel boats, and smaller skiffs came into and out of the docks like bees at the mouth of a hive. A wide river, almost a mile across by Cole's estimate, stretched far to the south where it seemed as though the jungle swallowed it up. "The way from here to Vandrad or anywhere else is by water or by air. Our choice, unfortunately, is obvious. At least for now."

Cole whistled to himself as he took in the sights. He watched a massive paddle-wheeled vessel with two tall stacks spewing coal smoke as it pulled away from the docks, heading south. The name on the side said 'the jungle's mistress.' People on its upper deck waved at folk on the shore or milled about pointing at things in the distance. Small skiff boats skittered about, driven by paddle, some with fishing lines poking out of them like whiskers. Cole noted how the water appeared almost black, but shone a brilliant blue in the few places where sunshine pierced the canopy of trees above and touched the surface. Behind him, Aislinn finished shutting down the truck and the telltale hiss of steam meant the bleed had begun. Retrieving her rag from under the seat again, Aislinn cleaned her hands and stood beside Cole, taking in the sight also.

"See that building down there on the water? That one with the mossy brown roof?"

Cole followed Aislinn's pointing finger and nodded.

"The one with the bigger boats coming and going?"

"That's the one. That's the marina. We'll rest in the inn for tonight, and tomorrow, we'll take a powerboat to Vandrad. From there, it'll be horse and carriage to the Errbryte estate. We should arrive just in time."

"In time for what? Will the Cirrus not wait for us?"

Aislinn shrugged and turned back to the truck. She tossed the rag under the seat and started around to the back to get her bags. Her uniform jacket was off, and her suspenders were looped down around her hips. Cole couldn't help but compare her to a swashbuckling pirate from stories. As Aislinn pulled her kit bag out of the back of the wagon she replied "They'll wait. At least I hope they will. But I don't want to miss the party!"

Cole approached and retrieved his own bag. "What party?"

"The alchemist's birthday, Cole."

Compared to the Swine and Ale back home, the Swampfish Inn in Stonesvale was huge. A massive carved wooden sign hung above the door, depicting what looked to be a cross between an alligator and some form of shark. The beast had a flat relief carved along its side, inside which were the raised letters spelling out Swampfish. The whole thing hung on chains that looked like they might snap any time, dropping the sign to crush unwary patrons below. As they walked up the stairs under the sign, Cole heard the telltale raucous laughter and the dull roar of crowd conversation from within. The whole building was wooden, with shaded glass windows facing out into the town.

It looked to have three full stories all in a uniform rectangle, but with a peaked roof above the entrance.

The heavy wooden front doors swung open just as Cole and Aislinn approached, and a handful of giggling women erupted from the door. Behind them, calls from other patrons beckoning them to return met Cole's ears. Aislinn managed to step out of the way as the girls surged out, but Cole was not so lucky. One of the girls bumped directly into him hard enough that he dropped his kit bag. The other two girls moved off to the side, still giggling, while the girl that bumped Cole stopped to help him pick up his bag.

"Ah'm so sorry!" She squeaked. "Ah didn't mean to hit ya. Bit too much to drink, ah guess."

Cole made eye contact with her at that moment, bent over and both holding on to his bag. She had a round face and a perfect button nose. Her eyes were big and accentuated by thin eyebrows and long natural lashes. Her black hair was cut to the length of her chin and parted easily in the middle, framing her face. She had a wholesome beauty to her, and it stole Cole's breath a moment.

"Uh..." he tried to collect himself but could feel his face flushing, which made his nerves worse. "It's Cole."

The young woman tilted her head inquisitively and hefted his bag a second before handing it to him.

"Ah think it feels more like clothes," she chirped as her friends behind her resumed their giggles and whispers to each other in hushed tones.

Cole and the young lady stood.

"Oh... no... I meant my name..."

Cole was starting to believe the embarrassment he felt was never going to end when suddenly Aislinn interrupted. "Becky? What on earth are you doing here?"

The young lady turned her attention to Aislinn as Cole returned his bag to his shoulder. She smiled and Cole felt the blush return to his face again.

"Beg your pardon, ma'am. Ah ain't Becky. Ah'm Cass. Cass Adder."

"Uncanny..." breathed Aislinn as she stepped forward to appraise Cass closer. "Becky is forever going on about all her cousins. I always thought it was just a part of her charm, yet here you are!"

Cass squeaked and threw her hands together. "You know mah cousin, Becky! Well, ain't that just somethin'."

Before the conversation could continue, the other two girls started to dart down the stairs toward the docks. They called back over their shoulders to Cass. "Let's go, Cass! We'll miss our boat!"

Cass threw her hands up in apology as she hurriedly backed down the stairs to catch up with her friends. "Shoot! Ahm sorry. Gotta go. Tell Becky ah said hi! Nice to meet you, Mr. Coal man!"

Cole awkwardly waved goodbye as Cass caught up to her friends and they sped off toward the docks.

"Did that just happen?" Cole said as he turned to Aislinn.

"Light Cole, just wait till you meet Becky Adder. She's the cook on the Cirrus. Then you'll understand why I'm so shocked."

As the pair entered the bustling inn, Cole asked "Does she look like Cass?"

"Cole," Aislinn said as the doors closed behind them. "I would swear before a court that that *was* her!"

The main lobby of the Swampfish doubled as its tavern, and the moment they were inside, Cole understood the reason for the peaked roof. From the front doors to the back of the building, and from the ground floor they were on to the roof three stories above was one giant room. To either side of the main foyer, a hallway led into the inn rooms beyond. This pattern was repeated on the floor above, where stairs at the back of the room on either side rose to an open ring walkway that looked down on the tavern below. The same pattern was repeated again for the third floor. Patrons leaned on railings looking down upon the tavern on both levels, cheering for a bard that sang a shanty from a raised stage in the center of the foyer. At the back of the foyer along the wall was the biggest bar Cole had ever seen, with three female and one male bartender manning it.

"I don't get it," Cole began as Aislinn led him across the foyer toward the bar. "This town is so small... why is this place so *huge*?"

Aislinn grinned. "Economics lesson, Cole! Stonesvale is a main point of access to and from the Grindlemoor, Vandrad, and the sea. Sure, you can reach Havelock from here by water also, and that paddle wheeler we saw earlier is likely heading that way, but more importantly, Stonesvale is the place where a huge chunk of the traffic going north to the Falcon Lake regions, or south has to pass through. Only a handful of these people you see live here, Cole. Almost all are just passing through like us."

Aislinn dropped her kit bag to the floor as they reached the bar and took up a seat on the stool beside it. "Small town, enormous Inn."

"Special Investigator Aislinn Elissan. As I live and breathe," cooed one of the female bartenders as she approached. She was an older woman, heavier set, with curly auburn hair. Almost every finger on both her hands bore a ring, and her bosom was so squished into her corset it looked as though it might pop out. "What a sight to see you on the ground."

Aislinn leaned over the counter and kissed the finger of that bartender's right hand when she offered it. "Eloise. Wonderful to see you! Jaggert working tonight?"

"Of course he is, dear! The usual then?"

Aislinn beamed. "Two, please! And two ales also. It's been quite a road."

Eloise danced away to fill their order but called over her shoulder as she did so. "With you, it's *always* a long road, dear!"

Aislinn shifted in her seat and drummed her fingers on the bar. Cole watched her mannerisms shift from her usual contained charisma to something more comparable to an excited child about to receive sweets.

"Jaggert and Eloise own the Swampfish," Aislinn explained. After the last two days, both Aislinn and Cole had come to read when one another wanted an explanation. "Jaggert runs the kitchen, Eloise the bar and the inn. Trust me, you're going to love this."

Cole turned in his stool and watched the crowd for a while as they waited for Eloise to return. The bard on his stage had shifted to a slower tale of lovers lost in the swamp, unable to find one another because of the darkness in the forest, and muddled minds from swamp gas exposure. He laughed a bit as he listened to the tale, unsure whether it was intended as a comedy or a tragedy. Secretly, he found himself wishing the doors would open and Cass would walk in, having missed her boat. Just as he felt the flush return to his face at the thought of Cass, he heard a pained groan from Aislinn.

Eloise had returned with two mugs of ale and set them down, one in front of Aislinn, and one in front of Cole. Aislinn's head was down. Beside her mug was a shining brass handbell with an intricate rope-weave handle. Aislinn tried to push it back to Eloise.

"El come on," she pleaded through gritted teeth. "Do you know how much that would cost me?"

Eloise shrugged and pushed the bell back to her with two hands. "You know why you have to, dear. You can add it to your tab."

"El my tab is already worth my life. I'll have to enslave myself to you to pay this off."

"Would that be so bad, dear?" Eloise winked at her. "Come on. Half of these men and women here are veterans. Ring the bell Elissan."

Aislinn sighed deeply and lifted the handbell above her head. She looked at Cole as she paused, bell raised.

"Pick up your ale, Cole. This will be interesting."

With that, Aislinn flicked the bell and the clarion call that rang forth seemed to echo off the walls and amplify in such a way that it gave Cole goosebumps. A cheer erupted from the crowd as almost every man or woman in the tavern lifted their drinks to the sky. Those without drinks lifted their fists. Cole followed suit, even though he had no idea what was happening.

"*To the Rise!*" The entire bar shouted in unison.

"*For the fallen!*" Aislinn shouted into the silence that followed. And then she rang the bell again, before setting it on the counter with a defeated look to Eloise. One of the other servers arrived just then, sliding a pair of bowls filled with shepherd's pie in front of Cole and Aislinn. Behind them, the entire inn had erupted with cheers and hollers and the bard launched into a shanty about cloudbreakers.

"What in the Light was that?" Cole asked as a line of patrons clapped Aislinn on the back on their way past to line up at the bar.

Aislinn took a long drink from her ale and wiped her mouth with her arm after. "That, Cole Vallen, was the cloudbreakers toast. My dear friend Eloise here just made me buy a round for everyone."

"To the rise, for the fallen," Cole repeated.

"Cheers to those of us who rise from the ground, and a drink to those who never come home." Shouted Aislinn as she was pulled up from her stool by thankful patrons and whisked off to be danced around the tavern before Cole had a chance to inquire further. Instead, Cole drank his ale and ate his pie as the merriment went on around him. Aislinn had been right. It was captivating indeed. He was experiencing a small insight into the world he would soon become a part of. A world with its own rules, traditions, and history; a world among people who had claimed the sky.

Chapter 13

The siren song

Hope

In the Kingdom of Verdos, a culture known for its stewardship of knowledge and advanced scholars, every noble estate that existed coveted a library. Among them, the library of the Errbryte estate was by far the most impressive. Boasting a collection of well over a hundred thousand books and scrolls, the library made up the better part of the second floor of the estate, with wide oak archways carved with intricate reliefs depicting Verdos and Akoyan history. Every inch of wall from the floor to the ceiling was bookshelves, and every inch within the shelves was filled with tomes. Floorspace in the center of the library was dominated by three round study tables arranged like corners of a square, while the remaining corner was home to a first-generation airship cannon on display. In the center of the room, a spiral staircase led up to the single third-story room in the building: Hiram Errbryte's master suite.

Two tall stained-glass windows adorned the western wall, looking out onto the estate grounds nestled within the thick jungle of the Eastern Grindlemoor. At the base of the southern window was a waist-height table topped with a rotating chalkboard usually adorned with scribbles. The chalkboard was currently wiped clean, but the ghostly markings of its master's eccentric mind remained, no longer able to be entirely erased. Below the north window sat an ornate horseshoe study desk, littered with books and scrolls, stopper jars containing specimens, and writing material. It was at this desk, that Hope Errbryte sat alone, attending to her studies.

She pushed an unruly strand of her bright blonde hair back to its place behind her ear and continued scribbling notes in her book. Almost immediately, the strand escaped and fell forward again. Hope sighed and sat back in her chair, defeated by uncooperative hair. She reached up and opened the pearl butterfly clip that had fastened her long hair back and shook her head. If hair could talk, she reasoned, it would probably be making that sigh that one makes when a corset comes off at the end of a long day. She tapped her pen against the desk, resigned to the defeat of her studies, and stood to wander the library as she often did when boredom struck.

Her fingers brushed the spines of her father's books as she paced in a circle around the room. She knew maybe a third of them, those that her tutors had bidden her to read, and those she had chosen of her own accord. Adventure tales and explorer journals were her favourites. Not hard to imagine, as Hope was rarely allowed to leave the estate unless her father was away on business. Three years ago, her mother had fallen ill and passed away. She had grown old and lived a good life, as Hope had been born late in their years. It was a sad time. Losing her mother had made the estate feel empty, and in the years since her father had only become more reclusive. Of course, the call of adventure would be Hope's siren song. For the trapped, it almost always is. Hope paused as her fingers lingered on possibly her favourite book in the library. She tilted her head to the left to read its embossed lettering, letting her long hair fall as gravity intended to where it nearly touched her belt.

Legend of Savage Harbour the title read; embossed lettering dusted with gold leaf to stand out against the book's dark leather jacket. Though perhaps her father eclipsed her fascination, Hope still bore the standard Verdosi love of literature and knowledge. Hope just happened to love the make-believe books a little more. Stories like the one she now slipped from its place on the shelf and held in her hands. She had read this particular book so many times that she could recite it if someone asked. Maybe not word for word, but well enough to know the story. In her mind, she imagined someone asking. *On the coastline to the east of the World Spine Mountains, where the land meets the endless void of the Great Blue waters, sits a town of ghosts, steeped in myth.* Maybe it wasn't exactly how the book began, but it was how she pictured it in her mind. Great jagged spires of rock worn smooth as glass by blasting winds and ocean storms, like the teeth of a serpent trying to swallow the land, rose from the crashing waves. An ominous almost otherworldly atmosphere where storms consistently blacken the sky, and only the fiercest people can thrive. Set against that backdrop, the story of a young boy called to the waters by an eerie song becomes the first to venture past the rocks and solve the mystery of Savage Harbour.

Hope held that image in her mind's eye as she slid the book back into its slot on the shelf. She thought about all the nights she lay awake, listening to the wind outside her window, hoping that she might hear a note or two of her own siren song. A song that would speak only to her, beckoning her onward beyond the rocks to adventure and freedom and experience. Hope rapped her fingertips against the book's spine as she lost herself in her daydream. She wanted adventure. She wanted to be the main character in someone's favourite story.

"Had enough of calculus already?"

Hope turned and looked up to watch her father descend the spiral staircase from above. He was a thin man, frail-looking, with short-cropped straight white hair. His features were sharp and elegant, and his skin had the same porcelain quality that her own did. He used a cane to steady himself as he walked, a remnant of the laboratory accident that had introduced him to his mother. Between the cane and the brace that helped his knee remain straight, he had a sort of lope to his walk that made his hair shake. That was one of Hope's favourite things about her father. His dancing hair, she called it.

"I finished the assignments the tutors left a while ago," Hope exclaimed proudly. "I was doing some writing. Well, sort of. More like sketching notes."

Hiram reached the bottom of the stairs and crossed the room to the desk. He thumbed through the papers on the desk and picked one up. Nodding to himself silently as Hope approached.

"This is good," Hiram whispered. "Interesting formula you chose to solve this. Not what I would have used..."

Hope leaned forward and offered a mischievous grin to her father. "But it's right!"

Hiram smiled and set the paper down as he repeated his daughter's words. "But it's right. I'm impressed, Hope. There are few uses for the Buckes Rubric but you found one I never thought to try."

Hiram slid a paper out of the way and read the notes Hope had been doodling in her book. "The eye blinks at me. It can see right through me. Right to my very soul..." Hope leaned forward to cover the notes, but Hiram picked up the book and continued. "I want to fight it, but it ensnares me. Ancient eldritch magic, born of the realm of lore, has taken control of my heart and I have become a slave to something far more powerful than myself."

"Dad, it's not even finished!" Hope giggled, reaching for the book playfully. Hiram spun gracefully, putting his back to her and securing the safety of his prize a little longer.

"Green fluid fills my chamber until I am floating, left to observe the world through a green haze. I am lost..."

Hope successfully snatched the book from her father's hands and snapped it closed. She grimaced at Hiram, though she failed miserably at communicating anger. Hiram smiled as he lifted his cane to point at a rare jungle frog floating in a glass jar full of green-tinted formaldehyde. One of many such treasures adorning the room.

"I fear the frog and his eldritch magic! We should burn him at once!" Hiram proclaimed to the cry of his daughter. She leapt to the desk, clutching her notebook to her chest and standing between the cane and her frog. She tossed her head with dramatic flair and bellowed in the most rapturous voice that she could.

"No Father! We cannot!"

Hiram didn't miss a beat, he dropped the cane and stepped forward, raising his hand as though he were holding a crystal ball.

"But why? What hold has he upon you, this dangerous frog?"

Hope laughed, unable to keep a straight face against her father's theatricality.

"I love him." She declared.

Hiram paused a moment and then, laughing, he stepped forward and hugged his daughter tight.

"You have a way with words, child. Perhaps if the alchemic arts are not to your fancy, there may still be a use for you with the Scholars at the archives."

Hiram kissed the top of her head as a butler entered the library. "Lord Errbryte. Visitors here to see you, sir."

Hiram stepped back from Hope and looked across the library to the butler summoning him. He was one of the new ones but trained well enough to know that 'visitors' without names meant unannounced individuals seeking private audiences. Hope knew that too, or rather she had picked it up over time in all her observations of moments just like this. Her father had tensed up. The happiness on his face was gone.

"I will see them in the gardens. Please fetch wine."

The butler bowed and vanished through the arched door. A moment later, Hope heard the tap tap tap of footfalls going downstairs to the main floor below. Her father turned to her and kissed her lightly on the forehead.

"Party guests already?" Hope asked.

Hiram shook his head. "Unlikely. Sorry, my dear. I have to go. I'll be back shortly."

Hope watched Hiram start to walk away, unable to stop herself from smiling as she watched his hair dance. "I'll be waiting," she called after him.

Without breaking his stride, Hiram looked back over his shoulder. "Alas, the frog shall live another day." Then he rounded the corner outside the arches and vanished from sight.

Hope listened to the k-thump k-thump sound as he descended the stairs. In her mind, she counted to twenty-five and then crept across the library to the arch. Outside the library was a wide hallway with a banister railing looking down on the ballroom below. Hope stole a glance to her right to make sure no one was on the stairs her father took, and then crossed the hall to stand against the railing.

The main feature of the Errbryte estate was its Grand Ballroom on the first floor. The second floor, which included the library, featured double staircases on both sides that allowed guests to reach a second level, wrapping around the entirety of the ballroom below like an open-air mezzanine. The ballroom was constructed for entertaining nobility and royalty alike, and the mezzanine gave people a place to retire and converse away from the music and conversation that generally filled the lower floor. There was a wide space at the south end between the stairs that was almost always filled with food and refreshments. Hope peeked over the railing to the ballroom below but realized she could not yet hear or see her father and his guests. Instead, a fruit tray caught her eye, and she dashed over to pop a strawberry in her mouth.

Just as she bit down on the delicious berry, she heard the ballroom doors open below her. She knew the path to reach the gardens from indoors was below her in the ballroom, so she had surmised she could witness her father's guests if she was stealthy enough up here on the second floor. She listened intently for the voices to move out into the ballroom below her. When they started to fade away under the eastern part of the mezzanine, and she heard the doors to the garden swinging open, she stepped to the railing to peek below.

The butler stood at the wrought-iron doors to the garden, holding them open as Hiram stepped through with his trademark hobble. His dancing silver hair sparkled with torchlight. It was dark outside in the garden, so the servants must have lit the torches. Such a clandestine meeting place, Hope thought to herself. A man appeared, followed by a second, and Hope watched as the butler ushered them out into the garden behind her father. The first man was attractive and young, despite his silver hair. He moved with a smooth gait. Fit. Well-dressed. Noble. Hope had never seen him before at father's functions. Odd.

The second man stopped and tapped the butler in the chest with the back of his hand. It was a familiar gesture. Or an arrogant one. His clothes were the same as the first, if not slightly less kept. His hair was a jumbled mess of dark curls. Hope leaned against the railing to get a better look. Perhaps it was her movement that caught his attention and made him turn. Perhaps he was simply taking in his surroundings. Whatever it was that made him turn, the man's eyes searched the upper mezzanine and landed directly on Hope. Her breath caught a moment in her chest, and she wondered if she should step back. Hide her face. Would her father be mad at her for spying on his guests? It was unlikely, so Hope did what she thought was best. She smiled at the man, and he smiled back. It was an unsettling toothless grin, and Hope noticed he was missing an eye.

Chapter 14

Home in the sky

Cole

By the time Cole and Aislinn approached the Errbryte Estate, most of the guests for the gala had already arrived. The approach to the estate was a cobblestone pathway fenced in by transplanted cedar trees, their huge girth standing out in stark contrast to the jungle trees beyond the grounds. Cole felt like a phase of his life was ending and a new one was about to begin as their coach rumbled across the cobblestone in time with the clip-clop of the horses pulling it.

For the first day after leaving Stonesvale, Cole had been left to his whimsy once they boarded their paddle boat bound for Vandrad. Aislinn was in a sorry state, and so had decided she would retire to their cabin and sleep it off. Cole had spent that day speaking to anyone he could or simply just watching the jungle pass by from the upper deck. He had met some fascinating people and witnessed the abundance of life that populated the thick canopy forest of the Grindlemoor. He had seen alligators, birds beyond count, a few small jungle deer, monkeys, and even a wondrous black puma lounging on a branch in a tree near the water.

The pair had spent no time at all exploring once they arrived in Vandrad, they boarded a coach and immediately departed for the estate. That final leg of the journey had taken them a little less than two full days, and Aislinn had spent every waking moment of it educating Cole on the history of Hiram Errbryte, his accomplishments, and the rumoured wonders of the estate itself. She had shared with Cole how rare it was for Hiram to open his estate to visitors, and how overly excited Aislinn was to see it all for herself. Of course, as interesting as everything the estate had to offer was, Cole was focused entirely on the Cirrus. As the coach trundled along, Cole got his first close-up look at the ship as they passed one of the huge trees and the view opened into a meadow at the outskirts of the grounds.

The Cirrus was tethered to the ground in the open meadow by a series of lines stretching out from its hull to the ground, making it look like a giant steel tent at a festival. There was no smoke issuing from its tall stacks, and no people visible on its decks. A ramp had been lowered from somewhere below its belly, which crossed the thirty feet or so of space between the ship's hull and the ground. A tree briefly blocked Cole's vision as they rolled past, but then there it was again, floating just off the ground in all its wondrous glory. They were close enough now that Cole could see through the bridge glass, just enough to spot a few details of tightly packed machinery and personnel stations. The hull number was clear as day from this close. C26. V.A.S. Cirrus. Second-generation cloud-class cruiser. Now, a crew of forty-eight.

Aislinn saw Cole staring out the window and leaned over. "Once we've arrived, we'll board and stow our gear. I'll make introductions, and then we can clean up and prep for the gala."

Cole swallowed hard. "I'm about to step onto an airship."

"Light save me..." Aislinn whispered as she sat back against the seat she was in. The pair of them had the coach to themselves from Vandrad, which suited Aislinn just fine. It had given her time to get Cole up to speed without having to worry about security or interruptions. She had more than a few trepidations about bringing Cole into the fold as she had, and the closer they came to their rendezvous with the crew, the more Aislinn had wondered if she had made a mistake. The boy was highly intelligent, and highly observant as well, but he was still so young. His obsessive interest in airships and the life of cloudbreakers worried Aislinn. He was naive, and Aislinn had her fair share of experience with the consequences of naivety in this life.

"This life, Cole... you have to understand," Aislinn had told him after she had nursed her hangover from the events at the Swampfish. "It may look glorious and romantic from the outside. I imagine that may even by design as far as the dogma you were fed is concerned, but the *truth* of service is not what the radios and posters make it out to be. It's not always adventure, merriment, and the ringing of bells. It is horror, suffering, sacrifice... and often more death than a sane person can handle."

Aislinn remembered the look on Cole's face when she told him that. He was reading her, instinctively, in the exact same way that Aislinn had been trained to get where she was in her career. In Cole's eyes, Aislinn could see her own pain reflected. For a moment, Aislinn worried she may have shattered the boy's impetus for this path, but then there it was. That sudden shift in Cole's body language. That relaxing of his facial muscles, the turn up at the corner of his lips, the change in shape to his eyes. Aislinn knew his youth was about to speak before Cole opened his mouth. "But that's when we were at war," he had reasoned. "It can't be like that still, can it?"

And there it was. The exuberance that belied a man not yet experienced in the world. Aislinn knew Cole would not understand. Even after the bombing, after losing Rikket, he did not yet realize. Everything he had been through had not left a mark on him, or he was ignoring it. And for that reason alone, Aislinn worried she had made a mistake. The world was at peace, just as Cole had said. He was right about that. But a cloudbreaker is a soldier. Their *business* is war, whether the world is at peace or not. Aislinn had seen enough of the world to understand that. There is always conflict. There is *always* death. Somehow Aislinn had to prepare Cole for that.

Trying to take her mind off the issue, Aislinn watched out her window as the carriage passed through the end of the tree-lined approach and the Errbryte Estate revealed itself in its entirety before her. The grounds were immaculately tended, with short green grass covering the land from the edge of the roadways and paths to the tree line of the jungle that hemmed it in. At the end of the approach, a laid-brick lot had been built with a stable-house off to the side, and stone pillars connected by chains fencing it off from the rest of the grounds. On the right side of this lot, a tower of wood and metal stood about two stories high, firmly planted in the center of a stonework circle that looked as though it may have once been a fountain. Beyond that, a pond provided a feature to the grounds and was surrounded by pathways and benches where Aislinn could see guests mingling and tossing crumbs into the water where happy ducks and fish consumed it.

The estate itself rose behind it all, a multi-story stone and wood mansion that suited its name. The entire first floor of the building was walled with carved stone bricks, shining a polished gray. The top floors were wooden, stained a dark brown and maintained such that the panels looked freshly installed. Three stories marked the highest point on the left of the structure, the second story carrying out further to the right, before dropping off to a single story at the farthest right. This made the mansion take on a triangular shape, with two more rectangular structures poking out from the front forming the entranceway. As the coach mercifully rolled to a stop out front of the stables, Aislinn drew a deep breath. "Alright, here we go."

When the carriage driver opened the coach door, he had to step back as Cole almost jumped out onto the ground. Aislinn apologized to the driver, and then the pair of them followed the driver around to the back of the coach where their bags had been stowed for the journey. A stable boy busied himself unhitching the horses and leading them into stalls inside the stable, as Aislinn and Cole turned away from the mansion and made their way across the lot to the meadow where the Cirrus was tethered.

The closer he came to the Cirrus, the more Cole realized its size was deceiving. The ship was far larger up close than he estimated, having only ever seen it from the distance over the fields from Lookout Rock. The bottom of the hall was wide and almost flat across its base before it carved sharply up into the side of the hull. The sides also had an unexpected taper as they neared the top, giving the entire hull a bottom-heavy appearance. Cole supposed that made sense for stability. The upper deck was rimmed with fencing posts that appeared to be hinged at the bottom, each one connected by three cables.

As they passed the first of the tether lines, Cole was amazed at how thick the braided rope was. The ropes seemed to protrude from the hull itself through small portholes with hatches that were flipped open. At the ground a tripod structure a little shorter than Cole himself was set up, becoming the anchor point for the lines. In its center was a cranking mechanism with three arms that were presently folded up against the structure's large internal cylinder.

"Boring anchor," Aislinn said when she noticed Cole's interest in it. "We use them when we're setting down somewhere without an airship dock." She pointed to the three folded arms. "Those drive the bore when they're flipped up. Think of it like a five-foot-long screw, but way thicker. Drills into the ground and holds the tether lines in place."

Cole counted ten tether lines, five to each side, and imagined three crew members per tether spinning the giant screws into the earth. "Amazing," he breathed in awe.

Aislinn continued past the tethers toward the ramp into the Cirrus' belly. "They didn't work so well in the desert though," she said as they passed directly under the ship. Its size continued to awe Cole. There was a charged feeling in the air, and Cole noticed the hairs on his arms and the back of his neck standing up. The air had a heavy clean scent to it, like the smell just before a lightning storm.

Continuing to answer Cole's questions before they were even asked, Aislinn explained. "It's the lift plates. Aether Steel plates inside the hull. Cirrus' steam engine runs an electric generator which powers the ship and the plates. That smell is called ozone. Charged air particles. The same thing is making your hair stand on end."

"How do lift plates work? I could never find much about them in books."

"For good reason," Aislinn stepped onto the steel ramp that led into the steel behemoth above. "Most everything about the lift-plates is a guarded secret. Only a handful of people in Akoy and Verdos know how they're made or how they work. All we know is when you run electricity through them, they become lighter than air. More electricity, more lift. Without their invention, there would be no airships."

The ramp was wide enough for three people to walk abreast and sloped at a comfortable angle. There was a roughly waist-height handrail on either side made of steel tubing. Two chain-driven arms to either side with a knuckle allowing them to fold were currently extended. The mechanism for the ramp to raise and lower. A cloudbreaker was standing with one foot up on the handrail, a brush in one hand and a bucket of grease in the other. Her black hair was tied back in a ponytail, and she was painting grease onto the knuckle of the ramp mechanism to their left.

"You missed a spot, Cheddar," Aislinn chided as they passed her. The woman turned her head to see who was boarding, and quickly shook it. Goggles atop her forehead almost fell, and her attempt to steady them with the hand holding the brush resulted in a dab of grease in her hair. There was much more than that already. "Oh! You got it!" Aislinn continued.

"Get lost in the woods, Elissan," Cheddar barked, even though Cole saw the hints of a smile on her face. "At least one of us works for a living, you bug-eater."

Cole laughed trying to imagine what made Aislinn a bug-eater. "Ignore the grease monkey, Cole," Aislinn said as she continued up the ramp. Behind them, Cheddar returned to her duties, but as she did, without looking at them again, she hollered: "Welcome back!"

Aislinn threw a two-fingered wave over her shoulder as Cole inevitably asked a new question. "Why bug-eater?"

Aislinn shrugged and adjusted her pack strap to a more comfortable position on her shoulder. "Peregrines can sometimes get a lot of bugs in their face during a dive. It's just something jealous people say to us because they can't fly." Aislinn winked to finish her statement just as the pair reached the top of the cargo area the ramp led to.

"This is called the hangar," Aislinn began as Cole took in his surroundings. The singular space made up almost the entire lower section of the ship from hull to hull. Catwalks had been built up off the deck itself, made from diamond-shaped bits of steel that provided a corrugated service good for grip when the ship was moving. In the hollow space below, a gentle hum emanated from large pads into which a mind-numbing amount of cables and piping ran into and out of. To either side of the hangar were tall racking setups with hinged doors. Most of them closed. Inside the open racks, Cole could see all manner of material from spare parts, to tools and dry provisions.

"Stores and warehousing are down here, and we can use this space for any other temporary need we have. Makeshift hospitals, troop transport, vehicles, or whatever else the mission requires." Cole listened intently, but his wide eyes were scanning the space non-stop. His exposure to the ship had only just begun, but already he was mesmerized by how efficiently every single inch of space was taken up by piping, cables, machinery of all sorts, lighting, and so on. He followed Aislinn straight down the middle of the space to where it ended in a flat steel wall with a single closed hatch in the center. The door had a circle wheel in the center that drove a mechanism connected to four arms that pressed pins into rings which held the hatch tightly sealed.

"Through there is the engine room," Aislinn said, turning instead to climb a staircase on their right that was hidden by the end of one of the warehouse racking. "You'll get your chance to see it later. I'll likely have you working with Lucius when we're underway. No better man alive to get you up to speed on airship engineering."

Cole rounded the railing at the bottom of the staircase and followed Aislinn up to the deck above. "This is two-deck," Aislinn continued. She pointed to their right as she stepped into the hallway that ran the length of the ship. "That way is aft, and that way is forward." Her left hand came up as the right one fell. "Don't worry if you don't get it right away, it's easy to be turned around in here until you've been aboard a while."

Aislinn started towards the aft end of the ship, even though she pointed over her shoulder toward the opposite end. "Forward end of two-deck you'll find communications, the captain's quarters, and the bridge. Down this way is the kitchen, the mess hall, the medical room, and the lounge. We'll go stow our gear and then I'll leave you in the mess while I debrief with the captain."

About fifty paces down the hall toward the aft end, Aislinn stepped onto another staircase and climbed to the deck above. This deck was similar to the one below, with one singular hallway running the length of the ship connecting all the spaces. As with everywhere else, not a single speck of area was unused.

"This is one-deck. Crew quarters, cannon bays, and the peregrine tubes. Before you ask, yes. It was on purpose to put people sleeping right beside the cannons. It means we can close for action faster." Aislinn wheeled to the left this time and started making her way toward the forward end. Cole was taking mental notes the entire time. He wanted to impress Aislinn and set his internal compass in record time. "You'll be bunking with me for now, unless the captain says otherwise."

Aislinn proceeded a third of the entire length of the ship, and they passed a handful of the cannon bays, which were dropped open rooms reached by a staircase of five steps. There was space for two men, one to load and a seated gunner. Mechanical lifts brought ammunition up to the loader from the stores below. Cole was surprised to see no cannonballs or powder bags. Instead, he saw cylindrical brass objects tipped with rounded points stacked horizontally in the loader mechanisms.

"What are those?" Cole said, stopping and pointing into the cannon bay. Aislinn turned back and approached so she could see what Cole was pointing at.

"Cannon rounds," Aislinn replied. She pointed at the cylinder, trying to illustrate with her finger as she explained. "See that brass cylinder there? It's called a casing. The tip is called a projectile. The casing holds the powder and primer inside, precisely measured. The round can be loaded and fired almost immediately now, no more stuffing wads or getting the powder mixed wrong. They're an Akoyan invention. The Whitehall family mostly makes them, with a few other smaller noble houses in the market now too. It's the same theory as a rifle cartridge, just much bigger."

"My Dad still hunts with a musket," Cole admitted.

"Most people do," said Aislinn, motioning for them to continue. The next door in the hallway on the right ended up being their destination, and Aislinn swung it open. Unlike the engineering space below, the doors to the quarters were simple standard doors with a handle. On the outer hull of the room, there was a glass porthole that let in the daylight and provided an incredible view looking down over the Errbryte mansion. From the porthole, Cole could see that the first story extending to the far right of the mansion was open in the center, like a long square hallway that surrounded a garden.

"Home sweet home," Aislinn said as she tossed her bag onto a waist-high bed set against the wall to their right. Above the bed was a series of shelves that extended to the ceiling. Set inside the top of that shelf was an electric lantern. Below the bed was a pair of slide-out lockers for storing gear and personal items. The shelving above and the lockers below the bed made it so that the mattress sat inside an alcove, with a curtain on sliders tucked away at the foot. Wool blankets covered the bed, as well as a down pillow. Both sides of the room had a mirrored setup, and Aislinn pointed to the empty bed across from her. "That one's yours. Obviously."

Cole took his bag off his shoulder and tossed it onto the mattress, acquainting himself with the space as Aislinn opened one of her lockers and began emptying the contents of her bag into it. Cole did the same, and in no time, he was unpacked. Slightly overwhelmed and curious about how comfortable his new bed was, Cole slipped into the alcove recess and laid down, stretching out on the mattress and pushing his head into the pillow.

"It's actually not bad," he whispered. Aislinn sat on the edge of her own bed and motioned to Cole.

"Look up. See that rocker switch above your head?" Cole nodded so Aislinn continued. "Flip it."

Cole flipped the switch and there was a subtle click followed by a whirring sound. The curtain that was bunched up at his feet slid closed faster than Cole expected, and he found himself in the dark, now closed off by a thick canvas sheet. Cole wondered if this was how a corpse felt when it was buried in a coffin, but he was oddly comfortable. Tight spaces never bothered him. Cole hit the switch again and the curtain slid open once more.

"Not bad?" Aislinn asked.

"Not bad." Cole swung his legs out of the bunk.

"Okay let's get you to the mess hall so I can talk to the captain. Then, we should clean up and change before the gala, so I'll show you where the heads are then."

"The heads?" Cole asked as he followed Aislinn out the door and back into the hallway where they turned to the right.

"Washrooms. The term came from old water ships. Bathrooms were always at the head of the ship, far away from the captain as possible so they didn't have to smell it."

"You're kidding," They rounded the stairs and headed down to two-deck.

"I am, actually," Aislinn admitted as they headed aft. "I have *no idea* why they're called heads."

The further Cole followed Aislinn toward the after end of two-deck, the more his stomach started to grumble. Even among the mechanical potpourri of odours he had been exposed to since stepping aboard, the smell that met him approaching the galley was intoxicating. It smelled of freshly baked bread, cinnamon, and sweets. Aislinn had noticed it too. "Becky's aboard for sure," she quipped. Cole felt his face flush.

"Becky Adder?" Cole asked sheepishly. "As in Cass Adder from Stonesvale that you thought was Becky Adder, Becky?"

Aislinn stopped at an open door and presented her arm in a flourish like she was introducing the star of a play. "The very same," she said. From inside the space, a cheerful voice with an unmistakable accent rang out.

"Ashes!" Becky Adder said as she stepped into the doorway and slapped Aislinn with a towel. "Yer finally back!"

Cole was speechless. There standing before him and wearing a cloudbreaker uniform, was the absolute twin of the woman who had bumped into him outside the Swampfish Inn. She was a little shorter than Cole, with an attractive round face and chin-length black hair that bobbed as she giggled and perfectly framed her face. It was like seeing Cass all over again. Instead of a blue jacket, as was customary for their uniforms, Becky Adder wore an apron that despite her profession was immaculately clean.

"Becky," Aislinn said as she motioned to Cole. Her mischievous grin did not go unnoticed and Cole felt his face flush even more. "This is Cole Vallen, my new initiate. Cole, this is Becky Adder, our *exceptional* cook."

"Stahp it, Ashes," Becky said as she turned to extend her hand to Cole. Her smile was wholesome and genuine, and her big eyes were captivating. "Hi Cole, ah'm thrilled ta meet ya. Are ya hungry? I hope yer hungry. Ah just put on a *special* treat fer the gala and ah'd just *love* to have some feedback. Want to give it a taste, Cole?"

Cole shook Becky's hand and she tugged him through the door into the kitchen, with Aislinn grinning like a fool as she did. Becky led Cole into a small tightly-packed kitchen that was just as well organized as her appearance. Every tool had its place, and the whole space seemed engineered for efficiency. On the right just inside the door was a large kettle cauldron, which sat beside a large flat-topped grill surface. A mess of insulated pipes ran into the space from behind the wall, so Cole surmised it was all steam-heated. On the left across from the grill was a serving counter with a big open window into the room beyond that was filled with benches and tables all bolted to the floor. At the back of the room was a hallway that veered off to the right and led to fridges and pantry racks.

Becky stopped Cole about halfway into the space, almost directly in front of the serving window, and picked up a pair of mitts that were hanging on a hook below the counter. She looked over to Aislinn, who was leaning against the frame of the door. "Don't be shy, Ashes. Come on in! Room enough for all of us!"

Aislinn shook her head. Cole could see she had been waiting for this moment, and under his breath, he cursed his mentor. "No can do, Becky Adder! I have a date with the captain. Cole will keep you company though, don't you worry!" With that, she turned to walk away, but then stopped and leaned back. "Oh. Cole met your twin in Stonesvale. You should ask him about it!" And then she was gone.

"Met ma twin," Becky mused as she removed a tray from the oven and set it on the grill top. "Ah don't have a twin. Leastways ah don't *think* I have a twin. Stonesvale, you say? Hrm. Wonder if Ashes is talkin' about ma cousin' Cass from Vandrad. She goes to Stonesvale sometimes. Has a thing for a bard that plays at the Swampfish last I heard. What was his name?" Becky's lips barely stopped moving, even as she pulled a spiral piece of cooked bread from the tray and set it on a plate. She reached for a shelf above the grill and retrieved a small jar. "Anywho, if it *was* Cass, she was always one of ma favourite cousins. Lovely lass. Quiet tho."

Becky drizzled a thin coat of honey from the jar over the spiral bread and handed it to Cole. It smelled of cinnamon. Tentatively, he accepted it and lifted the bun to his mouth. Biting down into the soft warm dough was an explosion of flavour. Sweet, with a doughy texture, and bursting with cinnamon and sugar from the honey. Cole moaned out loud, then quickly caught himself when he realized what he was doing.

"It's good, right? Ah call 'em Becky Adder's Sweet Cinnamon Honey Treats... but I might shorten the name, ah don't know. We'll see. What do you think, Cole Vallen?"

Cole could only nod. He was lost for words. Something in his gut, and not just the delicious treat he was consuming, told him he was going to like Becky Adder. A lot.

Chapter 15

Steps into a new world

Cole/Hope

Aislinn returned to fetch Cole almost an hour later. Becky had fed him two of her sweet treat cinnamon and honey buns, and the two had talked at length while she finished a second batch and had plated both up in preparation for taking them to the gala in the mansion. She had decided it was far past time for herself to get ready, so she had left to clean up and change, leaving Cole sitting alone in the mess hall reliving everything as he listened to the hum of the ship. That was when Aislinn walked in.

"How did it go?" she mused.

"I know why you did that, *Ashes*."

Aislinn rapped the table with her knuckles and then motioned to the door. "Come on, let's clean up. And don't ever call me that. Only Becky gets away with it."

Aislinn led Cole down to the hangar again where he was introduced to the quartermaster, a skinny tall man from the far north of Akoy named Remmy. He had a thick accent too, but a slow manner of speaking so he was easier to follow than Becky was. Together they set Cole up with two sets of uniform pants, cotton high-neck undershirts, a single pair of boots because there was only one in his size, a dress coat, a cold-weather coat, gloves, and a weapon belt - though Aislinn told him that would remain empty until after he finished basic training. With all his kit in hand, Aislinn led him back up to one-deck so he could put his new gear away, and then they crossed to the aft end of the ship where the heads were.

The heads were pretty much exactly as Cole thought they might be. There were toilet closets, sinks with mirrors mounted on the walls above, and a ceramic-tiled room with booths for showering. Each shower booth had its own dedicated curtain. There was no separation of sexes onboard the Cirrus, or any airship for that matter, as Aislinn explained. "A cloudbreaker is a cloudbreaker," she said, just as Cheddar walked past behind her. She was towelling her wet hair, now devoid of its coating of grease. "Regardless of their gender or sexual preference. We bleed the same blood, we wear the same uniform." Cole blushed as he stood beside Aislinn at another sink, and did his best to pretend he knew how to shave. Cole had not yet grown any facial hair, but thankfully none of the others seemed to care. He blushed more when Becky Adder stepped out of a shower in nothing but a towel. Cole swallowed and forced himself to concentrate on the mirror.

Hope Errbryte stood outside the front door of the estate, shaking hands and welcoming guests into the Errbryte estate personally. Her hair had been partially styled up into a beautiful bun atop her head, with curled ringlets hanging down to either side of her face. The remaining length was also curled and bounced behind her as she moved from welcome to welcome. She wore a silver and gold coloured corset with ribbons of red silk, over a flowing white gown interspersed with black filigree around the hem. The dress didn't quite reach the floor, and her heeled black leather boots peeked out from underneath. She was nobility, and she looked the part.

As the last of the guests she could see outside walked past her and through the wide-open doors of the mansion, she heard the band begin to play inside the ballroom. She glanced across the grounds, lingering a moment on the airship tethered in the meadow. At last, assured there were no remaining stragglers she had not yet greeted, she turned to make her way inside her home.

Cole and Aislinn were met in the hangar by Cheddar and Becky, and all four decided to walk to the gala together. Cole was wearing his uniform and felt pride oozing from every pore he had. His heart hammered in his chest, and he kept fidgeting at the high collar of his cotton shirt. There was no adornment of any kind on his single-lapel jacket, where Aislinn and the others were decorated with pins and service medals. It made Cole feel naked, and he had to remind himself his journey had only just begun, and this was the first time he had worn the uniform. He hooked a finger into his collar for the third time and pulled at it, stretching his neck around a bit.

"You okay?" Aislinn asked.

"Just a bit itchy," Cole replied and relented his pull on the collar.

Cheddar leaned toward Cole as she spoke. "You'll get used to it. Takes a while."

"Ah feel right as rain!" Becky beamed, and Cole could not help but think that she looked right as rain also. It was interesting to see that the only difference between the Becky he first met and this 'cleaned up' one, was the blue uniform coat and single decorative beret in her black hair. She was pretty no matter what she wore or how clean she was.

Aislinn started to slow her pace and held her hand out for Cole to do the same as they reached the brickwork lot. "When we get inside, I'm going to introduce you to everyone as my initiate. That's a rank, remember." Cole remembered the lesson from when Aislinn had delivered it during the boat ride to Vandrad. After she woke from her hangover, Aislinn had told him that officers such as herself can recruit individuals they deem worthy of service directly, granting the rank of Initiate without requiring completion of basic training first.

"Don't mention anything to anyone about what happened in Harrow's Town," Aislinn continued. "Say you're from there if asked, but nothing about the explosion or Rikket or anything else. Let me do the talking unless we get separated. If we do, remember; nothing about the explosion."

Cole nodded as they approached the open doors to the mansion. Becky and Cheddar were ahead and had already stepped inside, their heads swinging about and marvelling at the decor. "Got it, Aislinn. I understand."

"Affirmative," Aislinn corrected.

"What?"

Aislinn laughed. "You can say all of those words with one: affirmative."

Cole tried it out. "Affirmative."

Together, Aislinn and Cole stepped through the doors and entered the Errbryte Estate.

Hope stood beside her father, Hiram, at the head of the Grand Ballroom, below portraits of their family. Above on the eastern deck of the promenade, a five-piece string band featuring a harpist played classical Verdosi ballads that echoed throughout the hall loud enough to be heard but not so loud that it disrupted conversation. In the hall's center, a fifteen-foot-tall marble statue of Kalissa - the Akoyan Goddess of light and life - welcomed the people still streaming in. An ornate decorative brass chandelier hung above her head, bathing the statue in warm light provided by gas lanterns.

Hiram was making small talk with a pearl merchant out of Havelock while Hope talked with his wife. The man had built an empire that now operated a fleet of fishing vessels and was soliciting her father's interest in investing in an idea he had to farm oysters for their pearls. His wife was a jewelry designer who designed lines of necklaces and earrings from her husband's pearls. She was boasting about recently signing a contract to sell her jewelry to the Gisborne family in Gallenfort; a well-known noble family who made their wealth by producing clothing. She was insisting that she would love to create a custom piece for Hope. Perhaps for her next birthday or *other* special occasion. Hope did not care for the implications of that last part. Especially the way the woman accentuated the word other.

Nobles had a way of pushing marriage and romantic pairings upon their youth from an early age. Hope had never been exposed to that with Hiram. He was protective of her, and she appreciated it. While all the other girls she had spent time with during her younger years were already married, some bearing children, Hope was focused on her studies and making her father proud. Secretly, she wanted to be swept off her feet on a grand adventure, not bartered between nobles like a breeding horse. She wanted what she read in her books. That organic love that happens when you least expect it.

"By the *Light*..." were the only words Cole could say as he stepped through the double doors that led into the ballroom. At least a hundred people already milled about, forming groups of clustered conversation all around. Decorative red recliners sat against the wall to either side of the doors as they entered, separated from another identical set by a table between them. Guests milled about, some already seated on the recliners, sipping from the wines and meads that were spread about the tables. A massive ornate carpet covered the floor, almost guiding the crowd onward into the ballroom where a giant statue of a stunning woman wearing a crown of woven flowers had her arms outstretched and her head tilted like a mother beckoning her child. Above the statue hung a brass chandelier the likes of which Cole had never even imagined, full of lanterns each with their own flickering flame.

"Kalissa," Aislinn said as she pointed to the statue. "One of the goddesses of the Akoyan pantheon I mentioned."

"Light and life. Makes sense."

Above the room, a promenade deck ran around the second story, looking down into the ballroom below. A band played on the right-hand side, soothing classical tones reverberating through the room. Most of the railing space on the promenade was occupied by a smattering of blue coats with single lapels, among nobles and merchants alike. As Becky and Cheddar vanished into the crowd, Aislinn spotted someone on the upper level who waved when their eyes met. He had silver streaks in his black hair and a beard that matched. As he waved, Cole noticed he wore leather gloves, even with his uniform coat on.

"Come on," Aislinn whispered to Cole as she turned to head back the way they came. "Let's go upstairs. There's someone I want you to meet."

Hope listened to her father speaking to a scholar from the Archives as they discussed new findings in the fields of computational mathematics and material engineering. She was more than capable of following and understanding the conversation, and she idly smiled whenever the scholar would look her way and apologize for boring her. It happened a lot, but she would always correct him, and interject something about Parov's Theorem compensating for the material density that was confounding him or something similar. Hope enjoyed flaunting her intelligence when men spoke down to her. She was not a child anymore. She was not even a lady in the societal sense. She was Hope Errbryte, daughter of the world's smartest alchemist, and she enjoyed reminding people.

An unusual movement at the back of the room caught the corner of her eye, and Hope stretched her neck to see over the crowd beyond the statue at the woman who was waving. The woman wore the cloudbreakers uniform, that much Hope could see from the distance through the crowd. She did not recognize the woman or the attractive young man who accompanied her. They must have come in after she had resigned from her greeting duties. The woman was waving her arm, but not looking in Hope's direction. Instead, she was focused on someone on the upper promenade, near where the band was playing. As the woman turned and pulled her companion along toward the stairs, Hope followed where she had been looking. On the upper deck, she saw another cloudbreaker leaning on the promenade railing.

The man was standing alone, his arms draped over the edge. There were streaks of silver in his hair that matched his beard, and he wore leather gloves even in his uniform. She remembered him when he arrived. She had shaken his hand but had not thought it out of the ordinary to be wearing gloves. Now though, she watched as he idly twirled a crystal champagne glass between two fingers, dangling it precariously over the crowd below. Still wearing gloves, and yet with only two fingers, he was so dextrous with his grip on the glass. Curious.

Hope excused herself from the conversation with her father and made her way through the crowd toward the doors. She told herself it was her duty to personally welcome every guest, and now she had seen at least two she had missed. She would rectify that immediately. She was a gracious and welcoming host. Through the double doors and into the hallway, she turned to her left and lifted her skirt to climb the stairs up to the promenade without tripping. In her mind, she made up stories about why the man upstairs was wearing gloves. Stories that would make her eldritch frog laugh out loud in his jar.

"Lucius!" Aislinn called out as they approached him leaning on the promenade. The band played only a few steps away, so they had to lean close to speak to him. "Lucius, this is Cole Vallen. Cole, Lucius Parvelle. Chief Engineer on the Cirrus."

Lucius reached out with a leather-gloved hand and shook Cole's firmly. In his other hand, he was twirling a champagne glass but stopped when he saw Cole looking at it. "Boredom," Lucius shrugged as he stepped away from the railing and set the empty glass down on a tray that was sitting on an oak table. Cole noted there were quite a few empty glasses on the tray.

"Lucius here hates parties, don't you, old friend?" Aislinn chided as Lucius reclaimed his leaning perch against the promenade rail.

"Hate ain't a strong enough word. *Loathe* 'em. That's more like it."

"I'm not sure how I feel about them yet," Cole added. "This is my first one."

Lucius snorted, but in a friendly way. "Give it 'round a hundred more and you'll see. All the same, they are."

Lucius turned away from facing the ballroom and crossed his arms, leaning back against the railing. He looked Cole up and down.

"So," he said, tilting his head to Aislinn in a way that screamed *I told you so*. "Ya brought home a stray. Told ya not to, didn't I?"

Cole flushed a bit with embarrassment, but Lucius picked up on it.

"Don't worry, lad. Ain't your fault. It's her right to recruit ya, make no mistake. Aislinn and I got a history. Ole friends, you could say. I'm just bustin' her chops."

Cole could not think of a reply, so he stayed silent and simply nodded. His gambit worked, and Lucius turned his attention to Aislinn.

"Speakin' of bustin' chops," Lucius leaned forward closer to Aislinn so he could lower his voice. "Tell me some good news."

Aislinn glanced at Cole, and back to Lucius again. "We can't. The investigation and the trial were all the same as we suspected, and Cole can't remember much from that night at all. It's looking more and more likely we're dealing with a flash dart, but we have to prove there was a shooter."

Cole moved to Aislinn's left and set his hands on the railing while Aislinn brought Lucius up to speed in hushed tones beside him. He scanned across the crowd below and the promenade on the opposite side, trying to pick out familiar faces. He saw Cheddar down below, under the promenade across from them. She was standing with a group of cloudbreakers Cole hadn't met yet while they pointed fingers and appraised a suit of armour tucked into the corner below where the stairs rose to the other promenade side. Next, he spotted Becky standing near a door which he assumed led to the kitchens to his far right. She was chatting with a man wearing an apron who was holding one of her sweet bun treats. He seemed excited about it, and the two of them were rather animated as they spoke. Lastly, Remmy was on the Promenade opposite them, he appeared to be searching for something. Judging by the way he was holding his gut and the way he ran off down a hallway after a guest pointed in that direction, Cole surmised he was seeking a bathroom. Cole giggled a bit at the sight just as a woman's voice spoke beside him.

"Do you make a habit of sneaking into galas to laugh at guest misfortunes?"

Cole choked a bit as he turned to see a young woman standing beside him at the railing. She was looking in the same direction as him. He wondered how long she had been there. She looked at him playfully, shaking her head which made her blonde ringlets bounce. "Gastric distress is such a horrible thing. Poor man. Probably ate too many crawfish cakes. Rich food, they are. Goes right through you."

The woman turned and pointed at some small crackers on a platter behind them with a dollop of what appeared to be cream and a small piece of white meat sitting on top. "Those, by the way. So, unless you want to suffer the same fate as your friend over there, I'd suggest you steer clear." Cole swallowed and tried to remember if he had eaten any of them. The lingering taste of cinnamon in his mouth told him he was probably in the clear. The last thing he had eaten was Becky's sweet treat rolls.

A delicate hand reached out toward him. "Hope Errbryte. I'm the hostess for this evening." Cole took her hand. Her grip strength surprised him. She was dainty and beautiful, and yet still carried a strong presence. In a lot of ways, she reminded him of Seran Se'Baht Sable. There was a clear feminine charm, but underneath it was a capable spirit. Full of life and fire. He had been taken aback when he met Cass and again when he met Becky, but Hope was something altogether different. Like the statue of Kalissa in the ballroom, Hope had an aura about her. He felt like his hands clamming up, so he quickly released hers.

"Cole," he stuttered as he nervously wiped his palms on his thighs. "Cole Vallen."

Hope looked him over quickly, even reaching out and adjusting a fold on his collar, and fixing a part of his lapel that had folded over. "First day in the uniform, Cole Vallen?"

He swallowed hard and put on a resigned smile. "How can you tell?"

"You're serious," Hope said, an infectious smile forming on her painted lips. "I was only joking! Is it really your first day?"

"In the uniform, yes. I've been a clou... an initiate... for close to a week. We just arrived to meet the Cirrus late this morning."

"We? Oh yes! You must mean the woman I saw you with downstairs. The one *whispering* behind you? Well... it would be very rude of me not to greet every party guest individually. It's my job as hostess after all. Would you be so kind as to make introductions?"

Cole nodded, eager to take the attention off himself for a moment. He turned and leaned over to where Aislinn and Lucius were still speaking, clearing his throat to interrupt. When Aislinn turned her head to look at Cole, Cole backed up and held his hand out to introduce Hope.

"Aislinn Elissan, may I introduce..."

Aislinn snapped upright almost as if the Queen of Verdos herself was standing before her. She bowed deeply and then stood to accept Hope's outstretched hand. Lucius tried to hide a laugh, but it came out as a snort.

"Lady Errbryte," Aislinn said as she took her hand. "It is an honour. I have followed your father's work for quite some time."

"Really? So you're a scholar as well as a cloudbreaker, miss Elissan?"

"Please, call me Aislinn. And yes. I was raised an orphan in the Archives among the scholars."

"How fascinating!" Hope clapped her hands together. "I have always wanted to see the Archives. My father's collection is among the best in the Kingdom, but it pales in comparison I am sure. And if we're to be on a first-name basis, Aislinn, please call me Hope."

Hope leaned to her left over the railing and made eye contact with Lucius as he remained leaning against the railing behind

Aislinn. "Hello, Lucius. Is the gala to your liking? Can I have anything brought out for you? More champagne, perhaps?"

Lucius shook his head no, returning her infectious smile. "No thanks, I'm good."

"Lady Err... Hope," Aislinn stumbled as she stepped forward and took up her hand. "Would it be too much to ask if I may be introduced to your father? I would *love* to meet him."

Hope looked down over the railing and saw her father standing amid a crowd of nobles and merchants alike. He looked so hopelessly lost surrounded by the group, like they were wolves who had cornered him and were preparing their attack.

"Aislinn, I believe that is a fine idea, as it just now appears he may require rescue."

As Hope grabbed Aislinn's hand and started to guide her toward the stairs, Cole turned to follow. Just then his eyes found a face in the crowd below, entering the ballroom near the decorative sofas and the long rug. He was with a pair of other men, all appearing equally haggard. They were muscling their way through everyone, but not in a violent way. It was more the way bullies pushed their way through crowds. They reminded him of Edam Pyrell. Like they were trying to establish themselves as alphas amongst the pack. The man in the lead had unkempt curly brown hair, and as he swept up an entire bottle of wine from a table they passed, he opened his mouth in a wide toothless grin. His single eye sparkled the moment their gaze met, and for Cole, everything went black.

Chapter 16

A dark gift

Lucius/Cole/Aislinn

Lucius made it to Cole's side before anyone else. Luckily, he broke the boy's fall by catching him, preventing him from being hurt and easing him to the floor. Shortly, Aislinn and Hope were at his side too, kneeling as Cole convulsed into a fetal position with his fingers digging into and pulling at his hair.

"What happened to him?" Aislinn asked, almost shouting before she realized the band had skipped a beat, concerned about the scene unfolding before them.

"I don't know," Lucius replied. "Ya were walkin' away and he just collapsed."

"It looks like a seizure," Hope added, looking around the room aware of the attention they were drawing. "Does he have a history of them?"

Aislinn shook her head. "I have no idea. He was in an accident about a month ago and suffered a head injury, but this is the first time I've seen him do anything like this. We've been travelling together every day since."

"Well," Hope said as she bent over to examine him as best she could in the confines of the promenade. "He has stopped convulsing, which could be a good sign, but he seems to have gone rigid. Cole? Cole, can you hear me?"

Cole's eyes were closed but they suddenly opened and his eyelids fluttered. He went rigid, then limp, and then rigid again. His mouth opened as though he wanted to scream, but then closed and mercifully, it was like he suddenly fell asleep.

"He's not conscious. Help me get him to the library. If we stay out here, it will be a scene. We've already had enough attention. Aislinn, can you carry him?"

Without a word, Lucius lifted Cole and turned, carrying him cradled as one would a child - a large child - toward the south landing where he could cross to the promenade on the other side where the library arches were. Hope stood and waved to the band to continue, which they promptly did as Aislinn followed her fellow cloudbreakers. Hope addressed the nearby bystanders, thankful to notice that the commotion had not been witnessed by her father or anyone else downstairs it seemed.

"Just a minor medical issue. Prior head injury. No need to worry, please enjoy the gala."

Hope gave a curtsy once she realized her explanation had been accepted and quickly followed the others. Aislinn had already arrived on the far promenade and was approaching the library arches. She had moved ahead of them and was clearing a path. By the time Hope caught up to them, they were already inside.

Blackness lifts away and Cole is in the Swine and Ale. The smooth stool presses against his rump. He feels his weight on it. Feels the polished wood from years of use as though his bare skin were in contact. He can feel every movement of air in the tavern. Hear and isolate every voice. The smell of all the liquors behind the bar, in the mugs and glasses, and on the breath of every patron. It is all there. Every single sensation, like words on a page he can read. He knows which beards have wax. He knows the perfumes women are wearing. And he knows Rikket is beside him. He can smell the honey in the Prince's Light that his friend is pouring into his ale.

Time jumps, and suddenly Edam is standing before Cole. His mug is upturned above his head. Empty. Wait. No. There is a drip in Cole's hair he hadn't felt before. It never made contact with his scalp, but it is there. Then he is throwing the first punch. Left jab. No shoulder movement. Just a straight punch. The right side of Edam's chin. Impact on Cole's pinky and ring-finger knuckles. Then comes the haymaker. Wild right. Angry. Impact on the temple behind Edam's left eye. Cole can smell his breath as he exhales. Summer sausage and beans. He is unconscious before his head hits the bar. Here comes Peter's punch, but it never lands.

Time jumps again.

Cole is leaning against a table. His smile is wide. He can't stop laughing. Rikket is getting to his feet behind him. Someone shoved a cloudbreaker into them. Cole takes the ale sitting alone before him on the table. It's warm. Flat. Someone left it a while ago. He drinks it all anyway. There's a piece of bread, and some internal instinct tells him he should probably eat. He obeys and consumes the bread. Rikket has him again. Rikket is frustrated. His breathing is heavy. He seems to be scared of his father discovering the stolen liquor, at least as much as the Pyrell brothers catching up to them.

Time jumps.

Rikket is hauling Cole through the alley behind Swine and Ale. Cole can hear shouting. cloudbreakers are helping martial Jemmo keep peace and break up the brawl. They are almost two hundred feet away. Cole can still isolate their words. Jemmo is threatening stocks for the next person who throws a punch. There's a cat on a fence ahead. Orange tabby. It's female. Just a kitten. They pass the park on their left. There is the old lady who testified at the trial. She's sitting on a second-story balcony alone. She's knitting. The cat is hers. She's knitting it a sweater. Blue yarn. Specks of white.

Time jump.

Rikket has reached the cemetery. Cole can feel the alcohol coursing through his veins. He can feel when he slips in and out of consciousness. He can see everything in vivid detail, even though he knows when his eyes are open or closed. He knows Rikket has strained a muscle in his thigh. His gait has shortened on that leg by three inches. It's the side he holds Cole on. Cole isn't walking now. His legs don't work. He can feel the muscles no longer willing to move. That part of his brain has shut down. His body is protecting itself from the poison he ingested. He never realized what alcohol actually was. He can feel his liver trying to filter it from his blood, but he has consumed too much too quickly. His systems are shutting down, just like the power wagon engines. Preventing lasting damage.

Time jump.

Lucius found a suitable spot in the library between two of the round tables at the south end of the room. There was a bearskin rug on the floor. Gently, he laid Cole down on it. There had been a few moments during the traversal of the promenade that Cole had kicked slightly, opening his eyes a moment and then falling back into unconsciousness. After setting Cole down, Lucius made for the door.

"I'll keep watch," he said as he closed the doors behind him.

Aislinn was beginning to worry that Cole was suffering some sort of brain damage from his injury in the cemetery. Hope approached and knelt opposite Aislinn. She pressed two fingers on the inside of Cole's wrist and flipping her hair to get the curls out of the way, intently watched a clock across the library above her desk.

"What are you doing?" Aislinn asked.

"Shh." A moment later she released his wrist and answered her. "Something my mother showed me before she died." She pointed to the place on Cole's wrist where she had been pressing. Already, red spots from the pressure were starting to show. "You can feel the beat of his heart here. I watched the clock tick away fifteen seconds and multiplied the count of beats by four. It gives me his heart rate."

She leaned over Cole and placed her cheek near his mouth, using her hands to hold her hair from falling on his face. "His breathing is shallow, and his pulse is racing. This is strange."

Hope leapt to her feet and crossed the library at a run, as fast as her dress would allow. She quickly sped through a shelf of books, and then another. Finally, she found what she was looking for and drew it off the shelf. She opened the book and started flipping through the pages as she trotted back to Cole's side. She set the book down and held the back of her hand against Cole's forehead. She frowned. Next, she looked in his ears, gently opened his closed eyelids, and then looked closely at his nostrils. "Odd," she whispered, picking up the book again and flipping pages even faster now.

"What is it?" Aislinn asked.

"I have absolutely *no* idea."

At that moment, Cole's eyes opened wide and he tensed up. His mouth opened as if he were screaming, but his voice was just a whisper. After a moment, the silent scream erupted into a sound so loud that both Aislinn and Hope recoiled.

Rikket is talking to someone. He's saying good evening. There's another sound. Laboured breathing. There are two people with Rikket. Two men. One of them is in distress. His breathing is shallow, and rapid. Cole can hear the fabric of his clothing shuffling. He's shivering. Or convulsing. The sound is scratchy. Fabric against stone. Like Cole, the shivering man is on a bench. Cole is lying on his side on a stone bench in the gazebo. The temple windows are glowing in the darkness. There are priests inside. Cole can hear them, even with everything else around him. He can hear Father Ratly sweeping in the foyer. He can hear the whoosh as Father Impress slides prayer sheets into the pockets on the back of the pews. They had said they were preparing for mass. Rikket is pleading with the man he is talking to, explaining Cole's condition. He wants help. He is exhausted and scared.

"This is no place for you, boy. Begone from here." The man has said to Rikket. He is hiding his voice. Theatrics. Cole can tell by the subtle shifts in tone as he tries to force his throat to make unusual sounds. Rikket is unphased. He is still approaching the man. He continues to plead, asking for water and food. He is close now. Cole hears the fabric the man wears rustle. He is waving his hand at Rikket.

"You know not what you do, boy. Begone!" There is panic in the man's voice now. He is losing control of his phony act. The shivering man is getting worse. Cole can see the man on the bench opposite him. Just his feet. They are quaking. The fountain blocks the rest. He cannot see Rikket or the man he is speaking to. There is a shout. Rikket has closed the distance and the man he was speaking with has attempted to attack, but the sick man on the bench has made the first move. Cole hears a popping sound. A stopper is being removed from the glass. A flask? No. The tone is wrong. Higher pitch.

Cole plays every popping sound he has heard in his life. Only one comes close. It was a medicine vial his father had to take when he was sick with a parasite. Cole was only a child, but he is sure of his memory. The stopper came out of a vial.

Rikket and the man he was speaking with come into view. They are lit up as though lanterns have been lit. Were the priests lying during the trial? Did they see everything that happened? No. Cole can still isolate the sounds of Ratly's broom. They told the truth. This is something else. Cole can see Rikket now, to the left of the fountain. His back is towards Cole. He holds the other man against the post of the gazebo. Cole can see him now. His hood is back and his face is lit from the light. They are both looking toward the source of the light. It's on the other side of the fountain. It keeps getting brighter. Somehow, Cole knows it is the sick man.

Rikket is in shock. The false priest uses the distraction to push Rikket away and Cole gets a full look at him. Every single detail is frozen in time. He wears dark purple robes with a religious scarf. The symbols are old, Cole has never seen them before. Beneath the robes, Cole can see a bit of the man's leg and foot. Canvas pants. Tucked into high-top boots. They look military. Not a cloudbreaker. Something else. Cole can see his face now. He is grinding his teeth in anger. What little teeth remain in his mouth, that is. He is missing more than a third of them. Mostly from his bottom jaw. His face is scarred. Ugly. Especially around his left eye where only an empty socket remains. His hair is matted. In the light, Cole can see it is brown. Unkempt. Curly.

Time jump.

The one-eyed man is gone. Rikket is looking at Cole. The world around him is on fire. Cole's heart is racing. Rikket's eyes are full of fear. Cole can already see his skin starting to blister. The light itself is burning him. In slow motion, Cole watches as the air compacts in a sphere, moving outward from the source of the light. Fire, rolling and terrible, follows behind in a second wave. The shockwave hits Rikket first, at nearly the same time as the walls around him and the roof. The gazebo is torn apart. Cole watches as Rikket comes apart the same way. Rikket raises his left arm trying to shield himself from the light. Cole watches Rikket's arm turn to ash. The ash is thrown into his face and against his chest. His clothing burns away first, then his flesh. Cole can see his bones. See his organs as they cook. His body is moving now, thrown by the force of the blast. His head rolls forward. Cole knows he is already gone.

The fountain has protected Cole from the light and most of the fire, but Cole feels it as it hits the parts of his leg and lower torso that were not protected. The pain is intense. A searing burn sensation that then becomes cold. Cole can feel the moment his nerves die and the pain changes. He can see the shockwave wrap around the fountain. The barrier of hard air makes an impact on his chest. He cannot breathe. He feels his body sliding away from the bench. There is a thud as his back hits the half-wall behind him, and then another thud as the rest of the shockwave tears that away also. Cole is flying through the air now, propelled ahead of the fire that wraps angrily around the fountain. Cole can see it reaching toward him. It is coming, like angry fingers of flame, reaching out. Cole's right arm hooks against a short gravestone. It sets his body spinning horizontally in the air like a pig on a spit. He can hear the grass moving below him, disturbed by the shockwave. He can hear pieces of stone and wood whizz past, out into the darkness. Before he makes contact with the gravestone he can see it clear as day, lit by the fire behind him. He has rolled over in the air and now faces away from the gazebo. The fire is roaring. It is like it knows he has escaped. Cole feels his forehead smash into the headstone and everything goes dark.

Aislinn tried to recover from the shock of Cole's scream and quickly scurried forward to hold the boy's shoulder. Hope jumped to her feet and stepped back. As quickly as Cole had uttered the scream it was suddenly over. The doors to the library burst open and Lucius stood in the archway ready to assist in any way he could. Cole Vallen suddenly opened his eyes and sat up.

"Aislinn," Cole whispered, his eyes darting around the room. "How did I get in the library?"

Aislinn was completely perplexed, and Hope dropped her book to the floor with a plop.

"What in the Light... Cole, you..."

Before Aislinn could finish her sentence Cole leaned forward and grabbed his mentor by the shoulder. He blinked a few times, and for a moment Aislinn thought she saw the green colour in his eye flash. His voice carried a hard edge.

"I know what killed Rikket Sable."

Chapter 17

Blood on the hands

Ketrick

Eiffert Whitehall had become cocky. All the money and power they had accumulated building their network was getting into his head, and he had come to the gala wanting to flaunt that power. But when he saw the young cloudbreaker on the promenade, just before he collapsed and was rushed off, he knew he had made a mistake. Even with one eye, there was no mistaking the boy. Quickly, his single eye scanned the crowd searching for the telltale hair of his partner. He spotted him on the other side of the ballroom and headed straight through the crowd toward him.

Ketrick was standing with his mother Natalia and a few others. They were all grouped around Hiram Errbryte, speaking about the gala and other pleasantries. Natalia was a shorter woman, thin like her son, and wrinkled in the face befitting her age. She had the same silver-white hair that Ketrick did, a mark of their family, though with age hers had begun to take on a purple sheen most noticeable in sunlight. Despite her frailty as an elderly woman, there was a powerful charisma about her. She was a woman who had experienced life for good and for bad and had clawed her way to the utmost top despite it.

The Whitehall family was among the wealthiest industrialists in the empire of Akoy. They had begun in mining and eventually steel. They built the Core Forge in the foothills of the Rinda's north of Gallenfort and had single-handedly provided all the metals for the vast network of railroads that crossed the Forsaken Plains. As they expanded their operations in the early days of the war, they had built factories and facilities from one end of the north to the other, in both Verdos and Akoy. Then Ketrick's father had been killed in the war, and it was left to Natalia to hold what they had built together. Many cousins and rival families tried to tear her down, but Natalia faced and overcame them all. She proved a force to be reckoned with, and now her family was the prime supplier of arms and ammunition in the north, as well as steel and parts for the airships that won the war.

"Hiram," she cooed in her best high-society voice. "How do you do it? You have ten years on me at least, and yet time has been fairer to you, than I?"

Hiram smirked. It was the twenty-eighth time tonight someone had asked him that very question. "Lady Whitehall," he said with a sigh. "If there were a secret formula, you would be the first I would share it with. The world needs women like you if we are to keep this tenuous peace." The bystanders laughed.

Natalia stroked her hand across Hiram's shoulder. She was playing the game, even if she hated it. "Stop it you old flirt, we're much too old for that."

The conversation bored Ketrick, and he spent most of it simply downing glass after glass of champagne. The servers on Hiram's staff were diligent about bringing new trays. That suited Ketrick just fine. Hiram was beginning to look exhausted, and Natalia continued making comments about their shared age and the trials of the elderly. When a hand landed on his shoulder, Ketrick turned idly, expecting to be offered another drink. When his gaze met a messy-haired man with a single eye forcing a toothless smile, he almost dropped the glass he was holding. Natalia and Hiram both noticed him at the same time. Fortunately, no one noticed the flash of anger on Natalia's face, except Ketrick.

"Eiffert," Ketrick coughed in surprise which quickly became anger as he whisked his cousin away from the crowds. They passed through a dining area and then a kitchen. Still too many people, Ketrick pushed Eiffert through the kitchen and into a storage pantry behind it. Seeing the room was empty, Ketrick slammed the door and whirled on Eiffert.

"Idiot. What are you doing here? The gala is crawling with cloudbreakers."

Eiffert lifted his hands in a supplicating attempt to calm his cousin down. "I know, listen..."

Ketrick paced, ignoring what Eiffert was trying to say. "And you brought *muscle*? What were you thinking?"

Ketrick paused, realization dawning on him. "Who's loading the trucks?"

Eiffert shrugged. "Rest of the men. Ketrick, listen..."

"The rest of the men," again Ketrick ignored him and interrupted. "The rest of the men? And you were supposed to be with them, Eiffert. Light, I told mother you were in Gallenfort! You idiot. You know how much she hates you. I'm going to have to explain to her why I lied, and she's..."

Finally, Eiffert just blurted out what he had been trying to say. "Ket, the kid who survived the mess in Harrow's Town is here."

Ketrick froze. "What did you say?"

Eiffert swallowed. "The kid. The kid who was in the cemetery. He's here. I saw him upstairs."

Ketrick stepped forward so his face was mere inches from his cousin's.

"You told me he was taken care of."

"He was 'spose to be, Ket. The doctor told me he had no memory at all from that night. I paid the marshall off to make sure he went away. Just in case."

Ketrick shot forward just enough to make Eiffert think he was going to strike at him. Eiffert recoiled, though no strike came. "Then *why* is he *here?*"

Eiffert recovered from his flinch and simply shrugged his shoulders. Ketrick started pacing again.

"Are you sure it's him?"

"Pretty sure," Eiffert scratched his head. "I saw the green in his eye when he looked at me, right before he passed out. His cloudbreaker buddies carried him off, and then..."

Ketrick whirled and struck Eiffert this time. It was a solid slap to the side of his face without an eye. "*He saw you?*"

Ketrick was seething. He lifted his hand to hit Eiffert again. He wanted to beat his idiot cousin into the ground. But something stayed his hand. Maybe it was pity for the black sheep of his family. Maybe he still needed him. Instead, he wiped his hand across his face and then swept it back through his silver hair.

"Light, Eiffert. What a mess. *Your* mess. He's with the cloudbreakers?"

Eiffert rubbed his jaw as he stood slowly. "He's wearing the uniform."

"He's one of them? Oh, great. It's too early! If *he* finds out..."

Before Ketrick could finish his sentence, the door burst open and Hiram stormed in. He slammed the door behind him and poked his cane into Ketrick's chest, pushing him out of the way so he could face Eiffert directly.

"You were not supposed to show your face tonight. There is an *airship* parked on my estate lawn, and my ballroom is filled with cloudbreakers, and *still* you barge in? I have given you everything you wanted, and you have put it all in jeopardy. You are a fool!"

Ketrick stepped forward and pressed Hiram's cane down to the floor. He fixed the old alchemist with a raptor gaze and somehow turned his charming good looks into a cold menacing threat. "Hiram. Relax. You are acting a fool yourself. Remember that it was your idea to invite the Cirrus."

Hiram tapped his cane against the floor, turning his attention from Ketrick back to Eiffert.

"You know why I had to. They have all been on high alert since Harrow's Town and their flight path was a risk. I am done working for you. This shipment is your last," he hissed.

"Hiram," Ketrick began, still trying to get the alchemist's attention off his cousin. "We have a problem. The boy that survived in Harrow's Town is here. He's with them."

Still, Hiram kept his eyes on Eiffert. "Not my problem."

Ketrick stepped between Hiram and Eiffert, purposely looking away and moving in a precise and threatening way.

"Technically," he snapped his head toward Hiram. "It *is* your problem. We brought you into this to stabilize the formula. Have you forgotten? That blood from the incident, and the others like it, are on *your* hands, alchemist. All of this started because of you."

Hiram jerked as though Ketrick had slapped him. "Preposterous."

"Is it?" Ketrick asked. Eiffert grinned with malice on his face as Ketrick began to circle Hiram like a hawk.

"Your signature is all over the product," he continued as he crept around behind Hiram. "What other man alive could have stabilized the weapons? Isolated the mechanism for its operation? You know it all points to you. They know your curiosity just like we do."

Ketrick stopped in front of Hiram again, having completed his ominous circle. Over the sadistic man's shoulder, Hiram could see Eiffert trying not to laugh.

"And you know," Ketrick whispered. "We all work for *him*. We *all* have secrets in our basements, Hiram. You more than anyone. We need to fix this. Now. So, your party is over. Figure out a way to make the cloudbreakers leave. You need to remember what is at stake."

With that, Ketrick walked past Hiram, bumping him with his shoulder. He opened the door and stepped into the kitchen as though nothing had happened. Eiffert moved to follow but Ketrick stopped beside Hiram and whispered in his ear. Hiram recoiled at the foul smell of the man's breath.

"Play nice, alchemist, or I'll kill that beautiful daughter of yours myself."

Eiffert slipped away and moved to catch up with Ketrick, who was already across the kitchen, but he stopped and reached out for the handle of the pantry door. Over his shoulder, he looked back at Hiram a final time, speaking as he pulled the door closed.

"Maybe she would like a taste of your work?"

With that, the door clicked closed and Hiram was left standing alone in his pantry storage room, shaking as he fought to keep his balance.

Chapter 18

The secrets above

Cole

Over twenty minutes passed while Cole tried to convince the others he was okay and explain how he had reached his conclusion regarding Rikket's death. Aislinn had paced the library in thought the entire time, and Hope had barraged him with questions regarding his physical and mental condition from her book and two others she had retrieved in that time. Even Lucius had pressed, more than once, that what Cole had experienced was anything but natural, and he should likely see a doctor before they did anything else. Hope had scoffed at that. She was just as good as any doctor and intended to prove it.

"Lightheaded? Blurred vision?"

Cole sighed at her. "No. Nothing."

"Pain in your neck or joints. Headache?"

Cole paused. "Actually yes. A little bit."

Hope slammed her book shut and leapt to her feet. She crossed the library and began rooting through a basket of vials and flasks that clinked together as she searched. Cole could not help but notice how she made eye contact with a frog in a specimen jar when she found what she was looking for. She whispered something none of the others could hear, but Cole suspected she was thanking it.

"You said the false priest you saw," Aislinn said as she stopped pacing for Hope to rush past, preventing them from colliding. "He was wearing purple robes?"

"Dark purple, yes."

Hope set down a vial and a dropper. Removing the cap from the vial, she concentrated on siphoning out a measured drop of the liquid.

"That explains the fabric on the fence and the prints leading out of the cemetery then. It fits."

Hope grabbed the bottom of Cole's jaw in one hand while bringing the dropper close to his face like she was feeding a child. "Open your mouth and lift your tongue."

Cole did as instructed and she squirted the drop of tincture into his mouth. It tasted like peppermint and dirt. For the fifth time, she read his pulse by pressing his wrist and watching the clock.

"So, it was a flash dart?" Lucius asked. He leaned on the table that Cole was sitting on and chuckled at the grimace Cole made while trying to swallow the tincture.

Cole shook his head. "No. I already said that. There was no weapon. No shot was fired. The man on the bench just drank something from a vial he stole from the false priest."

"Still possible," Aislinn mused. "We never saw anyone eat what was in those darts."

Hope finished her pulse check and wrote a note in her journal. She pressed the back of her hand to Cole's forehead and smiled when their eyes met.

"Why would anyone wanna eat that stuff?" Lucius shook his head.

"Light, I have no idea," Aislinn stopped pacing and stretched her back with her hands on her hips. "So, we now know the false priest and the mystery vial were responsible for the explosion. The purple cloth I saw supports it. But... we can't prove any of it. And now you say this one-eyed shaggy man is here? Downstairs. Right now?"

Cole nodded.

"Why?"

Hope finally relented from her incessant inspection of Cole's medical condition and turned to face Aislinn. "He was here last night too, to speak with my father. He was with another noble I had never seen before until tonight. Ketrick Whitehall."

Lucius whistled.

Cole looked over his shoulder at Lucius and then at Aislinn, who had resumed her pacing.

"Is that important?" Cole asked.

"It may be," Aislinn answered. "Ketrick is the only son of Natalia Whitehall. She's the matriarch of their family. A very powerful woman."

"Whitehall is an old Akoyan house," Lucius continued for Aislinn as the inspector seemed lost in thought. "Made their fortune on steel and the like. Railroads. Now they make weapons. Almost all of them. And ammunition."

"That explains why they might have the flash darts. Reverse engineering maybe?" Cole surmised.

"Possibly," Aislinn whispered. "But why Hiram?"

Hope spoke up again, snapping her book closed and smiling again at Cole. "You're absolutely fine. I can't see a single thing wrong with you. If I hadn't been there to *watch* what happened, I'd have no concern for your mental state." She motioned over her shoulder at Aislinn. "Hers, though? I'm quite concerned."

Lucius burst out laughing. "It's like ya know her already!"

"Pardon?" Aislinn stopped her pacing and turned to face the others.

"My father is the single most brilliant alchemist in the north, possibly even the world," she paused. "Well, I can't speak for the Ciar K'hen, that's not proper. But the north, no question. *If* what you say is true there's no other person in the kingdoms that could reverse engineer this weapon."

Aislinn's shoulders drooped and her eyebrows sagged. "You don't think your father is involved, Hope?"

Hope turned away from Aislinn and busied herself with cleaning up her medical instruments, notes, and books. Lucius leaned forward.

"Best answer her, lass. Yer father is kinda like Aislinn's hero."

Hope drew a deep breath. "I don't know," She reached up and quickly wiped away a tear that had escaped her eye. Cole put his hand on her shoulder.

"It's okay, Hope. We'll find out together."

Hope smiled. "It's not that. I'm just afraid of what they did to him."

Lucius stood to his full height and crossed his arms. "You think they're forcin' him ta help?"

Aislinn took a few steps toward the doors. She had an intense look, so Lucius reached out and stopped her.

"Where ya think yer goin'?" the engineer asked.

"The false priest is here, Cole identified him. I'm going to get him and we'll make him talk."

Lucius shook his head but just as they were about to speak, the doors to the library opened and the Errbryte butler stood in the archway. He looked at all of them, before bowing when he saw Hope.

"Pardon me, Lady Hope. Forgive the intrusion, but Lord Hiram has stated he is feeling ill. All the guests have been asked to leave."

"What? Where is my father?"

"In the foyer my Lady," the butler said as he stood from his bow. "Making his farewells."

As the butler left, Hope dropped her head. Lucius walked to the door and peered out. On the promenade on the opposite side, the band was casing up their instruments. The rest of the upper deck was already cleared of people, so Lucius strode to the railing and looked over. He came back a moment later.

"Folk are clearin' out fer sure. Saw yer false priest down below too. Seems he's sendin' some goons out with everyone else."

Aislinn nodded to Lucius. "Follow them."

Without another word, Lucius slipped out of the library and disappeared down the stairs. Cole had slid off the table and was standing beside Hope when Aislinn approached. She put her hand on Hope's shoulder.

"I have to believe your father is being coerced, Hope. They know we're here and they know Cole recognized them. We *need* evidence if we're going to help prove his innocence. Does your father have a laboratory here? Facilities of any kind?"

Hope shook her head.

"Are you sure?" Aislinn pressed.

"I've spent my whole life in this mansion, Aislinn Elissan. I'm rarely allowed to leave, so I've explored every square inch of these grounds. If there were secret laboratories, I think I would know."

Aislinn sighed, frustrated, and then changed her approach. "Let's try a different approach, then. Where does your father spend most of his time?"

"Upstairs in his chambers mostly, or the garden if he needs air."

"Show me. Quickly."

"And if I do help you," Hope was bartering with Aislinn. "How do I know you will help my father?"

"Because, Lady Errbryte, I am possibly the only one wishing for his innocence as much as you are."

Hope hesitated before turning and leading Cole and Aislinn to the base of the spiral staircase in the center of the library. Hope stopped, looked back at Aislinn, and then headed up the stairs with the Cloudbreakers close behind her. At the top, they entered a landing and stepped out into the massive private chambers of Hiram Errbryte. Hope clasped her hands, doing her best to mask her insecurity, but Cole could see that her eyes were wide with concern. She looked like a child helping to steal forbidden treats from a panty. And yet, in the way she was unsure in her step, and the way she clasped her hands, there was excitement also.

Hiram's chambers were exorbitant, even for someone with his fame and reputation. The largest bed Cole had ever seen sat in the center of the south wall amid a pillared frame with silk drapes hanging from it. To either side of the bed were ornately decorated oak nightstands, and matching floor-to-ceiling wardrobe cabinets with brass fittings. The spiral staircase came out in the center of the room, and north of that the hide of an enormous tundra bear was splayed on the floor like a carpet. There was a study desk like the one in the library to the left of the bear rug, and to the right, a statue that made the hair on Cole's neck stand on end.

Cole was unsure why the statue was so unnerving. It was a giant serpent, mouth open and fangs bared. The whole thing was made of intricate brass, steel, and copper, and carved in such a way that it appeared animate and could move at any moment. The snake was coiled at its base with its head up and canted slightly forward. Twin flames flickered from its eyes, shining light outward directed by reflective hoods behind the flame. Hope saw Cole staring at the statue.

"It's just a fancy lantern," she said. "It was a gift from an artist long ago. Not for my father, but my grandfather. He was an explorer."

Aislinn had crossed the room and was sifting through papers on Hiram's study table.

"Benedict Errbryte. I read all his books too when I was growing up. Master Skyheart was a huge fan."

"The cartographer?" Hope asked as she approached, helping Aislinn determine what was useful and what was not among the scribbled notes on papers that littered the desk.

"The very same," Aislinn whispered, studying formulas on a scrap paper she had found that appeared quite old. "He helped raise me. He and Aldous."

"Aldous," Hope breathed, dropping a notebook to the desk with a light thud. "Aldous Corcoran. You *know* Aldous Corcoran."

"Yeah," Aislinn whispered as she passed the parchment she was holding to Hope, or at least attempted to. "What do you make of this?"

Cole felt that enough eyes were searching the desk, so he turned back to the statue for a moment and then began studying the paintings that hung from the north wall. Two smaller paintings hung in symmetry to either side of a huge floor-to-ceiling painting in the center. The smaller paintings were of older couples whom Aislinn assumed were Hiram's bloodline. The center picture was Hiram, Hope, and her mother. Hope was quite young in the painting, but Hiram and his wife already had years of their life upon them. Cole squinted at the painting and stepped closer.

"You *have* to introduce me, Aislinn," Hope was saying as Cole interrupted them.

"Hope, how old were you when this painting was made?"

Hope huffed and looked over at Cole and the painting. "I don't remember. Seven? I think?"

"How old are you now?" Cole asked.

"Cole," Aislinn laughed. "You never ask a lady her age."

"Ha ha," she chided back. "I'm twenty years old. Now seriously Aislinn. I need to meet him! He's written *all* my favourite books!"

Cole was ignoring them and fixating on the painting. He was doing the math in his head, and wondering how Hiram, in roughly fourteen years, had managed not to age a day. Then Cole glanced at the picture of Hiram's father, and then to the opposite side at his grandfather. Their clothes were different, as was their hairstyle, but they all looked more than simply alike. They looked like the exact same man.

"Okay," Hope was exclaiming. "I'll look at it if you promise to introduce me."

"Fine," Aislinn relented. "Now, please? What is this?"

Hope took the paper. "Scribblings. Old scribblings. I don't even recognize half the symbols in these formulas... but..."

As Hope's voice trailed off, Cole was kneeling. Something on the floor had caught his eye; scratch marks in the hardwood flooring in an arched pattern. Cole traced the line of the faint marks to where they disappeared below the frame of the painting. Cautiously he slipped his fingers around the frame and gave a slight tug. The painting and its frame swung outward.

"Aislinn," Hope whispered. "This math doesn't make sense. Granted, I don't understand a lot of these symbols... but it's hinting at a method to distill the essence of life itself."

Aislinn nodded and took the paper back from Hope's shaking hands. She carefully folded it and inserted it into a pocket inside her jacket.

"I thought as much," she whispered. "The symbols you didn't recognize? It's kir'ketechi."

"Ciar K'hen..." Just as Hope breathed the words, Cole had swung open the painting entirely, revealing a hidden door into a laboratory room behind the false wall.

"Hope," Cole asked over his shoulder. "How sure are you that you've explored *every* square inch?"

Hope gasped as Aislinn made her way towards Cole. "I... I didn't..."

Aislinn stopped and looked back at Hope.

"It's your father's private quarters, Hope. You couldn't have known."

Numb as though in shock, Hope trudged after Aislinn and followed her and Cole into the hidden room. A stone slab table sat to the left and two more like it were against the far wall. Tools of her father's trade littered the table-tops, as did specimen jars that would have made less acclimated people retch. An alembic bubbled away on a far table, with a blueish-purple liquid inside that burped an ethereal blue vapour on occasion which was quickly whisked away into more glass tubes. Hope's eyes were wide as she took it all in.

Most disturbing of all was a tall copper-rimmed glass tank filled with a greenish liquid that churned and bubbled, pumped into and out of the tank from tubes that ran into the walls and disappeared. A waist-height copper athanor churned beside the tank, pulling fluid from hoses connected to it that came up through the floor, and sending it into the tank to churn and bubble with the rest. A copper ladder rested against the front of the tank, and a swinging lid at the top looked as though it provided entry. Hope stepped forward, tears running down her face, and placed her hand on the glass.

"By the light," she whimpered almost inaudibly. "What have you done?"

Cole's reflection appeared in the glass. He was standing behind her.

"I never knew," she whispered.

Aislinn moved around Cole and Hope and squeezed past the athanor, careful not to burn herself on the hot metal. A window was open, and Aislinn leaned out.

"There are pipes out here," she said as she wormed her way back to the others. "They go down the side of the building into the ground."

Hope didn't answer. She stared into the glass, mesmerized by the bubbles and the churning fluid.

"Hope," Cole said as he put his hand on her shoulder. "I know this is hard. Where do those pipes go? What's below the estate?"

Hope swallowed and her eyes flicked to meet Cole's through his reflection. In the glass, the speck of green in Cole's eyes seemed to glow like an emerald.

"There are caves far below the mansion," she answered. "The estate draws natural gas from them for power. There are hot springs down there too, and we pump the water up for our bathhouse. I always thought those pipes outside were for a private bath. I never asked about them. I just assumed. There's also our family crypts beneath the garden... but beyond that, I can't imagine."

"Show us," Aislinn spun Hope around to face her. "Show us, Hope, and I will have Aldous write his next book about *you*."

In her eyes, the spark of adventure returned. Her fire was lit anew. Somewhere outside, whistling over the grounds of her estate in the darkness, her siren song was playing.

"We have to get to the gardens."

Chapter 19

The hunt begins

Lucius

It took every ounce of willpower Lucius could muster not to give up his suspicions when he shook Hiram Errbryte's hand on the way out of the mansion. Instead, he smiled, pretended he was too drunk to speak, and sauntered out into the yard. While guests continued to leave the estate behind him, Lucius grabbed Remmy and another cloudbreaker named Dakota as soon as he saw them. Quickly, he pulled them aside, keeping an eye on Ketrick as he did so. The slick noble was having a heated argument with his mother as she was climbing into a coach. He knew it. Ketrick was sending her away. Eiffert stood not far off, waiting along with his goons.

"Ow! Oi!" Chirped Remmy as Lucius released his arm.

"What's gotten into you, Chief?" Dakota asked.

"Listen and shut it," Lucius barked back as quietly as he could while still conveying his authority. "We've got reason ta believe that Ketrick Whitehall and that creepy mophead over yonder are messin' 'round with stuff they shouldn't. Aislinn's new pup implicated them in the explosion in Harrow's Town."

"Don't tell me Aislinn was right," Dakota began. He was sharp. A peregrine just like Aislinn, the only other one assigned to the Cirrus, but not the investigator his shipmate was. They all knew what flash darts were. Every veteran who survived the end of the war did. They immediately knew the gravity of the situation, and Remmy was already looking over Lucius' shoulder and keeping an eye on their targets.

"Looks like she was, but maybe worse than we thought," was all Lucius had to say. When Ketrick looked in their general direction, Dakota immediately grabbed on to Lucius as though steadying him from a fall and Remmy threw his head back and laughed. Ketrick kept walking, eventually meeting up with Eiffert and his crew before they turned and headed for a truck parked at the edge of the lot.

"Are we following them?" Remmy asked.

"We are," said Lucius as he turned his attention to Dakota. "First grab someone ya trust from the crew. Have 'em deliver this message ta the Cap'n. Ready?"

Lucius whispered the message in Dakota's ear and watched as he darted off into the crowd of people flooding out of the estate onto the grounds. Lucius glanced over his shoulder, watching intently as Eiffert and Ketrick boarded the truck while one of their goons set the valves in the open engine. Aislinn and the others had not come out yet, and the trickle was slowing. Most of the people flowing out through the front doors wore serving getups. And then there was the band.

"C'mon Remmy," Lucius said as he started making his way toward the group of musicians. "I have an idea."

By the time Dakota found Remmy he was standing beside an idling truck. The thin cloudbreaker had swapped his uniform for a long dress coat with tails and a white shirt with a bowtie. A moment later, Lucius appeared wearing a similar outfit. He clapped his gloved hands together and closed the back gate of the power wagon where all the band's instruments were. Remmy reached into the front seat of the truck and retrieved a jacket, pants and shirt, which he tossed to Dakota.

"Here," Remmy said. "These should fit you well enough."

Dakota immediately started stripping off his jacket and shirt. "This was your idea?"

Remmy shook his head as Lucius climbed into the driver's seat of the truck. "The big man's."

"C'mon! Change in the damn rig. We're loosin' 'em!"

With one leg in his pants, and one out, Dakota hopped to the side of the vehicle and tried to climb aboard, just making it in before Lucius had it rumbling across the brickwork lot. There were only a few power wagons at the estate, the rest of the guests had arrived either on the airship or by horse-drawn coach. The truck they were following was not so hard to follow. Lucius gave his quarry a long head start, but not enough to lose sight of them.

As Dakota finally got the last sleeve of his jacket on, he adjusted his bowtie while chiding his fellows. "What happened to the musicians, dare I ask?"

Remmy smiled, but it was Lucius who answered.

"Offered 'em a free trip on Aislinn's coach and a few paid nights in Vandrad."

"On Aislinn's tab?" Dakota asked. Remmy grinned even more.

"On Aislinn's tab," Lucius confirmed.

"Worth a week at least, right?"

Remmy started to laugh out loud as Lucius answered.

"Full month."

Chapter 20

The secrets below

Cole

Before leaving Hiram's secret room, Cole and the others replaced everything just as it had been, other than the parchment that Aislinn had put inside her jacket. They closed the secret painting door and crept down the spiral staircase back into the library. Despite the obvious potential danger, Hope insisted on taking the lead at every turn because if they came across her father, it would be less suspicious, and she could misdirect him. Fortunately for them, they never encountered a soul and were able to descend the stairs from the promenade to the first floor and cross the ballroom to the wrought-iron doors of the garden without incident. Further in their favour, the doors had been left open for guests to explore the garden during the gala, so Hope passed through them into the torchlight unimpeded. She stopped just inside the gardens and motioned to her guests to follow. She found them already at her side.

"There's no one here, Hope."

Cole's words made her blush. She chose not to respond to his comment, and instead led her peers down the tiled path rimmed in ceramic pots of roses, orchids, and other manicured flowers. Between the pots, trimmed grass and meadow wildflowers grew in a blanket of nature that covered the ground. In the center of the gardens were two statues, both holding torches held aloft in their hands. Hope paused a moment as she stood before the statues. She saw that Cole was looking at them also, so she explained.

"Koros and Kaderan. Twin daughters of Etmiel, the Akoyan Goddess of the wild. It was said that Etmiel never lay with humans like the others did. When she gave birth to her children, the other Gods demanded to know the father, but she never said. Most believe the father was a guardian of the forest. Like Nightcoat perhaps."

"Like from Legend of the Sunlight Prince?" Cole asked. "But he was a wolf."

Hope smiled and walked past the statues toward a big red oak tree that grew in the corner of the gardens. Aislinn leaned close to Cole as she passed him, following their hostess.

"So were the twins, Cole. They were werewolves."

The statues and a line of elevated ceramic planters made up the center of the gardens, and the path surrounded it creating a circle amid the greenery. In the southeast corner, a wrought-iron pergola contained a marble-tiled floor and protected a beautiful ornate fountain made from marble and spun with gold and silver throughout. The fountain had four bowls at the bottom, and the whole thing was carved with pictures of sea life and the ocean. Atop it, a wondrous figure held his hands aloft with water seeming to respond to his very will.

"Nidaro," Cole said before Aislinn or Hope could say a word. "Lord of Sea and Sky, but he vanished during the God War."

Aislinn and Hope looked at Cole in silence.

"I read a bit too," Cole shrugged.

Hope giggled and Aislinn gave a thumbs-up to Cole. Then Hope chose a path between two planters where some thick bush partially hid another iron fence, this time surrounding a descending circular staircase. She motioned to it as she swung open a gate with a metallic squeal. As Cole and Aislinn stepped past her and began descending the stairs, Hope unfastened her long skirt from the bottom of her corset, revealing pants and knee-high boots underneath, and tossed the skirt aside onto the grass. Then she reached up and pulled a single clip from her hair. The bun came apart immediately, and the full length of her golden hair cascaded down around her shoulders. She pulled it back into a ponytail and began fixing it in place using a stretchy bracelet she had been wearing on her wrist while Cole and Aislinn both stopped and stared at her.

"What?" Hope finished securing her ponytail and stepped onto the staircase. "No hero in lore has ever known when adventure called. I designed all my clothes for just such an occasion.

"That's not a bad idea," Aislinn said.

The three of them made their way down the stairs into the darkness below. The air became thick and musty, and they waited at the bottom for their eyes to adjust to what little light crept into the space from the small hole above. Hope fumbled in the dark against a wall to their north, while Cole and Aislinn explored as far as they were able in the darkness.

"It's around here somewhere," they heard Hope talking to herself behind them. "Ah! There."

A moment after she spoke, there was a scratching sound, and the flash of sparks briefly erased all the adjusting their eyes had done. Mercifully, a whoosh followed the second shower of sparks, and the concrete crypt came alive with the light of the torch in Hope's hand.

"You look like an explorer," Cole smiled at her. She beamed and curtsied in thanks, then joined the others in the center of the room.

The crypt was what anyone would expect from a family with as much history as the Errbryte's. The walls held niches marked out and labelled with the names of whom they held. The line went back seven generations, but only three generations were represented in the center of the room by raised sarcophagi. Everything was a dismal grey, covered in dust and cobwebs. There appeared to be no other passage out of the crypt beyond the spiral staircase. Cole approached the sarcophagi while Hope and Aislinn went to the outer walls and searched them intently.

Cole laughed when he overheard Hope say, "I'm finding the secret door this time," under her breath. Despite learning that her father was secretly experimenting with dangerous Ciar K'hen alchemy, she appeared quite calm. Cole knew nothing about her, but observing her behaviour considering current events made him wonder if the adventure was exciting her, or if she was simply in a state of shock. He was about to remind her that she was holding the only torch when she reached up and tapped her lit one to another hanging in a cradle on the wall. It whooshed to life as hers had, and she continued her search along the wall. Again, she lit another as she went, and then another.

Cole shook his head, smiling as he knelt to inspect the sarcophagus before him. There were three of them in the middle of the room, and Cole was kneeling before the one left of the center. The name on the plaque read Percival Errbryte, and the words Explorer and Alchemist were etched underneath. Cole stood and walked to the center one. Benedict Errbryte, Explorer and Alchemist. He approached the third. Hiram Errbryte, Explorer and Alchemist. This sarcophagus was canted open slightly. Empty.

"Your father had a sarcophagus built for him already?" Cole asked.

Hope never broke pace from her searching on the walls. "Of course. All rich men do."

Aislinn had stopped before a carved statue in a recess on the wall and was appraising it.

"She's right," Aislinn added. "It's quite common."

Cole left the sarcophagi and approached Aislinn to look at the same statue. It seemed out of place. On the top, carvings of winged people flew above masses of gathered people below. Children, women, and men were all carved in relief as though they were spilling out of the stone. Below them stood two pillars, and at the bottom, the same motif was repeated only this time the winged creatures looked like gargoyles and the spilling people were decayed and skeletal. In the center of the carvings were three slots that ran vertically up and down the stone. Sticking out of the slots were carved figurines on metal poles. As Hope lit the final torch just to their right, the figurine details became clear.

The leftmost figure was an elderly woman. Motherly and beckoning. She wore an apron over scrubs. The figure in the center was Hiram, right down to his cane and the brace on his leg. The final figure was Hope, dressed in armour with folded wings.

"This is new," Hope said, leaning past the others to appraise her figurine. "Why am I wearing that armour? It's awesome." Hope reached out to touch the figurine and found that she could slide the post easily within its channel. She pressed it down toward the bottom, where it clicked when it reached the end of the track. She practically exploded with glee.

"Secret door!" she squealed.

"It's a code," Cole said.

Aislinn nodded and pointed up at the carvings above. "That must be life. All those people look healthy and living, and those," she pointed to the bottom. "They all look dead, so that must be death."

"I understand it!" Hope exclaimed. She quickly slid her figurine to the very top of the channel. It clicked in place. Then she grabbed her father's figurine and slid it to the top. Finally, she grabbed her mother's and dropped it to the bottom. It clicked in place, and she slowly stood up. She waited a moment in silence with the others, then looked around the crypt.

"Did it work? Will it open?"

Aislinn tried pushing on the statue, but nothing budged.

"Can you try something?" Cole asked, afraid of disappointing Hope. "Place your father in the center."

Hope shrugged and slid her father's figurine to the middle of its channel, positioned directly between life and death. The wall clicked. Then it clicked again. A whirring sound ushered forth from behind the stone, and then a final click heralded the opening of a seamless stone door to their right which swung inwards into the crypt. Lamplight was spilling in from beyond. Hope hesitated at the door with Cole and Aislinn behind her.

"You guys," She whispered. "This is scary... but also kind of awesome, right?"

Aislinn and Cole squeezed past her into the room beyond, and she followed carrying her torch in two hands like a bat or a club. Inside, a series of iron bars walled in cells that had been carved out of the stone and dirt itself. Wooden beams and stone pillars held up the roof. There was a hallway on the other side that led to a junction further into the darkness. The makeshift prison felt more like a mine. Gas lanterns were hung on the walls. All of the cells were open and empty. The rusty bars looked as though they had not been used in a very long time.

As Aislinn crept across the room she surveyed the cells and her surroundings. She whispered over her shoulder as she passed the center of the room. "This feels a tad more scary than awesome, Hope. I'm starting to wish I had my gun."

Cole gave Hope a reassuring smile. "She's only joking," he whispered. Hope nodded, and Cole stepped over to one of the cells. The bars were rusted and covered in a fine layer of dust. There was a wooden bench inside, broken on one end.

"Empty," Cole said. "Looks like they have been for a long time."

"Same up here," came Aislinn's reply from the other end of the room.

Hope continued through the room with her torch brandished high. As she did, the dancing light reflected on something that caught Cole's attention. He knelt and extended his finger, rubbing it along the stone floor. When he lifted it, he rubbed his thumb and finger together. Blood. And it was still wet.

Chapter 21

Two paths

Lucius/Ketrick

Lucius watched as their quarry rounded a corner ahead of them and disappeared from view as they had numerous times before. The road was narrow and had no forks in this section, and Lucius knew there was no way their power wagon could leave the road. The forest was far too dense, and coupled with the swamp, it meant the only path ahead was the road. So, he had backed off a considerable amount. He wanted Ketrick and his friend to feel safe so they would make a critical mistake. They needed proof. Maybe even a confession if one could be beaten out of them, and Lucius wanted to punch something.

As Lucius rolled their power wagon around the corner that Ketrick had taken, he saw them still rambling on down the road ahead. The night in the Grindlemoor was almost more abundant with life than the daytime was. Insects chirped and nocturnal monkeys howled in the trees. Between the sound of the forest and the rumbling of the road with nothing to light the dark but truck lanterns, Lucius was becoming bored. The rolling road was hypnotizing. He wanted something to happen.

They had passed the last of the stagecoaches close to an hour ago, and Dakota and Remmy had both fallen asleep in the seat beside Lucius. The jungle seemed endless and imposing; the canopy of trees long ago growing over to enclose the road like a tunnel. Ahead, Lucius saw the telltale glow of the river as it seemed to shimmer in the darkness. Even with theirs and Ketrick's lights, the green-blue luminescence of the water was unmistakable. Many parts of this road came close to the banks of the water. At least it was something new to see. Lucius tensed suddenly, realizing that Ketrick was slowing down.

The truck ahead rolled to a stop in a part of road that was almost on the river's edge. There were only a short few steps from the road to the water. Shadows moved in the lanterns of their wagon. Ketrick and his chums had stepped out. Lucius reached across Remmy and punched Dakota.

"What?" the sleepy man asked before realizing what was happening. "Why are they stopping?"

"Dunno, but yer on," Lucius said before poking his thumb at Remmy snoring away in the middle. "Let 'im sleep. Sell it."

Lucius brought their truck to a rolling stop right beside their target. Two men were walking down to the water's edge with buckets. Ketrick was leaning against the side of their truck by the engine. Dakota leaned out, his slick black hair, white shirt, and bowtie sparkling in the light.

"Everything okay?" Dakota asked.

Ketrick rapped the engine compartment of their truck with his knuckles. As he did, someone climbed out of the passenger seat and came around to stand in the lanterns, unhooking the latches and opening the hood of the engine compartment. He was the one-eyed man Cole had identified.

"Topping up our water," Ketrick said stepping forward. He appraised Dakota and the snoring Remmy sitting inside the truck. Lucius leaned back so his face was in the darkness, but kept his hands on the steering wheel. "Long way to Vandrad, so better safe than sorry, we thought. It's a great spot if you need to do the same."

As if they had planned it, Remmy emitted a loud snore. Dakota smiled.

"Thanks, but we've had a long night. Just want to get home and rest."

Ketrick nodded and stepped back from the truck.

"Fair point, sir. You played well tonight. Thank you for that."

Dakota smiled and slapped the edge of their truck with his open palm.

"Appreciate the compliment, kind sir! You have yourself a wonderful evening!"

Lucius released the brakes, and their truck rumbled forward. Behind them, Ketrick was waving as Dakota looked back. Suddenly the lanterns on Ketrick's truck were shut off and Dakota found himself squinting to see in the darkness. Ketrick was mad about something, and Dakota could faintly hear him berating someone in the darkness. It was almost inaudible over the rumbling of their truck. The road started to bend a touch and just as it did, Dakota had a moment of clear vision upriver back toward the estate. There was a dark shape moving in the water.

"I think they have a boat coming," Dakota said once he was back in his seat. He was rubbing his eyes, still trying to refocus.

"Yer sure?" Lucius asked, continuing to guide the truck down the road and around the bend. Ahead of them was another turn to the left, where the road left the riverbank and headed back into the forest.

"Not entirely, my eyes weren't adjusted yet, but it looked like a big shape was coming down the river. Like a boat."

Lucius guided the truck around the turn to the left. Before them, the road went on straight for a very long time. Thinking as quickly as he could, Lucius bent down and removed one of his shoelaces. He tied one end around the steering wheel and the other around the frame of the cab to his left. Then he took the other lace and fastened it to the other side of the wheel and the gear lever. The truck was effectively locked in one direction now.

"What's the plan here, Chief?" Dakota asked, already taking off his suit jacket and the bowtie.

"Wake Remmy," Lucius said as he climbed out of the truck. "We're doublin' back on foot."

Dakota shook Remmy awake and then finished stripping his unnecessary clothing.

"What's goin' on?" Remmy asked, half asleep.

"They stopped and we passed them. We're ditching the truck and doubling back on foot. Drop the suit jacket and let's go."

Remmy yawned and started taking the suit jacket off. He opted to keep the dress shirt, vest, and the bowtie. He liked how they made him look. Dakota was just about to jump off the edge of the truck when Remmy called to him.

"Wait! Help me get the cello case from the back first. We need it."

"Why?" Dakota asked even though he climbed alongside the moving truck to the back anyway while Remmy did the same on the other side. When they met at the back, Remmy dropped the gate and slid the cello case toward them.

"Lucius and I put a portable repeater in it."

"Sly bastards," Dakota grinned as he and Remmy each took a side of the case. "Jump on three. One. Two. Three."

Cello case in hand, Dakota and Remmy bounced to the ground, running a bit and hopping as they fought to keep their balance. They watched as the truck ambled off alone down the road into the darkness of the forest, and then they hurried to catch up with Lucius.

Ketrick watched in the darkness as the barge slid up to the bank. His men on the shore took hold of lines thrown to them and quickly tied them off to trees, holding the barge against the bank so they could board. They had signalled the barge using the lanterns they had removed from the truck, but Ketrick was furious that his idiot cousin had taken both of them. It had taken the men far longer than comfortable to replace them on the truck to sell the lie that they were topping up their water to the coaches still coming behind them. They had finished just in time, fortunately, and one by one the carriages passed with little incident just like the musicians had.

It had been some time waiting for the last of them to pass, and the barge had to be tied up in such a way that it could not be seen from the road. Ketrick knew he had to show his face to every single carriage that passed. Any one of them could be his furious mother and he had no way of knowing which one in the darkness. He had waited there, for longer than an hour, leaning on the truck and waving at coaches in the dark while swamp mosquitoes fed on his blood. He vowed to return when he was lord of everything. Return and burn the swamp to the ground along with all the mosquitoes.

The barge had been hidden well behind the few trees on the bank by this section of the road. It was huge, so that was a feat. It sat low in the water, only a foot or two at most from the surface. The deck was laden with stacked barrels and crates, and a small crew cabin poked up toward the back. It had posts all along it on either side that normally carried lit lanterns, but all of them had been stripped long ago. They had done everything in their power to make this barge as stealthy as possible. It was made to run silent and invisible in the dead of the night.

Sighing, Ketrick decided there were no more coaches to wait for and he stepped forward, closing the bleed valve on the truck's engine and opening the fuel supply. Eiffert, who had been napping in the driver's seat sat up.

"What are you doin', Ket? I thought we were leaving the truck."

"I am," Ketrick said, closing the engine compartment and wiping his hands together. "You're not."

Eiffert climbed out of the truck and stood in the front beside Ketrick, bathed in the light. "What are you talkin' about?"

Ketrick whirled on him, poking his finger into his chest. "You made a *bloody mess* of everything tonight, Eiffert. What you did was *stupid* and now *you* are going to fix it or so help me, I will gouge your last eye out with my thumb! Now get in the truck."

Eiffert gritted his few teeth and spat as Ketrick turned away. Ketrick flicked his fingers and pointed at two men waiting on the bank.

"You five," Ketrick barked. "Get ready to release the barge, then go with him. Make sure he cleans up his mess."

The men obeyed and ran up the bank, untying the lines as Ketrick passed them and hopped onto the barge.

"You want me to kill the alchemist?" Eiffert called.

"No! For Light's sake," Ketrick slapped a mosquito on his neck. "You shade-cursed, half-brained, imbecile!" Mid-rant, Ketrick held his palm up and pointed to the smear of blood and dead insect in the middle of it. "*That's you*, Eiffert. *That's* how dumb you are. *No,* I don't want you to kill the alchemist. Just grab the damn girl. We'll need her to make sure he cooperates. Kill anyone else. *By* the *light,* it's no wonder no one likes you."

"Are we ready?" Ketrick asked one of the men onboard as he stepped further onto the barge. "Can we go?"

"Almost sir," came the reply.

"Ket," Eiffert called. "Where will you be?"

"Taking all this product to the facility, like *you* should have been."

"I'll see you there?"

"Bring me good news, Eiff."

"I will!" Eiffert hollered as he lost sight of his cousin amid the barrels on the barge. "I will!"

Off in the distance, Ketrick's voice came back. "Stop yelling! I can hear you just fine. Can anyone be that dumb?"

Laughter rumbled from the barge.

Mumbling, Eiffert turned and started making his way to the driver's seat.

In the jungle brush across the road, six eyes watched the whole scene unfold before them, completely unnoticed by anyone. As Lucius, Dakota, and Remmy watched Eiffert settle into the driver's seat, Lucius scurried back further into the ditch and whispered to his partners.

"You two have ta get on that barge. Wait fer the truck ta turn around then go. Be quiet. Blend in. When you know where they're going, set the repeater. We'll find you."

"What are you going to do, Chief?" Dakota asked as the truck engine rumbled to life. The gears whined and the machine edged forward, creaking as Eiffert cranked the wheel hard over.

"I'm goin' fer another truck ride."

They all ducked down into the brush as the truck's lanterns swung past them and pointed up the road toward the estate.

"Go!" Lucius hissed, and he made a beeline for the truck, silently jumping onto it just as it picked up speed and rolled away. Dakota and Remmy dashed across the road in the absolute darkness, cello case in tow, to where the barge was just beginning to pull away from the shore.

Chapter 22

Answers in the dark

Aislinn

Aislinn led the others into the hallway beyond the cells. Skeletal frames of wooden posts held up bracing beams in the ceiling, like rib cages holding back the dirt and stone above. The hallway walls had been filled with stone bricks, giving the passageway a macabre atmosphere. The ground they walked on was just that: levelled dirt. Behind Aislinn, Hope followed holding the torch aloft which provided them light in the darkness. Cole was in the rear.

When they reached the T-junction, Aislinn motioned Hope up so that her torch would illuminate the next hallway. To their right, the new hallway appeared to terminate at another junction. Their left continued farther than the torchlight shone, making the tunnel seem endless in that direction.

"Which way?" Aislinn whispered to Hope.

"How should I know?" she whispered back. "It's not like I knew the house I grew up in was hiding labyrinths and secret labs below it. I never could have imagined any of this existed."

"Despite the danger," Cole whispered having crept up to stand directly behind them. "You have to admit, it is kind of exciting."

Hope nodded her agreement as something caught her eye. She passed the torch to Cole.

"Hold this behind you, I thought I saw some light to our right there for a moment."

Once Cole had the torch back in the first hallway, Hope stepped out and stared at the far T-junction intently. She let her eyes adjust to the dim light without the torch in her hands, and she found that she could indeed see a flicker coming from the left side of the next corridor intersection.

"Extinguish the torch, Cole," she whispered. "There's light up there to the left of the next intersection."

Cole dropped the torch to the ground and stomped on it, rubbing the fire out with his boot. It flickered a moment and then the hallways fell into blackness. They blinked until their eyes had adjusted enough that they felt comfortable proceeding, and then with Hope leading, the trio crept down the hallway on their right heading for the second T-junction. The closer they approached, the better they could see, as faint light spilled into the space from the left. Hope stopped at the end of the hall and peered around the corner.

The left side of the new hallway ended about fifteen feet from the intersection, with a heavy wood and iron door that was slightly ajar. Light from inside the room was spilling through the crack between the door and its frame. The hallway to their right went on into the darkness where it suddenly stopped, opening into a gaping maw of darkness. Somewhere off in that darkness, Hope thought she momentarily witnessed a greenish-blue glow, but it was so faint that she decided it had to be a trick of her eyes. Aislinn had crept up beside Hope, and Cole behind her.

"What do you see down there?" Aislinn asked, noting that Hope seemed to be staring into the darkness to their right and not at the door to the left.

"I'm not sure, I thought I saw a glow but it was so faint. Maybe it was nothing."

A breeze wafted past them at that moment, coming from the direction where Hope was staring. It was almost as if the hallways were breathing. There was an unmistakable odour in the air: the fresh scent of water.

"I think the caves are down that way," Hope said as the breeze teased the ends of her hair. "I can smell water. The estate is built above caves, and a bit of the swamp comes in like an underground river. That's where the mansion gets its water, and methane pockets to power our heat and lanterns."

"Makes sense to me," Aislinn said as she crept past Hope heading toward the door on their left. "Shall we check behind door number one?"

Aislinn approached the door with Hope and Cole close on her heels. She tried to peer in through the crack but found it was not open enough to see through. Ever so gently, she pushed the door open enough to see inside. A foul stench wafted out, and all three of them fought back a gagging sensation. Now sure the room was empty, Aislinn pushed the door open the rest of the way.

Horror greeted them. There was no other word for it. Racks along the walls held meat hooks suspending carcasses in various states of decay. All of them were animals. Some appeared to be pigs, goats, deer, and even dogs. A long stone slab acted as a table against the left wall of the room. It was littered with surgical and butchering tools, sample jars with assorted organs and body parts, and a rack overflowing with ceramic and glass flasks. A similar table made from wood held aloft the disembowelled carcass of a cow on the adjacent wall. Two gas lanterns embedded in the wall above the carcass bathed the whole room in just enough light that it added to the gothic atmosphere. There was a large closed iron door on the opposite side of the room.

Aislinn and Cole moved through the room aghast at what they saw, but Hope was nearly in full hysteria. It was almost as though any of the corpses might suddenly animate and attack them. The horrid stench of the room was overwhelming. Hope was shaking, her hands clasped to her face, as tears streamed down her cheeks. Cole noticed her swaying on her feet and reached out. He grasped her in his arms just as he felt her knees buckle.

"Hey hey," Cole whispered, keeping her on her feet as best he could. Had she fallen on the horrid floor, her clothes would have needed to be burned. "I have you, Hope. You're all right."

Aislinn had reached the other side of the room and was examining a rack where the torso of a pig was held aloft by a meat hook. Strangely, there was no blood on the body. No organs or entrails of any kind. And no rot. Aislinn reached out and poked it with a finger.

"This is odd," Aislinn whispered as she began running her flat hand over the carcass.

"How," Hope choked on her words as Cole held her in his arms. "How could my father do all this? Why?"

Cole had been to many slaughterhouses before in his youth. Most of Butcher's Row back home in Harrow's Town had spaces just like this one. Or worse. He was surprised to see one hidden underground below a prominent alchemist's estate, to be sure, but for the most part, the room looked just like any other butcher shop.

"Hope," Cole said as he tentatively held her at arm's length. He wanted to make sure she was on her feet and not about to collapse again.

"Look at me, Hope," She did. Her blue eyes shone amid the dim room. "I know this looks bad, but we still don't know for sure what this is or what it has to do with your father. There may be much more to it."

"I think you may be right, Cole," Aislinn whispered, beckoning them to approach the pig carcass she was examining.

"Look at this," Aislinn was pointing to the skin as Cole and Hope approached. She pressed it with her finger, but the fingerprint did not bounce back like flesh would. Instead, it remained indented. "It's wax. And look here, the skeleton inside isn't bone either, it's *incredibly* intricate machinery..."

With his jaw hanging open, Cole leaned forward and pressed the carcass's skin as Aislinn had, leaving yet another indentation in the waxy hide of the pig. The carcass featured the full forward half of the animal, suspended on the meat hook between its shoulder blades. Its eyes were closed and its mouth open, and its front two hooves stuck straight out as though in mid-gallop. It was severed at the belly all the way across, with only part of its spine dangling out. As Cole inspected closer, he noticed the bone vertebrae of the spine was ceramic, interwoven with intricate strings of copper that glinted in the light. Inside its chest cavity was more of the same. The ribs were ceramic also. There were no organs.

"But," Hope whispered, desperately wanting to believe her father was not the monster she was starting to fear he was. "If these corpses are not corpses, what is that smell?"

Aislinn had moved over to the wooden table and was examining the cow. She covered her face with her arm.

"Some of them are real," she gagged.

Just then they heard a voice emanating from the next room. The iron door was too thick to hear what was being said but it sounded as though someone was issuing commands. Then there was another in reply, though the second one sounded even further distorted, as though something other than the door was also masking the voice. Hope immediately recognized the first voice when it spoke again.

"That's my father!" She hissed.

Aislinn dashed to the door and put her ear against it.

"Can you hear what they're saying?" Hope whispered again, leaning against the wall between the wax pig and the door.

"No," Aislinn replied, and then the door burst inward and Aislinn was thrown back against the table with the cow carcass.

An imposing set of armour stomped into the room through the open door. It had plates of steel interlocking across its torso, legs, and arms. Rounded shoulder pauldrons just barely fit through the door. From the tips of its toes to the top of its head, everything was covered in metal. Between the plates of armour, Cole could see a churning sea of gears, cogs, cables, and hoses. It looked more like a walking machine than a man. It was both terrifying and marvellous at the same time. With thunderous steps the machine strode into the room and planted a mechanical boot on Aislinn's chest, holding her to the ground as she screamed in pain.

"Do not resist," a muffled and inhuman voice ushered from within the machine.

Cole and Hope were too afraid to move, so they lifted their hands in surrender and stepped away from the wall. Hiram hobbled in through the door frame at that moment. He radiated malice, until the moment he laid eyes on Hope. He faltered, his cane sliding on the floor as he fought to keep his balance.

"Hope."

"Father," Hope wanted to run to him. She wanted to hug him and play-fight with him like they had in the library. Like they had so many times in her life. "Don't hurt her! Please. They are trying to help you. You have to explain all this."

Hiram swayed on his feet. He said nothing. His eyes were locked on Hope. His skin had gone ashen, almost the same colour as his white hair.

"Dad please," Hope pleaded as her voice cracked and tears flowed down her cheeks anew. "People have died. Please. *Please* tell me you are not the villain here!"

Hiram swallowed and his eyes dropped away from Hope. He took a deep breath and tapped his cane on the floor.

"New order. Let her up," Hiram said, and then again as he turned to walk back into the room beyond the iron door. "Bring them in."

Cole Vallen was the last to enter the room behind the others. Hope had followed her father first, and then Aislinn after the armour machine let her up. Cole followed behind the machine as it stomped through the door. He noticed it made whirs and clicks during its walk cycle, and hisses once the leg had landed resting on the ground. It looked as though the armour was wearing a backpack, with short stacks poking out of it much like those on the Cirrus but miniature in comparison. No smoke was emitted but Cole thought he witnessed a bit of a heat shimmer like one might see above a bonfire.

Cole got his first full look at the room beyond as the animated armour stepped aside. The space was entirely encased in steel. The walls, the floor, and the ceiling were all made of metal plating. Four steel pillars were erected in the corners, each featuring a human-sized cage with cables protruding from their tops. The base of the cages was like a tub, and from the bottom hoses ran out and vanished into the floor below. Taking up well over half the left-hand side of the room was a massive machine that resembled a telescope connected to two giant vats almost as tall as the room. There were copper orbs held aloft on beams and arms connecting to clockwork drive mechanisms, and at the base of the telescope object, a tilting metal slab that looked like it was made for a person.

Runic symbols like those in the book they found on the table in the previous room were scratched into the metal of the pillars as well as pathways along the floor leading to the tanks. Cole could hear a faint bubbling sound and there was a distinct hum in the air. He sniffed and made eye contact with Aislinn. By the look on Aislinn's face, she had smelled it too. Ozone. Just like under the Cirrus.

Hiram turned to face Hope, almost all of his weight rested on his cane. He looked defeated, his shoulders slumped, his chin twitching, and huge bags under his eyes. He sighed deeply and forced himself to look at his daughter.

"I suppose it was only a matter of time before you learned the truth about me, Hope. I am sorry it had to be this way."

"Dad. Please... no games. No puzzles. Tell me the truth. What is all this?"

Hiram shuffled over to the tilted table. He reached into a basket on the floor and produced a small slab of meat which he set on the table below the microscope object.

"It will be easier to explain if I show you."

Cole and the others watched as Hiram spun some dials on the machine and it lowered slowly until it was hovering inches above the meat on the table. He moved over to a lever on one of the tanks and grabbed it.

"Shield your eyes," he said as he pulled the lever. The machinery whirred and clicked, and a splash of bluish-purple fluid ejected from the machine onto the meat.

Chapter 23

Horror and History

Hiram

At first, the slab of meat began to glow, emitting a faint bluish-purple light that became more and more intense until suddenly it burst in a flash of fire and white-hot light. The sound was like a gunshot in the small space, causing everyone to recoil. When it was over, all that remained of the meat was a black scorch mark on the table, and Aislinn could not help but notice it was in the pattern of a star.

"I know," Hiram said as he stepped forward and placed a new slab of meat where the last had been. "It is quite the party trick. The reaction is even stronger when the meat is still alive."

Cole and the others watched as Hiram adjusted the dials and settings on the machine and then moved back to the lever. This time when he pulled the lever only a small drop of the liquid fell onto the meat. A vapour began to rise from the slab, and the meat emitted a soft bluish-purple light without exploding. After a short time, the effect faded, and Hiram held up the meat for all to see. It was completely intact and looked the same as it had when he placed it on the table.

"Father," Hope said as a tear rolled down her cheek. "What have you done?"

Hiram sighed and dropped the meat back into the basket at his feet.

"After the war was declared over," Hiram began as he leaned a hand against the table. "Natalia Whitehall came to me with a weapon that had been recovered from the siege of Matan Ba'al. A rifle. Nothing spectacular, just a steam-powered dart launcher. But the substance this rifle delivered was terrifying."

"Flash darts," Aislinn whispered.

Hiram tilted his head. "Is that what you call it? Good enough name as any I suppose."

"What did she want you to do with it?" Cole asked.

"Make more. She wanted me to synthesize the formula. Find a way to reproduce its effects and manufacture it."

Aislinn gritted her teeth. "I've seen firsthand what those darts do to people. Why in the light would they want more of that horror?"

Hiram shrugged. "After my initial experiments, I felt the same way. The first two formulas I attempted were shocking. I went to Natalia and refused to continue my research. But we agreed that if I could find a practical use for the formula I would. And so I did. The fourth formula has allowed us to miniaturize our steam engines. It reacts with bacteria and other organic material when exposed to water. Instant steam."

"So," Aislinn was on the verge of fury. Cole could see her shaking, and her fists were balled so tightly that her knuckles were white. "You used the weapon that killed so many of our people, that killed my *brother*... to make fuel?"

"*Technically*, no. I used a synthesized formula of my own design based on the mechanism of operation in the... flash darts. It's not the weapon itself, it's a new substance based on the principle of the original."

Cole could see Aislinn attempting to rationalize her anger. Her fist had relaxed. Slightly.

"The weapon used alchemy I had never seen before. Ancient and highly advanced. I could ascertain the original intent the more I understood it. It converts organic material to energy. In high enough concentrations, the reaction is as you saw. Catastrophic."

"Light and fire," Cole whispered.

"Yes," Hiram paused. "Light and fire indeed. What you saw here is the eleventh formula I have created. There were... side effects... if people were exposed to it in small doses. A drop, for example, as you saw with the meat results in no damage to tissue. As I am told, the experience of a conscious living subject exposed to the substance in such a low dose is quite euphoric. Reported symptoms include conscience altering hallucinations, overwhelming ecstasy, blissful intoxication. Quite addictive."

"And the Whitehalls know this?" Hope asked.

"Ketrick does. He was the one who discovered the effects. He claims it was by accident, but I find that unlikely given his proclivities. He came to me in secret and demanded I manufacture formula eleven in absurd quantities. When I refused and demanded to speak to Natalia, he..."

Aislinn stepped forward and thrust her finger at Hiram in accusation. "Enough. Euphoria or ecstasy aside, this stuff kills people the same way flash darts do. We've seen it. You gave them their weapon after all. Why?"

Hiram ran his hand through his hair and made eye contact with Aislinn as his jaw set.

"Because," he began as he shifted his gaze from Aislinn to Hope. "Apart from the scholarly obsession of seeking knowledge, Ketrick threatened to take away the one thing in this world that I still live for."

Hope cried and ran into her father's arms. Hiram smiled at Hope and then turned his attention to Aislinn. "While it is true that I have done... questionable things... many of which some might consider macabre, I have never done anything to hurt people intentionally. I had to protect what remains of my family."

Aislinn sighed and glanced at Cole and the silent sentinel of armour behind him.

"Okay," she said as she began to pace. "Assuming you are telling the truth about your coercion, I still have a lot of questions. How much formula eleven does Ketrick have? What is he planning to do with it? What is the deal with the wax pig in the other room and this walking steel? And why are you telling us now?"

Hiram left Hope's embrace.

"Well," he began. "I'm not quite sure in what order to answer those questions. Let me begin with Ketrick Whitehall. The man is cruelty incarnate. He has grown up in his mother's shadow amid a family determined to rip one another down from the pedestal of leadership. They treat one another like rats drowning in a bucket. Ketrick wants chaos and the substance is how he intends to sow it. Under his blackmail, I gave him the means to make his own formula eleven. I do not know how much he has in his possession now. Perhaps thousands of barrels."

"Thousands of barrels?" Aislinn gasped.

"Perhaps. Not for sure. A barge left here earlier with a little over a hundred barrels. That was the last I would make for him. As for why I'm telling you this, it is quite simple. I need you to protect Hope. Keep her safe. I have gone as far as I can in this duty, and with the cloudbreaker's assistance, perhaps I can stand up to them, knowing Hope is beyond their reach. In part, that is why I invited the Cirrus here. Finally, for the 'walking steel' and the 'wax pig'?"

Hiram passed Aislinn and stopped before the steel armour. He lifted a plate on its sternum and spun it, like opening the valve on a pipe. There was a burst of steam from its backpack, and with a whirring sound, the chest plates parted revealing a mass of waxy flesh and ceramic ribs protecting a clockwork heart that emitted a bluish-purple light.

"This," Hiram whispered almost too soft to be heard. "This is a favour to a very old friend. Like me, he was one of the most gifted minds in the north. Unlike me, he is no longer with us. No one alive knows where he went, or if he is still alive. But the day he disappeared, this showed up in my lab with a letter. He implored me to keep its secret safe. He feared the world was not ready for this discovery, and given everything that has happened to me, I know now, he was right. He called it the De'Ghova Engine. I barely understand how it works, but I understand its power."

"Lord Errbryte, sir?" Hiram spun the sternum again, and the machine's chest began to close as Cole stepped toward Hope. "Why did Ketrick agree to invite the Cirrus here? With all that's hidden here, why take that chance?"

Hiram shook his head. "I convinced Ketrick it was a good course of action. I knew no one could resist an invitation to my estate, least of which your captain and crew. We knew your flight path would have taken you over the Grindlemoor and you would have seen his barge, so he was easily manipulated. He and his cousin Eiffert have been tracking the ship ever since what happened in Harrow's Town. I had hoped to parley with your captain in secret to barter for Hope's safety."

Hope approached her father. There was venom in her voice, as well as sorrow. "One thing I don't understand, Dad. You say you initially refused to help Natalia with the weapon, yet you changed your mind. You made two formulas, before the black-mail. Why? I've never known you to change your mind about anything. Something had to capture your attention. What other reason did you have to keep researching?"

"Life, Hope. Answers to the greatest questions ever asked. I saw them in the formula as I unravelled it."

Hiram's chin lowered, and Cole noticed a deep sadness in his eyes right before Hope slapped her father across the face. Something unspoken had transpired between them, because next she sank into his arms in a tight embrace. Cole and Aislinn shared a brief look and Cole knew his mentor had seen it too. Hiram moved Hope away just enough to speak only to her.

"Hope," he whispered. "Listen. There's something else.. . someone even the Whitehalls are afraid of... and he..."

The sound of clapping broke the silence and everyone turned to see Eiffert Whitehall and three men enter the room. Eiffert was clapping, even though his right hand held a clockwork pistol. The other men were armed as well.

"Well, this is *certainly* a win for me!" Eiffert said, his toothless grin seeming even more ominous in the dim light. "Everyone who knows anything about Harrow's Town, here in one room with no way out. Plus, I can take the alchemist *and* his daughter back to Ketrick. How fortuitous."

Hiram ushered Hope behind him and stepped forward. "Leave them be, Eiffert, and I'll go with you willingly. This does not have to be a fight."

"Oh yes," Eiffert's grin widened. "It does."

Eiffert started to lower his pistol at Cole when suddenly one of the men in the rear launched into the air and hit the ceiling.

Before his body could hit the floor it was knocked sideways where it hit another one of the men in the back. The second man's pistol went off pointed at the wall and the round ricocheted causing everyone to duck. Lucius stood in the doorway reaching for the pistol that now lay on the floor before him. The third man who had been standing beside Eiffert spun and kicked at Lucius, forcing him to stagger back while the man who fired tried to get his bearings back.

In a moment, the room was in utter chaos. Hiram pushed Hope behind his armour and instructed the suit to protect her. Cole dodged to the side out of the line of Eiffert's aim just as his pistol went off, bouncing another round throughout the steel room until it bore itself into the side of one of the tanks. Aislinn ran forward but had to sidestep just as Eiffert fired a second round that deflected off the armour and struck Hiram in the thigh. Hiram dropped to a knee and Hope rushed to his side, but Hiram tried to push her back. Lucius and the two men at the back of the room were wrestling, as it seemed the engineer had been successfully able to disarm the men. Even with two of them fighting him, they were no match for Lucius, and he slammed one of them headfirst into the wall.

In the mayhem, Cole saw the malicious glint in Eiffert's single eye at the same time that Aislinn did. Eiffert's jaw clenched. His shoulders tensed and the muscle of his neck moved to the right, leading his torso to follow. It was all happening in slow motion. His aim moved right and lowered, and he fired. The bullet was meant for Hope, but Aislinn got there first. Cole watched

Aislinn's body suspended sideways in the air from her jump. He watched the spurt of red eject from his mentor's shoulder as she crossed in front of Hope. Then she crumpled to the floor at the feet of the armour.

"New order! Target Eiffert Whitehall!" Hiram was shouting. "Capture him!"

Faster than Cole would have believed it capable, the armour suit reached out and grabbed the pistol as well as Eiffert's hand. Where steel and wood ended and flesh began was no longer decipherable, and Eiffert kicked and screamed. Two other men rushed into the room past Lucius and the last of the initial men he still grappled with. They immediately opened fire on the armour suit, forcing it to drop Eiffert and defend itself. Bullets were ricocheting everywhere.

"Get Hope out of here!" Hiram was screaming at Cole. Hope was trying desperately to get Aislinn on her feet. The armour barreled forward, knocking down Eiffert and one of the new men. Lucius rolled away just as the steel behemoth smashed into the wall beside the door. Now free from Lucius, the third man picked up the gun Lucius had been reaching for and started firing at the armour. Eiffert was frothing at the mouth, screaming at his men to destroy the armour.

Hiram grabbed Hope's arm as Lucius arrived to help Cole get Aislinn on her feet. "Take the river, Hope. Get clear. I'll destroy the lab. I'm going to end this."

Hope's tears flowed freely. "No," she pleaded.

"Hope, there's no time! Trust me. Please. Go!"

Hope nodded. She dashed for the door, as Lucius and Cole followed with Aislinn dangling between them. Eiffert and the others were busy with the armour as it kicked and punched at them. Their bullets seemed to do damage, and its left arm started to slow. As soon as he saw that Hope and the others had cleared the room, Hiram stood.

"New order. Target the tanks. Destroy the lab!"

Eiffert dodged as the armour suddenly ignored all of them and lumbered past. His men continued shooting while they had ammunition in their guns. In the center of the room, Hiram stood looking at Eiffert calmly.

"What are you doing, alchemist?" Eiffert screamed.

"Ending it," he replied.

The armour drew back its fist and slammed forward into the telescope object and the tanks. Sparks flew, followed by fire. Eiffert turned and dove, just as the room exploded.

Chapter 24

Changing winds

Cole

Cole and Lucius had made it through the butcher room and well into the hallway following Hope when the blast wave hit them from behind. Though most of it had been dimmed by the rooms and space behind them, the force was still enough to knock them from their feet. They collected themselves quickly and continued through the remaining hallway into the caves at the end of the tunnel, spurred on by a fear of collapse from the explosions. Aislinn had been roused a bit by the blast and was keeping herself on her feet with Lucius' help, allowing Cole to help Hope find her way in the darkness. They had not stopped to recover her torch or find a new one. Instead, they relied on the faint glow of light seeping into the caves far ahead.

"I'm losing a lot of blood," Aislinn whimpered at one point when she tripped on a stone on the ground. Lucius caught her and held her up.

"You got more, don't you? Keep movin' Elissan. We'll plug yer leak as soon as we can see what we're doing."

On into the darkness, they marched. Hope was leading with Cole and the others following. More than once, Cole thought he heard Hope sniffling and wondered if he should console her, but he could not find the words. Instead, he silently followed her along, using one of his hands on the stone wall of the cave as a guide. The way narrowed at one point so much that they had to shimmy sideways through the gap, but mercifully they were greeted by daylight shining in from the mouth of the cave when at last they made it through.

The mouth of the cave had a bubbling pool of spring water that ran out into the sunlight beyond. It smelled fresh and earthen. Vine and other flora swayed in the gentle breeze coming in, making it seem as though the cave were breathing. As the group stepped out into the daylight beyond, they found themselves in a meadow where the spring formed a creek that meandered southward into the jungle. The golden sunlight of early dawn bathed the area in tranquil light, and the group chose a resting area not far from the mouth but hidden in some underbrush so they could ambush potential threats that may have followed them.

Lucius lay Aislinn down on the ground, and with Hope's help, they set to dressing the gunshot wound in her shoulder.

"Luck is on your side. The bullet looks like it passed through the muscle without hitting your clavicle. As fortune goes, that is the best possible outcome you could ask for."

Aislinn smiled before wincing as Hope began wrapping strips of fabric she had torn from her pant leg over the wound. "Funny, it doesn't feel like fortune," she whimpered.

Hope turned to Lucius, who was kneeling beside them. Cole was not far away, watching the cave mouth from the bushes.

"She needs medical facilities. Proper bandages and cleaning."

Lucius nodded and reached behind his back. He pulled out what appeared to be a large single-shot pistol and loaded it with a long round he pulled from his belt. He put his hand on Aislinn's good shoulder and stood. In three short strides, Lucius reached the centre of the meadow and stopped. He aimed the pistol in the air. The sound was more like a whoosh than a gunshot, and Cole and Hope watched as a trail of smoke marked the path of the projectile before it popped, and a shining star of bright red light hovered in the air.

Lucius turned back to the others as he placed the pistol back into his belt on his back. "Signal flare," he said. "Cirrus' is holding on station nearby. At least they should be... I asked them to. I'll send flares up every other hour till they come. In the meantime, want to catch me up on what all that was back there?"

Feeling more confident that they were not followed, Cole rejoined the group and was helping Aislinn sit up under Hope's watchful eye. Hope was holding her fingers against Aislinn's wrist, counting her pulse.

"After you left," Aislinn began, "We found a secret lab in Hiram's quarters and evidence that he was tampering with Ciar K'hen alchemy."

"Flash darts?" Lucius asked as he knelt with the group. Aislinn nodded, falling silent. Cole continued for her.

"Hope led us into crypts below the mansion, and we found a secret door..."

"*I* found a secret door," Hope corrected. Despite everything that had happened, Cole smiled.

"Right. Hope found a secret door, and we discovered Hiram's hidden lab. Where you found us. Hiram was there with that suit of armour, and he told us everything."

"Everything?" Lucius asked, clearly not satisfied with the information being shared.

"The Whitehalls are behind it all," Aislinn said. "Natalia brought Hiram the flash darts after the war and asked him to make them more. He refused, but eventually kept working on it for other reasons. Ketrick was blackmailing him for one of his formulas that he's selling on the streets as some form of intoxicant."

"You're kiddin'," Lucius shook his head. "Flash darts on the street as a damn drug?"

"He showed us," Cole added. "Dripped some on a piece of meat and it exploded, just like in Harrow's Town."

Lucius rubbed his hand through his beard. "Why would people want to take that?"

"My father said in smaller doses it causes euphoria and hallucinations, almost like visions, or something. He said it was highly addictive."

Lucius appraised Hope a moment before continuing. "Addictive, that's just great. So, a person has this drug, loves the feeling and wants more and more until they get their hands on too much and…"

"Light and fire," Cole interrupted. "That explains the man in the cemetery. He must have been meeting Eiffert, trying to get his hands on more. Rikket and I must have interrupted them and in the skirmish, the man got his hands on the whole vial and downed it all at once."

Aislinn nodded her agreement.

"Okay," Lucius began. "Invitin' the Cirrus here, they must have thought they could hide right under our nose, then?"

"Actually," Aislinn began. "That part was Hiram. He convinced them to invite us hoping we could keep Hope safe."

"That doesn't sound like a move Natalia Whitehall would make," Lucius replied. "She's much too smart for that."

"Unless," Hope interrupted. "Unless she doesn't know about the drug. She asked my father to make more of the darts, but he refused and they decided to make something together that would *help* the world, like the steam fuel. Why would she blackmail him into making weapons again and risk everything they had accomplished together? Dad said that Ketrick was cruelty incarnate. But he also said there was someone else. Someone worse, that even the Whitehalls are afraid of. That's what he whispered to me before the fight."

Lucius chuckled. "Wouldn't want to meet the person who can rattle Natalia Whitehall's cage. But it makes sense. She was plenty angry with Ketrick when Eiffert showed up at the gala. They fought when she was boardin' her carriage. Dakota, Remmy, and I dressed as musicians and followed in their truck. Found Ketrick and Eiffert stopped with some men by the river. They told us they were just fillin' their water tank, so we ditched the truck up the road a ways and circled back. That's when they split up. I sent Remmy and Dakota after Ketrick on their barge, and I hitched a ride on Eiffert's truck the whole way back here. I followed Eiffert and his boys through a secret door in a pantry below the kitchen."

"Awe," Hope whispered to herself. "*Another* secret door?"

"Wait," Aislinn sat up wincing. "You mentioned a barge? Did it have barrels on it?"

"Few hundred I'd say," Lucius answered. "Hard to be sure in the dark, but Ketrick mentioned it being a delivery Eiffert was supposed to make."

"Where are Remmy and Dakota now? Did they make it on the barge?"

Lucius shrugged. "I'm not sure. They were headed fer it when I snuck onto Eiffert's truck."

"Hiram told us about a barge with a hundred barrels of formula eleven on it."

"Formula eleven?"

Aislinn shook her head and waved off the question. "It's what Hiram called the drug. We need to get airborne. We have to find that barge and stop Ketrick before more people die."

Hope choked back a sob and dropped her face into her hands.

"Hope," Cole said as he grabbed her and hugged her to him. "I'm so sorry."

Hope whimpered as she tried to speak. "He did all of it to save me. They used me against him, and he died. To protect me!"

Cole tried to console Hope as Lucius looked from them to Aislinn.

"Ketrick threatened Hope's life," Aislinn explained. "It's how they made Hiram participate and make the drug. He said he'd given them the formula, so even without him they can still make it now."

Hope struggled and pushed out of Cole's arms to stand up.

"Maybe," she said through tears as she began to pace. "Maybe he's still alive! The armour broke his machine, and it exploded, but what if it saved him first?"

She froze in her pacing. "I have to go back. I have to go back! He might still be alive!"

Cole jumped to his feet in time to stop Hope from dashing toward the cave mouth. He held her tight as she fought him. Lucius stood and began reloading the flare gun.

"Hope," Cole pleaded. "Hope no, please. You can't. He sacrificed himself so we could protect you."

"Let me go! He might be alive... he might..."

Hope's fight waned, and she fell into sobbing gasps in Cole's arms as Lucius walked a few paces into the meadow. Just as he aimed the pistol skyward and was about to fire another flare, the steel hull of the Cirrus arrived hovering over the canopy of the jungle. The ship made a hissing sound as it vented excess steam, and began to slow as it approached the meadow. There was just enough space for the hull, so it lowered to the ground and began to drop the underbelly ramp almost on top of the group. Cole could feel the telltale tickle emanating from the hair on his arms and neck. Being under the lift plates once more brought a feeling of great relief as well as wonder.

When the ramp finally touched down where the group was waiting, Cheddar and Becky were standing on it. Lucius stepped on to the ramp and had a brief conversation with them, and soon Becky was dashing toward them. Cole released Hope and helped Aislinn get to her feet just as Becky arrived and took up Aislinn's opposite side.

"Oh Ashes!" Becky said as she began leading Aislinn toward the waiting ramp. Cheddar and Lucius stood waiting on the ramp to assist if needed. "Why'd you go and get yerself shot?"

Cole glanced at Hope, who was still looking at the cave mouth. For a moment, Cole considered going to her again, but then she turned her head away and started following toward the ship. Her countenance appeared to change as she saw Aislinn stumble slightly going up the ramp, and she rushed to catch up. Becky and Cole were holding Aislinn from each side, while Lucius and Cheddar brought up the rear.

"We need to clean and suture the wound," Hope was saying. "Do you have a medical room?"

Becky nodded. "We do. Ah'm the medic. Are you a doctor?"

"In a manner of speaking. My mother was. I learned from her."

Cole and Becky reached the end of the hangar where the ladder led above. Cole went first, helping pull Aislinn up the rungs as Becky supported her from behind. Aislinn was pale but she found the strength to climb mostly unassisted.

"Ya look familiar," Becky said over her shoulder to Hope as they climbed. "Did we meet at the gala?"

Hope blushed, now realizing that she had not personally welcomed Becky either. The bubbly young woman had somehow slipped past, and it made Hope wonder how many others she was remiss in her duties with. They had reached the top of the ladder and stepped out onto two-deck before Hope responded.

"I am sorry, I don't believe we did... I'm Hope Errbryte. Hiram's daughter."

"No kidding!" came Becky's cheerful response just as Hope stepped off the ladder and turned right to follow the others. They limped along with Aislinn in tow before stopping so Becky could open a door on their left. Hope stepped forward and took up a position supporting Aislinn so that Becky was free to open the door and prepare the room for them. Hope noticed a kitchen behind them.

The medical room seemed more like a converted closet than a functional surgical space, but there was a gurney bed tilted upwards at the head that they assisted Aislinn with laying on. There was enough room for Hope and Becky to stand on either side of the gurney, and the rest of the space was filled with cabinetry that was locked to protect the contents from the movement of the ship. Cole stood in the doorway and watched as the two women went to work on his mentor. Becky seemed more than happy to let Hope take the lead, so she began opening cabinets and pulling out material as Hope asked for it.

"Bandages and wash, please," Hope was saying as she began to untie the makeshift dressing she had applied in the meadow. Becky handed over a bottle of sterile water as Hope finished removing the dressing. Hope quickly washed off the wound, brushing away the dried and still-wet blood with gauze when Becky passed it to her.

"Here, Ashes," Becky handed Aislinn a cup of water and a small, stoppered vial. "For the pain."

Aislinn popped the stopper off the vial and downed the liquid, chasing it with the water from the glass just as Hope took a set of suture equipment that Becky was passing across. Aislinn coughed and laid back. Lucius appeared in the doorway beside Cole.

"How she doin'?" The engineer asked.

"I'll be fine," Aislinn said, smiling. Beside her, Becky was hooking up a blood bag to a pole beside the bed and preparing an infusion. "Becky gave me the good stuff."

Hope was wordless as she bent over Aislinn's shoulder and began closing the wound. The bleeding was barely a trickle now.

"Briefed the cap'n," Lucius continued. "We're in the air, heading south. There's still no signal detected from Remmy an' Dakota's repeater, but hopefully, we can spot this barge."

Aislinn nodded.

"Cole, head to the bridge. See what the captain wants you to do."

Cole nodded and slipped out past Lucius. He was unhappy with being sent away from his mentor but also ecstatic to be meeting the captain and seeing the bridge. He hurried down the two-deck hallway and as he approached the bridge, anxiety slowed his steps. There was chatter coming from the space, rapid briefings thrown out and curt answers from a stern female who must be the captain. Through the hatch at the end of the hall, Cole could almost make out the raised command platform and the windows beyond, with the forest canopy of the Grindlemoor stretching off to a distant horizon outside. Just as Cole was about to reach out for the hatch combing to steady himself as he entered the bridge, a distant thud shook the ship. Immediately, a cacophonous alarm sounded and all Cole could hear besides the ringing bells was the captain shouting into a broadcast.

"All hands to action stations!"

Chapter 25

Two is not enough

Cole

Cole stood outside the bridge of the Cirrus in shock. The wailing alarm assaulted his ears, and the captain's repeated command of hands to action stations echoed in between shouts of the crew as they ran through the halls for their assigned battle duties. Cole had never been assigned duties. All he had been told about his station aboard the Cirrus was that he would be working closely with Aislinn. His first actual flight aboard an airship was combat, and he was woefully unprepared. His eyes darted down the hall and he saw Lucius charging toward him. As the chief reached Cole and was about to say something over the blaring alarm, a new command was issued over the speakers from the captain.

"Brace for impact!" She yelled.

Cole mimicked Lucius as the chief braced his feet on the floor and pressed his hands against the wall. In the span of a breath, there was a deafening explosion in the aft end of the ship, and the entire hull seemed to jump and shudder. Cole's muscles fought to keep his balance as the deck jumped and the walls lurched like the ship was a bucking horse. He failed, as did Lucius, and the pair found themselves sprawled on the deck but uninjured. Inside the bridge, they could hear the captain shouting requests for damage reports and many voices answering back about various states of machinery.

"Chief Parvelle, contact bridge," the captain called out over the broadcast.

Lucius climbed to his feet and helped Cole do the same, then dashed to the bridge hatch and stuck his head through. Cole listened as the two conversed, but he could not hear anything they were saying over the alarms. In short order, the engineer was back at Cole's side and pulling him along. They stopped at the top of the ladder that led below to the hangar. Down the hall, they saw Hope poking her head out of the door and Aislinn standing beside her. Lucius thrust his finger at them.

"You get back in bed, woman. Yer just gonna get yerself hurt more."

Aislinn shook her head. "No chance I'm listening when you talk to me like that. What's going on? What hit us?"

"Rogue airship. No one recognizes the marking on the hull."

Aislinn's face went ashen. "An airship is attacking us? Was that a cannon round then?"

"No idea. I'm takin' the boy below to engineering. Need the hands. Captain says whatever they hit us with tore open the aft hull like a can opener. We're losing power. If we can't get her more, we're gonna drop."

At that moment, a Cloudbreaker Cole had not met yet slid down the ladder from one-deck and dashed past them heading for the bridge. Lucius motioned for Cole to head down the ladder. As Cole stepped off the ladder and out past the warehouse racking, Lucius dashed past heading aft where the massive hatch to engineering stood slightly ajar. If Cole had been impressed at all about the use of space within the airship, the engine room put it all to shame.

Beyond the hatch from the hangar, the engineering spaces were a labyrinth of machinery, piping, and tanks. Amid the maelstrom was a metal catwalk, stretching further aft to yet another hatch similar to the one in the hangar. The catwalk was suspended above a mass of churning pistons and rolling gears that hissed and squealed as they turned over among themselves like a nest of metal snakes. Occasionally, they issued forth quick bursts of steam, making the entire space slick with condensation and oppressive heat. Cole immediately understood the need for leather gloves all the time, as he quickly recoiled his hand from the metal railing he had grabbed for.

Lucius was charging ahead of him, his head rotating on a swivel as he passed gauges and meters. Cole thought about what Aislinn had told him about Lucius. Watching him appraise the condition of the machinery as he barreled across the catwalk supported the claim that there was no better man alive to learn airship engineering from. Cole even noticed his lips moving as Lucius appraised the machinery, almost as though he were conversing with the mechanical aspect of the ship.

In short order, Lucius had reached the second hatch and Cole was directly behind him. Grabbing onto the hatch wheel, Lucius leaned forward and pressed his cheek briefly against the metal. Then he stepped back and spun the wheel, disengaging the locks.

"This next space is the boiler room," Lucius yelled over the screaming churn of the engines. "If the door is hot, we're in a world of hurt. Always check before you enter."

The hatch creaked as it swung open, loud enough that they could hear it over the engines. Cole noticed that the bulkhead walls were buckled ever so slightly, bending the hinges of the hatch out of proper alignment. A burst of steam rolled past them and Lucius waved his hand trying to clear it.

"Cheddar!" He called out. "You in there?"

"Chief!" A voice called back from within the fog that filled the space. "I'm here. I'm trapped!"

Lucius vanished into the fog without a second thought, and Cole was frozen. He stood at the end of the engine room catwalk for a moment, staring into the white rolling void before him that had swallowed Lucius. It appeared to be a space not unlike the one he was standing in from what he could see. The room had been flooded with thick steam, making it almost impossible to see past the first few feet or so. The steam was venting into the engine room now that the hatch was open, and parts of the boiler room were becoming visible.

There was a catwalk again, moving straight forward beyond the clear air. Two huge tanks made up the lower part of the room, and Cole could just make out the beginnings of both. Above there were many more smaller tanks with piping and valves running between all of them. Gingerly, Cole stepped through the hatch into the room. There was hot liquid dripping onto his shoulder from above, and he looked up to see a pipe with a small gash in it that was spitting steam and water. It was splashing against cables and the bulkhead wall, before running down and dripping on Cole and the catwalk. Just then Lucius appeared from the fog, supporting Cheddar as she hobbled along beside him. Her right pant leg was shredded, revealing burned skin and some superficial wounds that trickled blood into the mix of oil and water that soaked her boots.

Lucius passed her onto Cole's shoulder before turning back to the dense cloud. "Get her to the hangar, then come back. Whatever they hit us with has ruptured tank five and poked holes in three."

Cole nodded and immediately turned toward the hangar with Cheddar leaning on his shoulder.

"Cheddar, right?" Cole asked, trying desperately to deal with his shock. "How bad is your leg?"

"Burned pretty bad. Got it pinned under a pipe when the boiler blew. I'll live though."

She smiled. "Cheddar is a nickname, by the way. My real name is Amelia, but no one calls me that."

Cole stepped through the hatch to the hangar first and then helped Cheddar step through while keeping weight off her injured leg.

"You must love cheese," he tried to joke, cringing when he saw the look on her face.

"That thing that hit us, you have to tell Lucius. It came right through the hull like it was nothing. Like a harpoon with a bomb on it. Blew up on the inside. I've never seen anything like it."

Cole nodded and swallowed. Fear gripped him as he led Cheddar to the base of the ladder to two-deck. There was a pile of soft gear bags on the deck under the ladder so Cole helped Cheddar sit down on it.

"Go help Lucius. I'll be fine here."

As Cole stood, he watched Cheddar reach up and pop a latch holding a small pack against the wall. The pack had a red cross painted on its front, and as Cole turned to head back toward Lucius, Cheddar was already opening the kit and emptying its contents on the deck.

By the time Cole had returned to the second hatch, much of the steam in the boiler room had dissipated and he could clearly see Lucius further toward the back of the space. He was bracing himself up on the first rung of a railing to reach pipes above and furiously tightening a coupler with a pipe wrench. As Cole approached, he got his first glimpse of the damage done to the ruptured boiler. Cole had a vivid imagination. He always had. But seeing the thick steel tank scorched and bent away like it was beyond even his wildest expectations. The steel was jagged, like the teeth of a river fish, bent out and away from its original shape. If not for the pounding in his heart Cole might have found it fake and even a bit funny. Lucius dropped to the catwalk with a thud and pointed to Cole's left with his wrench.

"Open that valve. Spin it clockwise until it stops."

Cole followed where the engineer indicated and located the valve. At first, it took a significant effort to move, but then it became easier, and Cole wheeled it until it stopped as fast as he could. As he did so, a rushing sound echoed from the pipes attached to the valve. Lucius moved past Cole to another valve on the same line and started turning it. A whining pitch echoed forth from the engine room in conjunction with the spins Lucius did on the second valve. Almost immediately, Cole felt a sensation in his stomach as though his body had become heavier momentarily. Lucius nodded to himself and passed Cole again to his original space, surveying the damage to the ruptured tank.

"What in the light could do something like this..." Lucius whispered, reaching up and pinching one of the folded-out teeth of the tank. The way it was bent out, it looked like it should have moved like paper under Lucius' touch, but it remained firm.

"Cheddar said it came through the hull like a harpoon," Cole said as he approached the chief. "Blew up on the inside."

Lucius nodded slightly. He looked lost in thought.

"Head up to the bridge," Lucius said to Cole, turning to look at him as he issued the command. "Report to the captain that we've lost boiler five and three is at half capacity. It's enough to fight, but we can't take another..."

The captain's voice over the broadcast interrupted them. "Brace for impact!"

Just as Cole bent to brace the way Lucius had shown him earlier, a sound of screaming metal filled the space. Steam sprayed into the room again, threatening to once more plunge the space into a thick burning hot fog. Before Cole could react, he heard a deafening clanging sound and looked up in time to see Lucius smash a sharp metal object protruding from one of the tanks with the wrench in his hand. Unable to make sense of what he was seeing, Cole could only stare as the chief bashed the harpoon with such incredible force that it was thrown back through the hole it made while entering. A dent almost the perfect shape of the wrench could be seen in the tank, and Lucius' hand came back empty.

A distant explosion rocked the ship from outside as Lucius helped Cole to his feet. Boiling water was pouring out from the hole the harpoon had made in the tank. Steam was rapidly filling up the space once more. Lucius was rushing Cole out of the space, and closing the hatch behind him before Cole could catch his breath.

"How did you do that?" Cole wheezed. He was not sure the engineer could even hear him over the sound of the engines, now spinning down again as they had before. Maybe Lucius was ignoring him. Either way, the chief did not answer as the hatch shut. He lifted his hand before him and shook it like it was injured.

"Lucius?" Cole called out. The chief lowered his head.

"Get to the bridge, Cole. Tell the captain we're shot. Tanks two and five are down, three will be down shortly."

Cole swallowed. "We have two left, right?"

Lucius fixed Cole with a stare as cold as the steel he worked on. "Two ain't enough to fight, Cole. It's barely enough to fly. We take another one of those harpoons, and it's all over."

Lucius' final words rang in Cole's ears as he sprinted through the hatch into the hangar. He barely registered Cheddar's pleas for an update as he vaulted the ladder to two-deck. He shot for the bridge, all the while hearing only two words repeating in his head.

"All over."

Chapter 26

The Peregrine

Aislinn/Cole

Aislinn recognized the telltale signs of power failure long before the second brace for impact was announced. Shortly after she had watched Lucius and Cole descend the ladder heading for engineering, she had made her decision. She was not going to sit out this assault. The pain medication that Becky had given her made her shoulder no more than a numb discomfort, even though she did not have full use of her arm. Hope had followed her up the ladder to two-deck, pleading all the way that she should be resting, but Aislinn had not slowed in the least. She made her way directly aft and stopped at a locker beside one of the peregrine tubes.

Hope's pleading caught the attention of Becky and a few other crew that were assigned to cannon positions. Becky herself was a loader, and as she saw Aislinn and Hope charge past her cannon bay, she climbed out to join Hope in preventing

Aislinn from attempting whatever brash heroics the peregrine was intending to perform.

Aislinn opened the locker, revealing a pair of pauldrons attached to a leather half-coat with buckles. She stepped into the locker and turned, threading first her injured arm and then her good arm through the looped armpit bands. Becky and Hope stood before her, aghast and pleading.

"Ashes ye can't do this, yer gonna kill yerself!"

Aislinn fumbled with the buckles across her chest. "I have to, Becky. I'm the only peregrine on board. It's me, or it's the ship."

Hope slapped Aislinn's fumbling hands away from the buckles.

"You already took a bullet for me!" She screamed. "What are you trying to prove?"

Undeterred, Aislinn continued trying to fasten the buckles, only pausing momentarily when the sensation of lift gave her butterflies in her stomach. Hope looked perplexed, but Becky knew right away what it was.

"See? Lucius has us fixed already."

"Won't be enough," Aislinn said, finally tightening and latching the buckle. She shrugged the gear up onto her shoulders and began fasting the belt. "You hear the cannoneers? We can't elevate our guns enough to defend ourselves. This ship wasn't built to fight other airships. None of them were. I'm the only chance we have, and you know it, Becky."

Becky resigned. She started helping Aislinn tighten the waist belt and her drop holster.

"I don't understand," Hope began. "Why are you helping her?"

Becky sighed deeply, taking a clockwork pistol from a rack in the locker and slipping it into Aislinn's drop holster on her left hip. "Because she's right. Ah hate her for it, but she's right."

"Look," Aislinn said as she clipped a strap in place to hold her pistol from falling out of the holster. "Airship cannons don't point up. There's never been a reason for it. We've never fought another one before."

Hope backed up as Aislinn stepped forward out of the locker. She rolled her shoulders to set the pauldron armour in place and ensure the backpack she now bore was in place. It was huge, spanning from the back of her neck to just below her waist. Two cylindrical tanks sat in the middle of the pack running the length of her back. Hoses led from the tanks to a mechanical valve and a cylindrical ejection port that pointed down. All of it was covered beneath thick folded canvas and metallic spines connected by covered gears. Hope could not help but liken the whole thing to the folded wings of a bat.

"So," Hope asked incredulously. "You're saying we have no weapons to fight back against another airship."

Before she could answer, the captain's voice boomed over the broadcast. "Brace for impact!"

Becky and Hope dropped to the floor and pressed themselves into a brace position against the wall. Aislinn stepped back into the locker and pushed her back against the backpack rack with her hands on either side of the door. They waited for the shock like the last time, but it never came. Instead, they heard a squeal followed by an echoing clang and finally a distant thud that lightly shook the hull.

"Must have been a glancing blow," Aislinn said as she stepped back into the hallway. Hope and Becky were climbing to their feet as Aislinn addressed Hope's statement. "And no. We have one weapon that can fight back. Me."

Aislinn turned and started opening a lockbox in the floor of the locker while Hope turned her gaze to Becky. She was pleading for a direct answer. Becky shrugged.

"Near the end of the war, we had ta face the possibility tha' the enemy could commandeer a ship. Rather n' destroy it, peregrines were trained ta disarm and board it in the air so we could take it back."

"Disarm and board it in the air..." Hope breathed, turning back to Aislinn. "By yourself?"

Aislinn stood and slung a bandolier with what looked like thick metal discs in pockets all along it. "I'm not going to board it. *That* I won't do by myself. I will disarm it though."

Aislinn pushed past Beck and Hope and stepped to a closed round hatch beside the locker. She spun the sealing wheel and pulled it open, revealing a large round metal tube sloping out and away from the deck. There was a wooden frame inside with small caster wheels and padding. Two metal handles were fastened at the top of the cart. Aislinn stepped inside and rested her chest on the cart, placing her knees into pads on the cart for them, and locking her feet into boot plates at its base. She turned her head back, looking at Becky standing in the hallway.

"Peregrine set," Aislinn said. "You have to do this, Becky. It's the only way and you know it."

Becky nodded silently and tapped a gauge on the wall beside the hatch. "Tube is green," she whispered and then closed the hatch.

Becky looked forlorn. She was unable to make eye contact with Hope. She flipped open a covered lever beside the hatch and grabbed it, hesitating for a moment. Then she pulled the lever and there was a hissing thump from inside the tube.

Cole was numb and out of breath when he stumbled through the open hatch onto the bridge. He had not been able to actually set foot in the space yet, so he found himself in awe as he tried to catch his breath. A catwalk suspended above a series of floating platforms was all that seemed to be keeping Cole from plummeting to the forest canopy far below. The entirety of the bridge was walled only with glass except for the ceiling. The singular catwalk that entered into the space led to a raised platform where the captain stood, swinging her head from side to side as she received reports from her pilots and bridge crew about the state of the ship, weapons, and the movement of the enemy. There were six stations on lower platforms below the captain and the main catwalk that Cole could see. Each station held at least two or three people, their faces buried in dials and readouts, their hands fastened tight to controls and levers.

"Mister Vallen, I presume?" came a stern voice that cut Cole from his stupor. The bridge had fallen eerily silent, and Cole looked up to see a red-headed woman with short-cropped hair peppered with grey staring at him. She wore the same blue coat as her crew, but her shoulders were adorned with epaulets trailing golden tassels. The mark of her rank as captain. Cole swallowed. He was unsure of the etiquette in addressing her, so he spoke as candidly as he was able.

"Message from Chief Parvelle. We lost tanks five and two. Three will go soon."

"What hit us?" the captain asked.

"We're not sure," Cole hesitated, shifting his weight. "It was like a spear... a harpoon maybe. Cheddar saw the first one come through the hull and then explode inside. Somehow, Lucius knocked the second one free of the ship before it blew up."

The captain nodded as one of the men on a lower platform called up at her.

"Rogue vessel is coming broadside, captain."

"Ahead full. Drop us and keep us at their bow, helm."

Cole felt the ship shift and saw the clouds outside the bridge window racing past as the Cirrus moved through them. He had not realized they were moving so fast. Inside the hull and down in the engineering spaces there had not been any view of the outside to indicate movement. There had only been the feeling of butterflies in his stomach when Lucius briefly fixed the engines.

"Power is dropping, captain. We're ahead full, but the generators are at max with only two tanks. We can't keep altitude."

"If they go broadside, it won't matter. We can't have their cannons turned on us. If we can stay at their bow, there's only the one weapon to worry about and we..."

"Captain!" Another of the bridge crew interrupted. "Starboard peregrine tube has been engaged."

The captain shot to the edge of her platform facing the right of the bridge. Cole heard the thump that followed and turned to look as the captain whispered under her breath.

"Light give you strength, Elissan."

Aislinn braced her legs against the cart the moment she heard the telltale hiss of the tube loading for launch. Her heart hammered in her chest, but it was anticipation, not fear. She reached up with her good arm and set her goggles over her eyes before gripping the cart handles tightly. There was a hard thump that assaulted her ears, and in the blink of an eye, the hull of the Cirrus was diminishing behind her and the empty sky opened before her. Clouds passed, blocking her view, and then were gone. She continued upward, moving at speed through the air until she reached the zenith of her trajectory.

The moment she felt her momentum change, Aislinn dropped the cart away and gripped the handles attached to either side of her hip belt. As the handles came free, she expertly threaded her fingers into the controls. At the same time, the mechanical arms on her backpack came to life, unfolding and spreading out into massive wings that caught the air and held her aloft like a bird. She searched the skyline for her target as she glided across the sky, catching a glimpse of it a few hundred meters away as it passed behind a thick puffy cloud.

"Perfect," she whispered to herself as she banked toward it. Her launch from the tube had given her just enough height to cross the distance, but she would need a tad more for the surprise assault she planned. She flicked her wrist and a levered trigger popped out of her right handle. She gave it a gentle squeeze and a burst of steam erupted from her backpack. The thrust shot her forward, and she used the speed to climb further, keeping the cloud between her and the rogue ship to block visibility. With a few more measured bursts of steam from her pack, Aislinn found herself in position high above the enemy vessel.

"So far so good. Here we go..."

Aislinn rolled in the air and moved her fingers through the control rings on her handles. The wings folded into the center, becoming a pair of triangles to either side of her. The result was incredible speed as she dove toward the ship. As she pierced through the cloud she got her first clear look at the vessel. It was larger than the Cirrus, painted a dark rusty brown with at least twenty guns per side. The whole upper deck was open, as though the operators had simply retro-fitted lift plates to a normal ocean-faring vessel. At the bow of the ship, they had fitted a large single-barrel cannon the likes of which Aislinn had never seen. The crew were scampering about as they loaded a new round of ammo in the cannon by hand.

Through the sound of rushing air as she approached, she could barely hear the surprised shouts of the crew on the upper deck. Aislinn could not make out what they were saying, but she knew that she had been spotted by their sudden change in posture and scattering as she bore down upon them. Satisfied with her trajectory and speed, Aislinn locked the control handles to her belt to free up her hands. The pain in her shoulder was searing again, but she fought through it and removed two of the discs from the bandolier, one in each hand. She flipped a switch on the top of them with her thumb and then threw them forward just as she shot past the ship's hull. The discs flew out and then suddenly snapped to the main gun, attracted by the magnets inside the mines. Just as the cannon fired another shot at the cirrus, the mines exploded, sending broken parts of the cannon across the deck and knocking two crew members over the edge.

Underneath the hull, Aislinn grabbed her control handles again and flipped the wings out to full, catching the air and turning her immense speed into lift as she soared back up and into the clouds. As she soared in the sky, Aislinn watched the harpoon round that was loosed before she destroyed the cannon impact the Cirrus near the very aft end. It was a death blow, and she watched helplessly as the ship spun and began to fall from the sky. Furious, she blasted steam and banked back toward the enemy vessel.

This time Aislinn didn't bother with a dive attack. Instead, she locked her handles at full wing with the steam jets running and ran herself at altitude alongside the port side of the enemy hull. Methodically she thumbed and tossed the magnetic mines as she passed the exposed cannons. Every single mine she threw hit home, and as she took control again and banked around behind the enemy, she watched with satisfaction as every port cannon erupted in a scrapped mess.

"Almost done," she said to herself as she banked into a dive.

Aislinn headed down the starboard side and did the same with the last of her mines. This time she realized she did not have enough mines to finish the job. She was going to have to board, even though with her injury, she promised Becky she would not. If there was a captain alive who could land a crippled ship safely, it was hers. The Cirrus was in good hands, and Aislinn had to make sure she did enough damage to prevent the rogue vessel from finishing the job. With a controlled blast of steam and last-minute deployment of full wings, Aislinn landed on her feet at the forward end of the rogue airship.

The harpoon cannon was a smouldering wreck. Her mines had attached at the base of the cannon and about mid-way down the barrel. As she had hoped, some of the ammunition was still lying scattered on the deck. As some of the crew who had been on the upper deck were regaining composure, Aislinn flipped off the safety catch on her pistol and collapsed her wings. She secured the controls and drew her pistol just as a man came charging at her. Two quick shots to his chest dropped him to a sliding halt on the deck, and Aislinn winced at the pain in her injured shoulder. She glanced around fervently and noticed a harpoon round sitting close enough to the cannon. She winced again and drew on all her strength to pick it up and shuffle over to the loading mechanism.

When Aislinn arrived at the cannon she frowned, realizing that the loading mechanism for it was jarred open by torn metal. Quickly, she set the round down and investigated the mechanism. She understood the basics of how cannons operated and was hoping that she could fire this one into a broken barrel. Instead, she found she was only able to insert the harpoon round partway and the rest of the loader was too mangled to function. Hearing shouts from behind her and more coming from below deck, Aislinn turned to see crew climbing up through a hatch toward the aft end of the ship. They were a haggard bunch, looking more like pirates than an actual airship crew. Ignoring them, she bent to examine the round.

"Come on," she hissed. "Think, Elissan!"

A shot rang out and a bullet whizzed past her and tore into the deck a few feet away. Deciding she had no time, Aislinn shot to her feet and stood back. She aimed her pistol and fired a few rounds at the harpoon. Whether by luck or by skill, one of her rounds hit the primer cap on the harpoon and it popped, knocking Aislinn back and jamming the harpoon round inside the shattered barrel.

Hoping she had done enough, Aislinn scampered to her feet and shot blindly at the enemy crew while she sprinted to the edge of the ship and dove off. As she fell, she holstered her pistol and took up her wing controls. In response, her wings unfurled and with a jet of steam, she was soaring away. The popping of gunfire behind her made her execute a few rolls and collapse maneuvers to make herself a harder target. No more bullets found their way into her flesh. She levelled out when she heard a boom behind her. She turned to see fire and scattered metal on the bow of the enemy ship. The harpoon had exploded inside the broken barrel, just as she had hoped it would. Her gambit was successful. The wrecked cannon had torn open the whole forward end of the hull.

Satisfied, Aislinn banked away and headed in the direction of where she last saw the Cirrus. The pain in her shoulder was horrible, and she wondered how much berating she was going to have to endure from Hope and Becky. It was hard not to smile. She knew Becky could not stay mad at her for too long. All Aislinn had to do was compliment her cooking and all would be forgiven.

Aislinn's thoughts were lost in the idea of Becky's sweet treats when the bolo weapon fired from the deck of the enemy vessel entangled her. She felt the sting of the sharp steel cables entwining her, just before the small explosives at the end of each cable tore apart her wings and her backpack. She was in free fall before she knew it. Piercing through clouds and open sky as she plummeted toward the forest canopy. Her broken wings and mangled pack dragged her in awkward spinning motions as she fell. Mercifully, her mind fell into unconsciousness as her body fell from the sky.

Chapter 27

Collecting the pieces

Cole

Cole's eyes fluttered open, and the first thing he noticed was pain. He decided that he was entirely too young to have experienced this much pain so often. He coughed and rolled onto his side, mentally checking himself over for serious injuries before he attempted to sit up or stand. Other than a head-to-toe ache, and perhaps a few areas that stung from cuts through his uniform, he was relatively unscathed. He sat up slowly, conscious of the protest of his muscles, yet also aware that nothing felt broken. Surprisingly, he felt better than he had waking up in the treatment center after the cemetery explosion.

Cole looked around to try and get his bearings. He was lying at the foot of a great tree that had been cloven off near its top, exposing the forest floor to the blue sky high above. Moss and undergrowth grew in abundance on the forest floor, possibly the reason Cole found himself relatively unscathed. There was no bog or swamp water nearby that he could see. There were only thick trees and a thicker underbrush. Jungle life sang a symphony song in the shadows below the canopy, so Cole surmised he must have been out of it for quite some time. Long enough at least for the chaos of the crashing ship to abate and life to settle back to its routine amid the forest.

Cole watched as a flock of brightly coloured birds trailing long wispy tails fluttered between the trees that had remained untouched by the crash. From down below on the forest floor, the hole that the ship had carved in the jungle canopy looked a lot like a fresh gaping wound and the sunlight that spilled in was blood. Branches and trunks alike had been torn asunder by the crash, and Cole found himself trying to remember what had happened. He trudged through the underbrush, following the scar in the forest, and shielding his eyes from the bright light when he reached spots where it found the ground. During one such moment of shielding, he noticed his glasses were missing. That explained how bright the light was.

Cole's foot splashed as he stepped on some soft-looking moss and he quickly recoiled before he lost his balance. He was lucky, as it were, that he had not put all his weight into the step and fell forward. The moss before him shuddered in a ripple that moved away from his footstep, and his boot was coated in a thin yet viscous layer of stagnant water that reeked of rot. He quickly scanned around and found an elevated pathway that skirted the bog, opting as well to pick up a stick and start poking the ground before he put weight on it. He saved himself from two more pools that way, as he followed the scar deeper into the forest.

Lower and lower the breaks in the trees became, and as the impact of the ship started getting closer to the thick bases of the trees, Cole started coming across pieces of sheared hull and debris. Even a cannon barrel stuck out of the earth at one point, ripped from the hull by impact as the Cirrus crashed through. It seemed as though the sun was close to setting when Cole finally rounded a large tree trunk and his gaze fell upon the wreck of the Cirrus on the forest floor.

The ship was barely recognizable as it lay amid the woods. Panels of its hull were folded back or torn off altogether, revealing the inside mechanics. The belly ramp had broken away on impact with the ground and now lay amid the ripped-up soil like a drawbridge leading to a ruined castle. The bridge windows were completely shattered, and the inner workings of the bridge appeared torn away like the bottom jaw of a great beast that had been removed in battle. The final tree that had stood against the last of the hull's movement had still broken above the impact, and its top end lay down over the shattered remains of the ship. Had Cole not been a part of the crash, and were it not for the pockets of fire that burned around the site, it would have been easy to assume the wreckage had always been here. Ruins of an old age.

With a sigh of relief, Cole noticed movement around the crash site. He shuffled more so than walked as his adrenaline caused the strained muscles in his body to stiffen. He had reached the broken ramp before anyone saw him approaching, and it was Lucius who first saw him hobbling toward them using his bog detector stick as a crutch. Cole noticed that the engineer was pretty banged up, and his right arm was hanging limp at his side, but that did nothing to slow Lucius at all as he bolted directly toward him.

"Cole!" Lucius shouted when he came closer. "Everyone! Cole made it!"

As Cole shuddered with emotion, he leaned against what was left of the ramp's handrails and let Lucius approach. Behind the engineer, combing the wreckage, face after familiar face popped into view. A few came running to greet him, such as Hope, Becky, and Cheddar, though Cheddar was less mobile even than Cole was with her injured leg.

Lucius stopped at Cole's side and put his good hand on Cole's shoulder. The old man wore a genuine smile of relief, but in his eyes, Cole saw weariness. He had a cut above his left eye, and dried blood matted his eyebrow and his eyelashes. Aside from the bruises and cuts, and his dead arm, Lucius looked mostly intact. Hope and Becky appeared to be the same, mostly minor cuts and bruises and nothing visibly serious. Hope hugged Cole tight when she arrived, as did Becky after and for longer.

"We thought ya were a goner," Lucius said as Becky released him and she and Hope started checking him over. "Soon as we came too and saw the bridge ripped away, we thought the worst."

Cole nodded, his memory racing. "I was at the back of the bridge when we hit the canopy. After the final harpoon hit us, I grabbed for the hatch when the ship started to spin. Next thing I knew we hit the canopy and the bridge was torn away. I blacked out in the fall and woke up safe on the forest floor."

"Lucky lad, Cole. Lot of us weren't so fortunate."

Cole swallowed. "The captain?"

Becky shook her head at the question. "Some of us found what's left of the bridge. It was a mess... none of them survived."

A tear ran down Cole's face. He noticed similar tears on Hope's face too but she was looking at the ground.

"Cole," Lucius began. "Aislinn..."

Cole's eyes lost focus at the mention of Aislinn's name. He swayed and caught himself against the railing. His jaw set, and a sickening feeling overtook him. He was experiencing another flashback like he had at the gala, only this time, something felt different.

A flash of white recedes and Cole is back on the bridge of the Cirrus. He is watching the clouds, the sky, the captain and her bridge crew. He hears the thump sound from the aft end of the ship reverberating in the hull and sees the captain lean forward. She watches a shape that is soaring away into the sky. He hears her say "light give you strength, Elissan," and he knows Aislinn has launched from a peregrine tube. He turns also and watches her soar up into the sky, through a cloud, and then another. He watches as she drops an object of some kind. It looks like a sled, with caster wheels and handles on a wooden frame. Aislinn's wings unfurl. She looks like a clockwork falcon. There is a jet of steam then, a trailing line behind her against the sky as she shoots further upward into yet more cloud. Then she is diving, wings folded like the peregrine falcon the boarders get their names from.

On her first pass of the enemy ship, it looks like she has accomplished nothing. She shoots right past the enemy hull, her wings unfolding again below the airship and carrying her around underneath. The cannon on the upper deck explodes. A cheer goes up among the captain and the bridge crew, but it is premature. A third impact rocks the ship, and they begin to fall.

Cole has managed to keep his attention on Aislinn to see her maneuver around the starboard side. He watches as the cannons shatter in fire and smoke. Her movements in the air are precise and elegant, and she swoops around the hull in tight arcs. He watches her destroy some of the cannons on the port side, but then she does something unexpected. She lands on the deck.

As the Cirrus begins to spin, Cole grabs onto the hatch combing to steady himself. The enemy ship comes into view, then out, then in again as the Cirrus spins in its fall toward the canopy. Cole finds in that moment that he has more conscious control of this flashback than his previous one. He finds he can freeze time within the memory and analyze details that his mind had recorded during the event. He plays with this a moment, watching the captain's hair and epaulet tassels wave with the motion of the ship. When the enemy ship is in view through the bridge glass, he stops the memory. He can see Aislinn. She is airborne, and banking toward them.

Cole lets the memory proceed until the next time the enemy ship is in view and he freezes it again. Aislinn's movement in the air seems odd. She has banked on an awkward angle and her steam jets are firing. No. Not firing. Not like before. The contrails have changed patterns. This is something else. Cole lets the memory creep forward, intently studying Aislinn before she goes out of view again. She is not in control. The enemy has hit her with something. Something that has tangled her. Broken her wings and backpack. She is falling, spiralling out of control.

The memory shoots forward to just before the Cirrus hits the canopy. It will be the last time Cole has a good view of the sky. He watches his mentor fall toward the ground. He calculates her speed, their trajectory, and her position relative to where the Cirrus is about to impact the forest. As his memory reaches the point of impact he knows with absolute certainty, that he can find Aislinn.

Lucius was shaking Cole's shoulder when Cole came too. He had not fallen on the ground in a heap this time and found himself still standing against the railing as he had before the flashback. He blinked and looked up at the others, the green in his eye almost shining in the waning sunlight. Becky looked the most concerned, and Cole realized that made sense because she had not been there to witness the first flashback during the gala. Hope and Lucius were still concerned, but looked more relaxed than last time.

"Was that another seizure?" Hope asked, stepping forward and putting her hand on Cole's forehead.

"Not like before," Cole said. "It was a flashback again, just like the gala when I saw Eiffert, but it was different this time. I had more control over it. I was back on the bridge before the crash. I could see Aislinn."

"What did you see?" Lucius asked.

"I think she's in trouble. I saw her bomb the enemy ship. She took their cannons out, and she was on her way back, but they hit her with something. Something that broke her wings and knocked her out of the air."

"Are you sure?" Hope asked.

Cole nodded. "Flashback was the same as the gala, where I saw everything that happened to Rikket. All in the same detail, only this time I could slow and even stop the memory. Focus on specific things."

Lucius whistled. "Useful talent..."

"Ah don't understand," Becky said. "How could you see Ashes?"

Cole shrugged. "It's hard to explain. It's like I relive the memory of bad things, in extremely vivid detail, like a picture book that I can read. Before I just had to watch, but this time, it's like I can turn the pages back and forth, even stop on one to stare a little longer. If that makes any sense. I could see the enemy ship and everything Aislinn was doing. She was incredible..."

Lucius helped Cole steady himself on his feet and looked him in the eye.

"Could you find her?" The chief asked.

Cole nodded, just as Cheddar had finally hobbled close enough to the group.

"What's going on?" Cheddar asked as Lucius turned to her.

"You were right," the old engineer answered. "Aislinn took out the cannons on the rogue hull. Has to be why they left the way they did."

Lucius turned to Hope and Becky. "Get medical supplies from the wreck and go with Cole. If he can find Aislinn, she will need your help."

Lucius called out to a group of crew who were picking through the wreckage nearby and three of them trotted over. "You three are going with Cole, Hope, and Becky. Cole is going to lead you to Aislinn. Find a stretcher in the hangar. Make one if you have to. Go!"

Cole took a deep breath as he watched Hope and Becky race off together toward the wreckage, and the three other crew followed before veering off toward what was left of the hangar. He glanced skyward at the waning light shining down through the trees.

"It will be dark soon," Cole said. "Might be dangerous travelling through the woods in the dark."

Lucius shrugged. "Do it anyway. If Aislinn is out there, she's likely hurt. She can't wait."

Cole nodded.

"What are we going to do, Chief?" Cheddar asked, leaning against her makeshift crutch.

"We'll find out if we can rig the radio in the comms room. We need to send a mayday."

Cheddar nodded and started hobbling toward the ship. Lucius turned and patted Cole on the shoulder again.

"Damn glad you made it, lad. Go bring our peregrine home."

Chapter 28

Wolves of the Grindlemoor

Cole

The sun had long begun to set when Cole and the others embarked on the trek to find Aislinn. The sky was awash in a pink and orange hue. What little light remained as the sky darkened was at least enough for the group to reach the end of the tear in the canopy from the crash. Beyond, the forest was already darkening, so two of the three cloudbreakers Lucius had sent along lit portable gas lanterns to light the way. One took the lead with Cole directing from behind, and the other took up the rear behind Becky. Hope followed Cole and the final crew member carrying the stretcher was in the middle.

In their silent line, they trudged through the dark woods, circling water and sloughs when they came upon them. All the while, Cole directed them to where he believed Aislinn would have made landfall. Progress was slow in the dark. The underbrush of the thick wood and the prevalence of bogs, ponds, and sloughs were a constant threat. Thankful for what Cole had shown him, the cloudbreaker leading with the lantern had quickly adopted the method of poking the ground ahead constantly with a stick. It was a simple gesture that had saved them from catastrophe more than once.

After hours, Cole called for the group to stop. He looked back, and then up at the canopy above. He made some mental calculations and then turned to Hope and the others as the back of the line caught up.

"She should be somewhere around here," Cole said, his eyes scanning the ground that was lit by their lanterns. "If we have more lanterns, let's light them up and search."

"Don't forget to stay in sight of one another," Hope added. "And check your ground. Find a good stick if you have to."

Creatures of the night sang in the darkness as the group lit two more lanterns and began to fan out in a search pattern. To ease his journey, the cloudbreaker carrying the stretcher dropped the gear and lit a lantern to mark it in the darkness. Hope and Becky also dropped their medical equipment as well, but Becky held on to a small first aid kit just in case. As they crept through the darkness seeking their fallen comrade, they called her name over and over, hoping she might be able to hear them and respond. Calling out also helped them keep vigil over one another, and methodically they stretched further and further into the darkness of the jungle.

As Cole patrolled, calling his mentor's name, he relived the memory of seeing her fall. He had been practicing all night since leaving the crash site and could now go back through his memories at will, even while maintaining a conscious focus on other tasks. He wondered where this new recall ability had come from, and why only select events and experiences triggered it. Through his concentration over the trek, he found he could recall the courtroom, Rikket's death, the Cirrus crash, and the fight with Eiffert and the others in Hiram's secret lab. But he could not do the same for events in his childhood, or other more recent events such as the Swampfish Inn. Resigned, he decided the best explanation was something to do with his head injury the night of the cemetery explosion.

"Aislinn!" Cole shouted again.

Suddenly, he froze as a chill ran down his spine. Two shining eyes stared at him from the darkness ahead. They were large and shone with a metallic yellow in the light of his lantern. They were not moving, just hovering in the blackness and staring right at him. Instinctively, he lifted the lantern and beheld a creature that took his breath away.

The great wolf bore fur the blackest Cole had ever seen. It seemed to ripple in his lantern light like shadow itself come to life. Cole's skin was ice and he swallowed. His hand gripped his walking stick tighter, and his jaw muscle tightened, but the wolf stood motionless. The creature seemed surreal, to the point where Cole almost wondered if he was hallucinating, but then it blinked and somehow he knew. It was real.

For a long time, Cole and the wolf simply stared at each other. Cole was racked in the indecision of fight or flight, the wolf was a stoic sentinel of shadow. But then the creature blinked again and turned its head. Cole thought perhaps it was about to depart, but he realized the creature was looking up and past Cole. It was motionless, and not threatening, and Cole could not help but feel like it was indicating something. Cautiously, he turned his head to follow the wolf's gaze.

Suspended in a tree entangled by vines and thin metal cables was Aislinn. She was a little more than ten feet off the ground, wrapped amid a cocoon of foliage and her broken wings. She was slightly upside down, and if not for the dried blood on her face and matting her hair, she looked quite peaceful and comfortable. In shock, Cole turned back to face the wolf but found only the empty dark jungle. He took a step toward where the creature had been and saw huge footprints in the soil. He could not imagined it. A black wolf had shown him what he was looking for.

Cole thought back to all the stories he had heard growing up. The tales and books his father had read him of the world's legends. Wolves of the Grindlemoor. The great Guardians of the Forest. He shook his head and pondered a moment, then drew a deep breath.

"I found her!" he bellowed into the night. "She's over here!"

Cole pulled his attention away from the tracks and the ghostly shadow wolf, and aimed his lantern up at Aislinn. He crossed to the base of the tree she was in and started looking for a way to climb up to her. Resigning to wait for assistance, he studied her face as she hung in her hammock of vine and broken wings. She squinted against his lantern light, and Cole saw she was breathing. She was alive.

The others arrived in short order and went to work immediately. Little was said as they worked feverishly to climb up to her and cut the vine that entangled her. When they had safely lowered her to the forest floor, they went to work removing the tangled wreck of her wings. They found a long steel rod embedded partly into the steam pack. It was like a short javelin but it had fixed fletching at its tail like those on an arrow. They were canted in a similar way to fletching, no doubt causing the javelin to spin in the air. There were also five thin metal cables attached, and at their end, Cole could see that the cable had been charred and frayed.

"It's a javelin rifle for sure," one of the cloudbreakers said as they pulled the pack and broken wings free of Aislinn. "Never seen one like this though. It's like a bolo of some sort."

"A weapon designed specifically for peregrines, no doubt," one of the others agreed.

The rest of the group backed up to give Becky and Hope space to treat Aislinn's wounds and stabilize her, while two of the crew went back to retrieve the stretcher and equipment.

"How is she?" Cole asked as Hope brushed the back of her hand against Aislinn's forehead.

"Not good, Cole. She's alive, but her breathing is shallow and her heartbeat is very weak. The wound in her shoulder looks like it opened up again, and her other arm has a compound fracture mid-wrist. We'll have to set the bone before we move her."

"Left hip is dislocated too," Becky added as she went about completing her assessment. "Lot of lacerations in her abdomen and thigh too. Ah hope there's no internal bleedin', but ah can't see no indication out here. We need proper medical resources. And soon."

Cole nodded just as the others arrived with the equipment and the stretcher. They administered medication and began bandaging what they could. One of the cloudbreakers helped Becky reset her dislocated hip, which caused Aislinn to grunt and roll her head in anguish. Seeing her in such pain caused Cole to grind his teeth, fighting the urge to break down. When they reset the broken arm though, and Aislinn screamed out into the darkness, Cole did shed a tear. He turned away from the group, his eyes shut tight. When he opened them again, two yellow eyes peered back from the darkness off in the jungle. This time, they were joined by others.

Cole watched the yellow eyes in the dark. One by one each pair blinked, vanishing into the black before reappearing again. The largest pair, which Cole assumed belonged to the wolf who had pointed him to Aislinn, seemed to lower and close a tad longer than a simple blink. Then they reappeared and rose again. After that, they all disappeared.

"What are you looking at?" Hope asked.

Cole jumped a bit. "Uh. Eyes. I think. Out there in the blackness."

Hope stared off in the same direction as Cole for a moment.

"I don't see anything," she whispered.

Cole nodded. "No, they just left."

He hesitated, then pointed at the ground where the prints were.

"This is going to sound crazy, but a huge black wolf showed me where Aislinn was. It was standing right there, where those prints are."

Hope looked down where Cole was indicating, then back at him.

"Are you okay, Cole?"

Cole blinked and turned to her. The green in his eye shone in the lantern light.

"Yeah, why?"

Hope knelt and looked closer at the ground.

"There's nothing here, Cole."

Cole shook his head and bent down to the ground. He traced with his finger where the prints he could see clear as day were.

"Right here. It's a wolf print. Can't you see it?"

"Cole," Hope said as she knelt with him. "Those are barely prints. If they are, they're months old."

Hope reached out and touched Cole's forehead.

"Come on, Cole," Hope said as she took her hand back. "We're ready to move her. We need to get back. You both need rest."

Cole sighed and stood. He looked from the deep prints on the forest floor to where the eyes were. Then he turned away and looked at his mentor, strapped tight to the stretcher that was now suspended between two of the crew with Becky attending from beside. He turned his attention to Hope, who was looking at him the same way she looked at Aislinn: like a patient in need of assistance. Yet other than some aching muscles, Cole felt fine.

"Okay," Cole sighed. "Let's get her back to the crash site."

Chapter 29

For the Fallen

Lucius

Lucius frowned as he listened to garbled static on channel after channel. Beside him, Cheddar toiled with some cables that led to a makeshift repeater the crew had built using damaged antenna equipment. She turned and twisted the long rods, watching the reaction on the Chief's face to see if it was picking up a signal. Eventually, the radio hissed and the static momentarily disappeared, so Lucius quickly keyed the microphone in his hand.

"Mayday, mayday. This is Chief Engineer Lucius Parvelle of the VAS Cirrus. We have crashed in the Grindlemoor south of the Errbryte Estate. Does anyone copy?"

The radio hummed. Silence answered back.

Lucius keyed the microphone and repeated his mayday call, which was again met by silence. He glanced at Cheddar and shook his head. She nodded back and immediately began shifting the antenna again. The radio went from silence to the garbled static once more and Lucius lowered his head. He tapped the microphone against his forehead in frustration.

Most of the crew had been up all night working on the radio rig, putting out the fires, and searching for survivors. They had found more bodies than the living crew. The reality of what had happened weighed heavily on morale, but Lucius had resolved to keep composure. He was the ranking member of the crew now, by seniority and title. The survivors were looking up to him, and he would not fail them. With his best friend missing, and his left arm almost useless, it was a monumental struggle to remain stoic.

Again, the radio static gave way to silence and Lucius waved to Cheddar to stop moving the antenna. He keyed the microphone and repeated his mayday. Nothing returned. He ground his teeth and prepared to send again but suddenly a voice crackled over the speakers. It was faint, like the sender was whispering. Lucius cranked the volume up as loud as he could and leaned closer to the speaker. It was Remmy's voice coming over the radio.

"This message is for the big Chief. Caught the boat. Heading south by south-east. Keeping the lights on. The message will repeat."

Lucius sighed and smiled. He looked over at Cheddar.

"Make a note of the frequency, Chedd. Just caught the lads' repeater. We'll come back once the mayday is received."

"You got it, Chief," Cheddar called back. She jotted some notes down in a journal that was sitting beside her and then returned to adjusting the antenna.

Static returned over the radio, and Lucius lowered the volume. Shortly, it became silent again and Lucius waved to Cheddar. There was resignation in his voice as he keyed the microphone once again. "Mayday, mayday. This is Chief Parvelle of the VAS Cirrus..."

Almost immediately a female voice answered over the radio.

"Chief Parvelle, this is Commander Gisborne of IAS Starfall."

Lucius pumped his fist in the air and cheered. Cheddar and some others nearby looked over.

"We got the Starfall!" Lucius hollered.

A cheer erupted from all the crew nearby, just as Lucius returned to the radio.

"Chelsea," he said. "By the light, it's good to hear your voice."

"And yours, Lucius," the reply crackled over the radio. "We received a mayday the moment the Cirrus came under attack. We've been searching all frequencies ever since. What's your status?"

Lucius paused. "Ain't good, Chels. Cirrus is down. Lost a lot of crew."

There was a long moment before the radio crackled back.

"Captain Syndical?"

Lucius shook his head as though those on the other end could see him. "Lost," he replied.

At that moment, a commotion at the edge of the crash site caught his attention. He glanced over at Cheddar, who was already hobbling as fast as she could in the direction everyone else was running. He followed their path to the edge of the clearing, and his breath caught in his throat. Cole and the others were back, and between two of the crew, a stretcher carried an unconscious Aislinn. By the look of relief on Cole's face, he knew already that she was alive.

"Lucius," the radio called. "We're on our way. Medical is on standby, and we'll drop a salvage crew. Leave the radio on this wavelength. We can triangulate your location."

"Received, Chels. Got a lot of wounded here. Sail hard."

"Confirmed. See you soon, old friend."

Lucius set the radio down and stood. The group had already reached a makeshift shelter that had been set up to give the wounded some protection from the elements. They were setting Aislinn's stretcher down across a pair of triangular stands when Lucius approached.

"How is she?" Lucius asked.

Hope looked exhausted as she replied. They all did. Becky was busy downing a flask of water that Cheddar had passed her.

"Not so good," Hope replied. "Cole found her hanging in the trees. She's pretty beat up, but she's a fighter. Broken arm, a dislocated hip, shot through the shoulder, and a lot of superficial cuts and scrapes. It's a miracle, but thankfully she's alive."

Becky finished her drink and passed the flask on to one of the crew who had been carrying the stretcher. Lucius approached Cole and put his hand on his shoulder.

"You did good, lad," Lucius said.

"Lucius," Becky said. "She needs a med bay. Fast. Blood, sutures, a surgeon."

Lucius nodded. "Starfall is inbound. Spoke to Commander Gisborne on the radio. Medical's prepped."

"The Starfall?" Cole whispered. He swayed on his feet.

Lucius steadied Cole. "Not a time to swoon, lad."

Hope helped Lucius ease Cole into sitting on a log near the shelter. His skin was pale.

"Feel dizzy," Cole said.

Hope accepted a flask of water from a crew member when he approached. She popped the cap off and handed it to Cole. "Drink."

Cole took the flask and drank long from it. Colour seemed to return to his skin in waves as he swallowed.

"Light lad," Lucius breathed as he bent down to examine Cole closer. "Ya look exhausted."

Cole shrugged. "I am. Can't remember the last time I slept. Guess it was when I fell."

Hope replaced the cap on the flask when Cole handed it back to her. She glanced up at Lucius.

"Okay, lad. Get some rest."

Hope smiled at Cole as she stood and then turned her back, whispering to Lucius as she stepped away.

"Chief, a word?"

Lucius let Hope lead him away from the group but kept an eye on Cole. The boy was leaning forward, his head in his hands. Hope stopped and looked back at Cole too, then met Lucius' eyes directly. Her face was expressionless.

"I'm worried about him," she said.

Lucius nodded. "I can see that. Rightly so, as well. The lad's been through a lot in a short time. He needs rest."

Hope shook her head. "That may be so, but I think there's something else. He said a wolf showed him where Aislinn was. He was so sure, he tried to show me the tracks it left but there was nothing there. Well, I shouldn't say nothing. There were tracks, but they were ancient."

"Hallucination?" Lucius asked.

Hope nodded and looked back toward Cole. He had slid down from the log and now sat on the ground resting his back against it.

"That's my suspicion," she replied. "It was eerie, Lucius. I mean, there *are* the legends. Wolves of the Grindlemoor and all that. But Aislinn mentioned a head injury back in our library. During an explosion, was it?"

Lucius nodded.

"And his best friend died during that explosion. We know that much from the library."

"What are ya driving at, Hope?"

Hope shrugged. "I'm not sure. He and Aislinn said there was no sign of anything bad from his injuries until he saw that man at the gala. Clean bill of health. I'm worried there may be some brain damage we're missing."

Lucius watched Cole slump as he lost the battle to keep his eyes open. He certainly didn't look brain-damaged. He looked like a teenage boy who was utterly spent.

"Look," Lucius sighed and turned to face Hope. "I don't know medical science. I'm just an engineer. But I know this," he pointed to Cole. "That lad has seen more darkness in the last six months than many cloudbreakers I sailed with saw through the whole war. His best friend died in front of him. His community blamed him for it. He was whisked off on a fool adventure and the first time he got off the ground he was shot outta the sky. He's only eighteen."

Hope glared at Lucius. "I'm twenty and during a gala at my home I saw a boy convulse and scream in agony only to be totally fine, after which all his *friends* ignored what happened. Then I was coerced into helping discover my father's involvement in an esoteric plot, before having to watch him sacrifice himself to allow us to escape."

A tear rolled down Hope's face and her lip quivered. "None of this is okay," she squeaked.

Lucius nodded. His face dropped, and his expression became solemn.

"We lost a lot of good people," Lucius whispered. "Crew, friends, family. We're all in shock and we're dealing with it in our own ways. I ain't sayin any one of us has it worse than others. We're all exhausted and runnin' out o' steam, but we have to keep the engines going, you know? Fly, move, fight. Those are the priorities a ship has to make. They trained us for that, but not you and Cole. You're both young and dealin' with all this for the first time. That's why we have to be strong for you. We can't fly. We can't move."

"Then what do we have left?" Hope interrupted.

Lucius looked up then and Hope saw a tear streak its way down the mud on his face. Hope had not realized how filthy and dishevelled he looked until that moment.

"We fight," Lucius continued, his gaze roaming across the field and all the activity going on around them. "Hope, sometimes bein' a cloudbreaker ain't about glory or always doin' the right thing. Sometimes it's just about towing the line when you need it taught. Bracing for whatever comes so the people beside you can rely on your strength. I don't know if Cole's gonna be alright. I don't know if Aislinn will. I don't know if you will either. But I trust in all your strength, and as long as I draw breath you can trust in mine. That's what we have left. Each other, and the fight that's in our hearts."

Hope took a long look at the Chief and then started to walk away toward Cole. Lucius could see the resignation in her posture, almost as though his words had shown her just how out of energy she was also. She stopped about halfway between him and where Cole lay and looked back.

"You know," she said as the corner of her lip turned up into a coy smile. "That was quite scholarly a thing to say. For an engineer."

Lucius chuckled but did not respond. His silence was communication enough. Hope nodded to him and turned back toward Cole. When she reached him, she sank to the ground and closed her eyes. Lucius watched them resting and then turned his attention to the shelter. Becky was busy fussing over the other wounded, and Aislinn was asleep on the stretcher. He strode toward the shelter but stopped before he reached it and turned to his left. He walked out across the clearing, rounding the trunks of mighty snapped trees until he was out of sight of the camp. He stopped at the edge of a small meadow beyond the crash site.

Before him, lying in the grass in carefully placed rows, was a multitude of black body bags. They were filled with the bodies of the slain, laid to rest for the moment until they could be buried as befit their service to their nations. The survivors of the crash had paid special care to ensure those who were lost were placed in the silence nearby, but also out of the way so as not to crush morale while essential duties were performed. Lucius fell to his knees and choked on his emotion that he dared not show the others. He wiped his face.

"I'm sorry," he whispered.

Lucius knelt in silence in the forest among the fallen for what had to be the better part of an hour. He wept, wiped his tears, and wept again. His jaw clenched and his teeth ground behind his pursed lips. His expressions oscillated from the tightness of rage to the crumpled resignation of mourning and back again. His eyes sought the sky and the field of bags in equal measure.

Eventually, he drew a deep breath and stood. He had been gone long enough to recover most of his strength. Cheddar needed help with the radio after all, and the others needed him for any other work that might need doing. Most importantly, he knew that if he lingered too long, he would be found here, lost among his emotions. As he turned to head back to the camp, he paused.

"To the rise," he whispered.

"For the fallen," came a female reply that made him jump. He spun to see Cheddar, leaning against her crutch.

"Light Ched," Lucius breathed. "Scare a man half to death like that."

Cheddar shrugged. Her long black hair was a tangled mess that still bounced with her shoulders. She had huge bags under her eyes.

"Been looking for you everywhere, Chief," she said. "Figured if you weren't in the hull you'd be out here. Just took my time getting to you is all."

Lucius smiled. "Thanks for that, Ched."

Cheddar grinned in response and indicated her crutch by lifting and lightly shaking it. "Don't thank me. Wasn't on purpose. I'm just not that fast right now."

Lucius turned to take one last look at the makeshift morgue, then he approached Cheddar and matched her slow pace back toward the campsite.

"Those of us still standing owe our lives to you, Chief," Cheddar whispered. "If it wasn't for the power you restored, it would have been a lot worse."

Lucius shrugged. "Don't do that, Ched. Cap'n flew the ship. If anyone saved us, it was her. Her and Aislinn."

Cheddar nodded. "Truth. But," she paused and stopped walking. "You carried me out of the boiler room, Chief. You came for me, right through that smoke and fire and steam."

Lucius froze. He turned back to look at Cheddar. Her squared features were stained with soot, sweat, and grease. Her hair was matted with the same. Tears were carving clean lines down across her cheeks.

"I owe you my life, at least," she said.

Lucius shook his head and approached her. His wounded left arm hanging lifeless at his side, he rested his right hand on her shoulder and sighed deeply.

"Listen, Ched. Yer a damn good mechanic, and an even better cloudbreaker. There ain't a soul onboard who wouldn't have done the same as I did. We're family, as far as I'm concerned. Every single one of us is a hero today," Lucius lifted his hand and pointed his finger over her shoulder at the morgue while he nodded. "All of us. Fallen or still standing. Right? We honour 'em. And ourselves. To the rise."

Cheddar nodded and raised her chin. She swallowed hard and wiped the tears from her eyes. The act smudged the muck on her face. The result looked almost like war paint.

"For the fallen," she said.

"For the fallen," Lucius repeated, and together, they walked back to camp.

Chapter 30

The Starfall

Cole

Cole woke to the sound of shouting. He stretched and his muscles protested in agony, in part due to the way he had fallen asleep against the log, but also because of wounds and whiplash from his fall. He realized Hope had nestled up beside him and fallen asleep also. Some of the ringlets in her hair had escaped the confines of her ponytail and now sat across her face partly shading her from the evening sun. Smiling down at her, a fresh burst of shouts and cheers caused Cole to crane his neck to discover the source of the commotion. His motion roused Hope from her slumber.

"What's going on?" She asked as she rubbed her eyes, sitting up even slower than Cole had.

"Not sure."

Cole climbed to his feet using the log to brace against the wobble in his legs. Golden light bathed the crash and the campsite, almost as though all the fires had been relit. A group of people standing nearby were talking and pointing into the air. As Hope climbed to her feet beside him, Cole followed the group's indications and saw a massive shape hovering above the trees. At first, Cole was intimidated. But as the haze of his recent awakening lifted, realization soon dawned on him and he read the painted lettering on the airship's hull. IAS Starfall.

The Starfall was every bit the marvel that Cole had imagined it to be. It was at least double the length of the Cirrus, with a wider hull that looked like two smaller airships joined side by side. It bristled with cannons along the lower portion of its hull, and above those, its massive vapour sails were folded in like the fins of a lionfish. Like the Cirrus, the Starfall sported a forward bridge slung low under its bow. The difference was that the massive, curved glass panels were separated by gilded beams that connected to a carved figurehead depicting a roaring dragon whose wings shielded the upper part of the bridge where it connected to the hull. The Starfall also had an aft bridge, which Cole could just barely see above the trees.

The enormous flagship was much too big to fit within the clearing caused by the Cirrus crash, so it took station hovering above the canopy. Unlike the Cirrus, the Starfall had an under-belly elevator platform that was currently lowering to the ground. Cole could see a compliment of people standing on the elevator platform. On the ground below, Lucius and Cheddar waited with a group that was slowly growing as others arrived to greet their brethren.

"That is a huge ship," Hope said.

"Indeed a marvel," Cole said as he turned his attention to Aislinn on the stretcher inside the tent. "A diamond in the sky."

Hope started toward the group waiting for the elevator platform.

"I see Lucius," she said. "Come on, Cole. Let's go greet them."

Cole followed Hope across the crash site past the tent to the open area where the group was waiting. They arrived and made their way through to stand by Lucius just as the elevator touched down. One of the crewmen on the platform lifted a metal gate and people started pouring off the elevator carrying equipment and supplies. A thin red-haired woman with white skin and a high-collar white coat made a beeline for Becky. She was carrying a large case and was flanked by two others with similar clothing and equipment. When she reached Becky, they conversed quickly before heading for the medical tent. Cole watched the gathered crowd part for them and then turned his attention back to Lucius when he heard a woman's voice address him.

"Chief Parvelle," the woman said. "By the light, it is good to see you unharmed."

The woman's voice alone was enough to strike Cole senseless, but when he turned his eyes upon her, he found himself truly speechless. She was taller than Lucius, by an inch or maybe more. Not a single auburn hair on her head was out of place amid the tied-up curls, and her emerald green eyes shone even in the waning light as though lit from within. She had un-blemished dark skin, like a farmer after months of tanning in the fields, which only made her eyes seem to glow even more. She was a rapturous beauty, like a statue brought to life. Cole swallowed and took his eyes away. He could not help but notice that everyone was reacting to her in the same fashion. Even Hope.

"Relatively unharmed," Lucius said to her, indicating his still-useless left arm.

The woman stepped forward and touched Lucius' arm almost reverently. "Lucius, how?"

Lucius cleared his throat. "Story for another time."

Catching a glimpse of Cole and the others standing beside him, Lucius took a step back and held his right hand out to the woman.

"Cole, Hope, allow me to introduce Commander Chelsea Gisborne, Executive Officer and second-in-command of the IAS Starfall. Chelsea, this is Initiate Cole Vallen and Lady Hope Errbryte."

Cole shook Chelsea's hand without saying a word, but he felt his cheeks flush. Hope stammered an attempt at a greeting also. Chelsea's demeanour was as statuesque as her appearance. She was completely unaffected by the behaviour of the group. Cole could not help but notice how precise her movements were as she shook his and then Hope's hand. Her grip strength impressed him too, and he found himself shaking the pain out of his hand when she turned her attention back to Lucius. Hope shook the pain from her hand also and shared a wide-eyed look with Cole. They were impressed.

"Walk with me, Lucius," Chelsea said as she began making her way toward the Cirrus wreckage. Lucius beckoned for Cole and Hope to follow, and they did, with Cheddar limping along doing her best to keep up.

"Tell me what happened."

Cole and Hope followed silently and listened as Lucius recounted the attack like he was giving a situation report. Cole thought perhaps that was exactly what he was doing. The facts alone, not the human element, or the emotion of the event. Just the cold hard facts sequentially from the arrival at the Errbryte estate to the moment they found themselves in now. Having lived it all, hearing it again but stripped down to the bare bones was surreal. Cole stole a glance at Hope when Lucius reported Hiram's involvement and sacrifice. She simply turned her head away for a moment, and then back, offering Cole an unconvincing smile. They finally stopped near the after end of the Cirrus' hull and Chelsea put her hand on the cold metal where the harpoon rounds had torn open the boiler room.

"In the whole of the war," Chelsea whispered. "We never lost control of an airship to the enemy. We were so arrogant. Why should our cannons point up? The sky was ours."

"Not anymore," Lucius replied.

Chelsea nodded and turned to face him. "Not anymore. Tell me, did anyone obtain a good description of this rogue airship? Was it one of our decommissioned hulls?"

Cole spoke up at that moment, shocked by the sound of his voice. "It was ramshackle, Commander. No markings. Partly wooden hull. It looked more like an Ocean vessel retrofitted for flight than a purpose-built airship. It had a single harpoon cannon on the foredeck. More than ten cannons per side broadside. And it was painted a dark colour. Not quite black. A deep brown perhaps."

Chelsea appraised Cole with a flat expression. She took a step toward him. "How did you gather this intelligence?"

Cole swallowed hard, uneasy in her presence. "I was on the bridge. I had a quick look as we were crashing, and..." his words cut off under her scrutiny.

"A quick look," she whispered and glanced at Lucius. "This is the boy, then? Elissan's charge?"

Lucius nodded. "He is. Has an uncanny memory at times. He was able to guide a team directly to Aislinn after she fell in the attack."

Chelsea stood over Cole and he felt ice prickle his skin. For all her beauty, she bore a commanding presence and it took every ounce of Cole's courage just to lift his eyes to meet hers.

"Impressive, Cole Vallen," Chelsea said after a moment. "Very impressive."

"What happens now?" Hope asked.

At that moment, Becky trotted over and stopped beside Lucius.

"Light these Starfall folk can work," she said trying to catch her breath. "All the wounded are on board already, Aislinn too. She's gonna be fine. Surgeon's already workin' on her. We'll be able ta see her in a few hours."

"Excellent," Chelsea said.

"Oh boy, y'all gotta see this *ship*! It's really somethin'. Lucius yer gonna just *love* it in there!"

Chelsea smiled as they started to walk back toward the tents and the elevators.

"Lucius knows every bolt, nut, and valve on board the Starfall intimately. Don't you, Chief?"

Incredibly, the old engineer almost seemed to blush.

Becky was beside herself as she bounced along with the group.

"Is that true, Lucius?"

Chelsea stopped and turned to appraise Lucius.

"I am sorry, Chief, I overstepped. I did not know you had not told them."

Lucius shrugged and Cole noticed his shoulders slump ever so slightly, as though he were ashamed.

"It's okay, Chels," he said. "They would have found out sooner or later. Go ahead and tell 'em."

Chelsea resumed walking toward the elevator. The whole group was silent as they waited for her to share why their chief engineer was so intimate with the Starfall. She had a mischievous grin on her face. Cole knew she was stalling to tease Lucius. It was clear they had a long history of friendship.

"Chief Parvelle here *designed* the Starfall," Chelsea finally said.

For the next few hours, Cole and the others helped the Cirrus and the Starfall crew set up tents and equipment for the salvage team being left behind to scuttle the wreckage. Chelsea and Lucius had boarded the Starfall to brief the captain and consult with high command on their next orders. Cole had been introduced to the senior peregrine aboard the Starfall, an intimidating dark-skinned Akoyan named Elios Rayos, and the pair of them had been working with Hope to set up a mess tent. Elios shared that he was a good friend of Aislinn's and that he had become a peregrine at the same time as her and her brother Bayne. Elios knew a lot about Aislinn, and Cole listened with rapt attention to all his anecdotes as they worked.

"So, there we were," Elios was saying as Cole finished threading the last canvas panel section of the tent together. "In the Crystal Sky for a refit rest. Two other ships are in the hangars at the shipyard, so the tavern is *packed,* right? And Aislinn and Bayne *really* want an ale. I mean, they're going to die of thirst if they don't get one soon, you know? But there's only one server on shift. So what does Aislinn do? She tells the Windshear crew that the Starfall guys said they're cowards. *Then* she tells the Starfall guys that the *Windshear* crew says they make love to goats."

Cole laughed. He could see Aislinn in his mind stirring up that kind of trouble. He was struck by images of her at the Swampfish Inn.

"Well," Elios continued. "Doesn't the *entire* tavern just become a mess of raving lunatics instantly. People are fighting everywhere! And while all that is going on, where is our dear friend Aislinn? She's collecting as many pitchers as she can hold from tables and rushing out the door with them. I tell ya, I've never drank so much for free in all my life!"

"You're kidding," Hope said through fits of laughter. "Where were you for all of this? Where was her brother?"

Elios stood and held his arms out like he was shocked at the accusation.

"We were helping carry pitchers of course!"

Elios clapped Cole on the back and winked at Hope as he stepped through the canvas curtain door of the tent. He waved to a group of crew standing amid crates by the elevator. When they looked his way, he pointed at the tent just as Cole and Hope had exited.

"This one is finished," he called. "Good to set up the chow hall now."

Cole watched the group of people begin lifting crates and equipment and making their way toward them. Off to his right, he noticed Becky approaching. In short order, the crews of the two ships had set up six tents for command, bunks, kitchen, and eating. They had also erected a long temporary hangar for larger tools and recovered parts from the Cirrus wreckage. Becky was coming past the command tent. She was smiling, and her eyes were locked on Cole's.

"Heya Cole! Hey Hope! Elios treatin' y'all okay?"

Elios smiled and held the curtain open for an approaching crew member who ducked inside carrying a long crate.

"He's great," Cole said. "He's been telling us stories about Aislinn."

Becky shot Elios a glare.

"Best be good stories, Rayos! You talk ill o' my Ashes and we gonna have words."

Elios held his hands up in mock surrender.

"Hey! It's Elissan we're talking about here. There's nothing *but* good stories!"

Becky nodded with a stern "Uh-huh," and then turned her attention to Cole and Hope.

"We're about done down here, so ah'm headin' aboard ta check on Ashes. Comin'?"

Cole turned and looked at Elios. The Peregrine must have sensed the implied request for permission because he instantly nodded his head.

"It's a good idea. We've done all we can down here. The salvage crew will set up the rest the way they want it. You head onboard. See how Aislinn is doing. I'll gather the rest who aren't staying and brief Captain McCray."

Hope and Cole thanked Elios and shook his hand in turn. Then they followed Becky across the campsite to the elevator. There were only two other crew members on the lift with them as they began the ascent toward the airship hovering above. As they lifted off the ground, and his perspective over the crash site began to change, the weight of what had happened grew heavier on Cole's heart. Seeing the torn trees, the scattered debris, and the upheaval in the ground from above was almost shocking.

Cole leaned forward and grabbed the metal railing of the elevator platform to steady himself.

A warm hand rested on Cole's back, and he looked to his right to see Hope leaning against the railing with him. She was rubbing his back between his shoulder blades as she too looked over the site below them. As the elevator steadily rose out of the clearing, they crested the top of the forest canopy and the world seemed to open up. A sea of green stretched out before them, rolling off in almost every direction, and the great peaks of the Rinda Mountains far away broke the flat horizon. Even the air was crisper above the canopy, freed from the closed-in thickness of the jungle.

Cole took a deep breath and smiled. He turned to say something to Hope but found her attention was locked somewhere off to the northeast, where foothills met the jungle. Her hand still absently stroked his back, so Cole closed his mouth and kept silent. He could not be sure because he had spent most of the early flight inside the bowels of the Cirrus, but he surmised she was looking in the direction of her home. It felt odd to Cole, that such serene beauty could play host to so much recent emotional turmoil. He took in a group of jungle birds below, flitting from tree-top to tree-top above the canopy, and wondered if his recent experiences would colour his trademark infatuation with the sky. One short glance skyward, just as the hair on his neck and arms indicated proximity to the Starfall's lift plates, and Cole knew. Nothing could ever corrupt his love of the sky.

Before a word could be spoken about the view, it was gone. The elevator platform slipped inside its recess in the Starfall's hull, and the endless sky was replaced with cold metal and wood. There was not a lot of difference between the Cirrus' hangar and the Starfall's beyond sheer size. Cole was immediately struck by the Starfall's use of space. It had room. Seemingly in abundance. The cluttered and practical use of every inch of room as seen on the Cirrus seemed absent aboard the Starfall. Though Cole could still see piping, cables, and machinery, it was eloquently hidden or built in such a way that it seemed an organic part of the ship. There was no claustrophobia within the flagship. It felt as much like a palace or a mansion as it did a warship.

Becky asked one of the Starfall crew that had ridden the elevator up with them if they could escort the group to the infirmary and the young woman agreed. She led them across the massive hangar to a stairway in the very center of the space. It was not a ladder, but rather an actual set of metal stairs, not unlike those one would expect to find in a building. There were five decks in total on the Starfall. Like the Cirrus, the bottom deck was a hangar and engineering spaces. The next deck up, called three-deck, had the bridge, command quarters, operations room, and the medical center. Cole was a little disappointed that the first deck they visited was their destination, but he knew he would have time for a proper tour later. He resigned to ask Elios for one as their guide indicated the door to the surgical room.

Becky stepped through the door first, followed by Hope and finally Cole, who nodded to their guide in thanks. Aislinn was resting on an elevated bed in the center of the room. There were no portholes or windows to the outside. Banks of cabinets to either side of the room held all manner of medical implements and supplies, and a big gas lantern with a huge reflective disc hung on a spring-loaded arm above the bed. Aislinn was dressed in linen robes and was covered to her breasts in blankets. For a moment, Cole thought she must be warm under those blankets, but then he realized he was a tad chilled. That was when he noticed the hum of the forced air in the room.

Hope approached Aislinn's bedside and inspected the bandages on her shoulder and the linen sling they had placed around her to immobilize her broken arm. Gently, she placed the back of her hand against Aislinn's forehead. At Hope's touch, Aislinn groaned and opened her eyes.

One by one, Aislinn looked around at the group surrounding her bed. Her brow furrowed a moment and then relaxed. She looked up at the surgical lamp above her, and then at the remainder of the room.

"Either I'm dead," she said hoarsely. "Or... wait. Am I dead?"

Becky giggled. "Ya ain't dead, Ashes. Yer on th' Starfall."

"What happened?" Aislinn asked, squinting her eyes for a moment.

"You were hit by something," Cole said. "Shot out of the sky. I saw you, from the bridge, just before the Cirrus went down."

"What did they hit me with?"

Cole looked at Hope as she started to fuss over Aislinn, trying to prevent her from sitting up.

"We aren't sure," Cole answered.

Aislinn relented against Hope's pressing and settled down into the bed.

"How did you find me?"

Hope leaned her head toward Cole. "Cole did the weird thing he does, like back in my library only with less seizure."

Aislinn glanced at Cole, her eyebrows raised.

"I could see you," Cole explained. "Like I could see Rikket. But it was different. Long story. But I led them right to you. Found you hanging in the trees..." Cole paused. "Or rather..."

Before Cole could say anything about the wolf, Hope interrupted him.

"You need rest, Aislinn. Questions can wait. The Cirrus crashed, and we survived. That's what is important. We're on the Starfall now, and..."

A broadcast over the intercom interrupted Hope and a man's voice boomed throughout the ship.

"All hands. This is Captain McCray," there was a long pause. "This has been a dark day for all of us, the crew of the Cirrus most of all. The war is supposed to be over, yet here we are, scuttling a downed ship and caring for wounded survivors. I have spoken with high command, and they assure me that the Ciar K'hen empire has denied involvement in this attack."

Cole and Hope shared a look as Aislinn whispered. "Not involved? But those were Ciar K'hen weapons."

"I won't waste words," Captain McCray continued. "An attack on one of us is an attack on all of us. We will hunt down that ship, and those responsible for these attacks. We are currently tracking a repeater set by the Cirrus crew dispatched by Chief Parvelle. We need to expect resistance. This will get worse before it is over. We are going in blind with little intelligence on our enemy forces, but I believe in all of you. I believe in this ship. The night is always darkest before dawn. Let's go light it up."

Chapter 31

Storm on the horizon

Ketrick

Snow and ice painted the tallest peaks of the southernmost Rinda mountains where they touched the coast of the Furious Sea. The arm of high summits and sprawling hills created the eastern border of the Grindlemoor. A chill wind ripped through the high elevation, bringing light snow down in sideways sheets. A guard standing his post on a tall concrete wall shivered and tightened his coat against the cold. The lantern attached to the wall behind swayed in the wind, its light driving away the bleak darkness of the high mountain night.

Amid the imposing landscape, the Whitehall facility was part fortress and part monastery. It was constructed of mostly concrete and stone and sat nestled against the high peaks which served to camouflage it as well as make it imposing. From the rampart walls that surrounded it, one could see out over the sea to the south, and the sprawling jungle of the Grindlemoor to the west. Aside from the huge fortress, the facility also boasted a large courtyard which was buzzing with activity. Even with the wind and the blowing snow, shouts of men and women hard at work could be heard echoing from the walls and the peaks. They were unloading barrels from trucks, placing them on wooden pallets four at a time before steam tractors would hall them off.

From a window within the fortress, Ketrick Whitehall looked down over the area. He was idly stroking the fur of an overweight gray cat that was curled up on a pillow laid out on the windowsill. The cat's loud purr was the only sound in the room, beyond what little shouting from below managed to overcome the wind and the window. The bottom of the window was three panes of simple transparent glass set in brass frames carved with filigree. Above those, a tall stained-glass art piece depicted a man in white doing battle with another man in black who appeared to be his twin.

Ketrick sighed and turned away from the window. He pulled on a high-backed ornate leather chair that was resting behind a monstrous oak desk and sank into the seat. The desktop was immaculate and held nothing more on its surface than a single journal, an inkpot, and a quill pen. A hearth blazed to the left side of the room, casting a flickering orange light across the cold space, adding to the gentle glow of the glass lanterns that hung from the ceiling chandelier. A row of bookshelves filled the opposite wall, and a white-furred bearskin rug decorated the center of the floor. Despite the opulence of the desk and the window, it was a remarkably simple room of stone walls and a heavy wooden door, which squeaked as it was opened by a man who entered.

"Master Whitehall?" the man asked, barely taking a single step into the room.

Ketrick leaned back and kicked his feet up onto the desk. "What is it?" he asked.

The man swallowed and took a few more steps toward the desk, stopping only a foot or so away from the bearskin rug. He looked down at the face of the dead bear, mouth open, teeth glinting in the firelight. It was like the carpet itself was snarling at him.

"The trucks are almost unloaded, sir," the man stuttered.

"Good. Has there been word from Eiffert?"

The man nodded. "He just arrived, sir. He's on his way to see you."

"He's alive then," Ketrick said, leaning back in the chair.

Eiffert shuffled in through the door at that moment, pushing past the messenger.

"Sorry ta disappoint you, cousin," he barked.

Eiffert was a mess. Blood matted his hair and covered most of his face, and there were burns along his neck. His clothing was tattered and dried with blood, and most of his leather jacket was singed and cracked. His right hand was a massed wad of stained scrap clothing wound into a tight makeshift bandage. He limped as he walked, dragging his right leg, which kicked the bear in the face as he passed. Ketrick dropped his feet from the desk and sat up. Leaning forward, he laughed out loud as his cousin stopped before the desk.

"Eiff, you look awesome."

"Don't feel awesome," Eiffert replied, his grimace flaking off some of the dried blood on his face.

"What happened?" Ketrick asked, leaning back into the chair once more.

"Found the old man spillin' everything to his daughter and the cloudbreakers. It got ugly. The old man had a suit with him, never seen anything like it. Near ripped my hand off."

"And?" Ketrick asked coldly.

"And what, Ket? Hiram blew the damn lab up. Killed himself and everyone else so the girl could get away. I barely survived."

"Sir?" the messenger asked meekly from the door.

Ketrick ignored the messenger. His attention was focused on Eiffert.

"So the girl could get away?"

"He blew the lab up, Ket!"

"She got away?"

"Sir?"

Both Ketrick and Eiffert wheeled on the messenger and shouted in tandem. "What?!"

The messenger swallowed hard and stood aside.

"Cerin Barunn is here to see you, sir."

The temperature in the room seemed to drop as Ketrick watched the man who entered the room. He was medium height, with a stocky build and a square face. His black hair sat atop his head in a mess of curls, and he bore a thick beard that was trimmed short to match. He wore clothing that looked more like armour, adorned with brass fittings and hardened leather padding with shoulder pauldrons that sported black tassels. On his hip he carried a holstered clockwork pistol, and on his other, he bore a sheathed rapier with an ornate hilt. As he strode into the room, the messenger slipped out through the door and closed it behind him with a click.

Cerin stopped in front of the bear and looked down at its snarling face. When he lifted his eyes back up to meet them, Ketrick noticed a sheen. A momentary flash of yellow, like a cat's eyes struck by light in the darkness. His voice was shockingly cold when he spoke.

"My. What a mess you two have made."

"Cerin," Ketrick began as he stood from the chair. "I can explain."

"Save it," Cerin barked. Eiffert and Ketrick both flinched.

"You had a simple part to play in all of this, Ketrick Whitehall. Guard Hiram Errbryte. Keep him safe from scrutiny, and ensure he kept up his end of the bargain. That was it. Simple."

Cerin stalked toward the hearth as he finished speaking and stopped. He reached out and his fingers lingered on an iron fire poker leaning against the stone. After a moment of silence, he picked up the poker and stuck the tip into the coals of the fire.

"But you were so ambitious," Cerin continued. "You thought you could use Hiram. Blackmail him. Threaten him to work for you, all so you could build your own little empire, out from under your mother's skirt. And you thought you could do this without any of us knowing? Foolish mistake, Ketrick."

"Cerin," Ketrick pleaded. "The money from selling eleven was *for* you. It..."

Cerin suddenly drew the poker from the fire and pointed the glowing tip at Ketrick like a sword. Sparks and embers scattered across the floor.

"Enough! This is over, Ketrick. You're done. I'm taking the Midnight Storm. My men are loading it as we speak. The Raider was damaged when we took out the Cirrus. Which we did, by the way, to try and cover *your* mess. We underestimated their peregrine, and she made a huge mess of the ship. The Raider is yours now. I expect it repaired and combat-worthy immediately. As for your *eleven*, I'm taking what will fit in the Storm's hold."

Ketrick's face had gone ashen.

"What about us?" Eiffert asked.

Cerin turned his attention to Eiffert.

"What do we get from all this? We made the drug. We built all yer weapons. We *bled* for you!" Eiffert had crossed toward Cerin as he spoke, waving his arms in the air. He now stood on the bear rug as he finished his tirade. The crackle of the fire was the only sound in the room, and then Cerin lowered the poker and replaced it in the coals again.

Emboldened, Eiffert continued despite Ketrick's protest.

"I fought them cloudbreakers, pretty much lost my hand to that suit. Got all that eleven out too. Which you say you're takin' now? And we get a broken ship to fix? That eleven is worth a fortune, Cerin. You can't have it all."

"He's right Cerin," Ketrick added. "It's not quite fair."

"Fair," Cerin echoed.

In a blinding flash of movement that sent even more sparks and embers scattering across the floor, Cerin spun away from the hearth and drove the hot poker straight through the base of Eiffert's neck where his collarbones met. The hot metal hissed and sputtered as blood and flesh alike boiled on the exposed tip. Eiffert's body crumpled to the ground atop the bearskin rug, the hot poker beginning to melt the rug's fur. The smell of burning hair and blood filled the room, as Ketrick turned his attention back to Cerin.

Despite the grisly display, Ketrick shrugged. "I'm not sad about that," he said.

"Indeed," Cerin said as he rubbed his hands on his pants. "I'm leaving you with the gift of your life, Ketrick Whitehall. I do it only as a favour to your mother. I trust you will be more thankful and obedient in the days to come."

Ketrick nodded in silence as Cerin continued.

"With the Cirrus down, I am certain that high command will have every ship looking for the Raider. It was not my plan to reveal ourselves this soon. We are fortunate this facility is not associated with you or your family. That may buy us some time, as long as they don't know where you are."

"My family? No one knows we're involved."

Cerin gestured to the corpse of Eiffert, whose blood now stained the white fur of the rug.

"Your man told you. Hiram told them everything and Hope Errbryte escaped the estate. I'm sure the cloudbreakers with her did as well. When we attacked the Cirrus, they had just touched down in a meadow southwest of the estate. They were picking someone up."

"But you said you shot the Cirrus down."

"Indeed we did," Cerin's nod as he spoke was so deliberate and filled with malice that it sent shivers down Ketrick's spine. "But that peregrine destroyed our cannons and there was too much risk in lingering to finish the job. There's a good chance there were survivors. It stands to reason you will be implicated in all of this and to be fair, you deserve to be. You have threatened all my plans, Ketrick."

Ketrick sank into the chair. His eyes were wide, staring at Cerin. "What should I do?"

Cerin clasped his hands behind his back and shook his head. "Nothing."

"Nothing?"

"Yes, Ketrick. Nothing. You will fix the Raider, and you will do nothing. When I am ready for you, I will send word. But until then, you will do..."

Cerin waited patiently for Ketrick to finish the sentence.

"Nothing," Ketrick said.

"Good man," Cerin replied.

The door opened and a huge man stepped in. He was dressed the same as Cerin, with clothing more like armour, although he carried no weapons. He was more than a foot taller than Cerin, with a barrel chest and arms like a normal man's thighs. His head was shaved bald to the skin, and he had a striking tattoo of a coiled cobra that wrapped from his neck up over his scalp to its hissing mouth above his right eye. Like Cerin, his eyes shone like a cat in the firelight. Unlike Cerin, they were a steel-gray colour.

"Captain," the huge man said as he stopped just inside the door. "Midnight Storm is ready to sail. Waiting on you."

Cerin nodded. "Thank you, Kort. We're done here."

Kort walked through the door without acknowledging Ketrick or even glancing at the corpse on the rug. Cerin started to follow him but stopped at the door. He turned back to Ketrick after a moment of silence.

"You put Hiram Errbryte out of reach. You put the cloud-breakers on alert. And because of you, I've had to show my hand far ahead of schedule. If you so much as set *foot* outside this facility without my word, Ketrick Whitehall, I will erase you and your entire family from the face of this world. Mark my words."

With that, Cerin left and closed the door behind him, leaving Ketrick alone in the room choking on the smell of his murdered cousin and the burning hair of the rug. He sat back in the chair and rubbed his eyes. Suddenly something plopped in his lap and he screamed out loud in a high-pitched squeal. The startled cat hissed and shredded his thighs as it attempted to scurry its girth away from Ketrick's lap. The room in silence once more, his lap stinging, Ketrick leaned forward until his face thumped to the desk. He rolled his head to the side and watched the cat as it licked its paws in the corner by the bookshelves.

"I'm not afraid of him," he said to the cat. The furry creature paused its licking only momentarily and then continued.

Chapter 32

The ultimate sunset

Cole

Of all the wondrous places Cole had seen within the Starfall, the aft combat bridge was his favourite second only to the upper decks, which were currently off-limits due to altitude. The aft bridge was only manned during action stations for combat and was part of the pressurized citadel within the hull. The space offered the only view of the sky where Cole could be alone to see it. Elios had shown it to him during their tour. Cole had come here often over the last three days that they had been in the air.

The space was not unlike the other airship bridges that Cole had seen. It was mostly curved glass panels set inside steel ribs that afforded unimpeded views out and below the ship. Catwalks and platforms elevated within the space were supported by girders attached to the window ribs. There was a rotating chair in the center of the upper platform, and Elios had told him that was where Chelsea sat during combat. With the executive officer manning the aft bridge and the captain at the fore, they had exceptional situational awareness and could command the ship with incredible precision. It was in that chair that Cole sat when he needed to be alone with his thoughts.

Usually, Cole was never bothered while he was in the aft bridge. Of all the times he had found himself staring out across the sky he had only run into another soul once. Cole had come to the bridge at night and was watching the stars and the moon when a crew member on rounds had poked their head in. They conversed for only a few moments and then Cole had been left alone. Today he had come to watch the sun setting on the horizon. The sound of the hatch opening that led into the hallway beyond told him this day would not afford him such privacy.

Overcome by curiosity, Cole peeled his gaze away from the scenery and spun the chair toward the hatch. Hope had entered and was closing the steel door behind her, spinning the wheel and locking it in place. She was wearing a cloudbreakers uniform. It was the only spare clothes to be found aboard the ship which would fit her. Cole thought the uniform was quite fetching on her. She had long ago lost the ringlets to her hair, and now wore it straight but pulled back into a ponytail with two wispy bangs left loose to frame her face. She smiled at Cole as she stepped onto the catwalk that led to the chair he sat in.

"I was looking for you," she said as she approached.

Cole smiled back and turned the chair sideways. He leaned forward and looked out the port side windows. They were floating high in the sky above the clouds. The puffy white blanket over the world below spread out to the horizon like a sea of soft cotton, every once in a while marred by the snow-capped peaks of the Rinda Mountains as they poked through. At the edge of the world, the sun was just beginning its dip toward night, and golden light sprayed across the sky and the highest surfaces of the clouds and mountains. Hope stopped at Cole's side and looked out at the scenery with him.

"It's breathtaking," she said.

"Give it time," Cole replied, gesturing with his left hand. "As the sun sets, all this will change colour. From golden to the wildest pink and orange, and when that is over? More stars than you've ever seen. Like diamond dust on the blackest carpet."

"That's quite poetic."

"Trust me. It still doesn't do it justice."

The pair sat in silence for a time, with Cole leaning forward in the chair and Hope standing at his side leaning on the rails that ran around the circular platform. The hum of the ship's machinery and the hissing of the circulated air within the citadel were the only sounds. Just as Cole had described it the sky began to change colour, from a golden hue to a vibrant pink-orange with shades of red. The angle of the waning light only touched the highest edges of the clouds and peaks below, and the shadow of night approaching underneath it all created a rich contrast that escaped description.

"It's like a painting," Hope breathed.

"Yeah. I don't think I could describe it to anyone if I tried."

Hope kept her eyes on the scene before them until the colours shifted from their vibrant hues to bluish-gray. Then she turned her back and rested against the railing, looking instead at Cole. His eyes remained on the sky, and the green spot floating amid the brown seemed to shine brighter in the dying light.

"How are you feeling, Cole? How's your head?"

Cole sat back then and looked at Hope.

"I'm okay. At least as okay as I could be, given everything that's happened."

"I mean physically. No more headaches?"

"No. None."

"Dizziness? Lethargy?"

"Lethargy?" Cole asked as he started to swivel the chair side to side.

"Tired. Even after sleeping a lot. Low energy."

Cole stopped swivelling the chair.

"No. None of that. Honestly, I feel great."

"Have you," Hope paused. "Had any more visions?"

Cole's smile faded. A forlorn look came over his face as he considered his answer.

"No."

Hope shifted uneasily.

"Cole, I'm sorry. But I need to know you're not seeing things that aren't there. I care about your health, that's all. I'm worried."

"They were there," Cole snapped. "They were there just as you are now."

"Cole, please. Don't get angry."

Cole stood from the chair and paced around it.

"I'm sorry, but how can I not? You don't believe me. I saw those wolves, Hope. I could smell their breath. See their footprints. The big one pointed its head *right* at Aislinn. I wouldn't have found her without it."

"Cole, try to understand from my point of view. I saw nothing. Not even the footprints you tried to show me."

"You said you *did* see prints."

"Well yes, but Cole, they must have been a year old. Maybe longer."

"So how does that mean I have the problem?"

Hope was shocked. "What?"

"You say I saw things that weren't there. What if it was *you* who could not see things that *were*? Is it possible that somehow the wolves appeared only for me?"

Hope swallowed. "I hadn't considered that."

Cole lowered his head. He approached Hope and reached out, placing his hand on the side of her face. His gaze buried deep inside her own.

"I see you. Right now. You're real. I smell your breath, just like theirs, only yours is more like cinnamon and bread."

Hope chuckled. "Becky made those sweet treats of hers."

"Did you save me any?"

Hope shrugged.

"Anyway, Hope. The wolves were real to me. I don't know why I could see them when no one else could. But I am *not* crazy.

It wasn't a hallucination, even though I'm scared it could have been. I have to believe it wasn't."

Hope was trembling. "Cole, have you read Wolves of the Grindlemoor?"

"Yes."

"Do you think..." Cole interrupted her by lowering his hand from her face and pacing back to the chair. He sank into it with a resigned sigh.

"It crossed my mind. But if it *was* a Guardian of the Forest, why was it helping us? The crash scarred a huge part of the forest."

Hope reached up and touched the place on her face where Cole's hand had been. She could still feel warmth there.

"Can I tell you something, Hope?"

Hope lowered her hand away from her face when he looked at her, nodding wordlessly in answer to his question.

"I think I'm cursed."

Hope flinched like she had been slapped.

"What?" she asked.

"Just something I've been told all my life, and I'm starting to wonder if it's true. My Mom had the same eyes that I do. Marked with a bit of green and otherwise brown. Folk back home used to say she was cursed, and that her curse passed to me when I was born with the same eyes. They say that's why she died in childbirth."

Hope listened intently as Cole continued.

"I was bullied all my life because of my eyes. They called it the Vallen curse. I had no real friends until Rikket, but then ..." he choked up a bit, swallowed, and went on. "Well. With everything that's happened, I'm sure starting to think the curse is real."

His eyes turned up to Hope. The shimmer of tears in them made the green shine all the brighter.

"Cole," she said as she held back her own flood of emotions. "I don't know what I believe."

"Is magic real?" Cole asked.

Hope shrugged. "People once thought so."

"What do you think?"

"I don't know for sure. Much of alchemy is science, but the older practices relied on things some might call magic."

"I mean magic like in the old legends."

Hope turned and looked out at the darkening sky. She wanted to hide the tears she could no longer hold back.

"My father," she caught herself in time to suppress a sob. "He used to tell me that all legend is grown from a seed of truth. He would say that the essence of all story can be found in its unravelling. True wisdom is born from seeing through the leaves and the fruit, tracing the branches to their trunk, and reading the roots until you find those seeds of truth."

Cole stood from the chair and stepped beside her. She let go of her fight to hold her grief back and fell into his arms.

"I miss him so much," she sobbed into Cole's chest. "I can't believe he's gone."

Cole held her tight and cried along with her. The images of Rikket that he had relived in the Errbryte library flashed through his mind, as did the slap and the look of rage on Seran Se'Baht's face when she blamed him for it. The sky darkened further as they cried together. It was a release of pent-up grief for both of them. Eventually, it was Hope who pushed away but kept herself within arms reach. She wiped the tears away from her eyes with her sleeve.

"Light look at us," she giggled despite her sobs. "What a mess."

Cole smiled and wiped his own tears the same way she had.

"Had it coming, I suppose. I think I might be surprised it took this long. We've been through a lot."

Hope put her hand on Cole's chest over his heart. She could feel the thumping of his heartbeat through his uniform.

"Cole, I..."

Cole stole her breath with a kiss before she could finish what she was saying. He was gentle, but passionate as he held her close and pressed his lips to hers. When he pulled away, both of them gasped for breath. They swayed, even though the ship had not rocked.

"I'm sorry..."

Cole started to speak, but Hope grabbed his collar and pulled him in again for another kiss. His hand cupped the back of her neck as her other hand did the same. When the second kiss ended, they held each other still in the same way. Hope was lost in Cole's brown-green eyes, and he in the sky-blue of hers.

"I do believe in curses, Cole Vallen," Hope said. "But I don't believe that you are."

"Is that why you kissed me?"

Hope giggled and slapped Cole's chest, pushing him away.

"You kissed me first."

Cole shrugged. "Then you kissed me back, so."

Hope took Cole's hand in her own as she leaned against the railing. He stood beside her, idly stroking the back of her hand with his thumb. Outside, the sky had succumbed to darkness, and the stars shone in abundance.

"Diamonds against the blackest curtain," Hope whispered.

"Told you."

Hope smiled. "Yes. You did."

"Cole," Hope said after a long silence. "What happens to us now?"

"What do you mean?"

"When we find the rogue airship. What if the Ciar K'hen are involved in some way, and there's another war? With you becoming a cloudbreaker, will you go off and fight?"

"I don't know. I hadn't thought of that."

"I hope it never comes to that."

Cole squeezed Hope's hand.

"We will have to see what happens," he whispered.

Cole thought back to all the times he had laid awake at night in his bed growing up. How he had yearned for his eighteenth birthday so he could enlist and go off to war and adventure. Thinking about it now, the idea made him sick to his stomach.

In the Cirrus attack, he had been given a taste of what war truly was. The shock, the loss, and the fear. He was no longer naive enough to believe that a single skirmish could hold a candle to the experience of an all-out war, but he was at last wise enough to extrapolate it. Aside from his father and Rikket, he never truly had anything to live for. He had always believed his life was forfeit and better served in sacrifice for others. Yet now he had Aislinn. He had all the other cloudbreakers. And he had Hope.

The ship's intercom hissed and Captain McCray's voice filled the silence.

"All hands, this is the captain."

Hope giggled and said, "We know," which made Cole laugh too. They tried to control themselves and listen as the captain continued.

"We have just received word that the Cirrus crew dispatched by Chief Parvelle have located the rogue airship at a fortress monastery in the southern Rindas near the coast. Ketrick Whitehall and a stockpile of the eleven taken from the Errbryte estate are believed to be there. This facility is high-altitude and may be heavily armed. We have no time to wait for assistance. We're going in alone. We must strike fast, or we risk losing the element of surprise. They shot down one of our own. Many of our brethren are now lost to us because of this cowardly action. We do this for them. Be prepared. If you don't have to stand, sit. If you don't have to sit, lie down. If you don't have to be awake, sleep. We attack at dawn. To the rise!"

Cole and Hope both threw their fists in the air as they shouted in tandem, "For the fallen!"

Chapter 33

Swift and decisive

Dakota/Remmy

Dakota shivered as he crawled up to the edge of the cliff he and Remmy were perched on. The cold stone and thin layer of snow seemed to sink through his clothes and flesh to chill his bones directly. From the edge of the rocky outcropping they were on, they had a full view of the fortress monastery below and the road leading up to it. Remmy had shuffled up to the edge first, and when he had signalled Dakota they were clear, Dakota had secured the transmitting repeater still inside the cello case and crawled to the edge beside his shipmate.

It had taken the pair the better part of a day and most of the following night, but they had successfully skirted the facility without being seen and climbed the mountainside to their current perch. For the most part, the climb had been uneventful beyond the difficulty of carrying the cello case and repeater up the steep ascent. In the late evening hours of the first night, Remmy had thought he saw the rogue ship leave and head down the mountains toward the ocean. As they looked at the facility below now, they could clearly see he had been mistaken. In the courtyard below them, the rogue hull was in full view with personnel scampering all over it like ants trying to dissect the damage and make repairs.

"By the light," Dakota whistled softly. "Something made a right mess out of that hull. It looks like all the cannons are blown to bits. Even whatever that thing on the bow is."

Remmy nodded his agreement and squinted his eyes to see better in the pre-dawn light that was just beginning to drive the dark away.

"They've been at it 'round the clock," Remmy said. "Is that hull one of ours?"

"I don't recognize it at all. It's nothing like any airship I've ever seen. Maybe a new type of ship the Whitehalls are building?" Dakota asked.

"Dunno," Remmy whispered. His attention was rapt on the facility far below. "Never seen a hull like that outside of ocean liners. Looks like mostly wood. Something tore it up good though. Think it was the Cirrus?"

"Maybe," Dakota replied. "Hey, you remember on the barge? Those guys were talking about the raider. You think it could be that ship?"

Remmy shook his head. "No idea."

Dakota watched the facility in silence for a time. A handful of guards patrolled the rampart walls, always in pairs. There were four towers that the walls connected as they closed in the central courtyard where the airship was docked. Each roof was metal and glinted with thin traces of snow and frost in the rising light. Dakota pointed at them.

"Look like those towers open to you?"

Remmy nodded.

"Mmhm. I'd say is likely. Whoever's doin' this is sure goin' to a lot of effort to protect whatever it is. Seems way beyond anything that Ketrick 'n Eiffert could pull off."

Dakota looked back behind them to where he had left the cello case. He had secured it open with a rope tying it to a tree at the base of the next rise in the mountain. They had found a small flat area with a small stand of four or five high-alpine trees to provide shelter from the wind. It was a great place to make camp and provide surveillance until their backup had arrived. Dakota watched the little green light inside the vacuum tube on top of the repeater. It would come on for twenty seconds and then shut off for five. Dakota counted for two cycles of the light going on and off again.

"Repeater good?" Remmy asked when Dakota returned to his surveillance over the facility.

"Light is green. Repeating every twenty-five, just like protocol."

Remmy shuffled his position trying to be more comfortable. "Wish they'd make 'em two-way," he said.

Dakota nodded. "No doubt. It sure would be nice to know when we could expect company."

"Or even if they got the messages," Remmy replied.

At that moment, the repeater made an audible click sound followed by a quiet whine that dropped in pitch until it stopped. Dakota looked back at the machine. The light was off, and it stayed off longer than it should. The pair shared a quick look, and then Dakota slid down from the edge until he was far enough away from the edge to crouch up and move to the cello case. He tapped the light a few times, then flipped the transmit switch on and off twice. Nothing happened. He picked up the transmitter unit and turned it over. Nothing was broken or out of the ordinary, so Dakota folded out the crank mechanism on the bottom and gave it a couple of spins. He turned the machine back over and watched the light. Nothing.

"Damn," he breathed as he set the machine back inside the cello case. Remmy slid down from the edge and shuffled over to join Dakota.

"What happened?" Remmy asked.

Dakota shrugged. "I don't know. Seems it just stopped."

The two of them worked on the machine together, following the protocols they knew of for a reset and trying to restart the repeater. Whatever they tried, the machine just refused to continue functioning. Eventually, they set it back down in the cello case and sat back in the snow. Remmy pulled out some rations from a pocket inside his coat and handed one to Dakota. They were chewy bars wrapped in cheesecloth. Dakota took it and unwrapped it as Remmy bit into his own.

"Where did you get these?" Dakota asked as he sniffed the bar.

"Found a box of 'em on the raft," he said as he chewed. "Ne'er be too prepared ya know."

Dakota sighed at the horrid smell of the bar but sunk his teeth in despite it. The taste was about as bad as the smell was. He almost gagged, but fought the urge and continued eating.

"Better n' dyin'," Remmy said as he finished the last of the bar. He picked up a bit of snow from the ground and used it to wash his hands, drying them against the thighs of his pants. When he was finished, he nodded toward the repeater.

"Worked for quite some time 'fore it broke," he said.

Dakota nodded and looked at the repeater also. It was strange seeing the machine silent after the last few days of steady transmission.

"It was sending the location since we rolled off those trucks and changed the message. They should have heard it. We'll stay as long as we can here, but if no one comes we might have to start thinking of a way off this mountain. "

A whooshing sound from above them caught their attention, and they looked up just in time to see Elios Rayos and three other Peregrines descending from the sky above them. They dropped perilously close to the treetops along the mountain, using the pre-dawn darkness as cover. As they approached the landing where Remmy and Dakota waited, they folded their wings in and spun so their feet faced the ground. Quick controlled bursts of steam from their packs slowed their descent so that when they touched down, it was as though they had stepped off a short chair or stool. With a series of whirs and clicks, their wings folded in and locked and they crouched down to approach the Cirrus crew.

"By the light," Dakota said as he reached out and clapped Elios' hand in his own. "You sir, are a sight for sore eyes."

Elios nodded at Dakota and Remmy as the three peregrines with him also shook hands with the Cirrus crew. One of the peregrines knelt on the ground near the cello case while another unclipped a long narrow duffel bag from his back. Remmy watched with curiosity as they set the duffle down and two other pouches with it.

"I guess you got our message," Dakota said to Elios.

"Chief Parvelle did. Passed the frequency over when we picked them up. We've been tracking ever since. Lucius said you might want a toy."

Elios nodded toward the duffel bag, and Remmy scooted over and started opening it. While Remmy was working on the bag, Elios motioned for Dakota to approach the ridge with him.

"What are we looking at?" Elios asked as they reached the edge.

Dakota pointed down at the facility below.

"We count sixty, maybe seventy people down there. Guards on the rampart patrol in pairs. They're pretty well-armed. Whitehall weapons, all of them. Javelin rifles too, or something like it anyway. Remmy found a crate of them on the barge. Looked like some kind of bolo spear, but grenade-tipped."

"What are they doing?"

"Mostly working on that hull down there. That or unloading barrels that came in on trucks from the barge we caught."

"Well, that hull is in worse shape than I imagined. That's good news."

"You know what tore it up like that?"

Elios smiled. "That would be Aislinn."

Dakota smirked. "Ha. Yeah, sounds like something she would do. I'm surprised it made it back here then."

Elios pointed at the rampart towers. "Do those towers open?"

"They haven't, not since we've been here. But we suspect they do."

"Well, we won't let them. That's what we're here for."

"If the Starfall *and* the Cirrus are here, they won't stand a chance."

Elios sighed and scooted back from the edge to rejoin the others. Dakota followed. As Dakota reached the back of the landing where the others crouched, he met the shining eyes of a grinning Remmy. He held a long precision rifle equipped with a telescope lens in his hands. Beside it was a larger spotting scope with a tripod and a stack of ammunition. Dakota took the gun when Remmy offered it and looked it over. It was a masterwork Whitehall rifle with a wooden stock and a long, machined barrel. Two spring-stabilized bipod legs were attached to its fore-end.

"Can you and Remmy provide support from up here?" Elios asked Dakota. "Lucius says you're one of the best marksmen he's ever seen."

"I won't let you down, Elios," Dakota replied.

"You can spot for him, Remmy?"

Remmy nodded.

Elios lowered his voice and reached out to rest his hands on Dakota and Remmy's shoulders. "Gents, you should know, the Cirrus was grounded outside the Errbryte estate. That rogue hull down there was responsible. A lot of good cloudbreakers lost their lives. Aislinn is in bad shape, but she's alive. So is Lucius, Hope Errbryte, the Vallen boy, and many others. We're still collecting the names of all the fallen."

Dakota's grip tightened on the rifle. The wood on the stock squeaked in protest and his knuckles became white.

"Keep that fire," Elios continued. "But stay grounded. Today is about answers. The Starfall is here. It's holding station above the clouds until I give the signal. We're going to storm that facility, level it if we have to, and we're going to get answers. Watch our backs?"

Dakota and Remmy nodded.

Elios motioned to his team and they crawled to the edge of the cliff. He turned back and gave a thumbs up to Dakota and Remmy, and then he and his team dropped off the edge. Dakota and Remmy scurried to the edge after them and immediately began setting up the precision rifle and spotting scope. Dakota watched as the four peregrines below unfurled their wings and with a short burst of steam, shot off over the treetops toward the facility below.

Dakota brought the rifle stock to his shoulder and settled into eye relief behind the scope. There was no need for the bipod mounts as the rifle easily rested against the rock on its downward angle. He made a few adjustments to the aperture for ranging and then began scanning the rampart walls through the telescopic lenses. Beside him, Remmy had set up with the extra ammo within his reach, and his spotting scope leveled at the facility.

"Two on the rampart by the tower closest," Remmy said.

Dakota centred the pair of guards in his scope as they exited a door in the tower closest to the monastery. They were directly in the path of the approaching peregrine team, walking side by side oblivious to the cloudbreakers. Dakota lifted the bolt on the rifle and slid it back. A round rose from the magazine below the chamber, and Dakota pushed the bolt forward with the round loaded into breach.

"Ready," Dakota replied.

One of the guards stopped and turned toward the court-yard to look at something happening below the wall. The other guard continued forward.

"Take the first guard," Remmy said. "Fire."

Dakota took his shot. The sound the rifle ushered forward was little more than a pop, yet far below, a spray of stone erupted from the side of the wall outside the rampart and below the target. The guard turned toward the noise from the impact and moved to the edge of the wall to look over. They were so far away, and high enough on the mountainside, that the sound of the rifle shot was masked by the construction noise and the sound of the forklifts and trucks.

"Impact on the wall low and left," Remmy whispered. Dakota made the corrections to his scope.

"Ready," Dakota said.

"Fire."

The second shot found its mark and the guard collapsed forward, tilting over the edge of the rampart wall and falling out into the dark woods below. The second guard who had been looking into the courtyard spun around.

"Secon' guard," Remmy said.

Dakota racked his rifle to load a new round and set his sights on the man now rushing across the rampart. The man was already yelling.

"Ready."

"Fire."

Just as the second guard reached the edge and looked over, Dakota's shot found its mark and the man fell over backward onto the concrete. Shortly after that, the four peregrines arrived at the wall and landed. Dakota watched through his rifle scope, careful to lead the sights away from his fellow cloudbreakers, as they collapsed their wings and split up. Two made their way to the first tower on their right. Elios and the fourth peregrine surveyed the second guard that Dakota had shot. Elios gave a thumbs up in Remmy and Dakota's direction and then rushed toward the second tower further down the rampart wall followed by his partner.

"Good shooting," Remmy whispered. He surveyed ahead of the second tower. "Two at port, comin' toward the second tower."

Dakota swung his rifle left and saw the guards Remmy was indicating. They were heading along the next section beyond the second tower Elios was heading for. Dakota set his sights on the one leading.

"Adjust up for range."

Dakota made the corrections.

"Ready."

"Fire."

The guard fell.

"Secon' guard."

"Ready."

"Fire."

As the last guard collapsed to the ground, Elios reached the second tower and ducked inside. The other two peregrines who had entered the first tower now exited and were scooting across the rampart section to join Elios at tower two. By the time they arrived, Elios and his man were already rushing past the second pair of downed guards toward tower three. All the while Remmy and Dakota tracked them, downing the guards who patrolled the rampart ahead of them systematically.

Dakota and Remmy watched as the four peregrines ran from tower to tower until they reached the final one on the opposite side of the courtyard. As three of the cloudbreakers ducked inside, Elios waited on the rampart, watching the Courtyard below. Steam tractors were bringing loads of equipment and supplies out to the construction happening around the airship. There was a large bi-fold door to the left of the stairs leading into the monastery. People and machines were coming in and out.

From his scope, Dakota saw Elios suddenly turn toward the tower. Two of his peregrines came out, but the fourth did not. The three of them jumped from the wall and used steam bursts to land safely on the ground in the courtyard. The first tower suddenly erupted in a ball of fire and shattered stone and metal. The second tower followed, then the third. The fourth tower remained standing. A claxon alarm began to ring and echoed off the mountainside, making it sound otherworldly. The courtyard was in complete chaos.

"They missed one," Dakota said. "I guess we'll know if they open now."

And the fourth tower did start to open. The peaked roof came apart like the petals of a flower, rolling out and revealing a mounted cannon system inside with four barrels. It was slow to turn, but the cannon barrels started moving in their direction.

"Can they see us?" Remmy asked.

"I don't know," Dakota asked, frantically scanning the gun platform for a target.

"Do you have a shot?"

Dakota saw that there were three men rapidly spinning wheels to move the cannons and another sitting in a chair behind a sighting device that appeared to be connected to the barrels. When the barrels moved, so did the whole chair the gunner was sitting in. Dakota tried a shot but his rifle clicked.

"Empty! Need a new magazine."

Remmy quickly fished a magazine out of the pouches beside him and handed it to Dakota who slammed it into the rifle and chambered a new round.

"Wait," Remmy said as he returned to his spotter scope. "They're moving past us."

"What are they aiming at then?" Dakota asked as he scanned the courtyard through his scope. He lifted his head from eye relief and looked at Remmy. "Do you hear that?"

Above them, the hull of the Starfall suddenly dropped through the clouds, piercing a hole in the thick cover. Sunlight from an early dawn above the clouds came with it. For a moment the ship was bathed in a radiant yellow-orange light that faded away when the hole in the clouds closed. The Starfall hovered above like an avenging dragon, drifting broadside and bringing its cannons to bear on the facility below. In the courtyard, Elios and his team fought with personnel that had surrounded them. Seeing the Starfall above, Elios waved to his men, and they started making their way towards the stairs leading into the monastery.

"We have to cover the peregrines!" Remmy shouted. "Two men behind that crate, between them and the stairs."

"Got them!" Dakota said as he loosed rounds that dropped both targets one after another.

The peregrines fought through some remaining personnel and started heading up the stairs.

"Coming up behind, beside that steam tractor."

Dakota's first round hit the tractor and sparked off, making the men duck. They looked around, unsure where the shot had come from. When they stepped out, Dakota dropped them. Moments later the peregrines vanished indoors. As soon as they had, the Starfall opened up with a broadside salvo from all cannons that decimated the rogue hull and a large portion of the courtyard. Most of the remaining people near it were scattered along with the debris.

"By the *light,* I'll never get used to seeing that," Dakota shouted. His ears were ringing from the barrage of the Starfall's cannons. Remmy was still glued to his spotting scope.

"There's still that tower cannon," Remmy said.

Dakota dropped into eye relief and quickly found the cannon again in his site. He tried to fire a shot at the operator, but the round ricocheted off the sighting device. The operator flinched.

"I can't hit the cannoneer!" Dakota shouted.

"I'm right here, 'kota. You don't have to shout."

"Sorry!" Dakota shouted back. "My ears are ringing!"

Dakota held his breath and tried to steady his aim. Another shot ricocheted off the sighting device. Dakota stretched and then relaxed his trigger hand. He took a deep breath, exhaled, took another, and then exhaled. When he had ejected half of his breath, he held the remainder and squeezed the trigger. The cannoneer in the seat slumped forward, and then the tower exploded.

"I got him!" Dakota shouted.

"It was a nice shot," Remmy agreed. "But the Starfall blew the tower up."

Dakota lifted out of eye relief and watched as the mangled barrels of the tower cannon crumpled down to the courtyard below. Behind his spotter scope, Remmy was laughing.

Chapter 34

Full broadside

Cole

Cole Vallen stood against the centre platform railing of the aft bridge on the Starfall. The bridge was fully manned, with Chelsea Gisborne seated on the swivel chair at its epicentre. They had just heard Captain McCray give the order to descend once they saw the explosions below. Elios' team had been sent to recon and destroy any anti-airship weapons the facility might have. Cole watched from the bridge as the ship descended from the bright light of dawn above to the darkness of the clouds and then below into dusk. The mountainside fortress monastery sat below them, nestled against a rugged peak. Fire and smoke billowed from three destroyed towers and Cole saw the rogue hull docked in the middle of the courtyard. He recognized every detail of the enemy ship, even the scars of Aislinn's attack on it.

"That's it!" Cole shouted and pointed below. "That's the ship that attacked us."

Chelsea leaned forward and spoke with terrifying authority such that her voice boomed throughout the aft bridge even though she was not shouting. An intercom device beside her carried her voice to the forward bridge where Captain McCray was waiting.

"Target confirmed. Vallen has positively identified the rogue hull in the courtyard below."

The intercom crackled and Captain McCray's voice rolled over it in response.

"Acknowledged. Helm to 119. Bring us broadside at level. Commander Gisborne, you are clear to fire. Make sure that vessel stays on the ground."

In the background, Cole could hear the helmsman repeating the captain's positioning order. Chelsea was already commanding her crew in the aft bridge.

"All port cannons, target the hull. Confirm range is clean."

A crew member sitting at one of the stations below Cole with their face pressed into a scoping lens called out in response. "Range is not clean! Peregrine Rayos and his team are pinned down. Commander, one of the towers is open. Four cannons are training on us."

"Stay on the ship," Chelsea commanded. "We'll deal with the tower after the rogue hull."

"Commander, someone is helping the peregrine team. I'm seeing evidence of marksman support. They're making their way inside."

"Peregrine Rayos must have found the Cirrus crew," Chelsea said.

"They have just entered the monastery, commander. The range is clean."

"Port cannons are locked on, commander. Target confirmed. Ready to fire on your order," another crew member said.

Chelsea leaned forward in her chair.

"Fire."

Cole gripped the railing anxiously just as the whole hull rumbled and lurched sideways. The side of the mountain lit up from all the barrels discharging at once, and almost immediately the entire courtyard below turned to fire and black smoke. Cole looked around outside through the windows. He noticed that the Starfall seemed to be drifting slightly, and surmised that the salvo had actually moved the entire ship. They had already stopped and were drifting back into their original position when Cole returned his attention to the facility below. As the smoke cleared, Cole noticed the rogue hull was mostly a scorched and burning wreck. He saw movement beside the wreckage. Two trucks were racing toward the front gate of the courtyard.

"Commander Gisborne," the scoped spotter below Cole said. "The tower is almost trained on us. I'm seeing sparks and the gunner is dodging something. I think our marksmen are trying to stop him."

"Let's do it for them, shall we? Target the tower. One cannon. The rest, prepare to fire on the rogue hull again. I want nothing left of that ship."

"Port cannons locked on, commander. Targets confirmed."

"Fire."

Again, the cannons roared. This time the tower disintegrated as well as what remained of the enemy airship.

"Commander Gisborne?" Cole said.

"Yes, Mister Vallen?"

"Two trucks are heading for the courtyard gate."

"Spotter confirm?"

"Confirmed," the spotter replied almost immediately. "Two power wagons, close formation, heading for the main gate out of the courtyard."

"Target the gate. Stop those trucks," Chelsea commanded.

"Cannons locked on," the gunnery director said. "Target confirmed."

"Fire."

Once more the hull shuddered and the mountains lit. The rampart gates erupted, sending stone and metal showering across the courtyard and the road beyond.

"I want confirmation those trucks cannot escape, spotter."

"Yes, commander," the spotter replied, moving his scope around as he waited for the smoke and debris to clear. "Both trucks have stopped. Occupants abandoning. Looks like the gate is destroyed, Commander."

Cole was in awe of the precision with which the crew worked together. Captain McCray on the bridge coordinating the ship's positioning and Chelsea in the aft bridge directing the guns was like watching an orchestra play. Everything they did was precise and calculated, checked and double-checked. Cole had grown up on stories of the Starfall's power, but he and Rikket had always believed it to be propaganda. Seeing the reality made Cole realize the stories did not do the ship justice.

"Mister Vallen," Chelsea said softly. Cole turned to look at her and found she was swivelled toward him and leaning forward in her chair. She curled her finger toward him, beckoning him closer. Cole approached.

"Commander?" he asked when he was at the base of her chair.

"How is it you knew about those trucks before my spotter did?"

Cole swallowed. "I could see them, commander."

"You could see them. From this height. Unassisted. Through all that chaos?"

"Yes, commander," Cole replied weakly. "I don't know how to explain it."

"What would you do next, if you were me?" Chelsea asked.

"Is this a test?" Cole asked sheepishly.

Chelsea did not answer. Instead, she bore into him with her breathtaking green eyes and waited. Cole blushed and turned away, his gaze quickly sweeping across the estate below. The towers were torn asunder and collapsed. Two of them were on fire. The rogue hull was a shattered and smoking heap, and the courtyard and rampart walls were a chaotic mess of shattered equipment, machinery, and bodies. There was still movement though, a small force of people heading toward the main door of the monastery. Cole watched as some of them fell before reaching the steps. They did not get up.

"The road," Cole said almost under his breath.

"Beg your pardon?" Chelsea asked.

"The road. The one coming up the mountain that leads to the facility. We may have destroyed their gate, but look," Cole pointed to the ruined rampart walls where the gate once stood. "There's still room for a truck to get through the rubble right there. It's small, but I think a good driver could do it. I can count three, no, four more trucks against that far wall of the courtyard. They don't look damaged yet. If the enemy regroups or overcomes Peregrine Rayos and his team, that road is their best chance of escape. Even with the air advantage, we could lose them if they make it to the tree line."

Cole turned to Chelsea. Her face was unreadable. "If we destroy the road, it won't matter how many trucks they have. Plus," Cole hesitated a moment. "Plus we could capture the functional trucks and not have to destroy them. If we need it, the road can be repaired after the battle."

Chelsea nodded and stood from the chair. She walked to the railing and looked down at the facility below. She was silent a long time, and Cole wondered if he had crossed a line. The rest of the bridge crew was quiet, looking at their commander and waiting for new orders.

"Spotter," The man at the lens jumped when she called on him. "Confirm remaining trucks in the courtyard. Is there space for one of them to get through the rubble at the gate?"

Cole felt the hair on his neck standing on end while he waited for a response from the spotter. Chelsea never took her eyes off the facility below.

"Confirmed, commander. There are four undamaged power wagons against the far wall, as well as the two that were abandoned. There appears to be a gap in the rubble, though it's little more than a path. It may be big enough for a power wagon to thread through the destroyed gate."

Chelsea rapped her fingertips on the railing.

"Gunnery, target the road beyond the facility. Have the cannons pick separate spots along the way down the mountain. Deactivate the road. Fire at will."

As Chelsea turned away from the railing and strode back to her chair, the guns lit up in rapid sequence but one at a time, not a full salvo like before. The ship shook, but softer, and the Starfall did not drift as it had before. One by one, eruptions of fire, dirt, and stone rose from the ground beyond the facility.

"Commander Gisborne," came the captain's voice over the intercom. "Why are we digging holes?"

"We are cutting off the only escape route for trucks, captain. Confirmed four functional vehicles below. Two more abandoned beside the target vessel may still be operational."

Chelsea smiled at Cole.

"I had a hunch we could use those assets."

"Well done, commander," came the captain's reply.

The cannons stopped firing and the smoke began to clear below. The road had been torn apart for a substantial distance as it led downhill from the facility. The bridge was eerily quiet. Cole turned his attention to the destruction below. He searched for movement, but the only thing moving was fire and smoke. He jumped when he realized Chelsea was standing beside him.

"Remarkable," she said.

Cole nodded. "I know. I can't believe how quickly it all happened."

"This is how most airship battles go, Mister Vallen, if appropriately prepared."

"I was expecting more of a fight. Is it actually over?"

Chelsea paused a moment beside Cole. Her jaw set as though she was going to say something but thought not to.

"Spotter, confirm the site is sterile," she finally said.

"Confirmed," came the response a moment later. "Target vessel is destroyed, no movement within the courtyard, all towers non-functional. Site is sterile."

Chelsea turned her head over her shoulder.

"Captain McCray, Aft bridge."

"Go ahead Aft," replied the captain.

"Site is confirmed sterile. The ground team is green."

"Acknowledged, commander. The ground team is green. Helm to heading 32. Docking altitude above the courtyard."

Chelsea turned to face Cole as the ship began descending and spinning toward the facility instead of being broadside to it.

Below him on a rocky outcropping with a handful of trees, Cole spotted Remmy and Dakota as they stood up from their spot on the edge of the rocks.

"For the record, Mister Vallen," Chelsea said. "I was referring to you when I said remarkable."

Cole did not know how to respond. His mouth opened and then quickly closed again. He stared at Chelsea, suddenly insecure without his glasses to hide his marked eyes.

"Your situational awareness alone is impressive," Chelsea continued. "But what you can do with those eyes is remarkable. I would have a hard time seeing the things you saw even if I had a spotting glass. That spotter there, the lenses he looks through magnify the ground more than ten times, yet he saw it all after you did. With your naked eye. That is more than smarts, Cole Vallen. You are blessed. That is a rare gift I have only seen once before in my life."

Cole swallowed hard and finally found his voice. "With Aislinn?"

"No. Not with Aislinn."

Chelsea turned and walked past Cole toward the hatch leading inside the ship's hull.

"Aft bridge dismissed. Prepare for grounding. We still have a job to do."

She stopped at the edge of the catwalk as the bridge crew left their stations and emptied through the hatch into the hull. When it was just her and Cole left in the space, she turned her attention to him once more.

"It was Aislinn's brother, Bayne Elissan."

Chapter 35

Thunder and Stone

Ketrick

Ketrick Whitehall had been leaning back in his chair with his feet up when the first tower outside exploded. The sound had rattled the stained glass and caused Ketrick to fall out of his chair. The pudgy cat had been sleeping on his pillow on the windowsill. He tore the pillow completely asunder trying to escape the boom. Ketrick had never seen the cat move so fast as he darted across the room and out the door into the monastery beyond. By the time the second tower blew, Ketrick was on his feet racing after the cat. He almost crashed into his messenger who was coming in the door at the same time Ketrick was heading out.

"We're under attack, sir!" the messenger said.

Ketrick gave him a look of pure disgust and then shoved him. The third tower blew up at that moment. A piece of the stained-glass window rattled free by the explosions fell to the floor and shattered.

"I can see we're under attack. Do you have anything useful to offer?"

The courtyard was a cacophony of shouting and gunfire.

"Is it an airship? Have the men prepare the flak cannons. Let's show them the surprises we've been working on here."

The messenger winced like a scolded child and pointed back out the window.

"Sir," he said meekly. "Those were the flak cannons. All the towers but one are destroyed."

Ketrick turned his head and looked to see three smoking ruins where his hidden weapon systems once were. The final tower to the right of his window was just opening. He could hear the shouts of personnel outside, and guns being fired. Then there was a flash of light and a brief whistling sound. The darkness inside his office became daylight momentarily as the cannon shells erupted what remained of the Raider. The concussion from the blast eradicated the stained-glass window, sending a maelstrom of debris flying into the room. When the force hit Ketrick and the messenger, it knocked both of them off their feet.

Ketrick sat up first and wiped blood from the many cuts on his face. The window frame was decimated, as was his chair and desk. He realized he and his messenger had both been thrown at least ten paces and were now lying right at the base of the far wall. Outside in the courtyard, all he could see was fire and destruction. He watched as the only remaining tower cannon turned on its target, but a second round of incoming fire destroyed it. As the ringing in his ears lowered, the sounds of screaming and yelling rolled over him, along with something else. Power wagon engines.

"Cowards," he whispered as he struggled to his feet. "Come on, we have to..."

The messenger was dead. The shards of glass embedded in his chest and face were likely more than enough to kill him, but Ketrick reckoned it was the awkward bend to his neck that finished the job. He was pressed up against the wall almost as though he were sleeping, but his shoulders were flush with the stone and his head hung limp and impossibly forward over his chest.

"Great," Ketrick said as he stumbled through the door. "I have to do everything myself."

As Ketrick fell into the hallway beyond the main chamber, another explosion rumbled the ground beneath his feet. He could hear his personnel shouting ahead of him, and the sound of their feet stomping the stone floors as they ran. He leaned against the stone for support as he trudged forward. Gunshots rang out, followed by more screams. Then a series of individual explosions outside. They sounded farther away. Blood stained the wall as Ketrick moved on. It was oozing from a wound on his upper left arm. Glass, most likely.

The room started to spin, and the torchlight that lit the stone halls began to fade. Ketrick reached the door at the end of the hallway and peered into the next. It was a short corridor that connected a staircase on one end and a chapel on the other.

Two bodies were lying on the stone in the hallway. Ketrick's personnel. He stumbled beside the closest one and dropped to his knees. His right arm was hanging almost limp at his side. It was the one that had smeared the previous hallway wall.

With his left arm, Ketrick searched the corpse at his feet. She was small and it was easy for him to roll her over. At her hip, she wore a holster. Her gun was still in it. Ketrick popped the tether that held the pistol into the holster and slid the weapon out. With great effort, he managed to force his right hand up so that he could rack the action and remove the safety. Armed, he struggled to his feet and started moving toward the staircase.

A man appeared just as Ketrick was closing on the stairs. He was wearing a blue uniform and a peregrine backpack. Despite his injuries, Ketrick's arm raised lightning fast, and he squeezed off three shots in rapid succession. Only one shot missed his target, and the peregrine slumped backward down the stairs.

"Can't go that way," Ketrick hissed. He was losing consciousness. He spun and headed away from the stairs toward the chapel.

Behind him, Ketrick heard a shout. The peregrines had found their downed comrade. He was struggling to stay alert and could not be sure how many voices he heard coming up the stairs as he reached the chapel door. He fell against the hard wood of the door, trying to push it open as someone behind him called out his name. In response, he threw his arm back without looking and repeatedly squeezed the trigger of the gun. He was firing blind, wanting only to scare off his attackers to buy himself enough time to enter the chapel and barricade himself inside.

The gambit failed. Someone tackled him from behind and together they fell against the floor inside the chapel. As Ketrick fell unconscious, the last thing he saw was the marble fountain in the centre of the chapel.

Chapter 36

Light and Fire

Cole

Cole stepped off the Starfall's elevator onto the shattered brickwork of the facility courtyard. He was followed closely by Lucius, Chelsea, and a handful of others. The ground was littered with debris, rocks, shattered stone, and parts of the rogue hull. The ominous ship beside them now looked little more than a mountain of scrap wood and steel, flames licking up from within. Light from the fire seemed to compete against the sun that was now rising. The cloud and mountain fog had lifted and mostly moved on, the only shadows being cast now came from plumes of billowing smoke.

As Cole stepped forward across the courtyard, he spotted Remmy and Dakota waving at them from the steps leading up to the main doors of the monastery. Starfall crew were carrying bodies of the slain facility personnel to a staging area off to the side against the outer wall. They were placing the corpses in rows, while other crew members put them into body bags.

"They will be identified," Chelsea said, having noticed where Cole's attention was focused. "Once our investigation is complete, the remains will be released to their families for proper burial."

Cole noticed a forlorn tone to Chelsea's voice, and a glazed look to her otherwise shining eyes. As good as she was at hiding her emotions, Cole could see the twitch in the muscles of her neck. The slight set and release of her jaw muscles. The tremor to her breathing.

"This is new for you," Cole said.

"Never fought our own before," Lucius answered on the commander's behalf. "Not like this. It's new for all of us."

They reached the base of the wide stone steps that led up to the monastery. From this close, the building looked ominous and far larger than it had from the bridge of the Starfall. Cole found himself staring at it. Double doors at least twenty feet high and made of intricately carved oak slabs with iron fittings were pushed open, almost beckoning them inside like the gaping maw of some gothic monster. Two towering structures stood on either side of the door. Above, a huge window was carved directly into the stone. It looked as though the window might have housed a stained glass at one time, now blown in and destroyed, leaving only the mangled spiderweb of broken cames.

A clapping sound pulled Cole's attention away from the building, and he saw Dakota had approached Lucius and clasped the engineer's hand. Both Dakota and Remmy looked haggard, unkempt and dirty. They were wearing cobbled clothing more akin to street urchins than cloudbreakers, though Cole noticed the edges of gala attire hiding below Remmy's cloak.

"Damn fine work leading us here, lads," Lucius said.

Dakota nodded. "Thanks, chief. Let's switch jobs next time. Sound good?"

Lucius smirked. "Trust me, lad. Ya don't want to go where I've been."

"Elios told us about the Cirrus," Dakota said as his head lowered. "Hard to believe."

Dakota took the rifle he had slung over his shoulder off and held it out to Chelsea. "Thank Elios for the rifle, commander. It's a beautiful piece of gear."

Chelsea waved off the offer. "Keep it. I think you've more than earned it."

Dakota slung the rifle back over his shoulder and smiled at Remmy. He glanced at the corpses being stacked against the wall. His expression faded and Cole noticed his shoulders slump.

"Hell of a thing, this is. A hundred years of war against the south and now we fight our own. Never thought I would be using a Whitehall weapon against Whitehall personnel," he said.

Chelsea patted Dakota on the shoulder as she passed him and continued up the steps. Cole started to follow her but stopped when he saw Lucius put his hand on Dakota's shoulder too.

"We did what we had to do, 'kota. Them or us, and they hit first."

Dakota said something to Lucius that Cole could not hear, and Lucius responded by patting the man's shoulder twice and then heading up the stairs to catch up with Chelsea.

"He okay?" Cole asked as Lucius reached him on the stairs.

"He will be," was all Lucius replied.

Inside the giant doors of the monastery, the group found themselves in a massive shrine hall with high vaulted ceilings. Curved beams made a cross pattern in the roof, carved out of stone and bearing intricate reliefs. There was no furniture in the room, only crates and racks of alchemical equipment. Cole recognized some of it.

"I've seen equipment like this before," Cole said to Lucius. "In Hiram's lab."

"Commander Gisborne," A woman called from the side of the room. She was standing by a table with a black body bag atop it. Chelsea and the others approached, and when they did, the woman opened the top of the bag to reveal the face within.

"That's Eiffert Whitehall," Lucius said.

Cole looked down at the man's face, stained with dried blood. His good eye was closed, but his missing eye was open like a cavernous hole in his face. For a moment, Cole had a flash vision of Eiffert wearing the hooded priest robes in the cemetery back in Harrow's Town.

"He killed Rikket Sable," Cole breathed. "He was the false priest that night back in Harrow's Town."

"Maybe Ketrick finally had enough of him," Lucius said as the woman closed the bag.

"We won't get answers unless we speak to Ketrick," Chelsea said.

Lucius grunted in reply but did not speak as they crossed the rest of the hall on Chelsea's heels. At the far end of the shrine hall, they found another double door, albeit smaller than the main entrance, that led to a squat hallway running perpendicular to the hall. One end of the hallway seemed to end in a simple alcove with candles and items of worship. The other ended in a closed wooden door. A large portion of the walls and flooring had blood stains spattered across it, and there were gouges in the stone from stray bullets. One of the Starfall crew that had been escorting Chelsea since they left the ship pointed to the door on their right.

"Ketrick Whitehall is this way, commander. Upstairs in a small chapel room. Elios is with him," she said.

Chelsea nodded for the woman to continue. The woman nodded in return, her curly fire-red hair bobbing as she did, and then led them down the hall to the door and opened it. Beyond the door was a spiral staircase, which they all followed in single-file before exiting into another hall like the one below. This hall had twice as much blood stained all over it, and more than twice as many gouges from gunfire. On their left about halfway across the hall was an open door, and at the far end they could see Elios and another of his peregrines standing over

Ketrick. They were inside the chapel, with Ketrick on his knees between them.

"Has he said anything?" Chelsea asked as she began to make her way across the hall.

"No, commander," the red-haired woman replied. "Not a word."

As Cole and the others followed Chelsea across the hall, they passed the open doors and Cole stole a glance inside. It was another hallway that ended in a simple alcove. Blood was smeared along the wall leading from tall double doors on the left to the door Cole was looking through. There was debris and broken glass scattered on the floor outside the doors. Cole suspected that was the room that had the stained-glass window.

Elios greeted the group when they stepped inside the simple chapel. He was standing on the left side of Ketrick, with his team member on the opposite side. Ketrick was a mess. Blood and ash matted his white hair, and he had lacerations on his face and neck that had long ago clotted, leaving a patchwork of dried blood on his skin. The right arm of his jacket was almost entirely red with blood. His clothing was torn almost everywhere except his legs.

Chelsea stopped only a foot or two directly in front of Ketrick. Lucius stopped to her right and Cole on the left with the rest taking up position behind her. There was a long silence as Chelsea simply appraised the man. Cole swept his gaze around the room, noting the relative simplicity of the carved walls. There were no windows. The only light came from gas lanterns in the center of the left and right walls. There was a marble water fountain that bubbled in the center of the room, and the back wall was entirely carved in relief. The statue depicted a man raising the sun in his hands while another cowered in robes below.

"Hope would love that statue," Cole whispered to himself.

At the sound of Cole's whisper, Ketrick twitched and lifted his head. He looked at Chelsea and grimaced.

"Ugh," Ketrick spat a gob of blood on the floor. "Gisborne. Are you still playing soldier? Or did you come to make me new clothes?"

Chelsea wore a stone expression. "Funny, Whitehall."

"I would offer you a kiss in welcome," Ketrick continued. "But I know you prefer women. That's what made you an exile, isn't it? Mommy and Daddy wanted a normal girl?"

Ketrick waited in the silence, a sinister smile on his face that faded when he realized he was not affecting her. His eyes flicked over to the red-headed crew member that had escorted them.

"Maybe she's your type. Maybe I could watch."

Chelsea's face held no emotion at all. "Stop it, Ketrick. Your desperate bravado is not impressing anyone. I know you're too stupid to pull all of this off yourself. Who are you working with?"

"Yeah," he spat again. "I know you, too. Stunning Chelsea Gisborne. Desperate to prove she's more than her looks. Ran away from her family to play soldier. Stain on the noble houses, you are. I won't tell you anything."

"Who killed yer idiot cousin?" Lucius demanded.

Cole noticed Ketrick wince like he had been slapped. His eyes moved off their escort and landed on Lucius for a moment, then darted back to Chelsea. His jaw was tight. His brow just a little pressed in. He looked afraid, but not of them.

"How do you know it wasn't me?"

Lucius laughed. Cole noticed Ketrick's teeth grinding.

"Ketrick," Chelsea said. "You are going to answer for everything you have done. For every. Single. Thing. I promise you that. Do yourself a favour. Comply. Maybe the courts will show you leniency."

"Leniency," he whispered as he nodded his head. "Alright, Gisborne. Alright. Without the Raider, I can't fight you or the Starfall. You win."

"The Raider, that's what you call your rogue hull?" Chelsea asked.

Ketrick nodded.

"And the cannon you shot the Cirrus down with," Lucius interjected. "That your invention too?"

Ketrick's sinister smile split his face. "Blast lance. So. It works."

Chelsea shook her head. "Coercing Hiram Errbryte into making drugs, building weapons specifically for destroying airships, going to war with the cloudbreakers..." she paused. "Why, Ketrick? What are your goals here?"

"Chaos," Ketrick replied. Far faster than any of them believed he could move in his current condition, Ketrick pulled something from his belt and stabbed the peregrine standing over him in the thigh. Elios quickly grabbed Ketrick by the shoulders and yanked him away. Ketrick was laughing sadistically. The peregrine he had stabbed stumbled backward toward the fountain, a shocked look on his face. His eyes and open mouth began to glow with a faint purple light.

Cole could see it all happening in slow motion. He saw radiating lines of crackling energy spreading out from the stab wound. He saw the man's eyes bulge, saw his mouth hang open in a wordless scream. Saw the faint vapour issued forth on his breath from his nose and throat. The light was building in his chest. Cole knew what would come next.

"Run!" Cole screamed, though for him it was a sustained bellow. Lucius had already grabbed Chelsea and was pulling her back toward the door. With his other arm, still mostly useless from the crash, Lucius had managed to push their escort toward the door. Elios attempted to drag Ketrick out but abandoned him at the door in favour of making his escape with the others. Cole himself was just spinning away to follow. He could perceive everything around him in slow motion, but his body was still stuck in real time. He felt sluggish, like trying to run against a fast current. Just as Cole was passing through the door frame, he felt something snag his pant leg and he toppled to the floor.

Cole looked down to see Ketrick sprawled out just inside the door to the chapel. He was already climbing to his feet. His laughter had stopped, and he was grinning like a demon. Behind him, the peregrine he stabbed was becoming brighter and brighter and had fallen to his knees against the fountain. Ketrick was backlit by the bright light emanating from within the chapel, casting him in shadow except for his shining white hair and his equally white, menacing grin. Cole was frozen. Tripped as he had been, he was now on his back just outside the door with nothing between him and the bomb about to go off but Ketrick himself.

"So," Ketrick hissed. "This is the boy who caused all our problems. Eiffert told me all about you. You should have died in that explosion."

Cole watched as Ketrick reached into a pouch on his belt that had previously been hidden under his coat. He produced a thin metal object with a glass vial inserted at the end of it. The opposite end was a long metal needle. Inside the vial, a purple-blue liquid sloshed.

"Well," Ketrick brandished the dart like a dagger in his left fist. "There's still time to fix that."

Cole heard Rikket's voice in his head at that moment, screaming at him to get up. He remembered the confidence of sucker punching Edam Pyrell, kissing Hope on the Starfall, and seeing the wolves in the forest. His whole life rushed into him at one moment, and as Ketrick stepped forward with the dart in hand, Cole found himself already rising to his feet.

The world was in slow motion again, but Cole felt less encumbered. He was faster than Ketrick. By the time Ketrick started swinging his arm down to stab at Cole, Cole was already connecting a left-hand jab into Ketrick's face. The punch staggered the man, and Cole seized the opportunity. In a fluid motion, his right hand ripped the dart from Ketrick's grip and spun it around. Cole screamed as loud as he could as he rammed the needle of the dart straight into Ketrick's chest. The liquid in the vial gurgled, and Cole watched it drain into Ketrick's dark heart.

Ketrick staggered and managed a sharp gasp before his hands found the dart still embedded in his flesh. He stared wide-eyed in shock at Cole. His eyes began to glow, and Cole's attention shifted to the peregrine beside the fountain. The peregrine was almost entirely bathed in white hot light, and Cole knew the fire was going to happen at any moment. He looked back at Ketrick, now well on his way to the same fate.

"For Rikket," Cole said, then leaned forward and shoved Ketrick with all his might.

Ketrick fell backward into the chapel and slid across the floor to rest on the opposite side of the fountain. Cole spun and started to run as fast as he could. Ahead, Cole could see his companions already disappearing down the staircase. He knew he did not have time to make it to them, so Cole turned and headed for the door to his right instead. As he entered the second hallway, he slammed the door closed behind him and kept running. He headed for the double doors ahead to his left. As he ran, the white-hot light bathing the hallway became yellow-orange and Cole heard the familiar roar of the fire he knew was coming. He kicked his feet forward and slid through the open doors of the hearth room on his back. The shattered stone on the ground chewed at his legs and back as he slid across the stone, coming to rest near the bookshelves.

The flash of fire came through shortly after, rolling into the room and dissipating quickly as the pressure was released outside by the huge open window. Another blast followed shortly after, bigger and more violent. The bookshelves rocked and fell over, as big chunks of stone in the walls melted and pushed into the room. Cole was buried by books and a falling shelf as the chaos erupted around him, but the explosions never reached him directly, nor did the fire. In short order, it was over, and the only sound was settling rubble and the ringing in Cole's ears.

Chapter 37

Dark side of Victory

Cole

The Starfall and their crew remained at the facility for three days after the battle, cleaning all the remains and documenting the evidence. Cole had suffered some torn muscles from the effort of his fight with Ketrick, as well as lacerations and bruising from his escape. He had spent most of their time at the facility in the Starfall's medical room in a bed beside Aislinn. Whenever the two found themselves awake at the same time, Aislinn would interrogate Cole on everything that had happened while she was out of it. Fortunately for both of them, there were only a handful of those moments.

On the morning of the third day at the site, Cole blinked his eyes open to see Hope standing over him. Becky was nearby, standing by Aislinn who was sitting up on her bed. Becky was fixing a sling over Aislinn's shoulder.

"Hi there hero," Hope teased as Cole looked up at her. "How are you feeling?"

Cole smiled. "I think I hate explosions now. And I'm not a hero."

"Ah hear different, Coleburn. Ah hear ya saved everyone from a flash dart."

Cole turned his head to Becky and then back to Hope. "Coleburn?"

Hope nodded. "Becky likes her nicknames."

"There," Becky said as she finished the sling on Aislinn's arm. "How's that feel, Ashes?"

"See?" Whispered Hope. Cole smiled and nodded as he turned to look at his mentor.

"It feels good, Becky," Aislinn said as she gingerly tried to move her arm. "Nice and snug."

"Like a bug 'n a rug, my cousin always says!"

"Cass?" asked Aislinn.

Becky laughed as she started to clean up her supplies from the end of Aislinn's bed. "No! 'Nother cousin. Limmy's her name."

"Limmy Adder?" Aislinn asked.

"Why?" Becky suddenly said. "You got somethin' against her?"

The room was silent, and then Becky let out a deep rumbling laugh.

"Gotcha Ashes! Her name's Angie, actually."

Aislinn shook her head and laughed with everyone else. Becky finished cleaning her supplies and put them away in a cabinet near the door. When she was finished, she turned and waved at the room.

"Be back later, okay?" Becky said before ducking out the hatch into the hallway outside. Her bubbly voice echoed back to them. "Get some rest! Oh, hi commander!"

"She's a character," Hope mused while Cole turned his head back to her. "I think I might start to like her."

"Give her time," Aislinn said. "And more of her cooking. She'll make you love her eventually."

Chelsea stepped into the room followed by Captain McCray and Lucius. Once Lucius was inside, he closed the hatch and spun the wheel to seal it.

"Good to see you are all awake," Captain McCray said. He looked crisp in his uniform, with golden tassels hanging from his epaulets, and not a single hair of his head or beard out of place. Cole wondered if the man woke up in such an immaculate state.

"I wanted to thank all of you for the part you've each played in all of this. I won't waste words rehashing your accomplishments, but I will say that commendations have been recommended and approved by high command, as well as the Emperor of Akoy and the Diarchy of Verdos."

Cole noticed the captain's jaw set, as though he was chewing on his next words.

"There is a dark side to this victory, however. One I am reticent to burden you all with. Our investigation into these events is turning up more questions than answers, and I fear we are just witnessing the beginning of a new..." he stopped and shared a look with Chelsea and Aislinn. "Or renewed... conflict."

Cole thought that in those last words, a weariness had fallen over the captain that only a lifetime in the toils of war could cause. He looked exhausted, right down to his soul.

"There was a whole complex dug into the mountain," the captain continued. "With a warehouse, a weapons factory, and what appears to be a fully functional airship hangar. We cannot confirm at this time, but it appears whoever Ketrick Whitehall's associates are may have another airship. Perhaps their own fleet. There was a substantial amount of weapons and ammunition that appear to have been liquidated before our arrival according to the ledgers we recovered. Also, we found no barrels of the substance reported by the Cirrus scouts that were delivered here from the Errbryte estate."

Hope lowered her head and Cole reached out to squeeze her hand.

"Hope," Chelsea said. "You should know we located evidence that your father may have survived the destruction of his lab."

Cole watched Hope's eyes snap wide open as her face shot up.

"We received word that excavation of the labyrinth below your estate was underway. They found the crushed armour, and some blood and torn clothing, but the body of your father was not there, and evidence suggests he may have escaped."

Tears ran down Hope's face and Cole squeezed her hand again. She swallowed hard.

"Where is he?" She squeaked.

"We don't know, Hope," Captain McCray answered. "But rest assured high command has authorized every cloudbreaker and airship loyal to the kingdoms to search for him. We believe he is a key in understanding all of this, and we will find him."

"What should I do?" Hope asked, her voice regaining a touch of her natural timbre.

"Go home," Chelsea replied. "Manage your estate for now. Command believes we need to keep as much of the nobility in the dark about this as possible for now. We have no idea if this ends with the Whitehalls, or if it goes deeper. I will use my contacts to help concoct a cover that your father is unwell, and that you will become his proxy in the meantime."

Hope turned her face to Cole. He knew the longing look in her eyes.

"What about Aislinn and I? What should we do?" Cole asked without taking his eyes off Hope.

Chelsea sighed. "Heal. As quickly as you can. You both are going to be essential in whatever comes next. Especially you, Cole. You've proven yourself invaluable. Command is already loading you on the next peregrine course in the spring. In the meantime, you and Aislinn will return to Harrow's Town and recover."

"Why am I going to Harrow's Town?" Aislinn asked. "I don't live there. I have no family there."

"Command thought you should recover alongside your initiate," Captain McCray replied. "Harrow's Town is isolated enough that you should be able to recover quickly with minimal notice from involved parties."

"You're hiding me. And the archives are not isolated enough?"

Captain McCray smiled. "It's not a suggestion, Investigator Elissan. It's an order. Recover with your initiate. In the spring, bring him to Gallenfort for his training. Which reminds me..."

Captain McCray reached into the pocket of his jacket and produced a pin with the cloudbreaker coat of arms on it. He walked to the edge of Cole's bed and held the pin out.

"Welcome to the service, Cole Vallen."

Chapter 38

A good team

Cole

The Starfall set sail for the Errbryte estate the following morning, but Cole and Aislinn spent most of the time either sleeping or staring off in silence. There had been some idle small talk, mostly when Hope or Becky came by for a visit. Hope had taken up Cole's proclivity for lounging alone in the aft bridge. She would share all the details of the sunsets and the stars when she would stop in on her way back to her rack. Cole could sense that she was being distant. She had not been the same since news of Hiram, or the request from command that she operate her father's estate. When the time came that the Starfall arrived at the Errbryte estate, Cole ensured that he was there to see her off.

There was another airship tethered to the grounds when they arrived and began their descent to the ground on the Starfall's elevator. They had been told they would not be staying, only that they were dropping Hope off. Becky had agreed to go with

Hope, posing as her new kitchen help. Hope had pretended to be coy about it, but Cole could see how happy she was to have the bubbly cook.

As the elevator touched down, Becky hoisted her bags up onto her shoulder and smiled at Hope. She did not say a word, she simply stepped off the elevator and headed toward the estate. Cole was still stiff, but he managed to step off without falling. He had been given a cane, but he was mostly swinging it around like a sword at this point. The Starfall crew had let Hope keep a uniform for the time being, and she was wearing it now as she stepped off onto her manicured estate lawn. Her hair was back in her beautiful ringlets, dangling down around her face and bouncing as she walked.

Cole walked almost halfway across the lawn with her, before they stopped at the edge of the brickwork road. Hope looked at the mansion, the grounds, and then back at the Starfall. She sighed.

"It feels strange to be back on the ground now," she said. "Not knowing when I'll see the world above the clouds again."

"You never know," Cole shrugged. "Might not be that long."

A flock of jungle birds flew over them above the trees. Both Cole and Hope followed their flight with their eyes.

"I'm scared, Cole," Hope whispered.

"About what?"

"Everything. About running the estate. About my father. About everything that's happened. About you."

"Don't be scared about me, I'll be fine. I'm looking forward to digging potatoes, to be honest."

"That's not what I mean," Hope sighed. "I'm scared that I can't do this alone."

"Oh," Cole said. He took a step away from Hope toward the estate and poked his cane against the bricks of the road.

"I know you can't stay," Hope continued as she stepped beside Cole. "I understand now. I've seen the world you dream of, and I get it."

She drew a deep breath and turned to face him.

"I just feel better when you're around. Stronger. Safer. We make a good team, Cole Vallen."

Cole smiled. "That's how I feel too. You know that night..."

"The night you kissed me?" Hope interrupted.

"You kissed me back," Cole laughed. "But yeah. That night. That was the first time that I can remember where the thought crossed my mind that maybe I don't want to be a Cloudbreaker."

Hope waited in silence for Cole to continue.

"I never had anyone I cared for like I care for you. Rikket was my best friend, but this is different. I only kissed one other girl my whole life. She ran when she saw my eyes. Plus, I never kissed Rikket."

Cole and Hope both laughed.

"But not you. Even when you thought I was crazy, you never ran."

"I never thought you were crazy, Cole."

"Brain damaged then."

"That's more accurate. Continue."

Hope was giggling, and Cole found it infectious.

"I'm trying to be serious and you're making fun of me."

Hope kissed him then, and they held each other in that kiss for a long time.

"Do cloudbreakers get time off? Like vacations or something?" Hope asked when they pulled apart.

"I hope so," Cole replied.

"You'll come to see me, right?"

"Absolutely I will," Cole squinted and held up a single finger pointed at the sky. "There's only one other place I would rather be..."

Hope slapped him in the chest.

"Hey! You didn't let me finish."

"Then finish, Cole Vallen."

"No more hitting?"

"No more hitting."

"There's only one other place I would rather be... but only if you're there with me."

Hope hugged him tight, and then held him at arm's length to look into his eyes. She reached up and touched his cheek below the green mark in his eye.

"You know, I really think you have the most beautiful eyes, Cole Vallen. I hope you never think of them as a curse again."

Cole smiled and kissed Hope one last time, before he parted and let her head across the brickwork road to the front door of her estate. Becky was standing by the door waiting for Hope, her bags resting on the ground at her feet. She smiled from ear to ear when Hope approached. Hope turned back at the door and waved at Cole. He felt his heart race and could not help the smile that crossed his face. That smile never left his face as he walked back to the elevator and it began lifting him to the Starfall. As he rose, he looked out to the tree line beyond the estate. The wolves were there. Watching him. For the first time in his life, he thought of his eyes as a gift.

Chapter 39

The journey home

Cole

"Ow," Aislinn whimpered as she bounced in the seat of the truck. "Are you *steering* for the potholes, Cole?"

The Starfall had dropped Aislinn and Cole off in Stonesvale Village in order for the pair to make the remainder of the journey home by power wagon. They had even purchased the truck outright so that Cole could leave it with his father. In Aislinn's condition, she was unable to drive, so Cole had learned quickly much to his mentor's chagrin. For most of their journey, she had shouted at him, cursed him, praised him maybe twice, and complained about every bump the truck made and how much it hurt.

Cole was sympathetic of course and would always slow down or pay focused attention to driving more carefully, but the closer they were to home the harder it was. He was excited to see his father and often daydreamed of the look Jasper Vallen might have on his face when he learned they now owned a power wagon. Of course, there was also the thought of seeing his son in a uniform, but Cole knew the truck would be the more welcome surprise.

As they rounded a corner, the south fields of Harrow's Town spread out before them. Cole slowed the truck and pointed off to their right toward the Northeast. Across the field, just as the tree line began, there was a raised hill with a prominent rock standing atop it.

"That's lookout rock there, on the top of that ridge. It's a part of the Simpren farm. Rikket and I watched the Cirrus approach from there when you first came to Harrow's Town."

Aislinn smiled at Cole's giddy excitement to be home. Though she was still in a lot of pain, she was regaining her strength rapidly and had been sleeping less on this final leg of their trip. Granted, she knew part of that was her anxiety at trusting the driving to Cole. Still, she was enjoying his energy and it lifted her heart to see him so happy.

"That feels so long ago," Cole said and his voice trailed off. He didn't speak again until they were passing into the town proper.

"Busy today," Aislinn said as Cole once again threaded the truck between clusters of pedestrians and horse-drawn wagons.

"Yeah," Cole said, picking up speed as they reached the ring road where they had more space. "Can't say I know why. No fairs that I know of this time of year, but it is close to the final harvest before winter. Maybe this is just what to expect now that the war is over."

"If the war is over," Aislinn corrected. Cole only nodded in reply.

Aislinn looked out at the people they were passing. Families with handfuls of scampering children, all of whom stopped to look in wonder at the truck as it rolled by. A young couple of attractive men in top hats and fine livery holding hands as they walked side by side. A man helping his very pregnant wife stroll through the ring road. A cluster of nobility standing outside the front of the courthouse. Aislinn turned to look at Cole and noticed he was looking at the building too.

"You okay?" She asked.

Cole nodded, his eyes fixed on the building. "Yeah, I'm okay. I guess I never thought about it until now..." he sighed. "What it would be like coming home. If they still think I was a part of it."

Aislinn looked back at the courthouse as they rumbled past.

"We'll make sure they know you weren't involved, Cole."

"I wish we could tell them the truth," Cole said.

"In time," Aislinn replied as she turned her eyes ahead. "In time we..."

Aislinn was interrupted when a shout bellowed out that caused Cole to instinctively slam on the brakes of the truck. The sudden stop jarred Aislinn pretty hard and she groaned.

"Watch it!" The voice shouted from ahead of them. A pudgy face appeared from behind a cart that had rolled into the ring road ahead of them. It was Edam Pyrell.

Edam froze stiff when he saw Cole behind the wheel and Aislinn sitting at his side. Cole realized then how he must look to them wearing his uniform and no glasses. His hair was even different than the last time he was in Harrow's Town. He wore it closer cropped and more professional now. Cole was also sure that with everything he had been through, he had also put on some muscle.

"You okay, Edam?" Cole called out.

Edam swallowed and nodded. "Yeah. Yes. Sir. Yes, I am. Sorry, I didn't mean to shout. Let me get this wagon out of your way."

Edam started pulling on the lead for his old mare that was tied to his wagon. Begrudgingly, she obeyed and the wagon started to roll out of their path. Cole smiled at Aislinn and then leaned out the side of the truck toward Edam.

"Edam," Cole said. "It's me, Cole Vallen."

Edam stopped in his tracks and blinked a few times, then rubbed his eyes like a child that was just waking up. He guffawed and then coughed.

"I know it was you," he said as he looked away. "Just bein' polite is all."

"Must be a first," Aislinn said quietly beside Cole.

"Are you sure you're okay, Edam? I didn't mean to scare you. I wasn't watching the road is all."

Edam shifted his weight. He was refusing to make eye contact with Cole. Cole wondered whether it was the uniform or the lack of glasses.

"I'm fine. This ole mare, she's not so fast no more is all. Hearing is gone. Don't do so well around trucks."

Cole sat back in the driver's seat and nodded.

"Alright. If you're sure. See you around, Edam."

Cole started rolling forward again, making their way through the rest of the ring road to the North exit. He leaned over to Aislinn.

"Is he still standing there watching us?"

Aislinn winced as she turned to look back over her shoulder.

"Like a stunned cow in the fields," she replied. Cole never stopped smiling the rest of the drive home.

When Cole and Aislinn finally rolled into the drive at the Vallen farm, Cole could see that his father was out in the fields working. He was standing alone except for three baskets about a hundred yards out. The old faithful wagon was parked on the edge of the drive, and the horses were tethered to a tree nearby with buckets of water and feed. Cole rolled the truck to a stop and looked out at his father toiling in the dirt. His back was to them, and he was so far unaware.

"I can make the rest of the drive," Aislinn said. "At least I think I can. Go see your father."

Cole relented without an argument and stepped down from the truck while Aislinn awkwardly shimmied over into the driver's seat. By the time she was rolling away toward the house, Cole was already a few yards into the field. He ran his hands through his short hair, brushing out some of the road dust and sweat. The late autumn sun was casting a brilliant golden glow across the fields.

Maybe it was the movement of the truck toward the house that caught Jasper's attention. Maybe it was the crunch of dirt under Cole's boots. Whatever it was, Cole had nearly closed the distance between them when Jasper turned. He saw the truck first, rolling up the drive toward his home. Then he turned the rest of the way.

Cole watched his father in slow motion. His heart was hammering in his chest, slowing the world down as it had so many times since the explosion that took Rikket. Jasper was wearing a vest with no undershirt. His dark skin was even darker with the summer tan he bore. He was skinnier than Cole remembered ever seeing him. Frail, and sinewy. Sweat glistened on his chest and forehead. His eyes locked on Cole and his eyebrows pressed together, raising in the centre as they did. His lower lip quivered and came up, and his eyes instantly watered up.

Cole stepped closer until he was a little more than an arm's length away. Only the partly-filled baskets of potatoes and some tools stood between them. Jasper nodded and kept nodding. Short, approving nods. Cole held his arms out, indicating his uniform.

"Hi Dad," Cole squeaked.

"Hi son," Jasper replied.

"I did it, Dad."

"You did."

Cole turned and pointed at the truck that was now stopping in front of their home.

"The truck," Cole coughed, trying to control the emotion in his voice. "The truck is yours, Dad. Gift... from the cloudbreakers."

Jasper's eyes darted over to the truck but barely lingered a moment before they returned to his son.

Cole pointed to the baskets.

"You, uh," he stuttered. "You want some help?"

Jasper smiled then and took a step closer to his son. A tear ran down his cheek, paving a clean path through the dust that had caked on his cheeks. Without another word, he pulled Cole into a tight hug and held him there. Cole returned it in kind.

"I'm so proud of you, Cole," Jasper whispered.

Cole cried in his father's arms.

"I miss him, Dad."

"I know, son. Rikket would be damn proud of you too."

Jasper let his son go and held him out at arm's length. He searched Cole's face.

"I like it without those glasses," Jasper said.

Cole smiled as he thought of Hope.

"Not a curse, Dad. A gift."

Jasper's eyebrows raised. "A gift?"

Cole winked at his father. "Tell you about it later."

Cole stood back and unbuttoned the jacket of his uniform. He shrugged the coat off and folded it, setting it atop one of the filled baskets of potatoes. Then he bent and picked up a spare pitchfork that was lying on the ground and moved over to the row beside his father. Jasper wiped the muddy tear from his cheek and smiled. Without a word, he went back to work as his son did the same beside him.

In the sky, a flock of crows passed over, squawking and chirping. Below them, Cole Vallen kept his eyes on the soil and dug potatoes with his father until the sun went down.

Chapter 40

The Storm of Savage Harbour

Cerin

The Midnight Storm drifted through the air above a tumultuous ocean that battered a shoreline of jagged dark rocks. When they broke, the waves threw spray tens of feet into the air, almost licking the bottom of the airship's hull. It was dark, the night sky made even darker by storm clouds billowing above. There was no rain, just the high winds and occasional flash of lightning common for storms in the area. The airship was significantly larger than its predecessor, with a similar metal and wood hull. Two blast lance cannons adorned the bow, mounted in a forecastle that allowed them maximum movement above and below. A third lance was mounted on the quarterdeck in the stern.

Like the Raider, the ship boasted a flat open upper deck making it look like a perfect fusion between an ocean vessel and an airship. The main deck was lit by gas lanterns set high on the two masts rising from the deck. Both were equipped with rolled-up vapour sails and tubing that led down below decks to the boilers. A superstructure toward the aft end separated the main deck and quarterdeck, with stairs on the outside leading to a pilotage atop the structure. There was a single hatch that led inside the structure, and much like the raider, there was a cargo hatch in the centre of the main deck between the masts.

Cerin Barunn approached the gunwale on the upper deck near the forward end and rested his hand on the wooden railing that topped it. His eyes scanned the horizon, as his other hand rested idly on the pistol in his holster. The wind was whipping his hair, and his stern face was lit momentarily by a sheet lightning flash in the clouds above. He glanced briefly skyward, inhaling deeply of the sea air, and then turned to look at the forward mast. A man was tied there, low and on his knees. His hands were bound behind his back. His head was low, his white hair whipping in the wind like Cerin's did.

"Savage Harbour," Cerin said to the man. Despite the wind and the sound of the surf below, his voice somehow carried like thunder. "This is where I was raised. Forgotten. In the void between Ciar K'hen and Akoy."

Cerin strolled over toward the man tied to the mast.

"We did alright. For a time. The ocean kept us safe. Our people know it. The war never made it to us, until the North took the sky."

Cerin knelt before the man.

"Oh, you don't really care for a history lesson. You're the smartest man in the world."

Cerin reached out and lifted the man's chin. Hiram's bruised face glared back.

"Hiram Errbryte. The great alchemist."

Hiram grimaced as Cerin flicked his hand, pushing his chin away and knocking his head against the mast behind him.

"I'm not afraid of you, Barunn."

Cerin laughed and stood.

"Of course you're not, Hiram. We both know I can't kill you."

Hiram turned his head and spit on the deck away from Cerin.

"No. I can't kill you," Cerin repeated. "But I will make use of you. Make no mistake. You will help me, and if you don't?"

Cerin knelt again so he could put his face inches from Hiram's. In this faint light of the lantern above, Cerin's eyes flashed yellow like a cat's.

"I will put that pretty daughter of yours this close. This. Close. Hiram..." even with the wind, Hiram could feel Cerin's breath on his cheek. "And I will skin her alive. Cut her into chum for the sharks while you watch. I will make you pray to die."

"You're a pirate," Hiram whispered. "You will lose. Everything."

Cerin shrugged as he stood up again.

"Maybe."

Kort appeared behind Cerin and looked down at Hiram, then back to his captain.

"Word from the mountain, captain," Kort said. His silver eyes were almost glowing yellow in the dim light. "Starfall arrived. They've destroyed the Raider and taken control of the facility. Ketrick Whitehall is dead."

Hiram laughed.

"See?" Hiram said. "You will lose. You have no more nobles to back you."

"Hiram," Cerin replied with a mischievous grin. "You underestimate me. This has barely been my opening gambit. I am just getting started."

Kort shifted his eerie eyes from Cerin to Hiram and back again before he spoke.

"She wants to speak with you, captain."

Cerin turned to face his second in charge, then looked back into the darkness toward the superstructure beyond the second mast. He beckoned at someone, and Hiram's brow furrowed.

"I want you to meet someone," Cerin said as his hand remained outstretched. A figure was approaching from beyond the light. "Someone very dear to me, and the reason I killed that wretch Eiffert with my own hands."

A woman stepped into the light between Kort and Cerin. She was graceful, serpentine in her movements, and beautiful. She had flawless dark skin and a head of curly white hair that somehow made her beauty even more ethereal. She was wearing a long dress, richly embroidered with silver and golden threads that sparkled in the lantern light. Hiram had never met the woman before, but he knew of her. She was Akoyan nobility.

Last he heard of her, she had married and moved somewhere in the north of Verdos. Realization struck Hiram as Cerin put his hand on her back and stepped her forward. It had been her son lost in Harrow's Town.

"Hiram Errbryte," Cerin said, his words radiating with viciousness. "Allow me to introduce my half-sister, Seran Se'baht Sable."

Epilogue

Lucius drew a deep breath as he reached for the handle of the public-house door. It had taken the weary chief the better part of a week to make his way this far north, and he was finally nearing the end of his quest. The tiny fishing settlement of Eastbank Village on the shore of Falcon Lake was a great place for a person to vanish. Unlike most small towns, the population here cared very little for the machinations of outsiders. They received travellers often enough, most of whom were on fishing or hunting trips in this remote region. As Lucius opened the door to the pub, he was rewarded for his insight. Only a handful of patrons sat in the room. Not a single one even looked up.

Relieved, Lucius crossed the small open room with its beams of hand-cut timber holding up a log cabin-style roof. The innkeeper behind the bar was idly rubbing the slab counter with a cloth. She looked up as Lucius stopped at the bar. Her hazel eyes were set within a face mapped with laugh lines and wrinkles. Lucius could almost read the happiness and the pain of the woman's entire life. She had strawberry blond hair, almost as ran-through with grey as Lucius himself. She smiled at him, and he smiled back.

"Food and drink?" the innkeeper said with a pleasing tone as she tossed the rag over her shoulder. "Or room first?"

"Room first," Lucius replied. "Been a long journey, wouldn't mind restin' my ole bones a spell 'fore I drink ya dry."

The woman grinned and laughed.

"I'm either going to love ya," she cooed as she walked to the end of the bar and scooped a key attached by a ring to a wooden tag marked with the number two. "Or I'm going to like ya. But just a little bit."

She handed the key to Lucius.

"I'll do my best for th' former," Lucius replied, winking as he took the key from her.

"Up the stairs at the end," the innkeeper said, pointing to a short hall past a fireplace to Lucius' left. "Can't miss it. There's only two rooms."

The woman's laugh was infectious and Lucius could not help but join her as he walked away.

"If I'm lost, I'll come find you," he said over his shoulder as he waved the key to her.

"Take your time, love. Just not too long. Got a chowder on the stove might need some help eating."

Lucius nodded as he reached the stairs, and without another word, he ascended the creaking steps to a hallway that led away from the main hall. Two paintings hung on the walls to either side of the hall as Lucius walked toward the end. Both depicted people fishing on Falcon Lake with the majestic Rinda mountains in the background. At the end of the hall, there was a nightstand table with an oil lantern and a door to either side. The door on the left was marked with a carved number one, and on the right was a number two. Lucius faced his room and unlocked it, slipping inside and closing the door behind him.

The room was minimalist and rustic, with a single straw-mattress bed, a desk with a wooden chair, and a stuffed leather armchair with an oil lantern on an end table beside it. Lucius smiled. A woman was sitting in the armchair, her long legs crossed, her shining green eyes almost glowing like emeralds in the lantern light.

"Waiting long, Chelsea?" Lucius asked.

Chelsea kicked her crossed leg a bit and lifted a book that was sitting in her lap.

"Not enough to complain. Finally had time to read," she replied. "How was your trip, Chief..." she paused, rolling the book in the air for emphasis. "What is it you go by now? Parvelle?"

Lucius scoffed and stretched his back to his full height. He leaned against the end of the bed so he could face Chelsea directly. When he spoke, his accent was gone and his voice carried a different tone.

"Parvelle, yes. Since I left the Starfall."

"Hrm. I don't like it. I like your real name better."

"Couldn't use it anymore Chels. You know why. Everything was getting too close for my taste."

,ea dropped the book in her lap.

_ .cius," she began. "I consider you one of my best friends. Within the service and without. When you asked for this..." again she waved the book. "Clandestine chat, I agreed without hesitation. I thought maybe you had something to get off your chest. I know you didn't ask me here to talk about names, so tell me. What's so urgent?"

"Aislinn's report," Lucius stated directly.

Chelsea dropped the book again.

"What about it?"

"The Errbryte estate. What she heard from Hiram before my intervention. What I saw."

Chelsea uncrossed her legs and leaned forward in her chair. Her expression changed.

"The De'Ghova engine," she whispered.

Lucius nodded.

"Well, now I understand the secrecy."

"I need your help, Chelsea," Lucius said as he began to un-button his jacket. He was slow to do so, as his left arm struggled with most movements.

Chelsea watched as Lucius removed his jacket and gloves. As the sleeves came back and dropped off his arms, the lantern light flashed and shone off what should have been his flesh. From the shoulders down, all the way to his hands and the tips of his fingers, his arms were artificial. Plates of copper, bronze, and steel were intricately woven over clockwork and mechanisms beyond either of their understanding. A web of banding and surgical screws was set into him just past his collar bones on either side where flesh met metal. His left arm made an almost imperceptible whine as he lowered it. Grinding and hissing until it came to rest.

"What happened?" Chelsea asked.

"Broke it during the Cirrus attack. Punched one of those lance things right out of the hull."

"You can't fix it?"

Lucius shook his head. "The sphere inside is cracked."

Chelsea stood and walked across the room. She reached out and touched the broken arm, feeling the jagged plates and sensing the grinding of the mechanisms within through her fingertips.

"Hiram told the others that thing was a gift," Lucius whispered. "He knew my dad. Had to. And he had his own engine, all this time. Sitting inside a suit in his crypts."

"What do you need me to do?" Chelsea asked.

"It's time I told the world who I really am, Chelsea. The war is over, things might be different."

Chelsea searched the chief's eyes.

"Are you sure?"

"I need to find out everything dad did. I need Hiram Errbryte. If I'm going to fix my arm, we need to find that engine."

"The reports said the suit was empty when it was recovered."

Lucius nodded. "I think Hope will help."

Chelsea nodded too. "We should also talk to Natalia Whitehall. She might know how we can get into Arbaness."

baness..." Lucius whispered. "The Floating Estate."

here might be answers there, Lucius. It's a logical step after the Errbryte estate."

"Well," Lucius said. "I suppose it's time for Lucius De'Ghova to go home."

About the author

Kenton J Moore was born in 1980 in British Columbia, Canada. The son of a helicopter pilot and a third generation farmer, he showed an early interest in reading and writing, but chose service to his country as his career in 2001. After ten years of service, nine of which aboard Canadian Navy ships, he now lives on his family's heritage farm where he spends his days dreaming up incredible worlds and stories based on his experiences. He works as an Inventory Analyst and is an advocate for mental health.

Cloudbreakers: Vallen is his fourth published work and the debut novel in his Airship Adventure series.

Learn more at www.kentonjmoore.com